THE LAST GOOD GUY

THE LAST
GOOD GUY

T. JEFFERSON
PARKER

G. P. PUTNAM'S SONS

New York

PUTNAM
— EST. 1838 —

G. P. Putnam's Sons
Publishers Since 1838
An imprint of Penguin Random House LLC
penguinrandomhouse.com

Library of Congress Cataloging-in-Publication Data

Names: Parker, T. Jefferson, author.
Title: The last good guy / T. Jefferson Parker.
Description: New York : G. P. Putnam's Sons, [2019]
Identifiers: LCCN 2019005507│ ISBN 9780525537649 (hardcover) │
ISBN 9780525537663 (epub)
Subjects: │ GSAFD: Suspense fiction.
Classification: LCC PS3566.A6863 L37 2019 │ DDC 813/.54--dc23
LC record available at https://lccn.loc.gov/2019005507

Printed in the United States of America
1   3   5   7   9   10   8   6   4   2

Book Design by Katy Riegel

For

Matt and Mary Ann

THE LAST GOOD GUY

1

///////////////////

THERE'S this scene in the old detective movies where the investigator sits in his office, waiting for someone to come in and hire him. He's a capable-looking man. His face has character. His office is functionally furnished and poorly lit. Light and shadow. The top half of the office door is smoked glass and you can read his name in reverse.

The door is ajar and you know a woman is about to come through it, and she will be pretty, interesting, and mysterious. She will tell the investigator a story and offer him money to find the truth in it, and when he does, nothing will be the same for either of them, ever again. Somehow, you are pulling for both of them, but you get the feeling there will be a winner and a loser.

She offered her hand and I took it.

Open face, assessing blue eyes, and curly light brown hair. Shapely, not tall. Fair-skinned. A red summer dress with white polka dots on it, red espadrilles, and a shiny red belt.

She removed a small white purse from over one shoulder, smoothed her dress, and sat. Her scent was light.

Her name was Penelope Rideout and her younger sister, Daley, had run away from home. Penelope had already filed a missing-persons report, but the police wouldn't act this quickly without evidence of foul play. Of which there was none. Penelope was sure that her sister had run away, because Daley had a "wild streak" and was mixed up with a "guaranteed loser" named Nick Moreno. Daley's favorite clothes, personal items, and toiletries were missing from home. She had not responded to calls and texts, and neither had the boyfriend. Penelope had sat in her car outside Nick's dark condo last evening and most of the night, hoping they would show. She'd then driven to Oceanside PD headquarters and filed the report. Nick was twenty years old. Daley fourteen.

"I'm very worried about her, Mr. Ford. She's precocious, and Daley doesn't always make good choices. The age difference alone is just wrong. I do what I can to guide her."

"How come her parents aren't here doing this?" I asked, resting my pen.

"Mom and Dad died ten years ago," said Penelope, eyes moistening. "In a car accident outside of Eugene, Oregon. A storm. I was eighteen and became Daley's legal guardian. The judge was skeptical, but my lawyer was good. Daley was four."

"I'm sorry."

She took a tissue from the purse and touched it under each eye, though I could see no tears. Neat nails, clear finish. Pushed the tissue back into her bag. She wore a slim wedding band and a sensible diamond. I did the math and came up with twenty-eight-year-old Penelope Rideout. Or twenty-nine, depending on her birthday. Twelve years younger than me, plus or minus.

"Has this happened before?" I asked.

"No. Never."

"When did you see her last?"

"Yesterday morning I dropped her off at school. When I got home from work around four, I saw she'd been there. This was not un-usual. I waited until evening. I've always tried to give her an appro-priate amount of freedom. When she didn't come home for dinner and homework, as is our agreement, I called. Texted. Her, and Nick. As I told you."

"What school?" I asked.

"Monarch Academy, Carlsbad. She's in the eighth grade. I held her back a year because I thought it was the right thing to do."

"Are you employed, Mrs. Rideout?"

"I'm a freelance technical editor. Aerospace and defense. Job shops, mostly. I make good money and take time off when I need to."

I asked her husband's name, and what he did for a living.

"Colonel Richard Hauser," she said. "He's a Marine pilot."

"You kept your maiden name."

"I wanted continuity for Daley. Because of Mom and Dad. It was all very hard at first. I'm also proud to be an Alabama Rideout and I don't want us lost to history. Daley and I are the last of our line who are young enough to continue it. Can you find her?"

Careful here. In my seven years as a PI I've never failed to find the person I was hired to find. Not that it's easy locating someone who doesn't want to be found. But it's my specialty. I have enthusiasm for such work because I lost someone close to me, who I know cannot be found.

"I'm good at what I do."

Those wide blue eyes again, waiting. "I certainly hope so. Daley means the world to me. To us."

I handed her the standard contract for an individual: eight hun-dred dollars for my first eight hours, partially refundable if I get re-sults in less. If not, the go-forward fees are set out, though I'll lower them sometimes. I've recently raised, steeply, my rates for most corporations and religious groups, and of course for political organizations of any kind.

Penelope Rideout squared the contract on the desk. Then brought a white phone from her purse and set it beside the papers. Next, a red checkbook. She looked up at me, then back to the paper, and began reading. The standard contract is three pages, single-spaced. I tried to keep it brief and unambiguous, but it's still a lot of words. She read every one. I watched her curls bob as she nodded and ran her finger along the sentences with a technical editor's concentration.

Through my office window I took in my view of Fallbrook's Main Street—a yogurt shop, an art gallery, a store specializing in vacuum cleaners and bicycles. A bank, a Mexican restaurant, a karate dojo, a women's boutique. It was September and hot. Jacarandas and orchid trees still in bloom. Fallbrook is a small, fragrant, old-fashioned town, a mom-and-pop place. We have characters. We have a peaceful side and a rough side. We are awash in classic cars, gleaming old vehicles sailing yachtlike down our country roads. We bill our town as the avocado capital of the world.

Finally finished with the contract, Penelope Rideout tapped the signature lines with her reading finger. "I don't have eight hundred dollars in cash."

"A check is fine."

"Do you deal with many dishonest people?"

"Not if I can avoid it. The cash policy helps."

"I've been cheated before. It makes you feel angry and at fault at the same time. Here are pictures of her."

She handed me the white phone. I scrolled across. Daley Rideout was pretty, like her sister. Same alert blue eyes, same curly light brown hair. Her face had an openness like her sister's, frame after frame.

I thought of my own siblings—a sister and two brothers—and how different we had been. We strove to be. Turf. Outta my face. But we always stuck together when things got serious. We're still very different individuals, the Ford gang. We still come together if we need to.

"That's Nick beside her, with the beard and the man bun," said Penelope. "He walks dogs for a living."

Nick was tall and handsome and looked proud of himself.

We traded phone and check. Her handwriting was loopy and childlike. I gave her a business card and asked her to send the pictures of Daley and one of Nick to my cell number in text and email.

"Did any neighbors see Daley come home from school?" I asked.

"No. Most of them work." Penelope sent me the pictures, and a moment later I heard them arrive on my phone. She bit her bottom lip, shaking her head as if in doubt or disbelief.

"You were recommended by someone I used to work with," she said. "I called him last night from my stakeout. Marcus Proetto. You located his daughter when she ran away. I did a brief Internet search of you after talking to him."

A year ago, Marcus had employed me to find his young daughter, who had given him and his wife quite a scare by heading to Lake Tahoe with a girlfriend. They were all of fifteen years old but had finagled Greyhound tickets from an adult friend of a friend. I corralled them in the Harrah's steakhouse and told their escort—a sleek, fast-eyed young man who had offered to buy them dinner—to get lost. He was unhappy about that. I boxed heavyweight in the Marines and am still happy to hit people who need it, and most men want no part of me.

"I've been told that the first twenty-four hours are crucial," Penelope said. "It's now been twenty-four hours, almost exactly, since I dropped her off at school."

I handed her a fresh legal pad and a pen and asked her to write down Daley's and Richard Hauser's contact numbers, dates of birth, Social Security numbers if she knew them, and the names and numbers of friends, relatives, and employers. Nick's contact info and condo address, very important. And anything else she could give me.

She wrote carefully and slowly, in silence. Curls bobbing again. When she was done, she pushed the note pad toward me.

"I have more of her friends' names and numbers at home on my computer," she said.

"Those might be helpful. What was Daley wearing when you dropped her off at school yesterday?"

"Monarch Academy has a code," said Penelope. "So a gray skirt just above the knee, and a white short-sleeved blouse. White athletic shoes. It was all in her hamper, though, when I came home from work. I don't know what she might have worn to leave home. She likes skinny jeans and tees with bangles and pop-star graphics on them—Pink and Taylor Swift and Alicia Keys. I noticed that she'd taken those three particular shirts. And a black tee with an image of Beethoven. You know, with all the hair. She took her retro canvas sneakers, too—pink and black. Her travel guitar and rolling carry-on were gone."

"What's Nick drive?"

"A white van with a papillon face painted on the doors. Larger than life, of course. For his business. Does this mean you'll find Daley?"

"It means I'll try."

I set my pen on the yellow legal pad. Penelope scanned my face with her blue eyes, waiting. In the good morning light now coming through the blinds I saw that her eyeliner was smeared and one side of her hair was a little flat and the chipper red polka-dot dress was finely wrinkled and darker under her arms. The long September night waiting in her car, I assumed.

"You've had quite a night, Mrs. Rideout. But you need to fill out missing-persons reports. There are four federal, three state, two local, and three private sites I recommend. Those pictures you have of Daley will be helpful, if you're willing to post them."

"Of course I am."

"I can have some coffee or tea sent up, if you'd like."

"Coffee with lots of cream. Thank you."

The Dublin Pub downstairs opens early for breakfast and I'm on good terms with the help. I tip heavily.

One and a half hours and a pot of coffee later we had filed the twelve missing-persons reports and made six digital pictures of Daley Rideout available for distribution.

We stood and I walked her to the door. "If I haven't located Daley by late afternoon, I'll want to see her room, and I'd like that longer list of friends and their numbers from you."

"Yes."

"Try not to worry, Mrs. Rideout. Most of these cases resolve quickly and happily."

"When I get an Amber Alert on my phone, it makes my scalp crawl," she said. "I memorize the child's description. I write down the car and license plate to look for. Now maybe I'll get one for my own sister."

"Amber Alerts are only for child abductions." These comforting words from Roland Ford, friend of the afflicted. I still catch myself talking like a cop sometimes.

"Do you have a little sister?" she asked.

I nodded.

"Imagine her gone, Mr. Ford."

"Call me Roland."

"Roland, she's the most important thing in my life. Get it?"

Through the window I watched her walk up Main Street, stop beside a yellow VW Beetle with its black ragtop up, then aim a key fob at the car. Noted the plates, because that's what I do. Saw the lights blip and her pale shoulder turn in the sunlight and the yellow door swing open.

2

///////////////////

I KNOCKED ON Nick Moreno's condo door and waited. This was an Encinitas complex named Las Brisas, the breezes, which at nine o'clock this morning were onshore, damp, and cool. From the ground-floor porch I could see the street where Penelope Rideout had parked for her night-long vigil. I pictured her half dozing, head against the rest and turned to the driver's-side window. Moreno's place had that nobody-home feel. I tried the doorbell again, heard the faint chime inside. The door was locked.

I followed a walkway around to the back gate. It opened to a concrete patio and a slope of ivy topped by a white vinyl privacy fence. Potted plants, a wound green garden hose, and a garage door, closed but not locked. I hit the lights, heard the fluorescent tubes buzz, saw the white van and the enlarged papillon regarding me pertly. Stepped up close and saw the van was empty. Stood there for a moment, looking at the tools of Nick Moreno's trade neatly stacked on a shelf: boxes of dog treats and plastic poop bags and paper towels.

One of the adjacent neighbors, Lydia, hadn't seen Nick in weeks. The other wasn't home.

The upstairs tenant was an affable young man named Scott Chan. When I told him my name and business, he said he hadn't seen Nick lately. When I asked about suspicious activity downstairs, Chan said not really, but the day before, he'd seen a silver Expedition SUV pull into the driveway. A round blue emblem on the driver's door, but he couldn't read it—bad angle. Two men got out and went into Nick's. This was around noon. Just a few minutes later, he heard them come back out. Saw them through his upstairs office window.

Then Chan looked at me, waiting, pursing his lips against something he didn't want to say.

"Was a girl with them?"

"When they came out of the condo, yes," he said. "She worked with him sometimes. With Nick. I don't know her name."

His description fit Daley Rideout's, down to her bouncy hair and bright blue eyes. He said she seemed to know the two SUV men. They were all talking. They seemed purposeful. She had rolling luggage and a guitar.

The men were in their late twenties or early thirties. One wore tan pants and a black golf shirt. He was big, looked strong, and had blond hair cut short on the sides and back but longer on top. The other wore the same clothes and a black windbreaker. Neat, clean-cut guys, Chan said. Could have been cops. Or Mormons. *Ha.*

"Did you go over to Nick's after they left?" I asked.

"No. No reason to."

"You didn't call the police?"

"Why would I do that?" he asked.

"Because you saw a very young teenage girl get into a vehicle with two men you'd never seen before. You watched through your window and you knew it looked wrong, which is why you didn't mention her until I asked you."

Chan slumped a little, then caught himself. "Look. I actually thought of calling the police. But the girl and the men looked okay with each other. They could have been family. There was no awkwardness. They got into the front and she got into the rear. Then the driver, the big guy, hopped out and went back into Nick's condo. A minute later he came back and drove away. Not fast, just regular. What would I tell police? That's intrusive. I believe in privacy, Mr. Ford."

"I believe in good judgment, Mr. Chan. Yours was bad."

"Did something happen?"

"Something always happens."

I gave Chan a business card with a fifty-dollar bill paper-clipped to the back. I always carry at least one such item in my wallet. It has paid off more than once. "If you see either Nick or the girl, call me. You'd be doing both of them a favor."

He looked down at the card and cash, shook his head, and sighed.

BACK IN THE garage I saw no signs of an alarm system. Rapped my fist on the door to the house. Waited, called out to Nick, and knocked again. Then picked the lock and went in through a small laundry room—guilty of breaking and entering, Your Honor—but driven by a certain quality of fear that I've learned to listen to. Learned as an Expeditionary Force Marine in Fallujah, going door-to-door, stepping into death's living rooms. Learned again as a sheriff's deputy on the not-always-friendly streets of San Diego County. And now, here in Encinitas, I stood listening to that special quality of fear, answered by the brash thump of my heart.

And by the muted drone of a TV coming from the floor above.

"Nick! Roland Ford here. I need to talk to you."

Not a peep. Just the TV above me, a man's still-faint voice followed by audience laughter. The kitchen was cool and the sinks were full of dishes. Coffeepot a quarter full. From the island kitchen I could see the dining room and the living room with the gas fireplace and the artificial logs. And the stairs leading up. The air conditioner huffed on and the blinds rattled softly.

From the foot of the stairs I called up again. Only the TV answered back. The steps were carpeted, and I took them quietly and two at a time. Lights on in the hallway. A home-office alcove to my left, with a view of another Las Brisas unit just a few yards away. A bathroom door stood open. I stopped at what looked like a guest room. Dog posters. Bookcases filled with paperbacks.

The TV grew louder as I approached the master bedroom. The door was half open and I could hear the sitcom clearly now, *That '70s Show.*

"Nick!"

The audience laughed. I pushed the door open and peered inside. A big TV hung on the wall, facing the bed. Nick lay propped against the headboard, facing the screen with eyes open and man bun in place, the remote cradled in his extended right hand. In his left hand leaned a glass tumbler. The bullet had caught him squarely in the forehead, centered just above his eyes. A big-caliber bullet, probably fired from a silenced gun—or half the citizens of densely packed Las Brisas would have heard and reported it. Certainly Daley Rideout and Scott Chan. Just a trickle of blood off his nose because Nick Moreno had died before he could even move. The headboard was a gruesome spectacle. On the TV, youngsters shot hoops and cracked jokes. The smell of blood.

Because a defenseless young man had been murdered, and because I was a licensed private investigator who had introduced myself to neighbors, tried to purchase information from one of them, then illegally entered another's domicile, I would have to call the police soon.

So I shot pictures of Nick with my phone.

And close-ups of the tattered pit bull–themed address book and the Labrador retriever appointment calendar I found on the office desk. I recorded his last three incoming messages on the landline answering machine. What I really wanted was his cell phone contacts, but his phone was likely in his pocket—it was nowhere else I searched.

I stood in the bedroom doorway again, considering "guaranteed loser" Nick Moreno. Twenty brief years. Someone's son, and I had to figure they had loved him and held him when he was hurt and fussed over which of his school pictures to order and what to get him for Christmas and if they should really let him have that puppy he badly wanted.

I also considered the other man who happened to be here—one Roland Ford, making a living off the dead.

Here to help a young girl who had taken up with violent men.

Here to satisfy a contract with a paying client.

I can cast my actions as virtues as well as the next guy.

I took out my phone again and put it on camera, then reversed the direction for a selfie. Looked down at my big and scarred and not beautiful face filling the little black screen. Took my picture. Felt that I needed to keep this moment. Ford, at another crossroads he hadn't known was there.

Then I went outside, locked my cell phone in the big toolbox bolted to the bed of my truck.

Walked back into Nick Moreno's home and used his landline to call Detective Sergeant Darrel Walker at the San Diego Sheriff's North Coast Station, which covers Encinitas. I broke off some toilet paper and wiped off the telephone handset. Put the paper in my coat pocket. Darrel and I had worked together once and almost gotten along.

Twenty minutes later I answered Nick Moreno's doorbell and looked into Darrel's unhappy face. Two uniforms and a crime-scene investigator with a rolling suitcase flanked him, all giving me their best grave expressions.

"Every time I see you something bad has happened," said Darrel Walker.

"Here we go again."

Darrel shook his head but not my hand, then stepped inside.

I WALKED HIM upstairs. The uniforms jangled heavily behind us and the CSI carried his suitcase rather than bump the cargo up the steps.

While they stood in the doorway of Nick Moreno's bedroom I stepped into the office alcove and looked out the window at the sunny September morning. Four road bikers sped by on the street below, clustered tightly, knees high and their chests nearly prone to the bike frames. A pickup truck slowly followed, a young couple in front and two surfboards resting on blankets on the tailgate. A red SUV came from the other direction, towing kayaks. I was once a cyclist, a surfer, and a kayaker. Then a college kid, a Marine, a boxer, and a sheriff's deputy. After getting knocked out in my pro boxing debut, I had a long talk with myself and took up ballroom dancing. I know. But even being large and heavy, I still feel light on the dance floor. Got third place in a waltz competition once, a nice little gold-finish trophy with a trim little dude and a woman in a lilting gown. There are few feelings as satisfying as another's body working in tandem with your own. The rhythm and trust. The aspirations to grace.

"Ford?" asked Darrel Walker. "Talk to me while these people do their jobs."

We sat in the small condo dining room. Darrel is bigger than I am, so the room felt even smaller. He records everything. I walked him through my morning and the new client with a missing sister who was mixed up with the man upstairs. Described what Scott Chan had seen, my concern for Daley Rideout, the suspicious arrival and departure of the men. Said that I'd found the garage door leading into the house open. And had heard the TV upstairs. I told him what I could, given that I had client privacy to respect and a job to do.

He asked me if I'd taken pictures and I told him no, I'd left my cell phone in the truck.

"So you called me how?" he asked.

"The landline upstairs."

"Convenient."

"Very."

"What else didn't you take besides pictures?"

"Nothing. I didn't touch anything but the phone and the garage doorknob. Even used TP to clean them up."

"You know I can arrest you."

"Except the girl took off with two men," I said. "After one of them put a bullet in that young man's head. Cut me loose to look for this girl, Darrel. You know what the minutes can mean. Everything I find I'll bring to you."

Dark eyes in a dark face, calculating. "I'll talk to the girl's sister and Oceanside PD. Probably get myself into a turf war. Maybe you should get out of here before I change my mind."

Climbing into my truck, I pictured Daley Rideout leaving with two men. I pictured Nick upstairs in his bed. I pictured Penelope's judging blue eyes. I turned on my phone, hit contacts for her number, then changed my mind.

3

////////////////////

I T was after one o'clock by the time I drove onto the Monarch Academy campus in Carlsbad. A sign at the entrance said:

MONARCH ACADEMY

Home of the

CAVALIERS

Academy chancellor Dr. Judith Stahl was a stocky, middle-aged woman with short dark hair and round wire-framed glasses. She frowned as I told her about my meeting with Penelope Rideout. She called Penelope and got permission to talk to me. She was still frowning a few minutes later as she led me down the steps from Oxford Hall and into the September sunlight.

"This is wrong," she said. "Daley should have been in American History at that time. I know she was here and on time yesterday for first period. I saw her. Academy security will get to the bottom of this."

Chancellor Stahl marched us toward the admin building from which we'd just come, heels brisk on the walkway. The campus was new construction, two levels of right angles, darkly stained lumber, and smoked glass. We backdoored our way to the visitor check-in counter. The same armed and uniformed young man who had signed me in and paged the chancellor for me was still on duty. He rose in respect for his boss. His badge said "Cates."

"Wayne," she said. "Get Baxter over here ASAP and come to my office."

"Yes, Chancellor."

Her upstairs office was spacious and cool, with views of the Pacific beyond the hills. Chancellor Stahl's secretary admitted Wayne, who quietly crossed the carpet and took a chair next to me, setting his laptop on his knees.

"Recap yesterday, and Daley Rideout," said Stahl.

Wayne looked up from the laptop screen. "She passed through student main security at seven forty-one in the morning. According to her teachers, she was in class for periods one through three. She didn't go through security for lunch in the commons. And none of her teachers after lunch flagged her as absent."

"Explain why," said the chancellor. "She was off-campus and in Encinitas by noon, according to Mr. Ford."

"Yes, Chancellor," said Wayne. "Her father, Richard Hauser, had signed on to the academy parent portal the evening before, and advised that Daley would be absent periods four through seven and of course lunch. Family matters."

"And he confirmed with a call later? Per Monarch procedure?" she asked.

Wayne consulted his screen again. "Within the hour, yes, he confirmed."

Someone did, I thought.

"But Daley did not check out through student security," said Stahl. "And you didn't see her leave? None of your people saw her leave?"

"That's correct. Very busy, the lunch rush."

"Then she could easily have left the academy alone and unaccompanied by an adult?"

Or accompanied by the wrong adult, I thought.

"I would have to agree, yes, Chancellor."

Chancellor Stahl was fiddling with a pen, which she now dropped to the desktop glass with a clatter.

I cleared my throat. "How often does a student steal the portal password and book her own vacation getaway? Have a friend play Mom or Dad for the confirmation call? Maybe do it herself?"

An incriminating beat of silence.

"Of course that can happen," said Wayne. "We ask them to change passwords often."

"We're an exclusive private academy," said the chancellor. "Not a supermax prison."

I asked about security video.

"Here," said Wayne, looking up from his computer. "It's all right here."

He leaned forward and set the laptop on the chancellor's desk, turning it so we could all see. I watched the screen quarter into rectangles, each showing a different entrance and/or exit.

My phone vibrated and I checked the caller number and name: Penelope Rideout. Let it go to message.

Wayne set the video calendar to the previous day, then sped the master clock forward to 11:40 a.m. In good, clear audio, the recorded lunch bell pealed through the campus public-address speakers. The lunch getaway lasted two frantic minutes. Boys and girls in their gray-and-white uniforms, slashing their ID cards through the turnstile readers, bursting into the parking lot to begin their fifty minutes of freedom. Juniors and seniors straight to their own wheels, underclassmen with moms and dads for getaway drivers, a jockeying battalion of high-horse luxury.

Cavaliers, baby.

But Daley Rideout was not one of them.

"I hate to keep being the bad guy here," I said. "But there must be other ways to—"

"Get on and off campus?" snapped the chancellor. "Of course there are. They can sneak out when no one is looking. They can climb a six-foot chain-link fence. They can squeeze past the turnstiles two at a time or just jump the damned things."

"They always find new ways past the video cameras," Wayne said with a chuckle. The chancellor glared at him with frank contempt.

On my phone I brought up the picture of Daley and Nick. Both the chancellor and Wayne nodded.

"He picks her up after school sometimes," said Wayne. "I spoke to her sister. She didn't approve, but Daley defied her. I think Daley defies her sister often, Mr. Ford."

"We should all get back to work," said Judith Stahl, standing. "Please escort Mr. Ford out, Wayne."

"I'd like to talk to some of Daley's friends," I said, not standing.

"We'd need to get Penelope's and their parents' approval first," she said. "And that can take some time."

"Time? Chancellor, Daley Rideout was last seen getting into an SUV with two men yesterday around noon, when she was supposed to be here at Monarch. I need to talk to some of her friends. Now. They might know who these people are and where they're going. Every minute counts."

She gave me a hard stare. "She has two good friends here at Monarch. I know where they are. I'll handle this, Wayne."

———

THE FOUR OF us sat at a picnic table in the shade of a coral tree in the now deserted lunch quad. Thin Alanis Tervalua regarded me from behind a wall of shiny black hair. Stout Carrie Calhoun was a corn-silk blonde with green, seldom-blinking eyes.

Trying not to alarm them, I told them who I was, then laid out the basics of Daley's activities the day before as best I knew them, ending with her being seen talking to two men in a silver SUV with a round blue emblem on the driver's door. The men were both late twenties or early thirties. They were clean-cut and conservatively dressed. I told them this had happened at Nick Moreno's place, omitting Nick's fate and Daley's departure with the men.

The girls watched me intently, Alanis with one brown eye not hidden behind her hair, Carrie with green, wide-eyed attention.

When they attempted furtive glances at each other, their cat was at least partially out of its bag. I heard the faint catch of Chancellor Stahl's breath.

"Nick is, like, a totally cool guy," said Alanis.

"He can be kind of edgy, too," said Carrie.

Their glances caromed, and I guessed that Nick was not their subject at all. "What about the men in the SUV?" I asked.

"Well, there's this club," said Carrie. "And sometimes these two guys in an SUV take us there after school. Connor and Eric. They drop us off, but mostly we just Uber there and home."

Carrie's and Alanis's descriptions of Connor and Eric were not unlike Scott Chan's version of Daley Rideout's escorts. And if they were the same men, it would account for Daley Rideout's apparent comfort with them.

Time to go fishing: "Do they drive a silver SUV?"

"With a sign on the door," said Carrie. "Of an eagle holding lightning bolts in its talons. It's their security company."

The sign that Scott Chan couldn't quite see?

My phone thrummed again: Penelope Rideout.

"You two girls are absolutely foolish, taking rides with men you don't know," said Chancellor Stahl.

Alanis shrugged, but Carrie brought some force to her voice. "Monarch teaches us to trust our judgment and be our own security guards," she said.

"Maybe we should revisit that policy," said Stahl. Then she looked at me. "They're talking about Alchemy 101. It's a teen club in Oceanside. Live music, big-screen videos, vegan menu. No smoking, no alcohol."

"Some of the people there are ugly," said Alanis.

"They are not," said Carrie.

"Not ugly-looking," said Alanis. "Looking ugly."

"What do you mean by that?" I asked.

Alanis shrugged. "At me. They look ugly at me."

Then an awkward moment between the girls, a stand-off I sensed they had had before.

"Did you see them yesterday?" I asked. "The Alchemy 101 men?"

They both nodded, and both looked at Chancellor Stahl with visible worry.

"We went to the sneak-out with Daley at lunch," said Carrie. "Because she asked us to. Because in a group you don't stand out to Mr. Cates. That's Wayne, the security geek. And Daley snuck through the hole in the chain-link that's hidden by ivy. And she got picked up by Nick in his van with the dog's face on the doors. Alanis and I watched Nick drive away and we waved. And just as we were about to head back to the quad, that's when we saw the silver SUV and the Alchemy 101 guys."

Who followed Nick and Daley to Nick's place, I thought.

"I take it the sneak-out is your latest way off campus without permission?" asked the chancellor. "Out there behind the visitors' bleachers?"

The girls pursed their lips and nodded glumly, more concerned with their fates as lunchtime conspirators than the possible fate of Daley in the company of two murderers. *Youth isn't wasted on the young,* I thought. *They just can't see over it.*

Chancellor Stahl walked me to the main exit. Her default expression was the frown, but it looked like one of concern more than disapproval. I dropped my visitor's badge back into the box.

"Daley Rideout is a troubled girl," she said. "Bright, but easily distracted. She tested at one thirty-one on the Stanford-Binet but only makes Bs. She has a list of Monarch infractions a mile long. Mostly absences. I don't know much about this Nick Moreno, except that he walks dogs for a living and is twenty years old to Daley's fourteen. So a child with a man. I have spoken with the police about this, though Mr. Moreno has broken no laws in associating with Daley. She's been here two years now and this is her third interaction with a man much older than she is. She is sexually mature. Which puts Monarch in a difficult position. Quite honestly, I don't think the sister can control her."

"Does she try?" I asked.

"She seems powerless. Penelope was just eighteen when her parents died. Daley was all of four. So they have a deep sisterhood. But is that the basis for competent stewardship? Not for me to judge. I can say that I'm worried about Daley and what has happened to her. And what might happen in the next days."

"What about the husband?"

"Distant and disengaged, from what I'm told. He's only been on campus a couple of times. Penelope says he travels a lot on business. What business, she hasn't said."

Parental kidnapping came to my mind. The most common form of child abduction on the planet. But Richard Hauser wasn't Daley's biological father, and there was no custody battle going on, at least according to Penelope.

I listened to Penelope's message from the road. Voice jittery. Detective Darrel Walker had come to the house. I called and told her I was just a few minutes out. She clicked off without a word.

4

////////////////

HER home was a forties beach bungalow on Myers Street in Oceanside just a few blocks from the Transportation Center. The fence around it was wrought iron and the gate swung quietly. The front yard was drought-proof gravel with pots of succulents and sturdy geraniums. There was one Mexican fan palm, tall and thin and needing a haircut. The slat cottage was mint green with white trim, and the porch had an oval rug for a welcome mat.

Penelope held open the screen door and I stepped into the living room. Her eyes were swollen and bloodshot. Baggy cargo pants and a black T-shirt. Ball cap, makeup gone.

"We're going to get her back," I said.

"I need more than words from you."

"Darrel Walker is a tough detective, and every agency knows what happened."

"My sister is abducted by murderers and you tell me how tough the cops are?"

"They'll do what they have to, and so will we."

"Meaning what? Meaning fucking *what*?"

She stared up at me for a long moment, a festival of pained emotions playing across her face. She balled her fists and shut her eyes and mouthed a silent string of words that I could make no sense of. It went on for a bit. A calming mantra, maybe. Or a prayer. Or a curse.

Then she took a deep breath. Her eyes and fists opened. "I shall now control myself. Penelope is in control again. See?"

"I need to take a look at Daley's room."

"Then I will take you to her room. I'm sorry for my anger."

"I feel some of that, too."

"I'm ninety percent lover and ten percent killer," she said.

"I'm German-English."

She studied me through a thicket of suspicion. "You have an unusual sense of humor. Here, a list of friends, and how you can contact them."

I pocketed the sheet of paper as she led me down a narrow hallway. Then a right turn into Daley's room. Good light coming through the window. An unmade bed, pink everything. A plush floor rug with dalmatian puppies romping. A mirrored closet, stuffed with clothes, sliding door half open. One wall with pop-star posters taped askew— Beyoncé and Selena, Justin and Bruno. An acoustic guitar propped in a corner, a nice Gibson. Another wall had been entirely painted in the blackboard finish popular with students, and apparently Daley had taken a serious shine to it: many-colored chalk swirls, yellow creatures with compound eyes, blue ponies with flowing orange-and-red tails, armies of tiny white ants marching over black, *The Scream* repeated several times in varying sizes, all faithfully re-created in violet and chartreuse.

From dalmatians to Munch, I thought. Part little girl and part "easily distracted" teenager. And what else?

Penelope allowed me to search Daley's room and her bathroom, which was just across the hall. I found no drugs, prescription or otherwise, no paraphernalia, no alcohol or tobacco. No birth control. There were more than a few energy-drink cans in the wastebaskets. She liked the same candy I do, anything with peanuts and chocolate, and plenty of it. No backpack.

On her desk were two small stacks of notebooks dedicated to different subjects from the previous school term. Her handwriting was sleek and aggressive, nothing like her sister's. Six books, stacked on top of one another, big to small: the Bible, the Twilight saga, the diary of Anne Frank. And a bright collection of ceramic Día de los Muertos skulls and colorful folk-art crosses. The center desk drawer was a tangled wad of cords and adapters.

The shower and bathroom counter were crowded with hair and skin products. Penelope told me that in addition to clothes and a few toiletries, and her carry-on rolling luggage, Daley had taken her laptop and a Martin Backpacker guitar that Penelope had bought her for her twelfth birthday. She played and wrote songs.

"Is she on social media?" I asked.

"I don't allow it."

"Does she have a smartphone?"

"Of course," said Penelope. "The child security software has never worked properly, but I examine it every night before she goes to bed. As agreed. I check it covertly, too. I prowl her friends' sites on my phone for signs of her. She's good to her word—no Facebook, no Twitter, no Instagram."

"Telegram or Snapchat?"

"No social media. It's a gateway technology."

"Gateway to what?" I asked.

"The evil in the world."

Of course evil predated social media by a few hundred thousand years, but what would have been my point?

"I learned a few things at her school that you should know about," I said.

On my way out of the room I saw what looked like kick marks on the inside of Daley's bedroom door. I stopped and felt the doorknob's outside lock.

"I lock her in her room at times," said Penelope. "Very reluctantly and very rarely. She doesn't care for it."

We sat at a small oak table in the dining area. From there I could see the living room, separated from the kitchen by a half-wall, and some of the front yard through the screen door. I watched the bikers and skateboarders and runners, and the steady parade of drivers heading home from their late-summer day at the beach.

"What can you tell me about Alchemy 101?" I asked.

"An Oceanside teen club. Daley likes it there."

"Do you like *her* there?"

"So long as I know where she is. I've been to it. The security is adequate."

"Do you know how she gets there?"

She gave me a skeptical look. "What do you mean?"

I told her what Alanis and Carrie had said about Connor and Eric, the silver SUV, and the rides to Alchemy 101 after school. How they just dropped the girls off and let them find their own ways home. How the men loosely fit an eyewitness description of Daley's escorts, who arrived and departed Nick Moreno's house in a silver Expedition.

"No. No, I don't know of these men." I saw the shame cross her face.

"People lie to me all the time," I said. "Even when I want to believe them."

"You seem too cynical for that."

"It's a weakness in my line of work, hoping that people are telling the truth. It usually doesn't last long."

While those maybe cynical words hung in the air I studied the small house, the worn hardwood floors and beach-rental furniture. Bare white walls. Tattered, poorly fitted blinds. An orange-and-red plaid couch, a cheap wooden side table, and a knockoff Tiffany lamp. A flimsy-looking wicker stand loaded with photos. Two blue director's chairs. A boom box on a sideways orange crate on the living room floor, some paperbacks and CDs propped inside.

"How long have you lived here?" I asked.

"A year. We rarely stay in one place for long."

"Because Richard is a Marine pilot?"

"Yes, as I told you," she said. "So Miramar for now. A Second Marine Aircraft Wing instructor. The Top Gun days are over at Miramar, but don't tell Richard that."

"I was One MEF," I said. Which is the First Marine Expeditionary Force that led the charge in Fallujah. We were aided by the 3rd Marine Aircraft Wing, which was headquartered at Marine Corps Air Station Miramar, then and now.

"Oh?" she asked. "MEF? I'm sorry but I can't keep up with Marine Corps acronyms."

"It doesn't matter," I said. But it did. "Is he in town now, your husband?"

"He's out at Fallon for a few days. Nevada."

"How is his relationship with Daley?"

A cool drift into her eyes. "Excellent. She has only a few memories of Dad. Richard is her father figure. There are uncles on both Mom's and Dad's sides, but, well, we moved around a fair amount. The three of us."

She retrieved a small brass picture frame from atop the kitchen refrigerator, handed it to me. Penelope, Daley, and a Marine pilot in his flight suit, all standing in front of an F-16. Smiles, wind in their hair, all three wearing aviator sunglasses. A happy moment.

"When did you and Richard marry?"

"November sixth, 2011. It was the happiest day of my life. When your husband is career, you go where they throw you."

I nodded, setting the picture on the table between us. My father had been career and we had gone where they threw us for years. Then he retired, but came back to consult for three times the salary and none of the deployments, transfers, and reassignments.

"How is your relationship with Richard?"

"Very good, thank you. Why do you ask?"

"To understand the forces in Daley's life."

"The strongest force in Daley's life is Daley."

"You described her as precocious but capable of making bad choices," I said.

"A textbook fourteen-year-old, I would say."

I wasn't sure there was such a thing. "The precocious part worries Chancellor Stahl," I said. "She says that Daley has had three 'interactions' with much older boys in the two years she's been at Monarch."

"She's still a virgin," said Penelope. "I spend tremendous amounts of psychic and physical energy making sure of that. I always have very pointed discussions with Daley's male friends. I scare them. Maybe because my ten percent killer shows through. I know I can't keep her protected forever. I'm doomed to fail, but I think Daley is worth the fight. Fourteen is too young. When I was that age I was happy. I loved horses and my girlfriends. I was still innocent."

I nodded but wondered if innocence had already passed Daley

Rideout by. Nick Moreno had died and Daley had left with the men who killed him. Without apparent struggle or coercion. *The girl and the men looked okay with each other.*

Penelope stood quickly when her phone rang, took it from a rear pocket, and looked down at the screen. "Richard," she said. "I need to take this."

5

///////////////////////

ALCHEMY 101 was in a strip mall in Oceanside on the inland side of Interstate 5. Oceanside is home to some one hundred and seventy thousand souls: Anglos, Hispanics, African Americans, Luiseño Indians, Asians, Pacific Islanders. Marines, ex-Marines, and veterans of all the branches. Surfers, anglers, motorcyclists, and a diverse beach-hugging citizenry too quirky to categorize. There's the California Surf Museum, the Oceanside Museum of Art, a good public library, and the Supergirl Pro Jam—the largest women's surf competition in the world. Oceanside is not one of your plush Southern California beach towns. Not enough mansions or gated neighborhoods. More woodies than Teslas, more wheelchairs than Segways. It's got street cred.

It was early evening by then, the western sky hanging orange and blue beyond the power poles. Alchemy 101 was in the middle of the mall, flanked by Reptile Republic and Blondie's Scooters. The mall's anchor store was a Dollar Tree. I noted Coast Donut, Discount Military, and Frank's Surf Shop.

Alchemy 101 had a neon Celtic-script sign in the entrance alcove and densely smoked windows. The sign was on, throwing its hot red letters against the darkened glass. At the booth I paid my ten bucks, got my right tamped with a red *A*. The sign said teens paid five. The cashier was a pleasant girl with pink hair and steel studs embedded the length of her right eyebrow who said, "Welcome to Alchemy 101, man."

I noted a ticket-booth decal saying that these premises were protected by SNR Security. The company graphic was a round blue emblem with an eagle gripping lightning bolts in its talons.

Interesting.

Inside, Alchemy 101 was larger than I'd expected. Well lit, the smells of incense and coffee. A stage at the far end, a dance floor, and booths along two walls. A snack bar and kitchen, and one entire wall of screens playing music videos, old TV shows, and what appeared to be Thoroughbred horse races from around the world.

Plenty of customers here already, young people sitting and standing around raised tables, mostly boys with boys and girls with girls. I noted some older customers—my age and more. Maybe they liked the alcohol-free bar scene. Maybe they liked young people. Maybe they were taking a look at the place where their children wanted to go after school or evenings, as Penelope Rideout had.

A band was setting up on the carpeted stage, a tall teenage boy facing an amplifier, tuning a yellow bass. The singer took her microphone from a case and slid it into its front-stage stand. Her hair was a downy orange halo and she wore a black sequined singlet, denim short shorts, black leggings, and red cowgirl boots. I did a quick surveillance, saw that SNR Security had salted the room with cameras.

I carried a tumbler of iced coffee to a stool by the entrance and sat with my back to the glass for a good view of the room. Used my phone to log in to the IvarDuggans.com site. IvarDuggans.com is the best of several big-bore online investigative services to which I subscribe, at some expense, and use often. Snoops 'R Us. If there's a Big Brother watching you, it's not the government, yet, but IvarDuggans.com and services like them. Their main customers are banks, collection agencies, insurance companies, and law enforcement. Their databases are massive and growing by the second; their engines are fast. Ivar-Duggans is especially good because they have twice the number of photos and videos that the other security sites have.

I came up with five Daley Rideouts nationwide. One in California. There she was, recognizable as the girl in Penelope's pictures but much younger. Longer hair, but curly like her sister's. A pleasant face. Three of the images had been plucked from Daley's Facebook page before vigilant Penelope had closed it down. At that time, Daley was eleven years old. The same for @onthemovedaleyrideout on Twitter, her last tweet being three years ago. On the move? Her posts and tweets were chatty and vague. In my small notebook I wrote down some of the names of her most consistent network friends.

Because of her age, IvarDuggans.com didn't have much on Daley Rideout. Born August 26, 2005, in Denver, Colorado, to Carl and June Rideout, deceased. Residences since Denver were Salt Lake City, Boise, Reno, and Eugene. The Rideouts had moved four times in the four years between Daley's birth and the deaths of Carl and June in a one-car traffic accident in Eugene in 2009. Following that, Penelope had become Daley's legal guardian and the Rideout sisters had lived five more years in Eugene. They had moved to Prescott, Arizona, in late 2014. Three years later, Daley and Penelope had moved to Phoenix. Then Oceanside.

I wondered about those years of frantic moving while Carl and June were alive. Work-related? Wanderlust? I was curious to see if Penelope's profile would have answers. As for Daley, unsurprisingly, she had no vehicle registrations, professional licenses, fictitious business names, tax liens, watercraft, or aircraft registered in her name. No known associates. And no criminal record, though even dogged IvarDuggans can't unearth sealed juvenile court, adoption, medical, or gun license records.

I looked down the list of categories left blank, pleased that not every bit and byte of information about young Daley Rideout was available to anyone willing to pay for it.

Oddly enough—very oddly—the same was true of Penelope: Her IvarDuggans biography was spotty.

Born October 14, 1990, in Mobile, Alabama, to Carl and June. Fourteen years later, the Rideouts moved to Denver, where the three Rideouts became four. After that, Penelope and her family lived in the aforementioned succession of homes—Denver through Eugene, four moves in four years—until the deaths of the mother and father. Annoyingly, IvarDuggans.com had the same long blanks for Penelope between Eugene, Prescott, Phoenix, and Oceanside—three moves in five years.

Penelope Rideout's education and employment histories closely paralleled her moves—and lack of them—around the country.

Elementary and two years of junior high school in her native Mobile. Mentions in both *The Mobile Daily* and *The Alabaman* of young Penelope's success at hunter-jumper youth competitions.

Then the southern girl skipped eighth grade and went west to Denver for her first year of high school. IvarDuggans provided no extracurricular news for that year.

She did her second year of high school in Salt Lake, her third year in Boise, one semester of her senior year in Reno, and her final semester in Eugene. Her graduation picture from Eugene High School showed a contained and pretty girl, with the same calm, adjudicating eyes that I had seen for the first time less than twelve hours ago in my Fallbrook office.

Penelope had graduated from the University of Oregon with a major in English and a minor in mathematics. In her graduation photo she looked composed.

Then part-time employment as a technical researcher/writer in Eugene, through 2011.

The year she married Richard Hauser.

Although IvarDuggans.com had no record of that union. Neither did TLO or Tracers Info. Very unusual. Information peddlers as sophisticated as these don't often miss things the size of marriages.

So I called him, Hauser, at the number that Mrs. Rideout had given me. Got one Suzanne Delgado, who had never heard of Richard Hauser and hung up. Checked Facebook and got eleven men with the same name, two of them approximately the right age but neither even slightly resembling the Marine colonel in the picture.

Went to the bar for another iced coffee. The band was doing a sound check. Nice and loud. I asked the boy-faced, dreadlocked barista about them and he told me they were a San Diego–based psychedelic garage band called Tin Lenses. I asked him if SNR was still in charge of security here, and he said yes, they stopped in every night.

Back at my stool, I tried to dig up the strangely overlooked Richard Hauser and found two such men who had been U.S. Marines in the last four decades, but neither was still active. Not colonels, not pilots.

I called an old Marine friend now stationed at Miramar, Master Sergeant Tyson Songrath. We spent a few minutes catching up, and when I asked about Richard Hauser, Ty had never heard of him. He certainly would have, if Hauser was actual: Songrath worked in aircraft maintenance and knew every pilot who'd come through Miramar in the last five years.

As soon as I hung up, the band kicked into its first song. Good timing. Fast chords crashed through the room. The singer's voice cut through them, high and clear.

Still online with my shameless snooping confederates, I quickly tracked down the basics on Carl and June Rideout (née Donegan). Carl had been a pleasant-faced, bespectacled man, an aerospace publications director, and she was a nurse, who looked very much like her daughters. He was a Mobile native, while June hailed from the Alabama hill country. Both from big families. He was a deacon in a non-denominational church; June taught Sunday school there. Carl had been ten years older than June, who had had their first child when she was twenty-one and their second at thirty-five. I wondered why they'd waited so long between children. Trouble conceiving? Trouble taking to term? A purposeful pause? They were middle-class people, old-school southern Democrats with a hint of prosperity via the Mobile Oaks Country Club.

A collision reconstruction report completed in March 2009 concluded that the single-car crash had happened on a stormy night, on northbound I-5, heading into Eugene. Carl had lost control of the minivan, crashed through a guardrail, and rolled the vehicle down a slope and into a creek running high with rainwater. No excessive speed. No alcohol or drugs involved. However, the right front tire of the van had blown out, and in all likelihood, the front-wheel drive, high winds, and rain-drenched highway had conspired to hydroplane the slightly top-heavy vehicle off the road and down the embankment. Carl was dead when the Oregon State Police arrived; June died that night in a hospital.

A family portrait taken just months before their deaths showed two wholesome, still-young parents and their two daughters, a teenager and a four-year old. They all looked loved. Mom and girls were conspicuously radiant.

However, I did have some questions for my employer—older sister Penelope—who was claiming to have married a man who didn't seem to have a history. None at all. And I had other questions for her little sister, Daley, who had just yesterday been seen willingly getting into a car with probable murderers and had not been home since. I looked at that family portrait again. A tingle came from the scar on my forehead—an old boxing injury that acts up from time to time. Sometimes a tingle, sometimes a chill, sometimes an itch or a burn. An expressive scar with a mind of its own. Always trying to tell me something. I wondered what.

An Internet search told me that SNR Security was a privately held, San Diego–based company now two years old, specializing in "Armed and Unarmed Personal, Workplace, and Job Site Protection." SNR Security was a member of the Better Business Bureau and the San Diego Chamber of Commerce, and endorsed by the Southern California Christian Business Association. I found two workplace racial discrimination suits, both dropped. No other complaints, controversies, or litigations involving the company.

I watched the young dancers, enjoyed the music. I might have been in a place like this twenty-something years ago. Partying like it was 1999. Even back then I liked to dance. A large but not completely graceless young man. I was twenty years old that year. Two years through a San Diego State University degree in history. I surfed and fished and had a steady girlfriend. Why history? Because when I read the papers and watched the news I couldn't make any sense of the world at all. Figured I needed some background. Soon as I had gotten a little, I joined the Marines and stepped from the pages of history into history itself. Fallujah. Where so much went wrong.

Alone there in Alchemy 101, I let the hours set their own pace. We widowers learn to do that. I scanned the newspaper on my smartphone. Nations rising and nations falling. Find the nuke. Our great American divide. The scandal du jour. All the heat and so little light.

Dinner was good, soup and a sandwich. I watched the customers on their way into the club. At 9:04 p.m. a silver Expedition SUV pulled into the handicap-only space out front, not ten feet from where I sat. The emblem on the door said SNR Security, and showed an eagle holding two lightning bolts. The driver got out, locked up, and knocked on the glass of the ticket-seller's booth, smiling at her on his way past. When he came inside I saw a sturdy guy, thirty or so, dressed in slacks and duty boots and a dark blue uniform blouse with a badge on it. A Sam Browne belt with Mace and a flashlight attached, no sidearm. He moved through the crowd to the coffee bar and started talking to the barista.

He accepted his drink in a to-go cup but didn't pay for it. He sipped it and slowly worked his way between the dancers and the standing audience, all the way along the full-wall video screen, which was now showing a hugely magnified, real-time Tin Lenses. The guard slipped backstage through a black curtain.

The orange-haloed girl in the singlet and shorts was giving the song her all. Boots planted, arms out, swaying in rhythm. The bass player watched her closely, his fingers tied to her movements as firmly as a puppeteers'. Through the amplified music, her voice rang clear and true.

Come on, shoot us a star
Play some electric guitar

So we can find where you are
In the Blue Rodeo

Ten minutes later, the security man came back through the black curtain, sipping his coffee, making his way toward the exit. I bellied up to the bar and bought a double espresso in a to-go cup, timing my return trip for a brush with the guard. He bumped past me, raising his cup to Dreadlocks as his badge glimmered in the brightly flashing strobe lights: Adam Revell.

I spotted him a few steps, then hooked around and followed him out. Gave him my back as I walked to my truck, digging the fob out of my pocket. Casual PI Ford, in no hurry and happily careless in the world. I saw Adam Revell behind me, reflected in my window, standing on the running board of the Expedition and waving goodbye to the ticket-seller in the glass booth.

6

///////////////////

I STAYED two cars behind, padding my cover with the beach town traffic. Took Interstate 5 through Carlsbad and Leucadia into Encinitas, then Encinitas Boulevard toward Rancho Santa Fe. Hills and open land. I'd done work here in this prosperous corner of San Diego's North County, multimillion-dollar estates with acreage, privacy, and plenty of room for horses and helipads.

Revell turned up Via Encanto, lightly traveled at this hour and leaving me exposed. I followed and fell back as he turned onto Matilija. Drove past it and U-turned, taking my time. Gave Revell his space.

Which gave R. Ford a chance to study the "Cathedral by the Sea" sign on the corner:

Home of the Four Wheels for Jesus Ministry
Where Christ Is King

When the SUV's taillights had vanished around a bend I started up the hill. Steep and wide. Up ahead I saw Revell sweep right, no signal, Matilija deserted. Again I loitered at the stop sign. Gave my mark some distance. Cut my lights and slowly followed him onto King's Road.

It was a private road, with thick new asphalt that randomly glittered in my headlights. From a steep, slow curve I saw the Pacific a few miles to my left, glittering much as the asphalt was, and the lights of the San Diego coast. I poked along, enjoying the view.

Rounding the next curve, I saw the Cathedral by the Sea, rising from a hilltop and bathed in light. It was modest in size, an asymmetrical construct of white marble and wooden beams bound together by stainless-steel cable. A copper roof flowed down nearly to the ground at one end, yet formed an upswept wave rising into the sky at the other. I wondered if the architect was now institutionalized. Concrete stairs and ramps led up to a tall, arched doorway. Inset windows of stained glass flickered with color. Above it all towered a large stainless-steel cross, lit by hidden floodlights to give it a supposed glow of its own. The Cathedral by the Sea was bold and somehow forbidding. I wasn't sure if it was expecting a worshiper or an invader.

The SUV rolled across a big parking lot, which was empty but well lit. I saw what might be an administration building, and a campus built around a stand of big Canary Island date palms, and a meandering grassy mall with fountains at each end, both still illuminated and tossing water in the night. Revell steered around the outbuildings and disappeared behind the cathedral.

I retreated to Via Encanto, backed my truck into a break in the thick chaparral, rolled the windows half down, and shut off the engine. I wondered how long it would take Revell to make his appointed rounds. Would he walk the grounds or just reconnoiter by SUV? It was hard to picture much trouble up on this swank but secluded hilltop church at ten o'clock on a warm Southern California night.

I found the Cathedral by the Sea website. Glancing from the phone to the road and back, I read:

Dear Faithful,

Please join us in worship of our Lord and Savior Jesus Christ, and in praise and thanks to Him for the forgiveness of our many sins. Our mission is to bring you to Our Lord. Come to experience fellowship in Him! Bring your children to our Sunday school, and encourage your teens to participate in our many activities. Next Sunday is surfing at Swami's—following our ten o'clock service, of course. Bring sunscreen, boards and joyful hearts! Sign up in the office, Moms and Dads welcome!

Pastor Reggie Atlas

Atlas's picture showed an earnest-looking man in his late forties or early fifties, with soulful eyes, shaggy blond hair, and a big, welcoming smile.

I did a Google search and scanned through the articles, blogs, and posts. The Cathedral by the Sea was just over a year old. Nice reviews from scores of North San Diego visitors when it opened early last summer. Hearty best wishes from the cities of Encinitas, Solana Beach, Del Mar, Vista, Rancho Santa Fe, and Oceanside. Optimistic notices on the religion pages of the local papers, and a good-sized piece in the *Union-Tribune*, written by a reporter I had once helped on a touchy story. Pictures of the pastor at home with his wife and children. Reggie Atlas had an easy smile and cheerful eyes and obviously liked cameras. He was forty-eight years old at the time of the story, a Georgia-born evangelist who had started small and ministered throughout the South by vehicle for ten years before establishing his first church. It went from modest to successful to very successful. Then the Lord had called him west.

I half read and half watched. Saw headlights on the cathedral parking lot asphalt, then the silver SNR Security vehicle, with Adam Revell barely visible behind the heavily smoked window.

I was surprised when he didn't backtrack down to the coast but headed east on Del Dios and onto I-15.

South to Santee, where he stopped for gas. I adjusted to the idea of a long night. I watched him from a competing station across the intersection, topping off my own main tank, an oversized thirty gallon. While the pump pumped, I got into the big toolbox bolted to the bed of my truck and claimed my night-vision binoculars, my holstered .45, and a small cooler stocked with jerky, candy, and drinks. Kept an eye on Revell. Set my provisions on the passenger seat.

Then off to I-8 East, which winds through the rough mountains and scorching desert and Imperial County farmland, tight to the Mexican border, then up almost to Tucson, where it joins I-10 for its long run to the Atlantic.

I varied my lanes and distance from the SUV, used the I-8 traffic for cover. Plenty of cars and tractor-trailers for that, even as we dropped down from the cool of the mountains to the September heat of the Imperial Valley and the dashboard clock hit midnight. Eighty-one in Ocotillo.

Onward to Coyote Wells, Plaster City, and Dixieland. Seeley and El Centro. Just past Buena Vista, the SUV got off at Rattlesnake Road and I had to slow way down as I came to the ramp and followed him off. He California-stopped at Rattlesnake, swinging left, which would take him through Buena Vista. I went right and continued on, his dust rising in my mirrors. I saw him make a right onto what looked like a dirt road, unlit, then disappear.

I made a slow U-turn and crept back along Rattlesnake, through tiny sleepy Buena Vista—part of it in California and the other part in

Mexico, with a twenty-foot-high steel wall to prove it. The gas station was closed. The convenience store open. A restaurant and a bar and signs for the post office and library. Houses scattered back in the dark, low hills.

The dirt road was wide and well graded. I cut my lights and used the nearly full moon, clear as a bulb in the north. Revell's dusty taillights shimmered far ahead. Headlights sprayed left and right in his turns. The shadows of creosote and ocotillo, leaning away from the moonbeams. Narrow dirt roads, one marked by a pile of rocks and another by a tire half buried in the sand. No signs, no mailboxes.

A trickle of nerves. Because there is no backup for PIs. No one to help you but you. No partners or departments, no cavalry to bugle in. You have your wit and skills, a phone that may or may not be in range, binoculars, a gun if you're licensed to carry one. Maybe a little cooler of food and drinks for those long hours on watch. Maybe even some luck. I believe in luck.

The road narrowed and got rougher. From the top of a slight rise I could see that the SUV had stopped, and the driver's door stood open. I glassed the low-beamed silhouette of a man dragging open a rickety barbed-wire-and-scrap-wood gate. A moment later he drove past it, then came back and escorted the wobbly gate back to its rustic post. Dropped a loop of chain over it. A breeze swirled around the SUV and it was gone.

The next gate was nothing like the first. Far ahead, bathed in the floods from a tall metal stanchion, the gliding wall of steel poles looked ten feet high. When it closed I saw the security guard accelerating away. And the metallic glimmer of two chain-link fences running in opposite directions as far as my night-vision glasses could follow.

The sign on the gate showed a fruit-heavy palm tree against a pale background. Beneath the fronds, heavy dark letters declared:

PARADISE DATE FARM
NO TRESPASSING

I sat tight. Watched the taillights rise and fall and grow smaller. It was twelve fifty-five. One minute later the gate lights went off. I gave the scene another good long look with my night glasses, saw no way in except through the gate, which I doubted would open to welcome the curious PI Ford.

Which meant you jumped the fence. I glassed it with an eye for electrical or razor wire. No and no. Ten feet was ten feet, but I could do it. There was a chance of my truck getting broken into by the time I got back. More practically, I tried to guess how far I would have to walk. All I had to go on was a low ridgeline that looked to be less than half a mile away. Over which the SUV had passed less than a minute ago. And from behind which shone soft light.

I lowered the glasses and thought about my first professional boxing match, Trump 29 Casino in Coachella, 2005. It was less than a year after Fallujah. Back then I was Roland "Rolling Thunder" Ford, a United States Marine Corps vet, weighing in at 210 out of San Diego, California. My opponent was Darien "Demolition" Dixon, a veteran not of war but of the ring.

I knew before the first round was over that I was outmatched. But when he knocked me down in the ninth, I refused to surrender. I got myself off the canvas and nodded to the ref and commanded my legs to move, and Darien promptly knocked me unconscious. I still remember seeing my mouthpiece sailing out through the lights. Next thing I knew I was on my stool, dazed in a not unpleasant way, seeing myself from the outside at the same time I was looking out at the crowd. I was learning something I'd never learned as a college student or a Marine: defeat. In that moment I became mortal. I've fought again since then, but never in the ring.

So my question is: Is it better to fight a fight you can't win or to give up and take the loss so you can fight again?

I found a stand of tangled greasewoods to watch over my truck. Spooked an owl that fell into flight when I opened the door. Worked the paddle holster into place inside my waistband, pushed the gun in snug, and snapped the strap. I loaded a small backpack with the binoculars, a compact thirty-five-millimeter camera with a great zoom, and a bottle of water. Pulled on some gloves. Chugged an energy drink from the cooler, locked up, and deployed.

1

////////////////

THE desert floor was flat, the sand packed hard for stretches, then softly rippled in the dunes. Lumps of creosote and brittle bush and scattered stands of mallow. A hundred yards away from the gate I climbed the fence, gloves a blessing but boots treacherous on the chain. Felt exposed as a moth on a wall. Easier going down.

A straight trot toward the ridgeline. Light good enough to see the rocks and dips and cacti. A breeze kicked up. Between the intermittent gusts I heard the far-off sound of a beehive, which reminded me that bees are commercially raised in the Imperial Valley but reminded me of other things, too.

Took me just fifteen minutes to make the ridgeline. Closer, but steeper than I'd guessed. The soft glow still came from beyond it. When I reached the top I took a knee, breathing deep and steady. Looked out at the date palms—acres of them—tall and droop-topped and elegant in the moonlight. Spacious rows for easy harvest. Medjools. I knew them from Iraq.

In the middle of the palms was an agricultural compound that looked more Mexican or Middle Eastern than Southern Californian.

Low-slung, boxy buildings in a loose circle around a packed-dirt campus. Built decades ago for the heat. The main house was a white two-story stack of rectangles, large and sprawling and flat-roofed. It looked added-onto over time. There was a packing house and a large corrugated metal hangar from which floodlights blanched the grounds in bright, buggy light. And a stately red barn with white trim, American-style. Three long bunkhouses stood on one side of the barn, facing one another in a horseshoe. On the other side stretched a row of eight squat cottages—white plaster, flat roofs, and hard edges. Various metal sheds for equipment and tools. A helipad.

Through the night-vision glasses I saw that not one but three silver SNR Security vehicles were parked in front of the main house, along with two late-model pickup trucks and two GM sedans. Parked within the bunkhouse commons were more passenger cars and vans and trucks. Eight in all. And three more outside the imposing metal hangar, the vehicles dusty in the downlights.

I heard the bees again, buzzing in the west and above me. Turned and lifted my binoculars skyward but saw nothing. Drones are hard to see at night. The breeze kicked up and covered the sound.

Tall ladders leaned against the walls almost everywhere I looked. The grounds were littered with wicker baskets, wound ropes, wooden boxes and bins. I glassed the palms and saw that some of the fruit was still wrapped in bags against rain, sun, birds, and bugs until harvest. Many of the dates had already been picked.

Suddenly, the roll-up door of the big metal hangar noisily clattered up and three all-terrain vehicles squeezed under it into the bright barnyard. Then three more. The dust swirled and the roll-up clanged to a stop and the ATVs circled and whined. The drivers wore silver helmets. They sped between the rows of the date palms, spread six abreast, as if practiced. When they hit the desert their headlights bounced more wildly and their engines groaned louder as they headed straight at me.

No way to outrun them, but I tried anyway. I was less than halfway back to my truck when the ATVs skidded into position around me. Headlights bore into my eyes, exhaust puffing into the night. Four in front of me and two behind.

The closest driver raised his hand and six engines went silent. Silver helmet and goggles. An M4 slung over his shoulder. His buddies exactly the same, except they had their guns pointed at me.

He lifted his visor. "Drop the pack."

I did.

"Who are you?"

"Roland."

"What are you doing here?"

"Bird-watching."

"How goes it?"

"The sun went down and I got lost."

"So you climbed our fence."

"Panic does funny things."

"Are you armed?"

"Yes."

"Toss it. Carefully."

I brought the gun from my backside, set it down on the pack.

"Are you the law?"

"I pay my tickets."

"If you can be honest with me, I might be able to help you. What kind of birds are you looking for out here?"

"Just one. Daley Rideout. I'll pay good money if there's been a sighting."

An indecipherable moment. Silence and a gust of breeze. The sound of the drone close overhead. My interviewer slowly unslung the rifle off his shoulder and pointed it at me. Remained seated. Raised a hand, head-high. The others dismounted their ATVs and drove their weapons into scabbards affixed to the roll bars. All of them looking at me. Young faces. Confident and knowing. Eagerness in their eyes behind the goggles.

"Roland," he said. "Get ready to suffer."

The five swarmed. I caught the first one with a left uppercut to the stomach, and down he went. Drilled another with a right cross to his solar plexus, and he went down, too. Three to go.

I swiveled left, fists up and chin tucked, but two men climbed my blind side and clamped my arms as the one in front pummeled away. The leader flew in on the headlight beams, jamming me high on the forehead with his rifle butt. It was the weight from behind that brought me down. Into boots and grunts and more boots and the metal stench of blood. I threw them off and struggled up as a smaller man swirled in, punching and kicking, a martial blur against which I launched a straight left jab that caught the bottom of his helmet instead of the throat I was hoping for. Felt my hand go wrong. You cannot win a fight against six determined men wearing helmets. Blood in my eyes and the crack of blows I couldn't see coming. Rising whoops and snarls. Wondering if they'd stomp me out. Someone tackled me at the knees and I was down, really taking it now, trying to lift my face from the ground, sucking the sand in with my breath as the kicks landed. Saw the combat boots right in front of me. They did a little hop, then one of them came at me like a freight train from a tunnel. Same boots as ours in Fallujah. Funny the things you notice before the world gives you up.

Stars above, jumping in my eyes. Slow bump of my shoulders on sand. Arms and back and butt dragging, boots off the ground and legs taut. Grumble of engines pulling me.

Can't be real. Close your eyes and it will go away.

Real. Very real. Bright lights. Motor hum and the slide of metal. The thick railings. Wall or gate. *Yes. I believe I saw a gate earlier.* Feel my back on harder ground, then the painful bounce of my head over what I guess is the gate track. Feet plop to the ground, legs contract. Above me sway the branches of a greasewood plant. I see the flank of a truck. My truck. My Ford. Roland Ford.

He kneels over me. A buddy or a ref or a corpsman or a priest. Helmet and goggles still on. Eyes blue and calm, floodlights streaming from behind him.

"Answer a few questions and you'll be free to hop on down the road. How does that sound?"

Move my head.

"What business do you have with Daley Rideout?"

A croak: "To find."

"Your basic, hardworking PI." He holds my wallet up for me to see, drops it on my chest. He has a snarling lion tattooed on his palm. "Who hired you to find the girl?"

I shake my head no. Crunch of ground. "No."

"Come on, PI. You've already half died in the line of duty. The crazy sister? Just nod that hard head of yours if I'm right."

I nod. Half dead is still half alive. And willing to stay that way.

He stares down at me. Twenty-something. Thirty. Pale, thick pink lips, the top one upturned by the goggles. Good teeth. White shirt with blood. Mine.

"Your partner killed the crazed Negro gentleman in Imperial Beach," he says.

I vaguely remember that. Back when I was someone else.

"I followed the story," he says. "And all the others like it. Your partner did the right thing and you threw him under the bus. One of your own. Making you just one more shit-lib."

Slaps me across the face, hard. Feels like a mallet. The wallet slides off my chest.

"But back to Penelope. She's reported Daley missing, I assume? Filed all the reports?"

Another sandy, crunching nod. I want to wipe the taut dried blood off my face, but it's too far to reach. Can feel the burn of an eyebrow gash. A split lip. An open forehead where the gun butt hit. Sand in all of it. Going to be a tough cleanup. Don't want to be there for that one.

"When I talk to my superiors, can I say that we'll never see you here again, Mr. Ford?"

"Back early tomorrow." A whisper. I try to laugh. Brings a wad of grainy debris into my throat. The cough is agony. A rib.

"Shame," he says. "We could use a man like you. And we believe we can change the world one man at a time. One woman, too."

Another whisper. "By date farming?"

"Hey, those Medjools blue-ribboned at the San Diego County Fair this year. Isn't easy. See, Ford, your takeaway here is, don't come back."

"Okay."

"I'd appreciate it if you don't tell the Imperial sheriffs. We have a good relationship and we'll deny even seeing you."

I grunt.

"I thought you'd see the light. This thing still has a charge and two G's—even way out here. I'd call a friend if I were you. Trying to drive yourself to the ER might be a little counterproductive right now."

He drops the phone to my chest. Slides off on the wallet side.

Then the howl of ATVs. Close my eyes, feel the sharp rain of sand on my face.

I take his advice and call a friend.

Will be a bit of a wait. But water in the backpack, which they leave beside me.

Water of life.

Burt on the way.

8

/////////////////////

MORNING. Home. Neither had ever looked better.

After two hours of poor sleep, the Irregulars got me onto one of the padded chaise longues on the patio, in the shade of a large palapa, with a view of the pond and the rolling hills beyond. My place for convalescence. Liz put a formidable bloody Mary on the table beside me. Dick ordered me to drink it. This in lieu of the pain pills from the ER, which in my jarhead stubbornness I had refused to take.

But I hadn't been able to refuse the El Centro Regional Medical Center diagnosis and treatments: a cracked lower rib, three stitches on the right eyebrow, four above the left ear, two more inside my lower lip, plus cuts, contusions, and abrasions galore. In the mirror I saw a swollen, half-blinded primate. Notes of plum and cherry. My insides ached, but no internal bleeding. The rib felt like a broken-off knife. Worse were the hamstrings and knee joints, well stretched by the ATV dragging, and my desert-flayed back. Ankle burns where the ropes had been tied. But worst of all was the stark humiliation of being reduced to this. Not just defeated but slaughtered in all but the dictionary sense of the word. It's sobering to realize how poorly defended you really are. What a joke your well-being really is. How little your life means to some people.

What entertained the doctors most was not my injuries but my non-concussion, which they couldn't square with the pronounced swelling of my head just above the hairline, courtesy of the fearless leader's rifle butt. Now topped by a bristling five-stitch railroad. My explanation of an unusually hard head, coupled with a boxer's ability to take a punch, meant little to the doctors. I didn't mention the occasional moments of wonder I experience since being knocked out by Darien Dixon. During these moments I feel exactly as I did sitting in my corner on the stool: dazed but somehow content, too. Post-KO wonder. The El Centro ER doctors asked me to check into their hospital for observation and I declined, and was eventually driven home by the capable Burt Short.

Now my tenants were fussing over me on the patio. I call my tenants the Irregulars because they are not ordinary people. Then again, is anyone?

I rent out the six casitas that face the pond because I enjoy occasional company, and because good affordable housing shouldn't go to waste. I inherited this hacienda from my wife, Justine Timmerman, who died four years and five months ago. She was thirty-one. The estate was a wedding gift from her family. It has a name, Rancho de los Robles—Ranch of the Oaks. The main house is two stories of adobe brick and rough-hewn timber, and well over a hundred years old. Needs some work. The surrounding twenty-five acres are oak grassland.

The Irregulars are a changing cast. Three of the originals are still here. Some of them are forthcoming about themselves, while others reveal little. I post the house rules, laminated in acrylic, on one of the palapa uprights for all to see:

GOOD MANNERS AND PERSONAL HYGIENE
NO VIOLENCE REAL OR IMPLIED
NO DRUGS
NO STEALING
QUIET MIDNIGHT TO NOON
RENT DUE FIRST OF MONTH
NO EXCEPTIONS

Liz, my grandmother, lives in casita six. Grandpa Dick lives in casita number one, as far from his wife as possible. Yet close. Dick is mid-eighties, Liz younger. They spend most of their waking hours together. Tennis. Travel. They bicker incessantly and sometimes fight, fueled by alcohol and decades of marriage. I used to think they were textbook examples of how to erode a relationship, but now I'm not so sure.

Burt Short lives in casita five. He actually is short, with an open face and a swatch of auburn hair that looks like a toupee but isn't. Merry eyes. He's built like a bull, big-shouldered, small-footed. Comments about his size activate him. A passionate golfer. He came up my drive in a huge red top-down Eldorado three-plus years ago, my first tenant, with a likable cool and a preference to pay in cash, which he always has. His past comes out in occasional bits and pieces—various employment, travel, fluency in languages, and arcane violence—though most of it seems subject to change. There are few facts about his past that I can bank on. But Burt helped me out of a very bad predicament not long ago, which left one man dead and another terrified—I hope—into silence. Burt and I became something to each other that night, though I'm not sure what. More committed than friends. Closer than partners. We refer to the event sometimes but have never discussed it in depth. I'm half of a secret organization that has no name or charter, and only one rule: loyalty. Sometimes he calls me Champ and sometimes I call him Shark.

Now, lying on the chaise longue with a view of the pond and the hills, I turned my aching head to the sound of Burt pushing a wheelbarrow full of ice cubes across the barnyard toward us. I'd been listening to him and Frank—the youngest Irregular—over the last ten minutes, breaking open the store-bought bags of ice piled high in the trunk of Burt's magnificent red Eldo, and dumping the clanging cubes into the wheelbarrow. The ice has formed a glittering mountain. Burt powers it across the barnyard. Now and then a few jewels slide off and land in the green late-summer grass.

Burt has a trauma remedy that he claims to have had great success with while helping to manage a stable of young boxers out of a gym in Oxnard. One of those men is now a WBC super-lightweight contender. Burt, Frank, and I watched him on ESPN last week. Driving me back from the El Centro hospital just a few hours ago, Burt said the ice bath wasn't his idea at all but an old-school English treatment for a boxer's broken bones, cuts, bruises, and—most important—spirit. He'd seen it work near miracles.

I was not looking forward to it. Rotated my swollen face in the other direction to view the antique claw-foot bathtub that Burt and Frank transported out here in the front loader of the Bobcat. It was already half full of ice, slowly melting in the September heat. One cold bath that was going to be.

Back to the Irregulars: the aforementioned Frank is one Francisco Cuellar, an eighteen-year-old Salvadoran boy I discovered early this spring, living down in a tree-shaded arroyo near the western edge of the property. A friend and I had been bird-watching and decided to follow some quail tracks from a wash down into a streambed. When we reached the bottom, fifty determined quail launched into the sky between the oaks and another fifty stormed into a thicket of wild buckwheat and prickly pear. Which left my companion, Wynn, and me and a skinny boy with a homemade quail noose in one hand facing each other wordlessly while the birds tore away.

"¿Quién eres?" I asked, as the feathers softly zigzagged down.

Frank—Francisco let Dick and Liz anglicize his name—has gained twenty pounds since coming out of the arroyo to live in casita two. He works off his rent one day a week, and I pay him a fair wage for another two days a week. With twenty-five acres, an aging ranch house, six casitas, outbuildings, and a pond, there is always work to be done.

He has an aptitude for auto mechanics, having learned from his father, who owned a two-man garage in the coastal El Salvadoran village of Puerto el Triunfo. His father was shot to death in his small office for refusing to pay protection money to the local MS-13 thugs. Francisco had watched through an open door. Over the months, as I've gotten to know Frank, when I listen to his broken English and study his expressions, I sense in him no desire for a life in the north but rather for a return to his home. And vengeance. He talks to his family and friends on his flip phone, and my Spanish is good enough to understand his anger and calculation. He is interested in weapons, and Burt has taken him under his wing for shooting instruction. Burt also helped him get a driver's license. Which Frank used to drive my pickup back from the desert in the wee dark hours earlier this morning.

Frank gave me his automatic smile as he helped Burt steady the wheelbarrow over the Victorian tub. The tub had been in the barn, covered but unloved, long before I met Justine Timmerman or first saw this place, one of scores of treasures left behind by generations of Timmermans. The property was just one of their many holdings in the American West. I tried to return it to her father and mother after their daughter died. The terrible plane accident happened scarcely a year after we were married. The Timmermans refused to take back Rancho de los Robles. Family is family.

Thinking of Justine, hoping that there was an afterlife and she was happy in it, I looked down at my beaten body, the clean white T-shirt I'd put on, the swimsuit, my bruised and abraded legs, the flip-flops, the blue ligature marks around my ankles. I felt helpless and witless and somehow at fault. I pictured Justine. *The weather is wonderful; wish you were here.*

Our fifth and newest Irregular is a young woman named Violet Drew. I could hear her and Liz playing Ping-Pong behind me, back deeper in the shade of the palapa. The ball ticked and tocked back and forth and I heard occasional yelps, but mostly I heard the steady effervescence of Violet's voice.

She moved into casita four last month, just in from St. Louis. She was twenty-four, a flight attendant. A native of St. Louis and a graduate of Southern Illinois University, Edwardsville. After three years flying for United Airlines in St. Louis, she had relocated to fly out of Lindbergh Field in San Diego. She was dark-haired, talkative, and antically nervous, often looking behind her as if someone was sneaking up.

Violet likes to run around the pond for exercise, and she does this at least once a day, sometimes two or even three times. Long, fast runs, too—half an hour or so. Her strides are graceful and strong. In keeping with her nervy personality, she looks behind her constantly. Behind and up, an airborne threat. Ponytail flying. Never breaks stride.

I think Violet is bearing secrets, but so far she's been a happy addition to the Irregulars. I respect secrets. They help keep me in business.

9

///////////////////

BURT AND FRANK finished preparing my ice bath. They muscled the Victorian tub to the sandy beach that surrounds the spring-fed pond, propping the claw feet up on cinder blocks so the tub wouldn't sink with me in it.

If the mid-September day hadn't been so hot, I might not have got into the damned tub at all. Burt gave me a stern look.

I toed off the flip-flops and managed to stand with the help of Liz and Violet. Holding my arms, they guided me across the patio and down the railroad-tie steps to the soft, sloping beach. We stopped at the tub, positioned to give me a pleasant view of the water, the hills, and the sky beyond. The sunsets from here are excellent, though I didn't think I'd last more than a few minutes in the sparkling bed. The tub was half full, and the ice had been dug out so my body could be instantly packed with cold. An unopened half-gallon of budget gin stood on the blue tile of the barbecue deck, beside a box of large freezer bags.

"After you're comfortable, we'll pack it in around you," said Burt. "Then we'll fill some bags for your face and head, and you will indeed feel as if you are in a freezer."

He cracked the seal on the gin bottle and twisted open the top.

Used his teeth to pry off the pour spout, spit it into the barbecue sink, and smiled. He had explained earlier that an ice bath without gin is thirty percent less effective.

I watched him pour the booze over the ice with lengthwise strokes, the liquid gurgling out. Frank stepped forward, pulled a garden trowel from within a clean blue shop cloth, and worked the gin into the banks of ice, carefully re-forming the body-hugging berms.

Using Liz and Violet for training wheels, I stepped in near the bow, eased down butt-first, and lay back, propping my head up on a pillow of ice. A sharp cold bit into me and my body ordered me to retreat. Burt and Frank raised bag after bag of ice, cubes clinking down over me. The women packed the cubes firmly until all I could see when I looked down was a blanket of diamonds glimmering in the sunlight. Not even my toes. I closed my eyes against the cold. Felt it sucking the warmth out of me. Where did it go? Listened to them filling the face-freeze bags. Violet warbling on about getting buried in the snow at Christmas by her brothers, *a frozen-stiff snow angel and then after a while I couldn't feel a thing. Which is what's going to happen to you, Roland!* They built up pillows between the tub rim and my neck and head. Lay the bags over my throat and face, lightly because of the cuts. Through two courtesy peepholes I looked out at the pond and the hills and the clear blue sky. Felt the ache within. Heart thumping like some separate beast. Could see the blurred Irregular shapes on the edges of my vision.

"Everything cool in there?" asked Dick. A chuckle.

"Don't make him talk, honey—you'll break the seal."

"I suppose. Ignore that question, Roland."

"Roland?" Burt's rough voice. "I always found it helpful to count up from one to fifty, then back down again. Slowly. What you do is, when you come to a number, imagine what you were doing at that age of your life. Take a moment. Enjoy it. Then move on, up your years and back down again. You'll get a few mulligans, since you're only forty."

Almost at the point when the full-body ache had become unbearable, it began to recede.

Seventeen: high school first baseman, a grand slam against La Mesa, in love with Trudy Yates, called me the "lovable lump" in the yearbook . . .

Twenty-two: Student Union at SDSU, history major, watching the Twin Towers collapse and burn . . .

Twenty-five: Fallujah. Avalos bleeding out in front of me . . .

From within these memories I heard Burt Short ordering the others to leave us alone so we could talk. On the periphery of my peephole vision I saw them moving away. Heard Dick and Liz grumbling, and Violet's tale about playing tennis when it was so cold the balls froze and Frank and Burt talking in Spanish that I couldn't quite hear.

Then it was quiet. My body was numb. Even the deep ache in my ankles was gone. I felt only a strange heaviness, meaty and alive, but not cold at all. It was as if the flames of pain in my eyebrows and lip and forehead and back had been doused.

Burt's voice came through the frozen blanket. "Do you want me to sic the Imperial County Sheriffs on them? There are pluses and minuses for you."

"Not yet."

"I understand. You may want to handle this personally. Go another round, in the style of Rolling Thunder Ford."

I didn't respond to that. My thoughts were clear but my mouth unwilling.

"Next," said Burt. "One Penelope Rideout came to your downtown office early this morning, while we were having our desert adventure. A helpful Dublin Pub barista directed her here. Through the front-gate intercom, Rideout told Dick she was looking for you, that she'd hired you to find her sister. That you weren't returning calls and her sister was still in the wind. An unsatisfied customer. Through the intercom, Dick took her numbers and ran her off."

I forced my memories into sluggish words. Told Burt about Mrs. Rideout coming to my office, yesterday morning about this time. About Daley, Nick Moreno, Adam Revell of SNR Security. About climbing the fence, the date farm, the ATVs. I felt completely disembodied, and my voice seemed to be someone else's, but my mind seemed sharp. I was under the impression that if I moved anything more than my lips I would break some spell that had been cast over me.

"So while Liz and Violet were picking the gravel out of your back, I called Penelope," Burt continued. "She'd settled down enough to tell me that her sister had called her early this morning. Very early. Daley said she'd cut school with friends, driven up the coast with them. Partied on the beach at San Onofre. Heard that Nick had been shot dead. Decided her friends weren't such good friends after all. No details. Ditched former friends, hitched a ride into San Clemente, and called her sister from a pay phone because friends had taken her smartphone. Penelope couldn't get you, so she called your cop friend Walker in Encinitas, who was out of jurisdiction but called confederates in San Clemente. Penelope made it to the San Clemente 7-Eleven in less than an hour, but the sister was gone. San Clemente deputies were on scene. The clerk told Penelope the same thing he'd told the San Clemente deputies—that the girl had been there until less than half an hour ago. She'd bought candy and an energy drink and talked on the phone outside. Then two guys drove up and they all argued. She got into a silver SUV with them, and off they went. About five minutes later the cops pulled up."

I felt like my body had vanished. Like I was just a brain having thoughts. "Nothing since, from Daley?"

"Nada."

"Amber Alert?"

"Declined. Mrs. Rideout pressed the deputies, but they told her it was for the most urgent cases only. That a truant ditching school to party with friends and getting into an argument made this less urgent. They offered to call in a county BOLO on the SUV, told her it was the best they could do."

I had a frozen memory of Penelope Rideout's anger at me for not returning her calls during my Monarch Academy interviews. Of her almost trancelike control of that anger, her clenched eyelids and balled fists and the silent prayer or spell or curse. *I'm ninety percent lover and ten percent killer.*

"How are you feeling, Roland? Warm yet?"

"Just a little."

"Then you've been in long enough. You'll feel like a new man once you thaw out."

"I look forward to that."

"I'll be damned," said Burt. "Champ, this may be troubling news, but based on Dick's description of Mrs. Rideout's car, I'd say she just drove up to the gate again."

"Yellow V-Dub ragtop?"

"None other."

A numb lifting of my head. Some of the ice bags slid off. "Ring her in and help me get into the house, Burt."

10

/////////////////////

As the shivering tapered off, I felt better. Dried my tight pink skin, got on workout pants and a zippered hoodie, and arranged my hair above my crime-scene face. Then went back down to the patio, where Penelope Rideout paced heavily in the shade of the palapa.

"Why can't I get you when I need you? I will not be ignored. I will not be—oh. Oh my God. *Look* at you."

"Do I have to?"

"What can I . . . I mean, what should . . . just, *what*?"

"Sit and I'll tell you."

We faced each other across the big picnic table. I gave her the pond view. I started with Alchemy 101 and ended with my ice bath. She looked back and forth from me to the bathtub on the cinder blocks near the water. I kept my saga brief and to the point. Tried a cryogenic smile, but it hurt. She wore a yellow summer dress and white gladiator sandals and Jackie O sunglasses.

"I just raised your pay," she said softly.

"Not necessary. Tell me about Daley's call, everything."

She gave me a more detailed version than she'd given Burt over the phone. Daley called just after three a.m. She was in San Clemente. She had gone to the beach at San Onofre earlier with friends. She was almost hysterical over what happened to Nick. Angry at her friends, who didn't know anything about it except he was dead but they would protect her. She said the beach looked weird because there were armed guards everywhere. She refused to say which friends she was with. She'd split and hitched a ride to 7-Eleven with a creep. Daley was terse and vague.

"She leaps before she looks," said Penelope. "I told her that I'd just been through forty-plus hours of worried hell over her, and she told me to come get her and make it snappy. Now she's gone again. I was so close to getting her."

"Who are Connor and Eric, and why is she with them?" I asked.

"I told you yesterday I don't know them."

"Do you know SNR Security?"

"I do not."

"Adam Revell doesn't ring a bell?"

Penelope stared at me from behind her dark glasses. I could see her eyes through the darkness. "I don't like your tone of voice."

"I don't like getting jumped by six goons, following a lead I got from you."

"You're very suspicious."

"Part of my charm."

"I fail to see it."

"Do you know this Cathedral by the Sea?"

A dismissive exhale. "I don't approve of it."

"Explain."

"I read about it when they opened their doors. It's in a funny-shaped building. Some of Daley's friends go there."

"Does Daley?"

"Yes, once. With two girlfriends. Just a few weeks ago, the last Sunday in August. He came at her aggressively."

"'He'?"

"The youth minister. I forget his name."

"He came at her?"

"Recruited her for the youth group. For the Cathedral by the Sea rock band. For a cycling trip to Mammoth. After one visit from Daley, they had her booked up every weekend for a month. I had a bad feeling about him and the church."

"Did Daley?"

"She thought the church 'had promise.' Her words. So I forbid her from attending again, and recommended St. Mary, Star of the Sea, in Oceanside."

"Because—"

"It's Catholic and I heard good things about it."

"Were you raised Catholic?"

"I've never set foot in a Catholic church. Or any other, in recent memory."

"Help me with your reasoning," I said. "You attend no place of worship. You won't let your sister go to one she's interested in. So you send her to the Catholics, though you know little about them."

She pulled off her sunglasses and set them on the table, her blue prying eyes locked onto mine. Eyes that told a story. A hard one. Beautiful but chilling.

"Only faith lasts," she said. "It can't be broken or taken away."

I wasn't sure of that, but my sureness wasn't the point. "And Daley's faith is supposed to conform to yours?"

"She's fourteen years old, Mr. Ford. I'm not only her sister but her guardian. Every decision I've ever made has put Daley first. That's my job on earth, and I take it seriously."

I'd seen overparenting, so why not oversistering? Considering what had happened ten years ago on that stormy night outside of Eugene, Oregon, maybe it was understandable. Maybe commendable.

But more important to me than Penelope's attempted management of her teenage sister was that Daley's world had just grown larger. Nick. Alchemy 101. The Cathedral by the Sea. Paradise Date Farm. All linked by SNR Security. By Adam Revell, Connor, Eric, and the six helmeted warriors who had easily laid waste to Roland Ford, PI. Why had they done that? Because I was snooping after Daley Rideout? Maybe, but they had been in some control of her, chaperoned by Connor and Eric. What threat was I? A leap, but an easy one: the sign on the silver SUV that Scott Chan had failed to read was that of SNR Security. They *had* her. I'd suspected that much when I saw the SNR emblem on the ticket booth at Alchemy 101. The attack at Paradise Date Farm confirmed it. If my beating was not to keep me away from Daley, then what?

I looked at the tub of ice melting in the sun. "Mrs. Rideout—"

"Penelope, please."

"Penelope, exactly what did Daley say about San Onofre?"

"Just that it was surreal and the old power plant looked like something from a science-fiction movie. Armed guards everywhere."

I knew the San Onofre nuclear power plant well. Almost every Southern Californian did. I'd driven by it thousands of times, in and out of Orange County.

I felt stumped by Daley Rideout's behavior. Wasn't even sure how to describe it. Erratic? Careless? Reckless? Quite a wake of damage her actions had left in the last two days, from Nick Moreno to me.

"Has Daley gone to San Onofre before?" I asked.

"Not that I know."

"For all your security efforts, there are sure a lot of things you don't know about her."

"You can ridicule me but not my efforts or intentions," she said. "I do feel terrible about what they did to you. But I hope I can still count on you as an employee and an ally."

Behind me, a cloud drifted across the sun. The daylight diminished and Penelope Rideout's blue eyes turned gray. A breeze pushed some of her curls onto her forehead.

"There's no Second Marine Aircraft Wing at Miramar," I said. "No Colonel Richard Hauser at Miramar, either. Never has been."

"Are you sure?"

"Pretty damned."

"Okay," she said. "I believe you."

"*Okay?* Then who's that in the picture on your refrigerator?"

Another catch of breath. Impatience or exasperation. She used both hands to put her sunglasses back on, wedding band and engagement ring glinting in the sun.

"Richard, of course. We divorced two years ago, before the move to Oceanside. Richard is a clinical psychologist. That's him in the picture, though. We rented the flight suit from a costume shop. For fun. The picture was taken at the Flying Leatherneck Museum, not an actual runway. We all liked it so much. The three of us happy and together. I don't have many pictures like that."

"So you leave it out for visitors."

"To document a failed marriage with a good memory. Get it?"

"Why wear the rings?"

"They simplify."

My face hurt. I felt mentally off-balance. The warmer my body

got, the worse everything felt. I wanted to be frozen again. I wondered if the concussion that should have come earlier was finally arriving. Decided that this pretty woman sitting in front of me was one
of the least trustworthy people I'd ever met. Like a talking doll. You
just pulled the string and she blabbed whatever was set to come out
next. I entertained the idea of a refund, a washing of hands, a day or
two in bed, and an easier, more satisfying case.

"Where is Richard now?" I asked, not sure I cared.

"He took a position in Eugene. With a healthcare chain."

"Which one?"

"I honestly don't know."

"The city where your parents died."

"I met him there, actually. In Eugene. After Mom and Dad."

"The number you gave me for him was bad."

"He's obviously changed it. I haven't called that number in almost
two years."

"None of the search services I subscribe to have a record of your
marriage to Richard Hauser, or to anyone else. They tend not to
miss little things like that."

"We eloped in Reno."

"You're beginning to exhaust me, Mrs. Rideout."

"I do that to people." She stood. Came around the long picnic
table and sat down beside me. Set her sunglasses on the table again.
The drift of time and scent. Leaned in and set both her hands over
one of mine. Warm where the ice had been.

"Mr. Ford, please don't give up on me and Daley. There's darkness
all around us. We need you. I know she's fallen in with very bad
people. I also know some of what you've done in your life, and gone
through, and been made into. And I admire you very much. I may
strike you as Little Miss Conduct, but I'm a good person. See?"

I saw her eyes from point blank then, the blue of the iris and the indigo spokes around the pupil. Kaleidoscopes of sunlight. A gathering, judgmental beauty in them. I didn't look away. Hadn't not looked away since I met Justine. Let this unsettling fact join the river of unsettling facts running through me at that moment.

We sat there, hand on hand for a while. A man beside a woman, a woman beside a man.

"I'll walk myself to the car," she said.

"I can manage that much."

Slow going, across the patio and up the railroad ties to the circular driveway, where Penelope's cheerful yellow Beetle sat in the shade of a central coast live oak. I saw Burt and Frank not-so-covertly watching us from the far shore of the pond, where they were fishing for bass in the cattails. I saw Justine gliding past them in the rowboat, wearing a swimsuit and the floppy white hat she always wore. Dick glanced at me from the porch of casita one, where he sat in his Adirondack chair, overcasually clipping his fingernails. And Liz, way down in front of casita six, happening to look my way as she laced her shoes, tennis bag beside her, racquets protruding. Violet studied me frankly from the front porch of casita four, talking on the phone.

"Apparently you get plenty of supervision around here," said Penelope.

"Only when I need it."

"Must be nice."

11

///////////////////////

V IOLET, FRANK, AND I sat in the Cathedral by the Sea that Sunday morning, a full house, color-stained sunlight slanting through the windows and a rock band getting ready to start things off.

It had been three days since my close loss to SNR Security. The colors of my face were a little less vivid, the swelling was down, and my stitches itched. The rib hurt only if I breathed. Daley Rideout had remained fully vanished since the call to her sister. Neither Darrel Walker, Oceanside PD, nor any of the several state and federal agencies I called would tell me anything other than that she was still missing and there had been no new developments in the case. Private investigators rank only slightly above registered sex offenders when it comes to need-to-know. Darrel, to his credit, seemed concerned about my split-decision loss to SNR Security, said he'd see what he could find out about the company.

When the rock band kicked in, Violet paused her story about hitting tennis balls with Serena at a fund-raiser one summer, folded her hands over one knee, and listened up. Frank, who rarely spoke English away from home, was silent. Fingering the straw Borsalino I'd worn to protect the public from my face, I watched Pastor Reggie Atlas stride through the camera flashes to the pulpit.

He was taller than I'd guessed from his pictures on the Internet, and he had an athlete's spring to his step. Tan and trim. He looked to be late thirties or early forties, but I remembered he was forty-nine now. God was taking good care of his pastor. God and our healthy Southern California lifestyle. Reggie wore crisp new jeans, a long-sleeved open-collared white shirt, and white athletic shoes. His messy blond hair gave him a boyish look.

I looked around at the packed room. Every pew full and enough people standing to drive a fire captain crazy. The mezzanine was filled to its railing.

Today's sermon was "Your Road to Damascus."

Atlas started off with an emotional call for God to bless our fighting men and women overseas, and for the congregation to help lift their spirits through the Onward Soldiers Fund, which was sending thousands of dollars' worth of material every month to U.S. military deployed throughout the world. Exactly $55,375 so far, said Atlas, which averaged out to over four thousand dollars raised right here by this congregation every month since the Cathedral by the Sea had opened last year. The funds were matched by the Western Evangelical Alliance, doubling their value. The church had sent hundreds of phones, tablets, and sunglasses, mountains of healthy snack foods, crates of sunscreen, Quick Cooler bandanas, and compact "military-grade" Holy Bibles to servicemen and -women in more than a dozen countries. He said that God in his wisdom had made American fighting men and women the best in the world. And that America, as God's chosen country, was obligated to defend this beautiful world from the godless, the evil, and the forces of Satan. In the end, God's will be done. As an ex-Marine, I felt proud to be called the best. Along with hundreds of millions of other young people throughout history who had heard a similar message and bought it.

Following his Onward Soldiers Fund pitch, Pastor Reggie took his sermon from the fields of battle to the personal battles faced by Christians. He said that the battle with outer enemies—such as those Satan-inspired terrorists in the Middle East—and our inner enemies—such as greed, selfishness, lust for money, and lust for the flesh—are all part of the same battle. He said that, like Paul, we each will face a reckoning on our various roads to Damascus.

Atlas had a rich tenor and his words came to life without effort. His pacing was subtle but dramatic, and he had a nice gift for highs and lows, starts and stops. Occasionally he allowed a Georgia accent that suggested credence and civility. And something of the backwoods, too, self-humored but canny. He used his hands less than most evangelicals I'd seen, keeping them close in to his body and moving them like a boxer. I've heard evangelicals called "charismatic," and this was a good description of Reggie Atlas. His delivery was powerful, articulate, and somehow humane. He seemed to feel the inner battles of which he spoke. He was admonishing his lambs but empathizing with them, too.

So when Pastor Atlas condemned the sins of "adultery and homosexuality," he expressed what appeared to be genuine sympathy for adulterers and homosexuals. And when he talked about the need for "strong borders and a great wall of faith" between America and her "fine but less obedient neighbors," he sounded truly sorry that some people could not be allowed to stay in "God's chosen land." When he said that abortion was an abomination to the Lord and should be punishable as a crime against all women and men, and that he would "cast the first stone with eyes gushing tears," I believed him, though

I wasn't sure whom he wanted to tearfully stone, the abortionist or the pregnant woman, or both.

Violet whispered into my ear: *"I don't agree with him on some things, but he makes me want to believe!"*

I glanced over at Frank, staring at Atlas with mute, beak-nosed stoicism.

I looked back up to the pastor. Violet whispered something to Frank. I wondered why she was always talking, running, or looking behind her. Never at rest. Was she afraid something bad would happen if she was still? If so, what?

Mom and Dad made us kids go to church until we were twelve, respectively. After that, up to us. We were baptized. I always liked the sermons. I daydreamed through them, sometimes, of surfing and girls and baseball. But I wasn't bored by the sermons. I was inspired.

The final part of Atlas's sermon claimed that public and private wars could be won with the same two things: faith and action. Faith required prayer, and action required courage.

He told a story of his early years preaching in rural Georgia, how after a day of carrying the word to the poor, he'd park his VW van down by a creek or in a campground or far out in a parking lot, and he'd set his cooler on a table if there was one, or on the ground, and he'd take the loaf of bread, then part the layer of ice cubes he'd buy every third night—only cost a quarter back then—and dig out the baloney and cheese and the condiments. Baloney and mustard made the miracle, he said. And it took lots of miracles, because he might take up two, even three collections on a good day, but he'd still barely have enough gas money to get to the next town and do it all again.

One night in a park he was mugged by three young black men, no more than boys, really, but plenty big and rough. This was back in the days when the townspeople still wore their hair big, with the combs in them. Reggie was eighteen, less than six months on the road as an evangelical. It had rained earlier and there were ticks falling off the trees. After the muggers had beaten him down and rifled through his van and taken what they wanted and thrown the last of his food on the ground, Reggie had lain there in the cold dirt with the ticks landing all around him, and steadfastly refused to pray. Refused to ask for help. Refused to thank the Lord for sparing his life. For sparing his eyes and his hands and his vehicle or anything else, because Reggie was angry at the Lord for betraying His servant into the hands of the wicked. The longer he lay there, the angrier he got.

By the time Reggie had washed himself off in a park bathroom and gotten the ticks off him, collected what food wasn't ruined, then put his meager possessions back in order and climbed into the driver's seat, he had one hundred percent retired as a preacher. He was done. It was over. He had failed his Lord and his mama and the old man and himself.

But the engine of his van wouldn't turn over, and the more he cranked the starter the weaker the battery got, until there was barely enough charge left to power the radio. He listened to it—to a country preacher he had always admired and who had gotten his own show—until his battery was completely dead. "Like my spirit," said Reggie.

It was late by then, and he scrunched down in the uncomfortable van seat and let his head roll against the window. It was early spring and the glass was cold. He had almost fallen asleep when he saw an old man walking across the park toward him. It looked as if he had emerged from behind a young magnolia, but Reggie wondered how the man could have hidden himself behind the slender, still leafing tree.

The man carried a black duffel and it looked heavy. He set it on the picnic table and came to the window. Reggie looked at his face through the dew-dripping glass. An older guy, long white hair brushed back. Blue eyes in a haunted face. Reggie tried to roll down the window, but they were electric and he had no power. He swung the door open and stepped out.

"I heard you preach today," said the man. "In the holler down to the orchard."

"Then you heard my last preaching," said Reggie.

"Looks like they got the better of you."

"Three on one. I'm tough, but I ain't that tough."

"What did they take?"

"If it was good they took it."

"Here."

The old man tugged lightly on the sleeve of Reggie's coat and led him to the picnic table. There, he unzipped the big black duffel and began pulling things out. Reggie said the man didn't rummage around inside, he just pulled certain things out and left others, as if he knew exactly what he needed and where it was. Reggie watched the collection pile up on the table: baloney—same brand as his—and bread and a few cans of pork and beans and a box of crackers, a can of condensed milk. Then a Falcons sweatshirt that didn't even look that dirty, and a bottle of body-and-hair wash, and a bath towel, white and folded and once belonging to the Holiday Inn. The old man rested one foot on the picnic bench and from inside a sock he pulled some money, folded and dented in the shape of his ankle. He set two fives on top of the towel. Then put the soap on top so they wouldn't blow away.

"I'm not taking this," Reggie had said.

"Or you can take it and get that battery charged," the old man said. "That was some really good preaching today. You got to me.

Maybe I'll see you down the road, Atlas. I hope you can keep carryin' the word."

And off he walked. Reggie Atlas never saw him again.

Murmurs and soft exhales from the congregation. I heard Violet sniffle softly. Saw Frank studying her with apparent concern.

Violet leaned in and whispered: "I want something like that to happen to me."

12

////////////////////////////

AFTER the service a crowd waited in the courtyard to greet Atlas. He stood smiling, pressed by his faithful. His casual attire was perfect for his adopted San Diegans—mostly shorts and jeans and tank tops and T-shirts, except for the older crowd. Kids released from Sunday school ran amok. Awkwardly cool teenagers gathered together on one side of the courtyard. Better dressed than their parents. I pictured Daley Rideout among them, a curly-locked wiseass with a pretty face and a high IQ.

From here you could see the Pacific glistening under a light bank of clouds. Justine, my wife, had died out in that ocean, not far from here. Flying her Cessna 182, which she had affectionately named *Hall Pass*. She'd bought it used on her public defender's salary, painted it pink. A failed fuel pump. No fault of hers. No fault of the ocean. But from that day on, I'd never been able to view the Pacific as pacific. To me it was dangerous and unforgiving, a thing to be feared. I felt the same way about the God that had let Justine die there, terrified and alone. I'm still trying to get over that. Trying to be a bigger man.

As part of being a bigger man, I bought a similar Cessna 182 not long after Justine died, and christened it *Hall Pass 2*. I fly it for pleasure and occasionally for business. When I'm up there in the cockpit, looking down at this earth, which oddly looks bigger the farther away from it you get, I feel Justine's presence, and some of the happiness that flying gave her. Some of the joy and the risk, too. Heightened alert. A part of me is still angry that I wasn't with her that day. That I let her go up there, alone. Another part is afraid that what happened to her will happen to me. Why shouldn't it?

There were tables of food and drink set up in the central park. Trays of turkey hot dogs and burgers, bowls of salad and pink boxes of donuts, all free. We bellied up but donated generously. The half-gallon tip bottles were filling quickly with bills.

I kept my hat down low, just in case Adam Revell of SNR Security had pulled a Sunday shift here. I wasn't sure that Adam himself was among my new friends out at Paradise Date Farm, but he certainly might be.

We sat in the shade with paper plates on our laps. Frank ate as much as a bear, though his manners were better. Violet talked about making tamales on a semester in Mexico her senior year at SIUE. Which led me to note that there were very few Latinos there today. Or blacks, Asians, or American natives. Which is not in keeping with most of San Diego County, as mixed and varied as most any in this republic, I'd recently read.

I wondered if Pastor Atlas's remarks about "our fine but less obedient neighbors" might be a general topic here. So I checked the Cathedral by the Sea reviews online.

Almost all of the comments were positive, but some were not:

My visit to the Cathedral by the Sea was very strange. I was made to feel as if I was not welcome because I am of Mexican descent. I will not go back.

Pastor Reggie is a racist jerk!

I saw almost no people of color, other than myself and my
girlfriend. The people were friendly to one another, but they
acted as if we were not there. Won't go back there again.

There were several vitriolic replies to these, mostly along the
lines of *If you don't like it here, why don't you go back to your own miserable country?*

After lunch we strolled along the rose garden, and under the Canary Island palms that stood, stately and pruned and calm, above us. Walked along a row of what looked like classrooms. The doors were open and I could see the walls inside, decorated with the student drawings and posters and prints that an elementary school would have. The congregation had thinned out by then, cars heading down the hill from the parking lot, church volunteers bagging the lunch debris.

We followed arrows to the office. I wanted to stop by, pick up some church lit, and see if I could get some clue to Penelope Rideout's pointed reaction to the Cathedral by the Sea.

The office was a two-story building that looked far more humble, and much older, than the swashbuckling chapel. Inside, it was cool and open and quiet. The floors looked like 1950s linoleum shined to brilliance by janitors. A sign on the front counter read "Welcome!" There were neat stacks of pamphlets, magazines, and the Cathedral by the Sea bulletin, *From the Lighthouse.* Behind the counter sat two neat desks and two rolling task chairs. And beyond them, a long hallway with offices on either side. Rectangles of sunlight shining in.

"So, what are we doing here?" asked Violet. "Privately investigating?"

I shrugged, wishing I'd been more clear when I'd briefed Violet what not to say on this excursion.

"Are we searching for God or bad guys?"

I held a finger to my puffy split lip.

Her expression froze. She nodded.

Frank listened and watched but said nothing, his standard MO when he's away from home. He was afraid someone would hear his accent, then question, arrest, and deport him. These things happen. He told me that if he returned home to El Salvador he'd be killed on sight, having witnessed his father's murder. Here in public, I knew I was harboring and employing an illegal immigrant, but I still thought that in this case, it was the right thing to do. Which made me a criminal, too, living in a nation of laws while holding an innocent man's life in my hands.

I helped myself to some of the church pamphlets set out on the counter. And this week's *From the Lighthouse*, which had a calendar and all the upcoming events. Picked up a glossy flyer about an upcoming "Special Appearance by Lamar Fleming of Houston, Texas." And another announcing the recent launch of Pastor Reggie Atlas's complete recorded sermons, available online through Four Wheels for Jesus Ministry.

"Wait for me here," I said.

Violet gave me a complicit squint and Frank nodded.

I went around the counter and into the hallway, my shoes squeaking on the polished floor. The offices left and right were marked clearly: Assistant Pastor Erica Summer, Activities Director Rudy Mercator, Bible School Administrator Patrick Clarke, Youth Minister Danella Witt. I wondered if this was the youth ministry director who had lavished attention on Daley. According to Penelope, who would have had to have mistaken Danella Witt for a man. But maybe Penelope had just gotten someone's title wrong.

All of their doors were closed until I came to Pastor Reggie Atlas, whose door stood open.

He sat behind a desk, his back to me, looking through a window that faced the courtyard, where the last of his ten a.m. congregation was disassembling. Rungs of sunlight and shadow through half-drawn blinds.

He pivoted. "Yes?"

"I enjoyed the service. My first time here."

"Thank you, and welcome. Come in if you'd like."

I met him halfway to his desk, where we introduced ourselves and shook hands. Strong and cool. I took off my hat.

"Looks like a bad one," he said.

"T-boned at a four-way stop. He never even slowed down."

His grand smile. "Good insurance, I hope. Do you live nearby?"

"Fallbrook."

"I have friends there. And some of my congregation, too. Please have a seat. I was preparing for noon fellowship, but I have a few minutes."

He pulled out a chair for me, then took up his own again behind the desk. We talked San Diego: weather, surf, drought, wildfire.

"So, why do I have the feeling you didn't come here to hear my message?" he asked pleasantly.

"I'm looking for a girl named Daley Rideout. She's fourteen and she came here once last month."

"Has something happened?"

"Yes, but I'm not sure exactly what."

"What relation are you?"

"I'm a private investigator, hired to locate her."

"Then this is very serious."

"I believe it is."

"I sincerely apologize, but I'll need to see some ID."

I got the wallet from my coat pocket, handed him a laminated copy of my license and a business card. He studied them, then handed back the mock-up.

"What day was she here?" asked Atlas.

I gave him the August date that Penelope had given me. I described Daley and said she had come with two friends, girls her age. I handed him my phone. He stared at the screen, scrolling along with one finger.

"Not familiar," he said. "Certainly possible, though. I'm sorry, but as you saw today, the young people really turn out. So long as you don't wake them up too early. The young are our future, Mr. Ford. They will multiply us into heaven. It wasn't like that when I started out all those years ago. It was always the old folks back then."

"I liked the old-man-as-an-angel story."

A raise of an eyebrow. "Not an angel, probably. But every word of it true."

"I believe you."

"Do you think that something bad has happened to the girl?"

"Disappearing at fourteen is bad."

"Are the police looking for her?"

"They are. Do you know Nick Moreno?"

Reggie Atlas sat back, placed his hands flat on the desk. "Yes. He was almost a regular here. I heard what happened to him from my singles minister. Ugly and sad."

"Do you know Alanis Tervalua or Carrie Calhoun?"

He shook his head.

"Daley's age," I said. "Friends."

"No. But you should talk to our youth minister, Danella. She's out of town now, but she'll be back on Friday."

"What about Penelope Rideout?"

Reggie shook his head again, then spread his hands in a gesture of mild surrender. "I'm sorry. Related to the girl?"

"Sister and guardian. Richard Hauser?"

"No again, sorry again."

A moment of near silence. Distant seagulls and murmurs from outside. Through the window I watched a man tidying up the courtyard. He was young and muscular, with a white buzz cut, a sun-flushed face, and pointed ears. No aloha shirt and cargo shorts for this deacon. Chinos and a black golf shirt and shiny black duty boots. Clean cut, All-American, and doing good deeds for fellow man.

"You've come a long way from the hollers of Georgia," I said.

A thoughtful look from Atlas. "I did the first years of my preaching from that VW van and a series of recreational vehicles. All through the South. I was too young to know any better. To know what a challenge it would be. As in my message today. I was absolutely consumed by the word of God. I got my first real brick-and-mortar chapel many years ago in a town so small you could blink and miss it. Now here—the cathedral of my dreams. Bills to pay, though. Leave it to Pastor Reggie to covet some of the most valuable real estate in the country."

"I see you have an online program."

"Four Wheels for Jesus. It does very well."

"And you've got quite a following on the social networks," I said.

He opened his palms and shrugged, a humble gesture. "'The word of God is quick, and powerful . . . and is a discerner of the thoughts and intents of the heart.'"

"Hebrews," I guessed.

A full smile then, and a knowing nod. There was something intimate about Pastor Atlas, something you-and-me about him. I'd noted the same quality in many successful salesmen.

"I feel powerless sometimes," he said. "There are moments, though. With the Lord. With my wife and children and my believers. When I feel the power of the word coming through me. Not from, but through. He commands my body and soul. Are you strong in Jesus, Mr. Ford?"

"I read the Bible when I was in college. It took me a year, but I was glad I did. That seems like a long time ago. So we've met."

"Well, that's quite an acceptable start, I'd say. Please, come worship with us whenever you'd like. Bring your friends and family. Jesus will change your life."

He raised his shirt cuff for a look at his watch.

"Who handles church security?" I asked.

"Security? I don't know which company, but I can find out for you. Why?"

"It's not important," I said.

He nodded slowly, taking me in with steady blue eyes. For a moment he looked every one of his forty-nine years, if not more. Then, through some personal light and magic, his youth reappeared. He sighed and stood.

"Well, please, if I can help in any way . . ."

"You've been generous, Pastor. Thank you for your time, and for the good sermon. I'm glad you kept preaching."

"I hope you're sincere."

"I'm usually too sincere."

"Should I be worried? Nick? The missing girl? This alleged car accident that happened to you? This violence in the air?"

"Just keep your eyes open. And call me if you learn anything that might point me to Daley Rideout."

"Yes, I'll do that. But, Mr. Ford, do you think my family and I are safe?"

I wasn't sure what to say, so I just looked at him.

"I know," he said. "You can't answer that. In a world like this."

13

////////////////////////

LATER that Sunday, Burt and I tracked down the San Clemente 7-Eleven clerk who had seen Daley Rideout early Thursday morning. Yash Chowdhury lived on West Escalones, a few blocks from the store.

He squinted at Daley's pictures on my phone, nodding. "She was upset. I felt bad for her. I thought of calling the police, but she seemed to know the people she was arguing with. So I decided not to. I see things all the time. There was nothing physical, no forcing. Her sister called the police, but they got here after the girl left. The sister got so angry, they almost arrested her."

Yash was early twenties, short and slim, with a head of black curls and a mustache. His wife, Riya, was studying medicine at UC Irvine. Their house was small and neat and smelled of incense and laundry detergent. Riya retreated to the bedroom to study while we talked. Burt and I sat across from Yash in the living room.

"The girl came to the store at three ten," he said. "I checked the time because I was bored. She was in a white van. It was a commercial van with no windows, not a minivan. Old. The driver was hard to see. A middle-aged white man. She got out and he rolled his window down and said something, but she didn't turn around. She came inside and went down the household aisle and watched the van leave. Then she went outside and used the pay phone."

According to Yash, Daley had been wearing skinny jeans with high cuffs, flip-flops, and a black hoodie that read "I'm not as stupid as I look" on the front. She had had a black backpack slung over one shoulder.

Yash said that Daley bought an energy drink and three candy bars—the same ones I'd seen evidence of in her home wastebasket.

"When she paid, she was distracted," said Yash. "And maybe angry. I asked her if she was having a good morning and she said it was none of my business. She paid and put the drink and candy in her backpack and zipped it up quickly. I had been reading a fantasy novel because the graveyard shift is slow, and she saw it and said, 'Why read that? Real life is weird enough, isn't it?'"

Then Daley walked out, and that was when Yash had seen the punchline of the joke on the back of her hoodie: "Are you?" Daley was halfway across the parking lot when a silver SUV pulled in and a man got out and started arguing with her. He was approximately thirty years old, an Anglo, dressed in chinos and a white dress shirt. He seemed to be ridiculing her, and she "got in his face" and defended herself. There was no physical contact, just words and gesturing. Then he opened a back door and she took the backpack off her shoulder and climbed in.

Yash said that the vehicle had writing on the driver's-side door, but he couldn't read it with the headlight beams coming through the store windows. The SUV pulled onto El Camino Real and headed south.

The police arrived five minutes later, asking Yash if he'd seen a girl who matched Daley's description. They described her accurately. It was three thirty-five. The officers didn't seem particularly concerned about the girl, and they bought coffee before they left.

They were sitting in their car when a yellow Volkswagen Beetle skidded into the 7-Eleven parking lot, went straight into the handicapped-only slot, and a "curly-haired woman came flying into the store. She was maybe twenty-five. Small and pretty."

Then the officers came back in and got into a three-way argument with the woman, and she broke away from them and started asking Yash questions about the girl. She said her sister was in trouble and she criticized him for not helping her, then she "verbally attacked" the officers for not getting there sooner, and they physically escorted her to their car and locked her in the back seat. Yash could see her, her face a blur behind the glass and the metal screen inside. Two more police cars arrived shortly. Their lights were flashing but no sirens.

They let the older sister out of the cruiser, and after a "ten-minute discussion," the police let her come back inside the store. Yash answered her questions politely and hoped she wouldn't start screaming at him, too. But she had calmed down by then, and Yash saw that she was not drunk or deranged at all but was very worried. She wrote her name and number on a complimentary snack napkin and ordered him, politely, to call if he saw her sister again.

I thanked Yash and handed him a business card. Told him the same thing Penelope had told him. "Or if you remember something that might help me locate her," I added. "But call the police first."

"Yes, of course."

The three of us shook hands.

"You forgot something," said Burt, looking up at Yash with his odd smile. Some of Burt's bottom teeth show a little when he smiles, and if he's looking up at you—which is often, because he's short—the smile looks half jolly and half diabolical. I might know Burt well enough to say it's mostly jolly, but I really might not. He has a strangely persuasive effect on some people.

"What did I forget?" asked Yash.

"Everyone forgets something," said Burt.

Yash frowned down at Burt, brow furrowed, as if trying to take the man and his question seriously.

"She asked if we sell burner phones," said Yash. "The younger sister. I just remembered that."

"And?" asked Burt

"No, we don't," said Yash. "I told her to try Walmart."

"Glad I asked."

"And I always remember everything," said Yash, looking puzzled. "There's nothing else to do with a job as boring as mine."

14

////////////////////////

BURT AND I walked south down the beach at San Onofre, past the prime surf breaks—the Point and Old Man's and Dog Patch. I'm almost a foot taller than Burt—I was six-three and two hundred ten pounds as the heavyweight Rolling Thunder Ford—and I take long steps. But I was moving slowly that day and Burt had no trouble keeping up with me over the rock-studded beach.

I told him I'd struck out with Pastor Reggie Atlas, but that he appeared to be worried for himself and his family. Burt took that in short stride.

"Any clear reason why?" he asked.

"Nick Moreno. A missing girl who had possibly visited his church not long ago. My face."

"Preachers know more secrets than shrinks."

"One long confession," I said.

"He's hiding something."

Which is what I had figured, too. "Aren't we all?"

"True," said Burt. "But trite."

The San Onofre Nuclear Generating Station shimmered in the sun up ahead of us, its two nippled domes rising like enormous concrete breasts from the sand. Thick black power lines laced the sky above the structure, lines that once carried rivers of electricity up over the Camp Pendleton hills and deep into Orange County.

No more. No more plumes of steam rising into the air. The station had been closed for six years now, following the failure of suspect Mitsubishi steam generators. The plant operator, Southern California Edison, claimed that the generators were defective and had failed years ahead of schedule. Mitsubishi disagreed and refused to replace or repair them. Which left rate payers on the hook for the plant closure and decommissioning, buying more expensive electricity elsewhere, and, most important, the four-billion-dollar cost of storing the waste.

No one in their right mind wanted it here. Not in our state. Not with Nevada and New Mexico offering to take it off our hands for a fee. Much the same story as other nuclear power plants across our land.

Now, as Burt and I approached, a mere eighteen hundred tons of deadly radioactive waste waited in limbo in temporary cooling pools and storage canisters buried somewhere down near the shoreline. All subject to time, design flaws, maintenance oversights, monitoring failures, leaks, earthquakes, tsunamis, and terrorist explosives.

But on a beautiful September afternoon like this, no one was thinking about such lethal surprises. Clear skies, mid-seventies, four- to six-foot waves and a mild offshore breeze to hold them upright. Pale green cylinders, thin-lipped and top-dusted. Crowded, as California breaks almost always are. I surfed until I went to war and never since. I don't know why.

We came to Old Man's, long the home of the San Onofre Surfing Club. Mom and Dad were active members back in the sixties and I joined myself as a college kid at SDSU. Ground zero of the club is the shack, which is just that, a rudimentary, unwalled frame of lumber for propping up longboards, holding up tarps for shade, providing a hint of cover for the occasional beer. Nearby, trees and tables and outdoor showers.

Surfers, mostly young, were hanging around the shack, some sprawled in the sand for warmth. Beyond the skeletal structure, the waves rolled in in near perfect symmetry. I talked to some of the boys, but only a few had been here on Wednesday afternoon, and none had seen a girl who looked like the picture on my phone.

Finally, one of them, barely a high schooler by the look of him, had been here late last Tuesday afternoon—the day after Daley Rideout had left Monarch. Yes, he said, he'd noticed a girl and two men who weren't club members or locals. He peeled off his wetsuit, teeth chattering and hair dripping, looking at my phone screen as I swiped through the pictures of Daley Rideout for him. He nodded.

"Her name's Daley," he said. "You a cop?"

"No. A friend. I was a member here once."

"Man, what happened to your face?"

"I cut myself shaving."

A look.

I introduced myself. He gave me a quick once-over, palmed his hair off his forehead with both hands, must have decided I was okay.

He described the men as "way older than her," and said he couldn't quite figure out their relationship. It was like the men were in charge of her but she wouldn't do what they said. None of them were dressed for the beach. Daley had on jeans and a sweatshirt that looked too hot for summer, and the guys looked like they'd come from work—long pants and collared shirts and, like, corporate shoes, you know?

"She was cool," he said. "She wanted a beer, but there was only water in the cooler. She wanted to know about my board, and if my wetsuit worked, then why did I have goose bumps and blue lips, and didn't it hurt to walk over the rocks to get in and out? The two guys, like, stood off, over there, looking at the waves and waiting. She asked if she could borrow my towel, but I didn't have one, so I got one from Sean and she took off her sweatshirt and laid down in the sun for a while."

"And her friends?" I asked.

"Just hung down closer to the water. Watching her and checking their phones. After half an hour she got up and gave Sean back his towel and went down the beach with them."

"Which way?"

"Toward the power plant. Kinda weird. I watched them go to the fence and I saw two of the guards come out. Full-on machine guns, man, I mean serious stuff. They looked like Army or Marines. I watched because Daley was pretty hot and I liked her. The guards walked along the fence, back toward the buildings and all the nuclear waste and stuff. The guards let her and the guys in through a gate. That really surprised me. I thought, *Wow, who'd want to go in there, get all like radioactivated?*"

"Did they come out later?" I asked.

"Not that I saw. I went out a few minutes later, looked over at that gate a few times, but I didn't see her again. Hey, if you see her? Tell Daley that Jake from the surfing club says hi."

"I promise to do that," I said. "Do you have a phone, Jake?"

"Backpack," he said, nodding to a green pack hanging from a nail on the shack.

"How about we trade numbers? If you see her again I expect a call from you."

Jake gave me his number and I logged it into my phone, then sent my number to his phone as a text. A beat later, I heard the chime from within the green backpack.

He dug some sunglasses from his pack and slipped them on. "She in trouble?" he asked.

"I think so."

"Does it have to do with your shaving accident?"

"To be honest, yes. Call me if *you* see her, please."

"Not a problem. She's for sure got a boyfriend, right?"

"I don't think so, Jake."

He smiled. We shook hands. His felt as cold as mine had just a few short days ago.

BURT AND I came to the security fence around the plant, standard chain link, twelve feet high. No razor wire at the top, no electricity to shock curious surfers, swimmers, fishermen, sunbathers, or dogs. But still the end of the trail for citizens such as us.

From there the domes loomed higher. Some of the buildings had been demolished and taken away and an air of uselessness hung over the plant. The deconstruction cranes stood at rest here on Sunday, their latticed booms unmoving in the blue.

The only sign of life was plant security, the heavily armed guards that Jake mentioned. I watched a pair of guards patrolling the southern side of the station, automatic rifles slung over their shoulders, fat sidearms, ammunition, batons, and pepper spray on their belts. Desert camouflage uniforms. Another two emerged from a cluster of buildings, strolling casually toward the western perimeter of the complex.

About halfway along the western flank of the compound, a

couple of Jeeps came side by side, with two more armed guards in each. Burt waved as they came down the road past us. I chose to look away. Watched a surfer catch a very nice left, barrel along, nothing fancy, just an honest longboard run.

When the guards were well past us, I popped the question.

"SNR Security, right?"

"Indeed," said Burt. "And such friendly men. They waved back."

"They just made up my mind about what to do next," I said.

"Try me."

"What good can come of a fourteen-year-old girl, her homicidal pals at SNR Security, a date farm where they beat visitors, and a decommissioned nuclear power plant?"

"No good at all," said Burt.

"I want you to find a way into Paradise and take a look around. I'd do it myself, except . . ." I pointed at my own face.

"I've been thinking about that, too. And I have some ideas."

We stopped and looked at each other. "I don't mean to sound wimpy, Burt, but it's pretty fucking unfriendly down on that farm."

"So I see."

We continued down the beach.

"But," said Burt, "I also see that this doesn't have to be our problem. Who are you, Roland? You are an employee. You have seen your job site now and it is a formidable place. Those apes at Paradise could have killed you out there. They probably should have. I would guess that more than one of them thought it might be the prudent thing to do, put you down nice and deep and far away, like we did to our troublesome friend not long ago. So here you are, alive and breathing. What I'm saying is, is this job of yours worth it? Is the girl worth your life? Mine?"

I'd been wondering the same. Soldiers and cops put their lives on the line. It's part of the job. A private investigator doesn't have to. You can save your own skin anytime you want. No court-martial or internal investigations. You can even call the cops and let them do the dirty work. However, a PI can take on risk. And the amount of risk changes with what you think about your clients. I've had clients I wouldn't jaywalk to help. And others I've taken a beating for.

"She's fourteen," I said. "And in the company of murderers."

Burt looked down at the sand, nodded, as we walked along. "Between the feds, the state, and the county, there are thousands of people dedicated to finding runaways like Daley Rideout."

"Yet some of those runaways still show up dead, or never."

Human silence then, just the crash of waves and the cries of seagulls and the soft crunch of our feet on the sand. The ocean blue now, not green. Shadows lengthening west to east, evening coming on.

"Then, of course, there's the sister."

"Yes," I said. "There she is."

"I'm sure you want to come through for her."

"I really do."

"I can see why," Burt agreed. "She's responsible for the girl. Very much on the hook. And quite an eyeful, too. All those curves and curls."

"She has my attention."

"I saw it in your postures at the picnic table. How you walked her to her car."

"None of you were exactly subtle."

"Friends aren't subtle."

"It's like catching something."

"Slow to win, Roland. It's a saying in sports."

"I know what it is."

"I'm not worried," said Burt. "You'll notice things in her that will slow you down. It's easy to fog things up with your own breath."

We continued past the power plant a few hundred feet, then turned around and headed back toward my truck. Strange to walk past all those eighteen hundred tons of nuclear waste buried in the sand just a few yards away. While you check out the surf, and think about your work, and about a woman you barely know and who has lied straight to your face and you still can't close your mind's eye on her.

"Now, so far as Paradise goes," said Burt, "I've printed maps we can use. There's an adjacent BLM parcel that Paradise doesn't own— dirt roads, occasional bird hunters and rock hounds. I'll be inside. You'll be able to keep an eye on me. I talked to our friend Clevenger. He's made some cameras we can have. You'll like these."

15

////////////////////////

WHEN we got back home, I was surprised to find the Irregulars and Penelope Rideout arrayed around the picnic table under the big palapa, apparently deep into cocktail hour.

Sundays are ceviche night at Rancho del los Robles. I gathered that Penelope had arrived earlier, unannounced, then honked from the gate until Dick had let her in. When Penelope saw the festivities shaping up, she'd offered to fetch the ceviche from our usual source, Rosa's Restaurant downtown. Thereby earning an invite to stay for dinner. She sat between Dick and Liz, one of Liz's "industrial-strength" margaritas in a stemmed balloon glass before her.

Penelope wore a summer dress on this summer evening—periwinkle, I believe the color is called. Hair up on one side, held by a flowered comb. Her white phone sat on the table in front of her.

They had saved me my place at one end of the table. I sat and hefted one of the two large pitchers of margaritas, poured away. A festive paper tablecloth and mason-jar candles, faintly fragrant.

Inspired by the drinks, Violet launched into a story of seeing her first and only bullfight in Tijuana a few years back—a *novillada*, or novice contest, that was particularly sickening if you were pulling for the bull, which she was. She had been furious at her date for bringing her to such a pointlessly gruesome spectacle and had broken up with him before they'd reached their Tijuana hotel, where she had then moved her things into a separate room, and the next day taken the Amtrak Surfliner all the way from Imperial Beach home to Santa Barbara.

"I thought you were living in St. Louis," said Liz.

"Exactly," said Violet, smiling. "But I was staying with friends in Santa Barbara that summer and I had to get away from that guy as fast as possible! And I still remember the name of the bullfighter who was the big draw that day—Adan Coreas. There are so many things that I'd like to forget, but once they get into my head . . ."

The ceviche was great, as usual—fish, shrimp, scallops, and octopus. Everyone had their stories. Even shy Frank offered up some harrowing tales of crocodile-heavy rivers and big jungle snakes and riding *La Bestia* up through Mexico to the United States. He had the Hispanic flair for understatement. *A small boa of constrictor, maybe twelve feet.* I caught Penelope looking at me, twice. Just after checking her phone. I looked back at her in the candle glow, her burnished bare shoulders and the light on her hair, and eyes that had taken on the color of her dress.

After dinner, Ping-Pong. Liz a good and graceful player, as many tennis players are. Violet's ponytail flew every time she looked behind her and up, for that airborne threat she seemed to fear. Penelope had fast reflexes and accounted herself well with her partners. Within the summer dress her body was beautiful. Burt's team won every game, which it almost always does. Once in a while I can take him in singles. Tonight, I kept myself on the disabled list, though it wasn't easy.

Then the Irregulars vanished and Penelope took up her place at the table again. We tried to make light conversation, but, set against the obvious pain and peril in our worlds, the small talk was awkward and witless.

She looked down at her phone for maybe the fiftieth time. "I brought some things over for you," she said. "I'll get them."

From her yellow Beetle she carried two large shopping bags, each a bright floral design. She set them on the table at her place across from me, and remained standing. The Ping-Pong exertions had knocked her hair loose, and curls dangled over her forehead in some disorder. The candlelight wavered on her face and gave her eyes a theatrical quality.

"This is a bourbon I'm told you like." She displayed the bottle using both hands, hamming it up like a game-show model. Set it on the table facing me. Then looked into the bag with a thoughtful expression, as if considering the order of things.

"This is a box of chocolates." She propped the chocolates against the bourbon. Inside the bag, she moved something with one hand so she could get to the next item.

"These are oranges, pears, and peaches. All organic. See?" She carefully set them on the table.

"This is just a sixer of Bohemia from Vons," she said. "My favorite. Now, this . . . I really hope you like this. It's to take the place of the one they ruined out in the desert. I got the XXL, but I can exchange it. If you don't like it I'll get you a different style. I've always liked snap-button Western shirts. Though I haven't ridden a horse since I was a girl."

She smiled goofily and shrugged. The shirt was folded neatly, with the plastic collar brace still in it. The colors were muted and rich. She propped it up against the bourbon opposite the chocolate.

"I like it," I said.

"For more practical things." She set aside the empty first bag and tugged the next one into place. Then presented the booty. "Behold: antibacterial ointment for your wounds. And a bottle of rubbing alcohol. I know you must already have these, but you could be running low. I'd be more than happy to change your dressings before I leave tonight. Thus, three different kinds of bandages, from butterflies to the big square pads with adhesive on the edges. Cotton balls. And painkiller spray made from aloe. Plus, I thought some of these cold-hot stick-on dealybobs would come in handy, but not over broken skin, of course. Now, this is *therapeutic* massage oil, says right on the label. I am volunteering to treat you with it, when you're up to such a thing. I hoped it wouldn't embarrass me to give this to you, but it kind of does. I've never given or received a massage in my life."

She smiled, a little embarrassed, by the look of it. Just like she'd said. "And there you have it."

"Treasure beyond compare," I said.

"Well, at least some stuff you need."

She studied her gifts in silence. Cut me a look, still embarrassed. Set the meds and bandages and cotton balls aside, then pushed them toward me.

"I don't know what to make of you," I said.

She came around and sat down next to me. "If you can turn, I'll touch up that face of yours and explain me to you."

I turned. Up this close, Penelope Rideout was authentically beautiful. She set one of the candles on the table next to us. The smell of melting wax mixed with her light scent.

"I'm not bad at this," she said. "My mother was an RN. And Daley was just one endless accident when she was little. Nothing serious. Let's start with the ding in your head."

Her hands came at me and I closed my eyes. Felt the rasp of the bandage, the dab of cotton, and the cool alcohol around the stitches. They'd shaved a good-sized island of my scalp.

"Like my haircut?"

No reply. The stink of ointment and the light swipe of her finger.

"Everything I told you about my husband, Richard Hauser, is true," she said. "I know because I made him up."

"Explain."

"In the beginning there was the accident. It happened in March of 2009. We were living in Eugene and we were a happy little family. Mom and Dad went to dinner for date night. Their date night was Thursdays. I made us girls chicken potpies and I did homework. I was a senior in high school. Daley sat next to me on the couch, watching videos on her gadget. She was four. It was raining hard, and windy. On the way home, Dad went off the road in our van and down an embankment and into the Willamette. The van slammed down into the rocks and the windshield broke and the van got swept around and sank. They both died. There, the forehead's done."

Her face up close. Eyes bright and analytical, in assessment, as they often seemed to be. Then her hands came at me and I closed my eyes again. Felt her fingers on my brow, applying the dressing.

"As soon as the troopers told us what had happened, that's when the fog set in. I could hardly even see through it. Way later, it got better. But it never lifted all the way. I still look at things through the fog sometimes. I tell you this unhappy story so you know what it was like to be me. Penelope Jane Rideout, eighteen. I got a good lawyer, a lot of insurance money, legal custody of Daley, the house, the cars, the investments, everything. All through the fog. I didn't know how to do what I was doing. But I did it anyway. And the vultures started circling."

And I understood. Things got quiet again. I felt the sting of alcohol on my right eyebrow, and the warmth of her breath on my face. "That's an awful cut, Roland."

"Awful people."

"Let's try an easy-change dressing."

"We'll show *them*."

"You make fun of things when they hurt. I like that about you."

"You invented the husband to scare off the vultures."

"I had to. You can't imagine how craven some of them were. Men who were married but unhappy. Men who were happy but willing to leave their wives and children. Men who were already grandfathers. Men who cried. Men who became violent. Men who unzipped. Men who would not go away. There were good men, too. More than a few. But they didn't understand me at all. I was just a girl sleeping with her little sister, chewing on my nightgown sleeve when the fog came in and the tears wouldn't stop."

She was still working on my right eye, so I opened the left.

"Who was Richard Hauser?"

"A boy I liked in kindergarten. There were several years and cities between us before I swiped his name and bought myself an engagement ring. It's a half-carat of cubic zirconium. I think that's so funny. I don't know why. But it makes me smile all the time. Very few people can tell the difference. I'm frugal—I mean, cheap. It cost me four hundred bucks instead of ten grand."

She held up her left hand to show me her thoroughly counterfeit ring. And the maybe-gold wedding band alongside it.

"Clever. Why did your family move so much?"

"Dad and Mom. Work."

"A publications director and a nurse."

"Always a job for Dad and plenty of offers for Mom. They were grass-is-greener people. Always better somewhere else. When Daley was born they really sped up. Maybe they felt trapped. Every year a new city. Greener grass."

I recognized some of that in my own parents. And Dad was career Navy for twenty years, so he had to go where they sent him. Scratched that itch for him. Mom the same way. Would still rather go than stay. I grew up in Navy towns, San Diego being the largest and longest.

She placed her hands on my cheeks. "Turn your head to the right."

Which left me with both eyes open, facing my home, a century-plus-old fortress of adobe brick, with just a few lights on and its usual air of entropy, if not neglect. It deserved better.

"The hard part about faking marriage is digging up an occasional real man when you need one," she said. "Socially, of course. I've managed. But really, people are always so willing to take other people's word for things, don't you think? I mean, it's really much easier to believe what someone tells you than it is to follow every little suspicion down the bunny trail to see what's *really* going on. Look at the couple with nine children locked up in the house, hardly fed them, chained them to the beds and starved them. Relatives? Neighbors? Nobody said one thing. Because they wanted to believe the family was normal, like the mom and dad said it was."

I felt the cooler air as the bandage came off, then the swipe again of alcohol and antibiotic. Heard the rattle of paper as Penelope opened a new dressing.

"Good as new up here," she said. "I'll work on that back of yours, if you can hack it."

I unbuttoned my shirt. She stood and came around behind me to help get it off.

"You have a nice body, Roland, but it hurts just looking at it."

"Glad I don't have to see it."

"Well, time to get tough, *hombre*."

I tried to let my mind wander as she lifted off one bandage after another, picked away at dried scabs and the newly surfaced grit. The mind won't wander at times like this.

"Ever married, then?"

"Nope."

"You're sure?"

I felt her hands stop moving. "Now you don't trust me."

"You're too good a liar to trust."

Silence.

"Look, Roland Ford—I just told you something true about myself. My big bad. Maybe that was stupid. Some people are better off the less they know. They prefer it. Insist on it. I hope that's not you. I chose you because you dig to the bottom of things and don't quit until you're there."

"At the bottom."

"Yes."

"Is that even good?"

"It's what I need."

"What else are you hiding?"

I felt her slap on a fresh bandage. She came around and studied me. Hooked a strand of hair behind one ear. Drilled in with those flat blue eyes of hers. Her judgment look. Then the flash of her never-distant temper.

"It must be tiring being you," I said.

"Now what?"

"Your anger. Your deceit."

"Mister, if this was a movie and I had a knife, this is where I'd throw it past your head and it would stick in the tree trunk behind you and shiver back and forth. And I'd have your full attention and my anger would have produced good results."

"Plenty of knives in the kitchen," I said.

A staredown. Her weighing things. Then a split decision. Close on the judges' cards. Her face relaxing in slow gradients.

"You'll trust me someday," she said. "You just watch."

Then behind me again, picking away at my wounds with what felt like slightly reduced empathy. I was glad she didn't have a knife. Not a word between us.

It seemed to take hours, and I was happy for it to be over. She sprayed on the topical painkiller and it cooled things off a little. She helped me back on with the shirt. Sat down across from me as before and buttoned me up. Leaned in closer. Eyes on me, her critical squint.

"There's nothing I can do about this lip," she said. "It's going to have to heal on its own."

Kissed it softly.

The yellow Beetle putting down the drive. Memories blowing in like a rainstorm.

16

///////////////////////

ELLISH HEAT, and the sun was barely up. Hot as Al Anbar
Province, except for the eighty pounds of gear I wasn't carrying.

I used the early light to dig a burrow in the sand behind a long-
fallen tree trunk in a thicket of dead and dying greasewoods. I laid
my shotgun on a bed of branches and my hunting vest over it. Set up
my telescope for a view of the Paradise Date Farm.

Then took a few minutes and treated myself to coffee from a thermos and a sunrise cigarette. Listened intently for the bee-buzz of the
little drone that had tracked me when I'd come here for a look
around. So far, no sound at all but the occasional doves flying overhead on squeaky wings.

It was a Tuesday, mid-September in the Imperial Valley, forecast
for 116 degrees Fahrenheit. Five days since I whupped those six flyweights in their matching silver helmets, less than half a mile from
here. My rib laughed at me as I worked myself into the burrow. The
lump on my forehead smarted under my breezer, the sweat burned
into my stitches, but the coffee and smoke made me think of
Fallujah—a vast, palm-lush, and hostile beauty.

My telescope was a gift from Justine. We'd spent some long and pleasant hours with it on new-moon nights, out in the hills beyond the pond, spying on the heavens. It's a powerful thing, and with the tripod legs pulled in and pushed well into the sand, the heavy scope was stable.

My foxhole was on a rise. Paradise Date Farm coalesced into startling detail before me: the main house and the large hangar. The red barn and the packing house and the cottages, all in their loose circle. Three silver Expeditions with the SNR Security logo on the doors were parked neatly outside the main house. Six cars stood in front of the long bunkhouse, windows cracked to defer the heat, half of them outfitted with children's car seats. A few more waited in carports alongside the cottages.

Four dark men loaded wicker baskets and ropes and boxes into the trucks. Long-sleeved shirts and ball caps. They stacked ladders in a long-bed dually, the faint clang of equipment and their voices reaching me across the still, dry air.

Through the open roll-up doors of the metal hangar I saw a row of ATVs, a Bobcat, and two full-sized John Deere tractors, all clean and well tended. Conversing just inside the door were three men wearing the same desert camouflage as the San Onofre guards, and a fourth man in tan slacks and a black golf shirt. He was tall, muscled, and blond, and seemed to have some rank on the uniforms. Hair longer on top and short on the sides, same as Daley Rideout's guardians. One of whom had shot Nick Moreno in his bed at point-blank range.

A moment later, Adam Revell came through the front door of the main house with an American flag tucked under one arm. The screen door tapped shut behind him. He wore the same blue guard uniform he'd worn to Alchemy 101 the night we'd become friends. He cut in front of two of the harvest workers as if they didn't exist, on his way to the flagpole that stood not far from the front porch. Then hoisted the flag adroitly, keeping it from touching the ground. Inside the hangar, the men turned to watch, one of the camouflage uniforms saluting casually.

AT EIGHT SHARP, a very old white pickup truck came to a stop at the speaker console outside the main gate. The truck was mine. I'd accepted it for payment from a neighbor whose missing cat I had located last year around Christmas. Looking for that animal had cost me some valuable hours, and in the end the cat had actually located me. Oxley. My neighbor really loves Oxley, and their reunion was moving. The not-quite-derelict truck had been sitting in my barn ever since, battery disconnected and covered by a tarp. It was old and beaten, but big enough to carry the tools of Burt's new trade: ladders, buckets, commercial sponges big as bread loaves, squeegees, extension poles, glass cleaner concentrate, rags, rags, rags. Grandpa Dick had once been a commercial artist and early in his career had done signage. He had used light-gray paint to give the door stencil a weathered and authentic look:

Imperial Window Cleaning
Since 1976

I watched the dust settle as the window went down. Saw Burt punching away at the keypad, his white painter's cap tilted up cheerfully. Frank sat next to him, staring impassively out at a vast desert so unlike his Salvadoran home. Burt talked into the intercom. We had predicted that getting past the gate would be easy. But getting a go-ahead to start work would be trickier.

What I'll say, Roland, once I'm in, is somebody from SNR Security called and told me to get out to this hellhole and wash the windows. I drove eighty miles and I'm not turning around now. Look at your damned windows. Might have to charge you the extra-duty rate. How would I know who called? The boss says where to go, that's where I go. And I don't come back without his money. This is cash or check, I'm sure you were told.

Burt rolled up his window and the gate arm rose. That smile of his. Frank said something and smiled, too.

The old white truck came bouncing into the compound and parked outside the main house. Two camo-clad SNR men approached it, one at each door. Burt slid out, cowboy boots puffing up the dust. Burt believes that his shortness gives him an advantage over most people in most situations. Says it has to do with uncertainty. Animals love him, especially dogs and horses. Francisco didn't move.

Muscle Blond from the hangar strode across the yard. Burt swung out his hand, but the man refused to take it. They appeared to introduce themselves. They were soon joined by a man and woman who came from the house. Pistols on their hips. The couple looked late twenties, he in jeans and work boots and a rolled-up plaid shirt. Tattooed forearms. The woman had a rural look—tight jeans and cowboy boots and a chambray work shirt. Yellow hair brushed up into a flattop.

A shadow crossed the ground in front of me. When I looked up, my rib screamed with pain, but there was no drone, only a large raven dipping in for a look at this strange human.

I sipped some more coffee, let my heart slow back down. Tried to think of something pleasant and drew a Penelope Rideout card. Penelope at my table in the candlelight, looking at PI Ford, only half covertly. I put that card back into the deck and shuffled. Came up with ten years of a faked marriage to an invented man. To keep the vultures away. It made some sense, but not enough. I could see it, but I couldn't see it. I didn't think I'd gotten to the truth of her yet. Only her beguiling surfaces.

By then, Burt was wrangling with Muscle Blond, Flat-Top Woman, and Tattooed Forearms, all at once. They loomed over him. He faced them, arms out, stubby fingers spread, his surprisingly big head turned up to them like a kid arguing with grown-ups. Muscle Blond shook his head decisively, Tattooed Forearms argued, and Flat-Top Woman set her hands on her hips. Burt gestured toward the house and appeared to curse.

Then drew his phone, dialed, and held it out to Tattooed Forearms, who wouldn't take it. Neither would Muscle Blond or Flat-Top Woman.

Burt looked up at each of his opponents as he waited for his call to go through. Then he was talking again, fast. He paced, checked his watch. Listening and nodding.

After a minute of this he gave the phone to Muscle Blond, who reluctantly put it to his ear, said little, then rang off. He tossed the phone to Burt and walked toward the hangar, throwing up his hands.

Which is when I saw the roaring lion's head tattooed on his palm.

Burt snatched his phone midair, jammed it into a back pocket, turned, and waved Frank from the truck.

Grandpa Dick Ford at Imperial Window Cleaning, an occasionally foul-mouthed geezer and not to be trifled with, had apparently spoken his piece.

17

//////////////////////////

THEY worked unhurriedly from building to building, carefully bracing the tall ladders, bearing down with dripping sponges, drying their squeegees between strokes. One of the uniformed guards followed them from wall to wall, watching for funny business, but was called away by cell phone just before the high square windows of the hangar were finished. Burt waved to him and called down as he walked off, and the guard waved back. Burt pulled a dry shop cloth from his pants pocket to scour out the dried-on bugs and conceal his phone while he took pictures through the glass.

When he climbed down, I saw a wasp nest stuck to the wall up near the eaves, where Burt had been window washing: Clevenger's handiwork, not a nest but a motion-activated video camera that could live-stream back to us through satellite and cell signals. Clevenger was a former Irregular, an Emmy-winning nature documentarian, a terrible Ping-Pong player, but a good man. He was working on a wasp segment for *Spy in the Wild*. When I told him about the beating I'd taken at a mysterious date farm in pursuit of a missing fourteen-year-old, Clevenger had insisted we take four of his handmade video cameras for a better look around. And a dedicated laptop to receive the feeds. No charge.

I kept an eye up for drones. The doves were flying in this

still-early part of the morning, out to get their water and feed from the Imperial Valley fields before the temperature put even them in the shade. Scores of doves, zero drones.

Sipped water, ate a couple candy bars, thought of Daley Rideout. I still couldn't figure out who was in charge—Daley or the SNR men who couldn't control her but wouldn't let her go. Much like Penelope with her spirited little sister.

I watched Burt and Frank. Frank, gangly and teenaged, seemed unfazed by balance issues, breeze, heat, or altitude. I wondered if he might start his own window-washing business, but Salvadoran refugees were out of favor in today's federal America. Asylum was rare and work permits few.

The farmworkers worked the Medjool harvest. High up in the trees, the men picked the ripe dates by hand and filled wicker baskets, then lowered them by rope to the packers on the ground. When their bins were full, the trucks carried them to the packing house.

Shotgun blasts came from my right, coming gradually closer and closer. Hunters hiding in the greasewood, like me. I shot doves with Dad when I was a boy, and I remembered how the birds would funnel through a certain spot, so you'd sneak over there when the skies were momentarily empty, hopefully unseen. Doves have good eyes. And once the first shotgun blast has broken the silence of dawn, the birds fly faster and higher and longer without stopping. By eleven a.m. all you can do is watch them fly out of range over you. By then it's too hot to be standing like a fool in one of the world's hottest deserts anyway, hoping to kill small birds for dinner with shotgun shells that cost twelve bucks a box when you could buy a whole cooked chicken for seven. As the shooters moved closer to me I knew I'd have to abandon my bunker, take up my shotgun—brought half for disguise and half for self-defense—and pretend to be hunting.

Burt and Frank finished the windows of the main house, the hangar, and the red barn. I saw two more new wasp nests, one on the barn and one more on the hangar, making two. Burt went back to get a few problem windows of the house, which meant photo ops that he'd not had with the guard standing watch over him.

Then on to the bunkhouses, which were small and low and looked to go quickly. Burt let Frank handle these while he used a spray bottle and shop rags to work on the dust-caked windows of the cottages. Seemed to spend a lot of time with those windows, working them over two times each. A new wasp nest appeared.

When he was finished he stood back as if to admire his work, then he hooked the spray bottle to his belt and pulled out his phone.

A moment later my own phone chimed. His pictures arrived slowly in this great sparse desert, three in all, apparently shot through a crack in the cottage window blinds: four garage-size freezers, white and clean. Five feet by four, judging by the look of them. They had been modified: intake hoses protruding from what looked like recirculation units fitted on their left-hand sides. A small timer/keypad beside each assembly. The freezers were spaced in the room for easy access. Hanging from nails in the walls were long-armed rubber gloves, protective suits of some kind, and military combat masks that defend against blowing sand, dust, and chemicals.

Burt: "How are the windows looking?"

I told him he'd missed a spot by the house's front door.

"Just in case my phone and I don't get out of here in one piece, you should have these pictures."

"What's in the freezers?" I asked. "TV dinners?"

"I doubt that. I couldn't contract for the interior windows, so we can't get inside. Later if ever, boss."

I watched and wondered. Looked at the pictures on my phone

again, shading the screen with one hand, trying to make sense of the freezers, suits, gloves, and gas masks.

A steady string of cars began arriving at about eight forty, all with children aboard. They parked near the main house and the kids hopped out with their backpacks and lunch pails. Several men, women, and children began emerging from the bunkhouse and the cottages.

The adults were all young, well groomed, and conservatively dressed. Something of an earlier America about them. Their children likewise. Backpacks and book bags. Some had hair still damp from the shower. Most of them stopped for a moment after getting out of the vehicles, as if stunned by the fierce morning sunlight. Then hustled to the big red barn.

A middle-aged couple stood before the open barn door and welcomed the children in. He was large and burly and wore a short-sleeved white shirt with a tie; she was almost as tall but slender, in a long summer dress. Her hair up in a bun. Much talking and shaking of hands among the adults as the kids disappeared inside.

The drop-off cars headed back toward the gate.

Two men in khaki pants and black golf shirts, wearing black boots and carrying duffels, came from the main house and got into one of the silver Expeditions. Adam Revell and another young man, both in blue SNR security guard uniforms, climbed into a second Expedition and followed the first down the road.

Everybody coming or going, I thought. Neat people. Brisk people. They seemed to have a purpose. Or at least a routine.

THE DOVE HUNTERS stumbled onto me a few minutes later, following a steady stream of birds flying straight over my position.

"Oh, sorry," said the older one. "Didn't even see you here." He eyed me suspiciously from behind yellow shooting glasses, considered my shotgun, and looked in the direction of my telescope, well hidden under dead branches and a handy tumbleweed.

Up came his son, certainly, same shape and sharp eyes, same yellow glasses. "How you doing so far?" he asked.

"A little slow here," I said.

"They've been flying right over you for twenty minutes," said Dad.

"Are you sure?"

"You should have your eyes checked," said Dad. "Seriously." His eyes roamed my face.

I shrugged.

A drone flew past in front of us, west to east, a couple hundred yards out. Right along the Paradise Date Farm fence line.

"Fish and Game," said Son.

"We don't know that for sure," said the father. "Those drones don't come out past the fence."

"Are they out here often?" I asked.

"The drones? Now and then," said Dad.

Took my time, didn't want to seem too interested. "Do you ever talk to the date farm people?"

"No," said Son, shaking his head. "Dove season is harvest time for them."

"There must be lots of trucks heading out for market," I said.

"Trucks come and go all the time," said Dad. "So do a lot of nice silver SUVs, and plenty of passenger cars. People living there. Not just workers. More than you'd think."

We exchanged hunters' pleasantries for a minute or two: How's the twenty-gauge Red Label swing? You shooting seven-and-a-halfs or eights? They had killed a rattler last week early morning, a big one, and told me to watch out.

"Well, nice talking," said Dad. "But get those eyes of yours checked. You could have had your limit by now."

"I'll do that."

"Later," said the son.

BURT AND FRANK finished up work at two. Loaded up the old white truck and stood in the front-porch shade for a few minutes, awaiting pay. Burt wore his sweat-soaked painter's cap in a mission-accomplished style, bill upward.

Finally a man came out and handed Burt a check. I recognized him. I'd watched him through the window of Pastor Reggie Atlas's office last Sunday, tidying up the Cathedral by the Sea courtyard after the hot dog, burger, and donut extravaganza. Same clothes. Same blond buzz cut, ruddy face, and pit-bull ears. Same black golf shirt and khakis and shiny black duty boots.

Burt examined the check and seemed to be trying to get Pit Bull Ears into a conversation, but no luck. The man looked down at Burt with undisguised amusement and I wondered if things would escalate. Burt hates being treated like he's short. It's one of the few things that gets to him.

But the man went back inside without incident, and the front door closed silently. Burt slid the check into his wallet with the bills. The window washers got into their truck.

A moment later the dust and the shimmering waves of heat swallowed that truck whole, and it was gone.

18

////////////////////////

Burt's hard-won pictures jumped to life on the computer monitor in my home office. Seven images in all, counting the mystery freezers. Burt was unhappy that he couldn't shoot the farmhouse interiors because the house was full of people. And that the barn windows were shuttered.

But he had managed to sneak four shots of the hangar's interior. Behind the tractors, ATVs, and other work vehicles that had been visible through the roll-up doors stood two long work benches. Hard to tell what kind of work, if any, was done on them. Bench vises, electric sanders/polishers, a drill press, a band saw, coffee cans of what looked like nuts and bolts, soldering guns, toolboxes.

Burt frowned at the screen, scrolled back and forth between the images. "I could only get four shots before the big guy came back in," he said. "Every time I tried again, there he was. A lion tattoo on one palm. He introduced himself as Connor Donald."

Connor Donald, I thought. Muscle Blond. My attacker. Leader of the pack.

I booted up my tablet and entered his name in the IvarDuggans .com search field. Then set the dedicated wasp-cam laptop on the desk.

And once again let my eyes roam Burt's shots of the inside of the Paradise Date Farm hangar.

"What's that in the background, Burt? It looks like a security-screen door. The perforated steel ones you can see through from inside but not from the outside."

"That's exactly what it is. Donald went in and came out four times that I saw. Used a key each time."

"No one else?"

"Just him."

How I would have loved to see through that security-screen door.

Burt and I turned our attention to the custom laptop that Dale Clevenger had built and loaned us. It was dedicated to receive the live feeds from his four wasp cameras. It was large for a laptop, very heavy, and encased in red aluminum. I'd opened it and propped it up at one end of the desk.

Clevenger's four wasp-cams were motion-activated and the batteries were good for eight hours of streaming. The power shut down automatically after thirty seconds of inactivity. You could check the remaining battery life for each camera. Dale had programmed the laptop computer so all four cameras could stream at once, the screen quartering itself to accommodate them. From Dale's computer, the live video could be sent to other devices, either live or later.

Wasp-cam one was up now, a view of the main house. We watched a silver Expedition roll into a parking place in front of the house and stop on a pillow of dust. Adam Revell and his partner got out and headed into the house.

"On the left is Revell," I said, "Daley's acquaintance from Alchemy 101 nightclub. And possibly one of the six helmets who put me in my current condition. The other guy I don't know."

A few seconds later, the screen split in half for the camera-one feed—two date pickers trundling from one of the storage sheds with empty wicker baskets in both hands. They were talking. Waves of heat shimmered around them. Dale Clevenger's video was very clear. As if on cue, camera four came to life on the laptop screen when an authentic wasp landed on it, legs straddling the lens, wings fanning in the sunlight as it checked things out.

By then, my disorganized thoughts were trying to advance, lining up like swells from different directions but headed for the same beach:

Daley Rideout.

Connor Donald.

SNR Security—khakis, black golf shirts, and silver Expeditions.

Uniforms and camouflage. Pistols, boots, and tattoos.

A barn full of schoolchildren and a cache of modified game freezers and protective gear.

An all-white lineup.

"Burt, who are these people and what are they doing?"

"They are Americans, acting out their version of the American Dream."

"But what does keeping Daley Rideout have to do with the American Dream?"

"It makes sense to somebody," Burt said.

But none to me. And more important, where was she and what had they done with her? A cool tingle came from the old boxing scar on my forehead. I tried to be open and receptive. I tried to quiet my mind and let the scar do its magic. Then it stopped. No tingle, no warning, no guidance. I'd failed to hear its message. My scar is no parlor trickster and will not perform on cue.

So I stared at my desktop monitor, at Burt's hard-won picture of the unrevealing interior of the metal hangar, confronting the terrible truth that Daley Rideout had been gone for nearly a week and I had failed to retrieve her. Seven days is statistically disastrous for abducted children. The small candle in this darkness was that she'd been seen alive more recently on the beach at San Onofre, and very early the next morning at a convenience store in San Clemente.

IvarDuggans.com had precious little information on Adam Revell, but an image of his California driver's license confirmed that I had the right guy.

Connor Donald was another story.

His picture was dated three years ago. Same casually handsome face. Shorter hair then. He was square-jawed, with a focused and present look in his eyes.

"Who would have thought that?" asked Burt. "Dumb-looking beefcake like him?"

Burt had already read the IvarDuggans bio. He reads faster than anybody I've ever known. He can absorb and retain the information on a book page or a monitor screen after looking at it for six or eight seconds. He once mentioned a speed-reading program his parents had given him for his fifth birthday, this plastic gadget with a long rectangular window through which phrases would pass as fast as you could push a lever. He said he got so fast it was like reading thoughts. He sold it to a friend and bought cherry bombs. He also claimed that his uncorrected vision was 20/10 and actually improving with age, attributable to homeopathic remedies.

"Give me a minute, Burt, will you?"

"A wet dose of arnica 6C and a daily euphrasia douche would help your vision a lot, Roland."

"Noted."

Our Connor Donald was twenty-nine years old, born in Strouds-
burg, Pennsylvania, graduated top of his class from a public high
school and got a football ride to Penn State. Quit the team after one
season, forfeiting the money to study physics and philosophy. Graduated summa cum laude, hired by JPL, moved on to Aero-Dynamics
in Orange County, California; then General Atomics of San Diego.

"A rocket scientist," I said.

"And more."

Four years ago, Donald had joined a Christian mission—Lions of
the Lord—in Somalia, sponsored by the Western Evangelical Alliance, which, I remembered, was matching the Cathedral by the Sea's
Onward Soldiers Fund donations one-to-one. The adventure had
turned into a nightmare when three of the missionaries and six of
their armed bodyguards were murdered by Somali rebels. I recalled
the gruesome horror, well covered by the press and media. One of the
slaughtered ministers was a San Diego woman.

I linked from IvarDuggans to a *New York Times* article about the
killings. There, Connor Donald talked at length about the day it happened. Surprise. Guns and machetes. Young men—just boys, by the
look of them.

"I don't know why they left me alive," he said. "Unless it was so I
could witness to the world."

Donald's IvarDuggans biography said that he left General Atomics shortly after the tragic African mission. He had apparently gone
unemployed for two years, until the founding of SNR Security.

The IvarDuggans SNR folder informed me that the security company was privately held and tightly guarded its public image. Donald
was believed to have been an original investor and possibly SNR Security's first chief operating officer.

Back to Connor Donald: His bio had not been updated for a year.

Last known address, Buena Vista, California, home of Paradise Date Farm. I thought again of the beating I'd taken out there, and of the snarling lion tattooed on Connor Donald's palm. Felt the cracked rib still aching in my chest, and the tight lump at my hairline.

Donald had no criminal record, no property or tax liens, no known associates I recognized.

An IvarDuggans query asked for "corroboration and updates on this subject."

"Nice career moves," said Burt. "From scientist to crusader to security guard to date farmer."

I'd been thinking the same.

"Everything's connected by SNR," I said. "Daley. Alchemy 101. Paradise Date Farm. Even the Cathedral by the Sea, which interested Daley and repulsed her sister. The SNR guy at Paradise who wrote you the check? He's part of the church, a deacon or an elder. I saw him there last Sunday."

Burt studied me with curious, unemotional eyes. He produced his wallet and handed me the check.

It was drawn on a Paradise Date Farm account at San Diego Valley Bank. Signed precisely by Eric Glassen.

"Okay," said Burt. "Another SNR connection to the church." A moment later, Eric Glassen's pugnacious mug was staring back at us from the all-knowing ether of IvarDuggans.

He was thirty-four, five years older than Connor Donald. And like Donald, Glassen had an unusual, almost contradictory, academic résumé—double undergrad degrees in mechanical engineering and history from UC Riverside. Grew up in San Bernardino. Surfed, had a rock band, played four years of varsity football as a cornerback.

He'd been arrested for assault in a bar fight when he was twenty-

two, charges dropped. At twenty-three, a DUI that stuck. Employment at manufacturing companies in Los Angeles, San Jose, and
Seattle. A brief stint in the UFC as a middleweight, professional record of 6-8, retired in 2014. Hired by Corvus Protection in 2015 and
SNR Security two years later.

"Looks like a tough customer," said Burt. "And that six-and-eight
record in the UFC couldn't have left him in a good mood."

As a fighter who had done some losing, I agreed.

19

////////////////////////

LATER that evening, after Burt had left, I did another Internet search for information on SNR Security. The SNR website gave me the paragraph I'd already seen: The San Diego company was two years old, privately held, and specialized in armed and unarmed personal and property protection. It offered no grander mission statement than that, no pictures or bios of company officers, no testimonials from satisfied clients, no shots of their headquarters, no phone number, no jobs tab, no links to more. The one-page site did have a street address and a "Contact Us" email address, and a background graphic of the SNR logo I'd seen on the door of Adam Revell's SUV—the eagle with the lightning bolts.

The more search words I tried, the more I saw how publicity-shy the company was.

SNR Security declined to comment for this story.

SNR Security could not be reached.

SNR Security did not answer our inquiries.

There was a humorous story by a *San Diego Union-Tribune* business columnist trying to find out what the letters *SNR* stood for.

SNR Security didn't return any of my ten emails over the next ten workdays.

So I decided to ask them face-to-face just exactly what their initials stood for.

In SNR Security's contemporary but sterile lobby, I was greeted by a smiling woman in a blue security uniform who smilingly told me that SNR had no public relations department per se, but she would certainly help me if she could.

Smiling, she told me that SNR didn't stand for anything specific— the letters were chosen because they were easy to remember.

When I asked to speak with her supervisor, she seemed sorry to tell me there were no SNR personnel available to talk to me at this time. She broke this news to me with a smile, and said their website had an email address, I just had to click on "Contact Us."

I shared with her my plight of ten unreturned emails and she told me she would look into it.

I told her I'd be happy to wait while she did so, but she told me, with a smile, that it would take some time.

So I sat in a contemporary but sterile chair and waited for less than one minute.

As if on cue—likely the old hidden-camera trick—a blue-uniformed security guard with a surfer's tan and a crew cut came through a door behind the reception counter, squeaked across the shiny marble floor in black combat boots, and asked me to leave.

He was not smiling. The gun at his side was black and fat as a family Bible.

I stood and asked him how he liked working for SNR, and he asked me again to leave or he would call the police.

"Why?" I asked.

"Because you are trespassing and have been asked to exit the building." He lifted a phone from his belt and arranged a thin speaker wire running down from a bud in his ear.

I smiled at both of them, and left.

I'm still not sure what SNR stands for. Say Nothing Real? Just because I happen to live in the city where they do business apparently does not give me a right to know.

I'm sure their security services are terrific. But they should get a more transparent name.

I SAT IN my office in the dimming evening light. Let my eyes wander across the bronzed pond and the hills and the sun melting into layers of orange and blue. But my mind did not enjoy the sunset. It was busy chewing on the problem of exactly where Daley Rideout was, and what she was doing, and what was being done to her. I felt frustration and a desire for violence, like a father might.

I wondered how SNR was controlling her. So many possibilities. The sex trader beats his new girl, then injects her with heroin or opioids to kill the pain. The beating breaks her spirit—because she's been told she's beautiful, and she's been touched tenderly, and she's gotten pretty gifts—and suddenly she's a bruised and aching girl, plainly despised by the man she thought liked her. The narcotic brings a soft cloud of relief and creates a craving for more. A dependence within hours, an addict within days.

But I had no convincing evidence that Daley had been befriended, seduced, or abducted for the sex trade. It didn't strike me as SNR-like. Hard to say why. They seemed more . . . sophisticated than that. In spite of the unsophisticated fact that onetime missionary Connor

Donald had likely shot Nick Moreno in the forehead as the young man watched TV in bed. And that they'd beaten me just for saying Daley Rideout's name.

But there are so many methods of control that don't require powerful narcotics or physical force at all. I remembered Daley's apparent familiarity with the two SNR men as they boarded the silver Expedition at Nick's condo and drove away. I thought of her ignoring two SNR escorts as she talked with surfer Jake at the San Onofre Surfing Club. And of her arguing with two SNR men in the parking lot of the 7-Eleven in San Clemente—arguing but not resisting—then willingly getting into their vehicle.

As I pictured that scene playing over and over again, I believed that at that moment in the 7-Eleven parking lot, under the bored but curious gaze of Yash Chowdhury, the clerk, the balance of power between Daley and her not-quite-abductors had changed. They wouldn't lose her again. No. And the easiest way to control her? Take her phone, put her in a remote house or building, lock the doors, and post some guards. SNR had plenty of those to choose from.

On my desk, Dale Clevenger's big red laptop suddenly jumped to motion-activated life. Camera three: Two adults I'd seen earlier—Tattooed Forearms and Flat-Top Woman, both of them with guns on their hips—came from the house with two young boys and a girl. I guessed them at seven, five, and three years old. The boys wore white shorts, black canvas sneakers, and plaid shirts buttoned all the way up. The girl wore a pink dress and shiny pink shoes. Her hair was pulled into a yellow ponytail and she carried in both hands a baby doll easily half her own size.

They stood around the flagpole and the boys lowered the flag that

Adam Revell had raised early that morning. They were careful with it, stretching it out for the long folds, then gradually stepping closer as the triangle of stars and stripes thickened.

The older boy presented the flag to the woman and the five walked in loose cadence back into the house, boys first, adults next, girl trailing behind, all of them just steps ahead of the dark.

AN HOUR LATER I was driving back up the coast to San Clemente, headed for the last place I knew for certain that Daley Rideout had been seen.

I could sense her out there, this girl I'd never met. Both a moral duty and a paycheck. She was close, but drifting from my reach. One moment I felt puzzled but hopeful, like a dog returning for a buried bone that had disappeared just hours ago: *I will now dig again*. The next moment I felt only foolish and beat-up.

I pondered what Penelope Rideout had said about my willingness to dig to the bottom of things. And that she had chosen me for this labor because of it. It had made me proud, the choosing. *I will now dig again*. I wanted to do it well and show her the quality of man I was. I wanted her to truly see me. And here it came again, the forbidden jump of my heart. Forbidden why? Justine? Enter the cave of your past, and ask the ghosts that sleep there.

Light fog clung to the coast. Just off Interstate 5 the new Camp Pendleton Navy Hospital loomed in lighted glory like an immense barge floating on a wide black river. I've never set foot in it. My brethren were treated in other VA hospitals, and I had visited three of them and sat beside their beds and slowly walked the halls of rehab with them. Waited for appointments with them. San Diego.

Long Beach. Phoenix. Separate but related hells. Two are doing just fine now. One is not and never will be. There is nothing sadder or more infuriating to see than a once strong young man or woman surrendering their desire to live. We warriors kill ourselves off at roughly twice the rate of the rest of you.

I pulled into the 7-Eleven parking lot, saw Yash Chowdhury behind the counter. Parked around the dark side of the building, where I wouldn't take up a prime spot.

Got a big cup of coffee and paid Yash. He hadn't seen Daley again, though her sister had been in earlier this evening. And two hours before her, a man who looked somewhat like the man who had dropped Daley off here that late morning had been here, too. He had told Penelope about seeing this man, but wasn't sure enough to call me or the police.

"Daley is very popular," said Yash.

"The van driver," I said.

"Yes. He came in, bought a hot pepperoni stick and a thirty-two-ounce beer. He said he was looking for a girl. She had been here very early last Thursday morning. I told him I was working then. He described her. And the hoodie that she wore, with the humorous question on it. He said he was her uncle."

Late forties, said Yash. Short, stocky, medium brown hair, wearing shorts, a light blue Hawaiian shirt with outriggers and coconuts on it, and leather flip-flops. Needed a shave. Runny blue eyes.

Yash didn't like his attitude. He told the man he didn't remember such a girl. The man left. Didn't give a name or leave a number.

"And the sister?" I asked.

"We talked and talked," said Yash. "She was nothing like the first time I saw her. When a customer needed to pay, she stepped aside and drank her Slurpee. The Raspberry Blast stained her gums red, so we laughed. What a positive spirit she has. But so worried. She's very conflicted."

I was still trying to figure her out, but at least I had to agree with Yash's assessment of her.

20

/////////////////////////////

I worked the city of San Clemente from north to south, on both sides of I-5. A searcher, all motion and hungry eyes. Drifting fog and stars. Good strong coffee from Yash. Camino de Estrella, Pico, Palizada. Nice neighborhoods, homes built close together down by the ocean, not so close up in the hills. Light retail. Not much traffic. A sleepy beach town.

I was fooling no one, not even myself. I knew my chances of spotting Daley Rideout were too small to matter. But just big enough to create hope. So I drove, looking for that tiny dot of hope, smaller than a taillight but big enough to see. I studied the pedestrians. The faces in cars, briefly lit, then gone. Kept my eyes out for silver Expeditions and old white panel vans. Because Roland Ford digs to the bottom of things.

South all the way to the city limit. San Onofre Nuclear Generating Station loomed half-lit in the middle distance, its spent fuel rods cooling in their casks. Cooling for the next hundred thousand years. Protected from earthquake, tsunami, thieves, and terrorists by SNR Security, who would not be interviewed for this story. Who had jumped me near a desert date farm for mentioning a girl's name. As the pain faded, my thirst for vengeance grew.

Downtown. Avenida del Mar. Pedestrians out on this summer night. Not as many as in Laguna or Newport to the north, or La Jolla or Encinitas to the south. Here in downtown San Clemente you don't even have to pay for parking. I cruised past the restaurants and cafés and the folksy little shops, half of them already closed. Backed into a parking space for a good view of the street. Right in front of the Mongkut Thai restaurant, and through my cracked window the air smelled very, very good. Salt air and spices.

Thought I'd sit for a minute before I left my truck, hit the street, and made my long-shot rounds with pictures of missing Daley.

That was when I saw Penelope Rideout's bright yellow Beetle parked across the street and ahead, ragtop up, a light slick of fog on the windows.

Well, now.

What brings you here on this late-summer night?

A few minutes later she came around the corner of El Camino Real. Opposite side of Del Mar, slowly walking toward her car, hugging herself against the cool, looking through the storefront windows. Skinny jeans and white sneakers, a black cowl-neck sweater, hair loose and curled by the damp. The small white purse over her shoulder.

She stopped in front of the first store she came to, put both hands to the glass, and pressed her face up close. It was a touristy T-shirt shop, closed. She spent some time looking into the dark store. More than I would have. Maybe she liked the humorous shirts.

No. *Not looking for shirts,* I thought. *She's doing what I was doing—looking for her sister.*

From across the avenue she came toward me, lingering window to window, door to door. The Seagull Café was open and Penelope went in. I watched her through the glass, picking her way along the booths with a frankly accounting air, looking for something specific. She disappeared into the dining room, then came back into view as she approached the cashier. Asked questions. Most of the answers were headshakes or no's. She pointed. To the 7-Eleven? Held out her phone. More headshakes and no's, but also concern. Penelope stepped aside so a customer could pay. She scanned the dining room while she waited. When the cashier was free again Penelope asked her more questions and I could see some annoyance in the woman's face.

Penelope came out, pocketed her phone, snugged the cowl, and continued. Measured, purposeful. If the business was open she went in. If not, she stared through the windows. Stared long and patiently. As if she could draw out the object of her desire with the desire itself. *The humble seed of hope,* I thought. The same seed that had brought me here.

She worked past me without a glance in my direction, down Avenida del Mar, crossed just before the library, and started back my way. Went into the coffee place, came out a few minutes later with steam trailing out the lid hole. The optometrist, closed. The yogurt shop, open. Penelope through the window glass, interrogating a young man who looked eager to help but kept pursing his lips, shaking his head. He looked at her phone pictures and shrugged. Seemed to offer her a yogurt, which she declined.

I watched her approach, but she didn't look my way. My truck windows are almost illegally dark. Her face looked tired and drawn. Hugging herself again. By the time she walked into Mongkut Thai, she was directly behind me. I could see her in my oversized sideview mirror, starting in on a hostess with a colorful brocade dress and a welcoming smile.

I watched them in the mirror, the hostess's no-longer-smiling face and Penelope's backside as she asked her questions. I wanted to go help her, but that seemed like a crude intrusion. I felt sneaky and ashamed sitting there in the dark, watching my client struggle. Wearing out her luck against the odds. Pressing her hope so hard it began to dull. That was my job. But I didn't move. Just watched her and the hostess, oddly proportioned in my mirror, conversing in the angled half-light, half-dark lobby. *Objects in mirror are closer than they appear.*

A moment later she was crossing Del Mar again, an easy trot to avoid the traffic, heading toward her cute yellow convertible.

I followed her a few cars back to the I-5 ramp off El Camino Real, then south. She drove at exactly the speed limit, middle lane if it was open, signaled her changes. Always a pleasure to tail a model citizen.

She cruised past San Onofre and through Camp Pendleton along the fog-dusted Pacific. Past the dark hills and the shining hospital and into Oceanside, where I expected her to exit for home. Where I would leave off and let her return to her domicile unfollowed.

But she continued south, all the way to Encinitas. Wound her way toward the Cathedral by the Sea, where Daley had been showered with attention by the youth minister whose gender Penelope had somehow gotten wrong.

I let her get some distance, watched her pass the church's sign on Matilija, signal, and come to a complete stop at King's Road. Turned and continued toward the church.

I followed to the first rise and pulled off the road. The coastal brush thumped and scratched at my truck as I squeezed in. Got my night-vision binoculars from the console and shouldered open the door, my cracked rib shrieking. Pressed my way through the buckwheat and manzanita to the top of the rise.

In the shorn fog stood the Cathedral by the Sea. Shapeless but graceful. Walls of marble and wood snugged together by shiny stainless-steel cables. The upswept copper roof. Outdoor and inside lights on. Double doors open wide. Through my field glasses I saw Pastor Reggie Atlas standing in the doorway, a man and a woman coming out, stopping to say goodbye to him, all cast in eerie green sniper's light.

Penelope swung the Beetle wide into the big parking lot, keeping to the edge, as if for cover. She followed the curb past the central campus with its stately Canary Island palms and the classrooms and administration building, but stopped well short of the cathedral. Her lights went out and she waited, half hidden in the near dark, just as I had done at the 7-Eleven. Eight other vehicles in the lot.

People continued to leave the cathedral, all stopping to speak to Atlas. I recalled the Cathedral by the Sea calendar from the *From the Lighthouse* bulletin that I'd picked up on Sunday—Adult Bible Study: "By Jesus Chosen." I glassed Penelope, black cowl unfurled high, face upturned and motionless.

Twenty minutes later, the Bible students had left. Pastor Atlas went back inside. The last of the cars trailed out of the lot toward King's Road. Only the yellow Beetle remained, a muted swatch in the foggy half-dark.

Penelope got out, shut the door, and locked it with a fob. Zipped the fob into her purse as she headed up the sidewalk toward the church. Hugged herself again and leaned forward, as if into a head-wind. Resolve over dread, force of will.

She climbed the steps and approached the open doors. Stopped at the threshold and said something. A moment later, Pastor Atlas came to the door and stopped. Ten feet apart.

In the night-vision green he spoke to her and she spoke back. No introductions that I could see. Something familiar in the exchange.

A conversation resumed? She terse; he patient. Jab and feint, thrust and parry. Then an escalation, inaudible to me, but I could almost hear it in their postures—the accusatory aim of Penelope's finger, the sad-faced appeasement from Reggie Atlas.

He looked past her, frowning. Then turned slightly and opened his hands in a welcoming manner, inviting her in. Penelope hunched in her black sweater, the white strap across her back. It looked like she was deciding whether to accept the invite.

With a suddenness that caught me by surprise, she yanked a silver cross from her purse and raised it at Atlas. Held it high. A vampire movie. Atlas looked disgusted, then flummoxed and hurt. He was mouthing a defense when she turned, ran to the steps, and started down. Fast and sure on her feet, white sneakers in descent, white purse swinging, and the silver cross still in hand.

Which was when a silver SNR Expedition pulled into the lot from King's Road.

The driver cruised the perimeter, just as Penelope had done, heading for her car. About halfway there, he must have seen Penelope running, or the light on in the cathedral, or Pastor Atlas standing at the top of the steps. The Expedition cut across the vacant lot and swung to a stop in the handicapped parking as Penelope ran for her car and Atlas stopped halfway down the marble steps.

Adam Revell climbed out of the SUV, Atlas yelling at him, his words muffled by the heavy air. Penelope almost to her car, horn chirping and its lights flashing once. Revell caught between them, unsure what to do, looking at the fleeing woman, then to the pastor.

Atlas's next words cut the night air: *Get over here, you dumb sonofabitch!*

Penelope's car swerved sharply, then plowed for the exit, horses whining.

I broke brush to my truck, cranked it to life, and crunched backward through the scrub onto King's Road. Threw her into drive, shot across the road, and tucked into the far shoulder. Plenty of room for Penelope to get by.

Headlights in the rearview.

SHE HAULED BUTT back to the interstate, where she tossed the speed limit and passed the slower cars. Still signaled her changes. I followed her home, watched her pull into the garage. The door lowered and a moment later the front-yard security flood came on but the house stayed dark.

I studied the small green bungalow in the patch of light: fence and porch and the ragged central palm. The living room blinds opened, then closed again.

I tried to interpret the hexagrams. But sometimes you need a place to start.

Time for an audience with the riddle herself.

I called her and she picked up.

21

////////////////////////

W E sat in her small living room, the knockoff Tiffany lamp beside the sofa casting varied light through its stained-glass shade. Penelope took the plaid couch with the lamp next to it and I got a director's chair.

She stared at me, lamplight and shadow on her face. "How long have you been following me?"

I explained my mission in San Clemente, Yash, cruising the streets—my last known address for Daley. My surprise at seeing Penelope there, interviewing the shopkeepers on Del Mar. My decision not to interfere. Following her first to the Cathedral by the Sea, then home.

"You think it's okay, spying on your employer?"

"I had your back. You know Atlas, don't you?"

She looked at me sharply, then away, sending her curls back with the shake of her head. "I already told you that. I met him in late August. When I was checking out his church. On behalf of Daley."

"No," I said. "You told me you met a youth minister who 'came at' Daley."

"He did."

"The youth minister is a woman."

"Maybe my youth minister was her assistant."

"Maybe he's related to your ex-husband."

"In what possible way?"

"As another character you've made up."

Silence between us then. She turned to me with her knife thrower's stare.

"Okay," I said. "Let's try this again. Do you know Atlas, Penelope?"

"What did you see and hear tonight?"

"Short answer? Everything."

"Hiding in the hills with some fancy military scope?"

"Zeiss night-vision binoculars. Good ones."

"I will not take the name of the Lord in vain. Much as I'd like to right now."

"Let it rip, Penelope. I do it all the time."

"Then goddamn you."

"Say it like you mean it."

"I mean it, all right."

But I saw the anger angling away from her. Before it had really even gotten started. Wasn't sure what had come in to replace it. She gave me a long, empty look.

Then sighed and stood, walked to the window. Twisted a wand and let the floodlight in.

"I met Reggie Atlas twenty years ago. I was eight. Mobile, Alabama. He was a guest preacher at the Pentecostal and he visited our Sunday school. Led a prayer and talked to us about growing up in Jesus. Twice a year, he'd come guest-preach. The rest of the time he was touring in his van. He had named the van 'Four Wheels for Jesus.' He ministered all over the South. He was starting to draw good crowds."

She gave me a slack look, rare from her. The door-to-door search for Daley and the run-in with Atlas had taken something out.

"We got to be really good friends," she said. "Wrote letters, and emails, and talked on the phone. Wrote Bible essays and poetry to each other. Lots of poems. We both loved dogs and horses. Talked about everything. His family and mine. Jesus and His plans for us. He came through Mobile six years running. Always led a Sunday-school prayer for us kids. The van became a bus. Always had a nicer bus. Bigger and fancier."

She sat back down on the couch and leaned forward, resting her elbows on her knees.

"One year, he let me see his new bus. Just me. We prayed and talked and read scripture, and he gave me a beautiful red rose and asked if I'd like to drink the blood of Jesus with him. And I said yes. I would have said yes to almost anything. I was fourteen. Brave. Foolish. And Reggie was the warmest, strongest, best-looking, funniest man I knew except for Jesus and Dad. I felt wild when I was around him. He said the pills would relax me. He said that we could never experience a love like ours again. That it was a gift from God to us. That the love I felt for him was real. The blood was sweet red fruit juice with a funny taste at the end. We talked and prayed. I got dizzy. He touched my face. Baptized me from a beautiful silver bowl. Led me to his bed. I went of my own free will. Shall I keep going, Roland? I know you get to the bottom of things. But how much truth is good for you?"

"Go on."

"I remember some details. Trying to escape him. His hands. I was numb. My fists were light as cotton and he was heavy. Very hard to move or even breathe. Pain. Fear. Wondering what Jesus thought of me. Wondering what the world outside would look like later. I slept for hours after."

In our silence I heard a car pass down the street outside. Distant voices on the sidewalk. Penelope addressed her entwined hands.

"Later, he told me the pills were morning-after pills. A double dose. So it all could be our secret. We could love each other like this whenever we wanted. And there would be no more pain, only pleasure. Forever. Us. Amen."

The voices from outside grew a little louder. Figures on the sidewalk, footsteps. A soft laugh. Penelope waited for them to pass by before she spoke again.

"But they failed. The pills."

Then the consequences, raining down.

"Daley," I said.

"My beautiful daughter."

I hadn't noted a strong resemblance between images of Daley Rideout and Pastor Reggie Atlas, but I hadn't been looking for that. Maybe I'd only missed the obvious.

"Does she know?"

"Oh, no, Roland. She's been my little sister for as long as she's had memories. Dad and Mom and I made her world that way. At first they wanted to give her away. I wouldn't do that. I prevailed. I had ten times their power of will. It's been my only weapon."

"Does Atlas know?"

"He was the only one who knows. Now you."

It took me a while to fit these pieces together. They were huge and almost unbearably heavy. But they fit.

"Reggie has followed us since Daley was born," said Penelope.

"Followed?"

"He, or sometimes people who work for him. They found us in Colorado, right after she was born. Found us in Salt Lake, Boise,

Reno. In Eugene with Mom and Dad. Everywhere we went. Now here at the end of the continent."

"What does he want?"

"At first, my silence. Which I was willing to give to keep him away. He knew that I could destroy his marriage and his career. A simple paternity test of Daley would ruin him."

"Why didn't you talk? Tell your story?"

"For Daley. For Mom and Dad. For me. He took pictures of me that night. After."

"Did he offer you money?"

"Often. I declined. He threatened to kill me if I told. Four times he threatened to kill me, to be exact. And as Daley grew, Reggie changed. She's my age now. The age I was."

I let that idea sink in for a long moment. "Your age now. And?"

"He wants to make her believe in him like he made me believe. I know this."

"How do you know this?"

"I stared into his soul as he raped me, Roland. He wants her also. He's more evil than you understand."

It hit me like a fist to a kidney.

"You think he's got her."

"That's why I went to the Cathedral by the Sea," she said, wiping an eye with her sleeve. "That's why I hired you. That's why I wander around a town I don't know, opening doors and looking through windows. I pray every second that she's simply run away because she's young and spirited and capable of bad judgment. That Reggie is not behind it."

She rose and closed the blinds and turned to me, cheeks slick in the weak light. That hard blue stare. Judgment and anger returned.

Shame, too. Pupils tight and black as peep sights, aimed inward. Not at the world. Not at me.

"I hate pity, Roland. But thank you for having my back tonight. I felt that someone was watching me. I honestly didn't think it was you."

"You've never gone to the police?" I asked.

"I tried to, in Denver and Eugene," she said. "But I couldn't tell them the whole truth. And they couldn't do anything with harassment and stalking accusations I couldn't prove. I sensed intense suspicion of me. One detective was different. He informally interviewed Reggie. The detective ended up apologizing to him. Late that night, Reggie threatened to kill me if I did that again."

"When and how did he threaten you?"

"Four times over the years. As I said. Exactly four. The first time was Denver. The most recent was Prescott."

"Can you prove it?"

"No," she said. "Always by phone. One time he heard me trying to record a conversation with a digital recorder. It was loud and obvious. After that, he would just listen and breathe. I knew what it meant. The four times don't include the breathing calls."

"Does he still call?"

"Often. He offers money."

"What did he tell you tonight, at the cathedral?"

"That I was insane, as always, and he'd call the police on me if I trespassed there again. I thought you were listening to us with some fancy gadget."

"I watched. I didn't hear."

I stood. Somehow the occasion required it. Like swearing an oath. Or paying last respects.

I was suddenly aware of how alone in her world Penelope Rideout was. A stranded creature born of a violent past, buoyed only by her own deceptions. And I felt my own aloneness, too—just a man in a small house beside a great sea, drawn by the simple need to earn a living.

"Please sit, Roland."

She sat back down on the couch, turned off the lamp. We waited in the near dark for a good long time. I didn't know for what. Part of me couldn't wait to get away from this once broken girl. But part of me wanted to stay with the woman she had become. Help beat back her demons. Be there for her. I could do just that. I wanted to.

Minutes, an hour, more. A night bird in the palm with a voice like knocking wood. Another car on the street. Always another car on the street in these crowded California beach towns.

"I'll pay extra if you stay here tonight," she said. "I want you nearby. This couch pulls out. I'll get you sheets and a pillow. Booze in the cabinet, ice in the fridge."

She disappeared into the dark hall and a light went on and I heard a closet open.

I looked at the front door, the easily thrown deadbolt. Saw the glint of my truck. Saw in my mind's eye the interior of that truck, with its familiar dash lights on and its gauges gauging and its headlights showing me the road home. Home. The Irregulars, if I wanted company. Privacy, if I wanted to be alone. The hills, if I wanted nature. All presided over by the welcome ghost of Justine. But . . .

I went into the kitchen, poured a long-night bourbon, and leaned against the counter with it. Fluorescent lights shivering overhead. Felt the terrible weight bearing down on the woman of this house, but couldn't think of one useful thing to do for her or her daughter. Her daughter. Of course. Under my nose the whole time. Under everyone's. Plain sight. You want to believe. You want to trust. You have things to do and people to deal with. So you see what you want to see. Until you don't.

And what if she'd made it all up?

Again.

She looked in from the living room, set an armful of bedding on the couch, and turned to me.

"Thank you."

She waved, awkwardly, as if unsure what type of wave this circumstance called for. Part "Hi" and part "See you later." Then headed back down the hall.

I sat up late. Sipped that drink. Thought about many things past and present. How one thing leads to another, then back again. Sometimes. And other times not at all. Remembered meeting Justine Timmerman, Esq., at a holiday party in the Grand Hyatt Hotel downtown one stormy winter night. One look and a few words. The acceleration of life. Felt that acceleration again, now.

I moved the bedding to the coffee table, took the pillow, and dozed uncomfortably. Dreams vague and meaningless. Up with sunrise, rib aching. Death's sparring partner looking back at me from the bathroom mirror.

My next move had to be Detective Darrel Walker.

22

////////////////////////

I AM actively disliked by most San Diego sheriff's deputies because of a shooting death I was party to ten years ago. I didn't fire, but my partner did. When the smoke cleared on that cool December afternoon, we deputies were alive, and an unarmed nineteen-year-old black man lay dead in an alley behind a strip mall. His name was Titus Miller. We knew him in the way that cops know citizens with histories of derangement, homelessness, and occasional violence.

I still replay that scene, frame by frame, though I try hard not to. It plays me. The sunlight streaming through the clouds above us like a graphic on a sympathy card. Titus combative that day, cussing our orders to stop and raise his hands. Screams and bright sun. Titus backpedaling away from us in his oversized coat and his scavenged athletic shoes, one red and one blue. Pulling something from his waistband and dropping into a one-knee shooter's stance. This black object glinting in the sunlight in both hands and five shots from Jason punching the life straight out of him. Titus probably dead before he hit the ground. The wallet in his hands, still chained to his belt.

My partner's name was Jason Bayless. A good enough guy, though hard to figure. Never gave up much of himself before the shooting. Nothing since. A family man. We'd worked together only a few times. Most SDSD deputies patrol solo, due to modest budgets and large territories to cover.

Jason had seen a gun in Titus's hands and I had seen a wallet and that was the very gist of it. The complications came later, during the internal investigation. He honestly believed he was defending his life. And mine. I honestly believed Titus was brandishing his wallet, likely as a prelude to showing ID. My words damned Jason. Excessive force. He quit the department within the year and went into practice as a private investigator. Same as I did. We crossed paths just last year on a difficult case, and Jason did me a solid that helped save some lives. I owe him. We tried to talk out Titus but accomplished little. He told me that if he's ever in the same spot again, he'll do the same thing. I told him I would, too. Some mountains will not be climbed.

So, as a black man and a San Diego sheriff's detective, Darrel Walker listened dubiously to me that hot, humid September morning as I told him about Alchemy 101, SNR Security, my still obvious licking at Paradise Date Farm, Reggie Atlas, and Penelope Rideout's ugly story.

He entered something on his desktop keyboard, glanced at the monitor. All I could see from where I sat were the back-end cables and connectors of his electronics, and Darrel's somber face studying the screen.

That screen had his full attention, interrupted by brief looks down at the keyboard. *Tap. Tap.* As I mentioned before, Darrel is bigger than I am. Hands like catcher's mitts. They should make XXL keyboards for guys like us.

"What was your takeaway on Atlas?" he asked.

"Convincing," I said. "Seemed concerned for this missing girl. Said he didn't remember her visiting his church. He was aware of

Nick Moreno, a semiregular. He wondered if my 'car accident' was really an accident. He asked me if he should be worried about his own well-being."

"Big of him," said Walker. *Tap. Tap.* Dark eyes moving back and forth across the screen.

"Reggie Lee Atlas," Darrel read. "Evangelical minister, Georgia born. Married, four children. Board of Western Evangelical Alliance. Honorary degrees. Got the calling at eighteen. Drove a bus around the South. Name of the bus and his ministry was Four Wheels for Jesus. Guest appearances and his own programs. Actually used a tent early on. Grew his followers. Things took off in 2005 when smartphones boomed. Lots of social media. Four Wheels for Jesus went online about a year ago—sermons from Pastor Reggie Atlas. Reggie picked to lead White House prayer breakfast. Bought the Encinitas property two years back, tore down the old meditation center, built the cathedral, and opened for business a year ago. Plans to expand. Plans for Four Wheels for Jesus cathedrals in Texas, Florida, and Georgia. *Forbes* guessed Four Wheels for Jesus Ministry assets at twenty-two million last year."

Darrel looked at me over the top of the screen. "I had no idea he's raking it in like that. You figure his nonprofit tax exemptions must be good as—well, gold. The church buildings and real estate alone are worth twelve million. No complaints against Reggie Atlas. No civil or criminal filings. No lawsuits. Not a whiff of sexual misconduct, harassment, anything. Squeaky-clean, Roland."

"Do you doubt my client?" I asked.

"I doubt everyone. Including this pastor man who thinks he hangs out with Jesus."

"Has anyone seen Daley since San Clemente?" I asked.

Darrel's eyes found me over the top of his monitor again. "Not yet."

I didn't quite believe him and he didn't quite care. Later, I'd ask that question again. He sat back, put his hands behind his head.

"After I talked to her last week, I did some digging on Penelope Rideout," he said. "The sister—or now, possibly, the mother. She came up clean. Good family, public schools. She was appointed legal guardian of her sister after the death of their parents. A car accident. I got the ODOT report on that accident. Used to do those myself, accident fatality investigations. Nothing suspicious about it. Penelope managed to finish college. An aerospace technical writer. Job shops. Moved around a lot. Stayed single. But just exactly how Penelope managed to pass her daughter off as her sister for fourteen years isn't clear to me, Ford. Maybe you know something I don't."

I'd been thinking about that, too. The key was, Penelope hadn't done it alone.

"Her mom and dad engineered it," I said. "They were conservative southerners. Churchgoers. No abortions, especially not for their girl. Adoption? Well, why give away what you already love, sight unseen? Keep the child. Start the coverup early and move fast. Keep ahead of the gossip. Daley gets a normal-appearing girlhood. Penelope gets to help raise her daughter. It would account for all the family moves after Daley was born. The new neighbors didn't have time or reason to question things. Nothing to question, by the look of things. June Rideout was only thirty-five when Penelope had Daley. I saw a picture of her. June looked young for her age. Easily a mother of two. You wouldn't even stop to think about it."

Darrel leaned his elbows on his desk and worried a yellow pencil in his large black hands. Stared at me. "And what was Atlas doing all this time?"

"Building his ministry and tracking Penelope and his daughter," I said. "Demanding Penelope's silence."

"And she?"

"Trying to dodge him," I said.

"Penelope thinks he's after the girl now?"

I nodded.

"You believe he'd do that?" Walker asked.

"It's not something that people like us can understand."

"His own daughter?" asked Darrel, disgust in his voice and on his face.

I let the obvious answer go unspoken.

"What if she's lying about all of this?" asked Darrel. "According to your story, she's been lying successfully for fourteen years."

"I believe her."

Darrel set the pencil on his desktop. "Do you *want* to believe her?"

"Does it matter?"

"You bet it does, so don't fool yourself. I've met her. She's convincing. Beautiful, too."

"I believe her, Darrel."

A sigh and a dry smile from the detective. "My mom likes Reggie Atlas. Never misses Four Wheels for Jesus on her damned phone."

One of Darrel's Explorers came to the cubicle with two cups of coffee, set them on his desk, told Darrel that one of the lieutenants needed him when he was finished. Darrel thanked him for the coffee and said he was almost done.

I still hadn't gotten an answer to my biggest question, but before I could ask it again, Darrel surprised me.

"SNR Security is a secretive bunch," he said. "Privately owned. Won't talk to the press, as you've probably discovered. Won't talk to law enforcement without a warrant or a subpoena. But here's the kicker—they don't like black people or Muslims very much. I'm a Black Law Enforcement Union member, right? So-Cal chapter. Have been for years. We have a good relationship with the Southern Poverty Law Center. Long story short: There's a list of complaints against SNR longer than any other private security company in the whole damned country. Everything from verbal abuse to physical assault. SNR won't hire blacks or Muslims, and they won't work for black- or Muslim-owned companies. This, according to complaints filed with us and the SPLC. SPLC has yet to take legal action. They have to choose their battles. That's why the private databases have nothing on SNR."

I tried to make sense of discriminating against Muslims and people of color often enough to raise complaints. Maybe legal action. Bad publicity for a company trying to guard its privacy. No upside at all that I could see.

"So," Darrel said. "Let me know when you've got SNR all figured out. Right now, I have to run."

"Has anyone seen Daley since the 7-Eleven?" I asked again. "I figure you've been in touch with your counterparts in San Clemente."

Darrel weighing me, sharp eyes in a heavy face. A distant tug of brotherhood between us, but maybe not enough to count for much.

"A girl who looked like Daley Rideout was seen at the Blue Marlin in La Jolla, two nights ago. So says the manager. Daley was with three men and a woman. All older, relationships unknown. They ate dinner in one of those upstairs cabanas that have the privacy curtains you can pull."

"To hide the missing child you're socializing with," I said.

"The general manager is Yvette Gibson. Tell her Darrel says hello."

"I owe you, Darrel."

"Yeah, you do." He drummed his big fingers on the table. "Roland? I don't want to believe Penelope Rideout. It would confirm my worst opinions about the human race. But I do believe her. So this favor is just Darrel Walker betting his conscience. Keep me in the loop."

23

///////////////////////////

YVETTE GIBSON met me in the lounge of the not-yet-open Blue Marlin, a prosperous restaurant in a jewel-like town. She was one of the most striking women I'd seen, tall, elegant, and ebony-skinned. Hair up, a sleeveless silver dress, and sharp short boots. No smile. I told her hello from Darrel and still got no smile.

She walked me through the stainless-steel stools and bistro tables, past the huge aquarium that divided the dining room. Hundreds of fish, big and little, locked in that hypnotic round-and-round thing they do.

We climbed the stairs. Through the smoked-glass walls I saw the Pacific surging against the rocks below and sailboats clipping atop the spangled sea. One of my favorite writers is buried down there.

Upstairs, the restaurant offices and an outdoor patio with heaters, a long grill, a bar, and several cabanas. We stood amid the cabanas, white-and-green-striped, with heavy canvas draperies you could close for privacy.

"Mr. Ford, I am not in the habit of discussing my guests with investigators of any kind. All I can tell you is what I told Darrel. A girl had dinner here on the patio two nights ago. A party of five. She looked like a picture Darrel's deputy showed me on his phone. I'd never seen her before, here or anywhere else. They had dinner between seven and nine."

"What name was the reservation under?"

A heavy stare. Assessing the damage to my face. "Darrel said the girl is in trouble," said Yvette Gibson. "On the missing kids websites."

I nodded. "She's fourteen and bright. Challenging the status quo at home and school."

"This girl didn't look like an eighth grader," said Yvette. "Expensive clothes. Makeup and lipstick, but not heavy. Carried herself well and seemed comfortable with her people. But she was by far the youngest one of the group."

"Did you talk to any of them?"

"I did not."

"Did you overhear any conversation?"

"They drew the privacy curtain after cocktails were served."

"Did the girl drink?"

"A virgin Moscow Mule. I won't tolerate underage service here. I looked at the check after Darrel's man left."

"May I see it?"

"No. I can't do that kind of thing."

I nodded. "They picked her up at a friend's condo after lunch, Tuesday of last week. She hasn't been home since. 'They' being two young men of questionable moral character. Dangerous men."

The heavy stare again. "You're not playing very fair, Mr. Ford. But maybe that's your nature."

"She's up against something, and time is short."

She sighed, shaded her eyes from the midday sun. "They used a corporate credit card. Signed by the man who made the reservation. Adam Revell."

"He's one of the girl's acquaintances."

"Might he have been the gentleman who did that to your face?"

"Which cabana?"

I followed her over. It was one of eight, its privacy curtains tied back and the tables and chairs neat and clean for the day's first seating. We stood under the canopy and I pictured Daley and her SNR escorts.

"Middle chair, facing west," said Yvette. "The woman beside her, three men across."

In the shade of the canopy I called up the photo gallery on my phone, found the downloaded IvarDuggans pictures of Connor Donald, Eric Glassen, and Adam Revell. She identified Connor Donald and Revell as two of the three men in Daley's party.

I found the Four Wheels for Jesus Ministry website photo of Pastor Reggie Atlas. "I know he wasn't there that night, but . . ."

She took a long look, shaking her head. "He looks familiar, but I see hundreds of faces a week."

I explained Atlas, his Cathedral by the Sea in Encinitas, his popular streaming sermons, his thousands of online followers.

"I go to Jah Love in El Cajon," she said. "We're lucky to get fifty people on any Sunday."

On a long shot I found my downloads of the oddly old-fashioned family taking down the flag at Paradise Date Farm that evening.

Yvette Gibson swiped the screen with a slender finger, studied the image. Scrolled forward. Scrolled back.

"Yes. The couple," she said. "They were dressed much nicer, and not wearing guns. Visibly, at least. Who are these people?"

I explained SNR the best I could: a private security company with accounts all over the country and ties to the Paradise Date Farm in the Imperial Valley, and the Cathedral by the Sea. Where, I pointed out, Daley Rideout had apparently attended at least once. Yvette handed my phone back.

"Mr. Ford? I have a thirteen-year-old girl. She's looking for some kind of grown-up trouble, just like I was at her age. So much of it out there. This girl Daley. Maybe she's looking for that kind of trouble. I'll call you and Darrel if I see her again."

I followed her downstairs and into the lobby. A frogman was in the aquarium, changing out a filter. Some of the fish fled in schools, others nosed closer to him with what looked like simple curiosity.

"I want you to tell me how this turns out," said Yvette. "No matter how it breaks. You do that, Mr. Ford, I'll buy us a drink and get us a quiet place to talk."

I said I would.

Standing in the shade of the Blue Marlin awning, I wondered where our fun five had gone after leaving here. Was Daley free to go her own way? Or was she a willing captive?

I called Howard Wilkin, one of my acquaintances at the *San Diego Union-Tribune*. I'd helped him out with a story last year because I trusted him. A big story, biggest of the year for San Diego, if you measure in terms of life and death. We made thirty seconds of small talk. One of the things I like about reporters is they're always in a hurry. He thought about my request for a moment, then said he'd get back to me with Reggie Atlas's home address.

I called Darrel Walker, disappointedly unable to confirm that Atlas was at the Blue Marlin with Daley Rideout that night. He told me maybe we had the good pastor all wrong. Which meant that Penelope Rideout was an even better liar than I'd thought. Darrel told me to keep up the good work.

———

BACK HOME, BURT was glued to Clevenger's wasp-cam feed from Paradise Date Farm—nothing unusual going on there.

Then I called Penelope. No answer, so I left a message.

On my way to the truck, my phone rang. I figured Wilkin or Penelope, but I was wrong. Didn't recognize the caller number. Sometimes you catch a break.

"Ford Investigations."

"Mr. Ford? This is Alanis Tervalua. We talked last week at school about Daley?"

"What's up?"

"Daley still won't answer calls. She's on all the missing-children sites. We want to talk to you again."

24

I SIGNED IN at the security desk in the Monarch Academy office and talked briefly with Wayne Cates, who eyed my battle scars suspiciously but said nothing about them.

"Good news from the Rideout family?" he asked.

"We're working on it."

The girls and I sat at the same picnic table under the coral tree in the same September heat. I told them Daley had been seen at a restaurant in La Jolla two nights ago. They looked at each other when I said that. Then back to me, disbelief on their faces, as if the stakes had been raised when they weren't looking.

"Everything we told you last week was the truth," said Alanis.

"But we didn't tell you everything," said Carrie.

I waited, looking at them in turn. Alanis with a one-eyed stare from behind her shiny black hair. Carrie with her wide, green, seldom-blinking eyes.

"Okay," said Alanis. "Daley was kind of with Nick, like we told you. And Nick was . . . murdered the same day Daley left here. So we know it wasn't Nick that abducted her. But there was a secret guy that Daley had also been talking to. For maybe, like, a couple of months. While Nick and her were, like, together, sort of."

"No," said Carrie. "They'd been *talking* for three months when she first told us. But Daley had known him for years. Off and on. They were like ghosts flying through each other, she said." She shrugged. "That was how she described it—like ghosts flying through each other."

"But she swore us not to say anything about him," said Alanis. "Not to anybody. She wouldn't even tell us his name. Like we'd know him. Or like he was important."

"She wouldn't tell us how they met, either," said Carrie. "But it wasn't online, because her sister wouldn't let her use her phone for that. Right? So we don't know his name and we don't know how they met."

"What do you know about him?" I asked.

"That he's old enough to be her father," said Alanis.

"No, *grandfather!*" said Carrie.

"And she thinks there's something spiritual between her and him. Daley said that before she met him she felt like a puppet in the rain. That talking to him was like turning off the rain so she could turn into a girl instead of a puppet."

"She actually said turn into a *woman*," said Carrie.

Alanis swept aside her hair and cut her friend a look. Then back to me. "And know what else? Daley said this secret old man was the first person she'd ever met who didn't make Jesus Christ seem funny."

"Like a joke," said Carrie. "Who didn't make Jesus Christ seem like a joke."

"What*ever*. Why do you always miss my points?"

I said nothing for a moment. Watched Alanis Tervalua's cyclopic stare collide with Carrie Calhoun's wide green eyes.

"Sorry, Lana."

"Always have to win."

"I know. I just get excited."

"So there you go again."

"Sorry. I'll be quiet."

Thus, silence. Just the breeze in the coral tree leaves and the droning sound of a Cessna 182 lowering into Carlsbad Airport. I recognized the sound of that plane without even looking, the very plane in which Justine had met her terrifying, solitary, unnecessary end. This time I didn't look up. Sometimes the throaty growl of that Lycoming engine brings joyful memories, and sometimes brute loss.

"Where is she, Mr. Ford?" asked Alanis.

"Two nights ago she was with Adam Revell, and Connor, and some others."

"So she's okay, then?" asked Alanis. "Is she going to go home soon?"

"I don't think she's okay," I said. "We need to find her. Tell me about Adam and Connor."

"We're kind of friends," said Carrie. "I mean, we all knew each other from Alchemy 101. Like we told you last week."

"I was never kind of friends with those two," said Alanis.

"But we haven't been to Alchemy 101 much the last few weeks," said Carrie. "There's something kind of off about it. Daley thought so, too. But it's hard to say what."

"I can say what," said Alanis. "They hate on you with their eyes."

I stepped closer to what I thought was the deep end, touched my toe to the water. "Do you go to the Cathedral by the Sea?"

"Once," said Alanis. "Same creep-out I got from Adam and Connor."

"Twice," said Carrie. "Both times with Daley."

"Tell me about that."

"Cool building. And—you know how churches are, everyone

smiling and forgiving you ahead of time. For stuff you don't even know you did. That cathedral has all these activities for teens. They want you at Surf Day and Snow Weekend and Mountain Camp, on and on."

"But you've never done any of those?" I asked.

"Not my deal," said Carrie.

"You were there twice with Daley?"

"She's interested in activities because of her sister," said Carrie. "Who's even more stricter than my own mom. Taking away her Facebook and all that. I mean—you can't ever say I told you—but Penelope locks Daley in her room sometimes. After nailing the window shut. I've seen the nails. And I've seen Daley's foot marks on the door where she's kicked it."

"The more her sister wouldn't let her do things, the more she felt trapped," said Alanis. "So she'd hang out with Nick. And she'd sneak off to Alchemy 101 with Adam or Connor."

I pictured Daley in all her teenage frustration, paying her five bucks, getting her hand stamped, and losing herself in Alchemy 101. Music, dancing, and plenty of other girls and boys to hang with. And I imagined her at the Cathedral by the Sea, being wooed by the youth minister—or maybe by Atlas himself, her own very, very secret father—hoping that her meddlesome sister wasn't about to bust her.

"Did either of you ever meet the pastor, Reggie Atlas?"

"Once," said Alanis. "He shook my hand with both of his. But I saw something in his eyes I didn't trust."

"Daley introduced me to him," said Carrie. "He was nice and kind of reserved. Like older guys can be. I mean that as a compliment, you know?"

"So Daley knew him?" I asked.

Carrie pursed her lips, green eyes scanning my face. "Well, I guess at least sort of. She was the one who took me to the cathedral my first time. She'd been there before, but not often. We had to make up this double lie to her sister and my mom so Daley could get away that morning."

"What was Daley's opinion of the pastor?"

Alanis shrugged. "Never said anything to me."

Carrie was nodding along. "Me neither. You don't think he's got something to do with Daley, do you?"

"No, I don't."

In my profession, I tell lies to get to the truth. People expect it and I don't mind doing it. Except lying to the trusting. Trust is hard to betray. Ask anyone who's hidden a diagnosis from a child, or cheated on a spouse, or had a faithful pet put down.

Maybe someday I could do better. Tell them not a lie but the truth: *Hey—Daley is back now and she's fine and she can't wait to see you.*

"How can we help you?" asked Alanis.

"Please let us help," said Carrie.

I put one of my big mitts over one of each girl's hands, small and warm as sparrows. I looked intently at them with my older-guy eyes in my older guy's beat-up face. They looked back at me in their young, unique, and peculiar way, and they were afraid.

"Stay alert and together when you can," I said. "Keep your eyes and ears open. Stay away from Adam, Connor, Alchemy 101, and the Cathedral by the Sea. Call me quickly if you see either of those men, or if something seems wrong. If anything is out of place."

"It's worse than we thought it was," said Alanis.

"And we thought it was pretty bad," said Carrie.

I waited with them in the Monarch Academy parking lot until Alanis's father came to take them home.

Checked in with Burt again. Nothing unusual at Paradise Date Farm. Burt was worried that camera four had malfunctioned. "Hopefully it didn't just drop off the wall and land in the barnyard," he said.

Very hopefully, I said, and rang off.

I GOT SOME take-out from Thai Thai and took it to my office. Sat and ate while the air conditioner hummed, watching Main Street in the midday heat. Not much traffic. We don't have much hustle-bustle in Fallbrook, except when school days start and end. Instead, we have classic cars, avocado orchards, and citrus groves. We have a terrific Christmas parade. And a nice 4-H show every year, if you want a lamb, a goat, a calf, or a pig. We have a handsome new library, a high school whose mascot is still a warrior in a feathered headdress, four bars, five tattoo parlors, just a few downtown traffic signals, one tennis club, thirty-eight churches, and a Christian Science Reading Room.

I thought back to a week ago, last Wednesday, when Penelope Rideout had walked into this office and begun her improbable tale. Enlisted me for her dangerous mission and sent me into the beating of my life. Puzzled, deceived, and angered me. Flirted and feinted and danced away. Into a private place of mine that had long been closed for repair. Years since anyone had come near it. But there she was.

I heard footsteps on the stairway, coming up. A figure arrived outside my door. A white shirt and a white hat, both pebbled by the glass.

He paused for just a moment, then stepped in and closed the door. "Mr. Ford."

"Pastor Atlas."

"Your face looks better."

"You came all the way here to tell me that?"

"I need to talk to you about Penelope Rideout."

"That's funny. As of Sunday, you'd never heard of her."

"May I sit down?"

25

///////////////////////

A TLAS sat, crossed his legs, and set his hat over one knee. The hat was a white Parabuntal fedora, crisp and clean. He wore what looked like the same trim jeans, white shirt, and white athletic shoes he'd worn to preach on Sunday. Same shaggy blond hair, now dented and darkened above his ears by hat and heat. Same hopeful blue eyes.

He looked around the office, gazed out at Main Street, then turned his attention back to me.

"Penelope Rideout has been telling a story about herself and her sister, Daley, for almost fifteen years now. I was probably the first to hear it. In the story, Penelope, a trusting girl, falls for an itinerant evangelical preacher. Who befriends, drugs, and forces himself upon her, resulting in Daley. Is this approximately what she told you?"

"She said the preacher was you."

Atlas stared at me for a long moment. The sunlight through the blinds hit the side of his face and brought a pale blue glow to one eye.

"Only part of her story is true. I was, in fact, an evangelical minister, traveling mostly by bus in the South, when I met Penelope Rideout. That was 1999. She was eight years old. After that, she came to hear me preach once, sometimes twice a year, until 2004. Then she didn't come to any of my services again until late 2005. At which time she told me that she had had a daughter from our union nine months earlier. Allegedly this happened in my bus, involving the blood of Jesus laced with a date-rape drug, damning photographs, and a failed morning-after pill. I was thirty-five years old at that time. Married, a father of three. I had been preaching from my bus, and as a guest pastor, for seventeen very long years. And was on the verge of establishing my very own first church."

A dark mood seemed to have come over him. He lifted the hat off his knee and leaned forward, out of the light.

"Go on," I said.

"Mr. Ford, you couldn't stop me now if you wanted. Penelope began accusing and harassing me not long after Daley was born. I don't know if there's a complete answer as to why. I saw that she was mentally ill. I read in the psychiatric literature that sibling rivalry can compound psychosis in the young, leading to more serious de-rangement. Later I learned that an additional sudden psychological trauma—such as the death of a parent, or both—will often incite a psychotic break. But as a man of God, not of medicine, I looked for answers in her soul. I saw a very bright, excitable, deeply unhappy girl. Filled with love. But with a blind, almost monstrous focus on herself. Creating a new self at the expense of her genuine self. And, of course, I looked into my own soul. Was I responsible? Had I some-how created this break with reality, or encouraged it to happen?"

The pastor regarded me. Challenging or observing? Waiting or pre-paring? He would have been impossible to read across a poker table.

"Did you?" I asked.

"After we first met, I saw Penelope Rideout once or twice a year, when I delivered a sermon at her church. And I also talked, prayed, discussed scripture, and sang with her and the rest of the Sundayschoolers. I corresponded with many of the young people through brief notes, occasional postcards. I've always focused on the young. As the future of our planet, and the future of my ministry. When she first accused me of fathering Daley, I felt like I was being taken down by the devil's own hound. A huge black thing, dragging me by the throat across cold ground toward the pit. Did I encourage Penelope's break? No, Mr. Ford. I tormented myself for years with that question. And the answer is no. I do not see how that is possible."

"Nothing she could have misinterpreted?"

"She misinterpreted everything."

"No private tour of the Four Wheels for Jesus bus?"

Atlas sat back down, set the hat on his lap, and placed his hands over the ends of the chair arms.

"It's very strange to feel filthy in my innocence. In denying my guilt. When you mention my bus in such a context, the bile rises in my throat and my stomach knots. When I hear the words *Four Wheels for Jesus* in this light, I feel that Jesus is being whipped and spit upon because of me. In some very strange way, Penelope has won. Like a suicide bomber. So, Mr. Ford—there were no private tours of my bus. I'll tell you something that shouldn't surprise you. In those early years, my wife and young children often toured with me. Driving those buses across the country, camping and setting up those tents and preaching and touching the poor and the humble, were among the happiest and most rewarding years of my life. Sleeping bags and microwave food. Hot dogs and burgers and donuts. We were poor as dirt, but we were carrying the Word. We lived the Word. Penelope Rideout's lies—her vengeance—can't take those years away from me."

"Vengeance for what?" I asked.

"Refusing her attentions."

"Have you threatened her?"

"My dear Lord, with what?"

"Why don't you take a paternity test?"

"That was my wife's first reaction, too, Mr. Ford. I've been demanding one for fourteen years now. Very privately, as you must understand. Penelope won't allow it. She claims that it would shatter her sister. But she knows very well what it would prove. Or I should say, what it *wouldn't* prove."

"Why are you here?"

"I want you to find Daley. Bring me to her, or her to me—however you do this kind of thing. Then help me convince her to take a paternity test to prove medically that I'm not Daley's father. This all has to happen in absolute privacy. I have a ministry, a reputation, and a family to protect. Absolutely no publicity of any kind. I will not enter the social arena of hate. A sealed secret. Daley, Penelope, and me. You will be the impartial enforcer and referee. You can oversee the test. If you would like, I will hire a nurse or doctor who can be trusted. You will make sure the blood is drawn properly and the test is done perfectly and without incident. It would take less than five minutes."

I tried to think my way through his delicate proposition. It was perilous but possible. I thought it strange that he showed so little concern for a missing fourteen-year-old girl, beyond her ability to help him prove his case. "And?"

"And after that, maybe the three of us—Daley, you, and I—can convince Penelope to get the help she desperately needs. She has driven her own sister into the night. Look at the violence that has followed her. Think of what can happen to an undefended girl in an evil time. The police can't find her. The agencies can't find her. Even you are having your own troubles in that regard. Mr. Ford, you can see that Daley Rideout needs a capable guardian, and Penelope is not that."

In Pastor Reggie Atlas, I was up against a real pro when it came to selling ideas you couldn't prove. I considered his youthful-for-his-years face, his boyish hair, his eager blue eyes. Faithful eyes. Hopeful.

"I've been hired by Penelope to find Daley," I said. "I can't take money from two people for the same job."

"Then terminate her contract and name your price," said Atlas. "With a bigger budget you can hire some skilled confederates and find Daley faster. That would be a good thing for everyone. Daley would be protected, I would finally be exonerated, and Penelope could save her hard-earned dollars."

"You are a convincing man, Pastor Atlas."

"I'm a tired man, too, Mr. Ford."

He stood somewhat stiffly, tapping his hat on his leg as he walked to the window. I wondered how many hours he'd spent performing. I wondered if preachers, like actors and undercover agents, occasionally got lost in their roles. He looked out at Fallbrook.

"Reminds me of small towns all over America," he said. "They all look different, but there's a sameness to them. The people tend to be good people. Things are slower. Down there I see a barbershop with an old-fashioned barber's pole outside. I see a candy store. Down the street, a hardware store. Joe's Hardware. What a great name for a hardware store. I like an America this size."

"There was a sex-and-torture dungeon in a house just a few blocks from here," I said. "Chains and mattresses. Wall fasteners and hand tools. A couple set it up. The cops shut it down when a young woman died there."

He turned. "Why do you bring that up? What is the point you're trying to make?"

"That faces can hide secrets. For a while."

"But why focus on the evil?"

"I like dogs and children," I said.

"Meaning what?"

"I appreciate innocence, too."

Pastor Atlas gave me a look that said I should be dunked as a suspected witch. Or maybe just locked in stocks right down there on Main Street, where the dogs and children I like so much could torment me.

"I'm tired of trying to hold up the whole of grim humanity," he said.

"Then drop us. We might not need you."

"Jesus hears every word you say."

"Oh, he's heard worse from me."

Atlas sighed, looked out the window again.

"Mr. Ford, I'm tired of defending myself, my family, and my ministry from a troubled woman and her dangerous delusions. I need your help to put this all to an end."

"Why start now?"

He put on his hat and gave the brim a rural tilt, then sat back down and pulled his chair closer.

"Start? I've tried before. This isn't the first time Daley has run away. She ran away from home in Denver, Salt Lake City, and Reno, too. And in Eugene, Prescott, and other cities and towns. Now Oceanside. Every time she escapes, Penelope comes after me again. I'm not hard to find. She hires a PI or a lawyer or worse. Suggests without evidence that I have kidnapped her sister. Or simply had her abducted. Or . . . sweet Lord, there's no end to Satan's imagination. To tales of me and my bus and the blood of Jesus mixed with drugs. As you know, firsthand. Did your version include the baptism from the silver bowl, or the robes sprinkled in holy water? One day, some well-meaning person will believe her, and my reputation will be functionally ruined. Thus I come to you."

"When was the last time you saw Daley?"

"Late August. She brought a friend to the cathedral."

"Just a few days ago, you didn't remember seeing her."

A brisk nod. "The mind investigates while the body sleeps."

I was familiar with that phenomenon. "And before that?"

"Four years ago. When she was ten. It was the first time I'd actually laid eyes on her, outside of pictures sent to me by her sister. This was before I opened the cathedral. Penelope brought her to my event at a convocation in Las Vegas. They sat in the very back. I was terrified. It was the most difficult sermon I've ever given. I had no idea why Penelope was there. No idea what she might do."

"What *did* she do?"

"Nothing, praise the Lord. They left before the service was over. I had trouble sleeping for weeks. So worried what Penelope might be planning. Inconsolable, even to my wife."

"Did you communicate with Daley after that?"

Atlas held my stare for a long beat. Then smiled. "Yes. I answered an email. It arrived on my webpage not long after the Las Vegas show. She wanted to know if Jesus could love a girl who fell asleep almost every night before finishing the Lord's Prayer."

"What did you tell her?"

"Yes, I told her. Of course Jesus loves you. I think I suggested she say her prayer earlier. Such as after dinner, or maybe even first thing in the morning."

"Did you ever tell her that you two were like ghosts flying through each other?"

Atlas frowned amiably, shaking his head with some good humor. "I'm sure I did not."

"Did she write again?"

"Every few months."

"And you wrote back?"

"Wouldn't you?"

I shrugged.

"Mr. Ford, will you find Daley and arrange the test? You are my best hope."

I thought about my decision, but not for long. "I'll let you know when I locate Daley Rideout. Until then, you can keep your money and I'll stay in the service of Penelope under the conditions set forth."

He stood. "Quixote had a wooden lance. All you have is a wooden head."

"It's good hard wood."

"It looks a little beat-up right now. Car wreck?"

I could have said something about Reggie's connection to SNR Security, but I didn't. No good reason to reveal what I knew. No reason to train a searchlight on myself.

"Call me immediately when you find Daley," said Atlas. "Better yet, bring her straight to me. That paternity test is the right thing to do, and you know it is. No matter who's signing your checks."

At the door, he turned. "Has Penelope mentioned her husband, Richard?"

"Yes, she has."

"She made him up. He never existed."

"I came to the same conclusion."

A beat as he studied me. Spun his hat in his hands. Then a small smile. "Have you been spending some extra time with Penelope?"

"Only what's required, Pastor. Why do you ask?"

"I'm concerned for your soul."

"Save it for the choir."

"I'm willing to pray with you right now. I could use some strength. So could you."

"Not necessary, thanks."

"It is so much more than necessary. But I respect your decision."

That smile again, boyish and conspiratorial. "Penelope is beautiful, isn't she? So bright and open. So sexual. Always has been. And, boy, she knows it. She offered all that charm of hers to me, more than once. Threw it right at me. She was fourteen and I was thirty-five. I won't deny that I was tempted. I prayed like a condemned man. Prayed, and prayed again. Jesus stepped forth and offered his hand to me. Now you know how I answered Penelope, and you see where it got me. Paul said it best. He said, 'Put to death therefore what is earthly in you: immorality, impurity, passion, evil desire, and covetousness . . . On account of these the wrath of God is coming.'"

"I hope He takes His time."

"I'll say a prayer for you."

I watched him leave and then walk up Main Street. Tipped his hat to a mom walking a baby in a stroller. Got into a sleek Mercedes Sprinter painted in high-gloss copper and black, with "Four Wheels for Jesus" airbrushed in racing-yellow script along its flank.

I sat back down just in time to watch my sleeping computer monitor wake up.

Burt Short's bold italic Times New Roman 14 font hit the screen in a drop-down:

LIVE AND URGENT FROM PARADISE FARMS
BURT

26

///////////////////////////

Dust rising in bright light and the strangeness of things happening without sound.

Clevenger's motion-activated wasp-cam streamed beautiful video, startlingly clear. I recognized the bunkhouse with the modified freezers in the living room and the gloves and white hazmat suits hanging on the walls.

The front door had been propped open. Connor Donald and Eric Glassen crossed the porch and disappeared inside. A forklift pulled up to the front porch, Adam Revell in the cage, four wooden crates stacked two-on-two waiting on the forks. Flat-Top Woman with the gun on her hip stood talking to him, her mouth working silently.

I put Burt on speaker as I watched Clevenger's wasp-cam feed.

"None of the usual activity earlier," said Burt. "No SNR vehicles coming and going. No Paradise shipping trucks in and out. No kids to the barn with their laptops and backpacks. They cleared the decks for this, whatever it is."

Back to my desktop monitor: Connor Donald and Eric Glassen coming from the cottage, wearing long black rubber gloves and hazmat masks. Flat-Top Woman on her way inside. Adam Revell hopped down from the forklift and followed.

"I didn't know you need heavy gloves and hazmat masks to handle dates," said Burt.

Flat-Top Woman and Revell came out a moment later, suited up like the others.

Wasp-cam four gave us a good look at the wooden crates, each bound with three metal bands. No brands, labels, writing, or numbers on them. Pine? They looked to be nearly five feet long, a foot wide, and a foot deep.

Revell and the woman took one end of a crate, squatting and straining mightily, horsing it away from the others. Connor and Eric took the other end, and the four of them—two on each side, short-stepping, backs straight—carried the crate toward the cottage.

"Clearly not TV dinners," said Burt. "What can it be now?"

The heaviest material per volume I'd ever handled was ammunition in Fallujah. A 420-round steel can of .223-caliber M4 ammo in each hand put you in a hurry to get where you were going. Hoping you got there before the steel handles bit you. But one of these wooden crates at Paradise wouldn't hold more than ten of those cans. Four adults? It looked like they were hauling something a lot heavier than that.

"Metals?" said Burt. "But why freeze them?"

"Gas under pressure," I said. "To keep it contained."

"Unstable chemicals. Isotopes."

"Of course," I said. "Things that date farmers and security guards depend on in their everyday lives."

They got up the low porch steps and crept inside on their eight straining legs, like a giant spider.

A minute later they came out, rested in the porch shade, then went to the forklift for round two. Revell lifted his mask and wiped his forehead on his sleeve before taking his corner of the crate.

Flat-Top Woman was breathing hard. Donald and Glassen had sweated through their black golf shirts.

A few minutes after the last delivery, the four were back on the porch, breathing heavily and conversing, their hazmat masks and gloves left inside. Revell pulled the cottage door shut and locked it.

"Heavy crates in high-performance freezers," said Burt. "Guarded by a publicity-shy security company that has a regional office in San Diego, accounts across America, and does not hire blacks or Muslims. Speculate, Champ."

"Maybe later. I have a story to tell you about Penelope Rideout, Daley, and Reggie Atlas. Conflicting versions of a possibly very ugly truth."

THAT NIGHT I sat in my truck on a turnout of a narrow road, with a view of Pastor Reggie Atlas's home in Rancho Santa Fe. A rural road, no lights, the moon a waning quarter whisked by clouds.

On a gentle hilltop sat the house, well lit. Large and Italianate, stone walls and a bell tower and cypress trees lining a winding drive. Why do so many Californians want to live in homes that look Italian? Are there California-style homes all around Rome and Milan? I saw that a pasture sloped to the road. White estate fencing, screened, and a white gate with a speaker/keypad column, car-window high.

Adjacent to the house was a big three-car garage, door open but unlit, three cars inside with room to spare.

I listened to the radio on low, studied the grounds with my night-vision glasses, elbows steady on the window frame.

A sudden buzz and rattle in my cup holder. I put Penelope Rideout on the speaker, returned my phone to its place, and turned off the radio.

"I'm sorry," she said. "That was an awful lot to lay on you. I was covering new territory, Roland. It was harder than I thought. I'll hang up right now if you want."

I spoke softly. "Atlas said it never happened and you won't allow a test to prove it didn't."

A few seconds went by and I thought Penelope really was about to hang up.

"I know what happened, Roland. It is written in me. But I don't want *her* to know that truth. I understand I'm not permitted to even think such a thing about lofty truth. It goes against what we're taught from the very beginning. And what it said on the Grecian urn. And all that about setting us free. But the story that Mom and Dad and I invented for her is more likely. Things could easily have happened just that way. And it's better. It frees her from knowing that she's the result of wickedness done to me. It gives her solid ground to stand on, and a simple history to be a part of. Something to build a life on, other than self-loathing and anger."

"He said you went after him years ago, and he refused you."

A catch of breath. Then the matter-of-fact cold in her voice. "I could kill him for saying that."

Then came Penelope's self-description riding the breeze through my open windows: ninety percent lover and ten percent killer.

"Roland, he's trying to justify his own monstrous behavior. Did he ask you to find Daley and bring her to him?"

I saw Atlas come from the house. He went a few yards down the walkway, stepped under the leaves of a magnolia tree. He wore his regulation jeans and white shirt, but tonight he was barefoot.

"Roland?"

"Yes, he asked me to bring her to him."

Atlas lit a cigarette. The smoke rose and spread.

"And what did you say back?"

"I'll bring her to you, as contracted."

"You don't believe Reggie Atlas, do you?"

"I believe that Daley is in danger."

The sound of Penelope breathing. "You do believe him. You believe I brought this all upon myself and Daley. You big dumb man. Isn't my word good enough?"

"You've given me a lot of words, Penelope. Some are more truthful than others."

"Yes, I have," she said. "What a terrible mistake I've made. But you're still under contract with me. Daley is mine and you will deliver her to me, as written."

And hung up.

The phone screen went to black. Atlas smoked his cigarette under the magnolia. He pulled a phone from his pants pocket and I could see the faint light on his downturned face. He worked it with one hand, read the screen, then tapped a command.

Penelope again:

"Roland Ford, you're not a big dumb man at all. You're a huge, stupid ox."

I waited for her to end the call. Instead I heard her breathing again, this time faster and louder.

"For an ox," I said, "I'm of average intelligence."

"I'm going to get the better of you someday."

She hung up again.

As I raised my eyes from the phone to the house, I saw that a vehicle had stopped at Pastor Reggie Atlas's pearly white gate. It was a silver late-model Cadillac CTS, the ones with the stealth body panels and fighter-jet front end. Wrote the plate number in my notebook. Rolled down the driver-side window.

Atlas ground his cigarette butt into the grass at his feet, tapped something into his phone, and the gate lurched to life. The car started up the drive, curbside motion lights coming on to show the way. Atlas stayed beneath the tree until the Cadillac came to a stop a few yards short of the garage.

In my night-vision binoculars I watched the driver's door swing open and a tall, slender old man unfold from the front seat. He looked to be eighty, with brisk white hair brushed back over a creased, hawklike face. Sharp nose, thin lips, bushy eyebrows. A brown suit, cut and cuffed in an older style. Expensive, by the look of it. White shirt, red tie. He was familiar, in a distant, secondhand way.

Penelope, back for thirds: "I'm sorry for what I said. Please find my daughter."

And just as suddenly, gone.

Old Hawk lifted the trunk lid and left it open, then walked to the magnolia tree. He conversed with Atlas in a terse, all-business kind of way. I wasn't close enough to hear their words or even the sound of their words. Guessing from Atlas's gestures—his open hands and interrogative expressions—he was asking for something. Old Hawk seemed to listen patiently, but nothing in his posture or movements gave me any indication of positive or negative. To Old Hawk, Reggie Atlas could have been a branch to perch on or a mouse to eat.

Old Hawk tapped a finger against Reggie's chest. Words from a dry smile. Atlas poked the older man back and said something in return.

Old Hawk marched long-legged into the garage, turning on the lights, and opened the trunk of a gleaming black Mercedes AMG sedan. Lifted out a metal Halliburton case and walked to his car. Set the Halliburton in the trunk and closed the lid with a touch of a button.

Reggie stepped from under the tree and joined the old man by his car. The two men talked for less than a minute, then Old Hawk climbed into his Cadillac. The silver sedan made a wide turn and headed down the drive.

I followed him through the winding roads of Rancho Santa Fe to Del Dios Highway, and all the way to Escondido. Plenty of traffic for cover. Out on the east side of town the homes got older and smaller, and the business signs turned to Spanish and the barrio said *hola*. The silver CTS proceeded comfortably down the avenue, went right on Holiday Lane, then made a sharp left and stopped at a gate.

End of my welcome. I drove past, made a U-turn, and came back in time to see the CTS heading up the drive. It was narrow and curvy but paved. No buildings or dwellings, only a poorly kept grove of orange trees. The Cadillac's headlights raked through trees with thin branches, sparse leaves, and small stranded fruit. More oranges in the dirt than on the trees. On top of the hill stood what looked to be a cluster of buildings surrounded by trees that nearly hid them from sight. A few lights through the foliage. When the Cadillac was about halfway to the top, security lights came on along the road, leading the way through the dark to the buildings within the trees.

27

////////////////////////////

FBI Special Agent Mike Lark was not quite a friend but much more than an acquaintance. We had had the same boss, though at different times in our careers. Her name was Joan Taucher. Joan was a tough and complex woman, and her death last year—shot by a terrorist on my property—rocked Mike's world and mine considerably. I killed that terrorist, a few seconds too late to save Joan's life. A soul-bruising series of events. I will take them to my grave.

Mike Lark had been not only Joan Taucher's FBI understudy but her lover, too. I hadn't seen him since her funeral, late last December. Now he looked more than nine months older. Mid-twenties. Same short blond hair, but leaner in the face and harder in his brown, Taucher-like eyes.

We met in the pay lot at Torrey Pines State Beach, shook hands. I told him I'd explain my most recent facial improvements later. We headed north on the dry, low-tide sand. Plenty of surfers on the small waves. Walkers and runners and kids with beach toys. On this mid-September day I could feel the change of seasons coming on. Just a liner of cool in the air that hadn't been there a week ago.

The license plate number I'd taken down from Old Hawk's CTS

had led me to Lark, whose FBI database had swiftly revealed the registered owner of the car, and his history.

"Alfred Battle is the godfather of San Diego's once formidable white supremacists," said Lark. "Two years ago returned from Idaho. Even Hayden Lake was glad to be rid of him. He told the media here he was 'returning to the land of the mud people' to live permanently. 'Mud people' being blacks and Hispanics. He bought his old spread up in Escondido, where he held the Aryan rallies and conferences in the seventies and eighties. Hoping to recapture his glory days, like everyone else. He has informal rallies on Sunday mornings. Bills them as the 'White Power Hour.' Guest speakers, glossy propaganda, fruit punch and sandwiches. Late in the morning, though, so he's not competing with church. I stopped by with a couple of other agents one Sunday and they were happy to escort us out. We've got nothing actionable on him. We'd love to shut him down, but it's a free country. He's got the city and fire permits, the porta-potties, plenty of parking. It's a big compound. Views to the ocean, much too nice a place for him. Battle's a hateful sonofabitch and it shows. A nasty dude in his day. Yet he's never spent a night behind bars. What else do you want to know about him?"

"I'd like to know why he picked up a Halliburton case from Pastor Reggie Atlas last night," I said. "For starters."

A sharp-eyed question from Lark. "You're sure it was Reggie Atlas?"

"I'm sure."

"It tracks. If Battle worked for a college, you'd say he's in development. He raises money. He lectures, gives these long, booming speeches. He writes propaganda blogs on Reddit and 4chan and any other Internet platform that will have him. Agitates. Riles people up. Big in Europe. He's a modest trust-funder himself. His wife has the deep pockets, though—Marie. An heir to the Knippermeir family fortune—Knippermeir's Breakfast Meats. She's the nominal owner of most of Alfred Battle's portfolio. Law-abiding, a generous donor, protected by money. Reclusive. There have been questions about her mental health, over the years."

I thought that over for a moment. "You think we have a briefcase full of cash meant for the Cathedral by the Sea, but actually going to Alfred Battle's haters?"

"They'll take money anyplace they can get it," said Lark. "They prefer Bitcoin, but church dollars spend well, too. Plus, the Cathedral by the Sea gets the big tax breaks, which drives our lawyers bats."

"Is Battle on your watch list?"

Lark stopped, picked up a flat black oval rock, and skipped it over the incoming soup. I wanted to do that, too, but my rib shrieked at the thought. Mike gave me a long look.

"Probably," he said. "There's social buzz about the Cathedral by the Sea discriminating against blacks and browns. That catches our federal attention. Hate crimes give us certain, well, latitudes. Nothing actionable yet, like I said."

"Atlas insulted Mexico in his Sunday sermon."

"Why are *you* looking at him, Roland?"

I told him about runaway Daley Rideout, the murder of Nick Moreno, Daley's link to Adam Revell of SNR Security, and my discussion with said security guards when I surprised them at Paradise Date Farm. Also about Penelope Rideout's and Reggie Atlas's sharply divergent stories regarding Daley's nativity, and her most recent sighting at the Blue Marlin restaurant in La Jolla. Told him that I'd staked out Atlas's house and Alfred Battle had come up in the net.

Mike mostly frowned at the sand as he walked and listened, but again, he studied me intently when I spoke of Reggie Atlas.

"So you really don't know if the girl is being held against her will or not," said Lark.

"She wasn't at first, but now I'm not so sure," I said. "She left for school that morning, came home at lunch with Moreno, changed clothes, packed, and went to Moreno's condo. Followed by Connor Donald and Eric Glassen of SNR. She knew them. She and some of her girlfriends had accepted rides from them after school to an Oceanside teen club. More than once. She left the condo with them, after they'd killed Moreno. Left willingly, too—although she couldn't have known what they'd done to him at that point. Later seen on the beach at San Onofre, possibly partying with friends. Who either scared her or pissed her off or both—no details. Maybe they said something about Nick. They took her phone. I think they were SNR handlers, based on a description from a surfer who talked to her— possibly Connor and Glassen, possibly not. She surfaced late that night in San Clemente, apparently trying to ditch them. She called her sister from a 7-Eleven in San Clemente to come get her. Or her mother. To be determined. Then left, possibly with the same SNR handlers she had gotten away from. Vanishes completely for days. Last seen at dinner with SNR people from Paradise Date Farm, at an expensive restaurant in La Jolla. She flips and flops, Mike. I don't get her."

"Drugs, fear, and hunger," said Lark. "Throw in some expensive clothes and fancy restaurants and it will take the fight right out of her. Pimps 'R Us."

"I don't think these guys are sex traders," I said. "They're up to something else, but I don't know what."

We picked our way around a spit of boulders buffed to ovals by the centuries. A huge raven overtook us from behind, shadow first.

"Who do you believe?" Lark asked. "Penelope or Atlas?"

"Neither all the way," I said.

"It's a sad story, if what she says is true."

"Oh, I think she's telling mostly truth."

He squinted to acknowledge the way I'd contradicted myself. "Then you'll return Daley to her?"

"I believe so."

"But she won't allow a paternity test," said Lark. "Which means you still won't know who the mother or father are. That doesn't sound like you, Roland, not getting to the truth. Good former lawman that you are."

I knew he was right. And once again—for probably the thousandth time since that night in Penelope's house, when she'd told me the story of the lovestruck girl and the lust-bitten preacher—I tried to weigh her story against Atlas's.

"I'll make sure to get a test," I said.

"You can't," said Lark. "Only the court can order it."

"I'll find a way."

Mike raised a doubtful eyebrow. "Unbelievable what some people will do. If Atlas did what she says, I mean."

I had nothing to add.

"I wish Joan was here," said Lark. "She'd have some choice words on Atlas. On human nature in general. Get into a lather over it. Then she'd say something critical of herself and make me laugh."

I laughed softly, first time in a long time, knowing exactly what he meant. We continued north in a long silence, lost in separate remembrances. Taucher was a fierce cop. Devoted, indefatigable, principled, and resourceful. Haunted by an opportunity that her San Diego FBI had missed in the days before 9/11. That ghost seemed to swirl around her, and she made little effort to deny it.

She told me once that she thought about the FBI's having an informant living with two of the hijackers—but, thanks to CIA silence about these men, no knowledge that they had been linked to al-Qaeda—"every damned day of my life." It showed on her face and in the way she spoke and in the ceaseless energy she brought to her work. She had loved her job and her city—she'd grown up here in San Diego—and the attacks on our republic had left Joan Taucher feeling like a mother whose children had been betrayed. She was ferocious and, somehow, I have come to believe, cursed. She left her dying blood on me. A lot of it. All I could do was try to talk her through the divide. But I had tried that in Fallujah and had already lost my faith in words.

Mike skipped another rock. Went three hops into the mouth of an oncoming wave. "This is what we do . . ."

". . . and this is where we do it," I said.

One of Joan's favorite lines.

She made it sound comprehensive and sufficient. A simple reason for being. I'm not sure how it sounded from Mike and me. My mind is a looser thing. Private First Class Avalos died in a Fallujah doorway holding a small plastic cross in one hand. Titus Miller died pointing his wallet at me. My wife, Justine, told me once that she was not afraid of dying, but she was afraid of being forgotten. And I will not forget her. Nor the others. Taucher among them. This is what I do, in addition. Not forget. My private promise. Nonverifiably of use to anyone. Maybe Joan was expecting us to fill in the details. According to our own needs. How could she have not? If I'm not making sense, it's because I sometimes can't.

"SNR has four freezers full of wooden crates at Paradise Date Farm," I said. "People coming and going all the time who have nothing to do with growing dates. They're running a children's school of some kind. Silver SNR vehicles everywhere. They beat me senseless just for being there and asking about the girl."

"Slow down, Roland," said Mike. "Start at the beginning. Crates in freezers? Crates of what?"

By the time we got back to my truck I'd told Lark almost everything I knew about Paradise Date Farm. I could see the concentration on his face as he tried to collate the strange intelligence.

"Can you feed that video live to me?" he asked.

"Can you give me what you have on Atlas?"

"FBI property is . . ."

"And call me immediately if Daley Rideout pops onto your radar?"

Mike frowned, following a squad of pelicans as they V-ed through the sky. "Joan said you always tried to get more than you gave."

"I'm a sole proprietor."

Lark considered me for a beat, then nodded. "Deal."

"Thank you. I miss her."

Lark inhaled deeply, looked toward the diminishing pelicans, then to me. Again, that moment we'd shared once before, at Joan Taucher's funeral. He didn't have to say the words for me to hear them: *You were with her and I wasn't and she didn't make it but you did.*

"I do, too, Roland," he said. "I hope you find the girl. And I hope you get some payback from those guys who dinged you up like this."

Nodded and smiled my anguishing little stitch-lipped smile. "Me too," I said.

I sat in my truck and checked messages. Watched Lark pick his way out of the crowded parking lot in his assigned Bureau take-home, an unmarked white Chrysler with a not-quite-hidden light package built into the roof. Younger agents get the hand-me-downs. He stopped for a family of four scuttling from the lot toward the sand, bristling with beach chairs, towels, and toys.

Then a buzz of phone, and Penelope Rideout's name on the screen.

"I found something of Daley's that might help us," she said. "When can you be here?"

28

///////////////////////////////

She opened the door before I could knock, let me in with an appraiser's squint and an air of conspiracy.

Her living room floor was strewn with school papers and art projects, girls' clothes and toys and precarious stacks of CDs. Plastic horses. A plastic castle. The ceiling fan jostled papers and doll hair.

Two open toy chests—a pink *Cinderella* and a yellow *Beauty and the Beast*—sat on the coffee table in front of the plaid couch, some of their treasures relocated to the floor.

The boom box was now on the half-wall that separated the small living room from the kitchen. Penelope nodded me to the couch, sat in one of the director's chairs, and aimed a remote at the player.

I sat as a young girl's whisper came from the speakers:

This is a very dangerous thing to do. Penny is the world's greatest sister, but she wants to know everything I do and say and even think. I need something that is just mine. She would totally destroy this CD if she found it. Penny's always afraid. Of, like, everything, but especially men. I wish I had a mom and a dad. Alive, I mean. But I have only my sister. She loves me, but she smothercates me. I think she misses Mom and Dad more than I do because she was older. I was four. I remember the police and the woman coming to our door. It was raining.

Penny totally shut down my Twitter and Facebook. Which means I have to, like, make new accounts, but then she'll sneak in and shut me down. Again. I tried to get my own credit card a bunch of times, but I always make a mistake and get busted. I should not have said I was a neurosurgeon, probably.

This CD is like an old-fashioned diary, but I talk it instead of write it. My teachers all say I'm a very good writer for my age, but talking is faster and I can hide a CD easier than a notebook. I can even make a copy in case Penny finds the original. Hide the copy in the attic where Penny hates to go. Because of mice.

I'm outta here.

After a few seconds' pause, the recording clicked off.

Then on again. A shuffle of what sounded like papers, a quick patch of static, then Daley Rideout's clear, articulate voice again:

I'm back!

So, the reason I'm making this CD is because I don't have anyone to talk to about certain. Very. Personal. Subjects.

I mean, Bellamy and I are best friends forever, but I've moved a lot so I know that forever isn't long since Penny keeps blocking my social media. And there are some things I don't want Bellamy to know. We are, like, the two different sides of one coin. She can be very judgmental, especially about boys.

For example? James, who I want to talk to but he's always got other girls with him. He's older. I don't know why I like some boys, but I do. Not all. But the ones I like, they make me feel happy when they're around. Powerful, too. One thing that I know about boys? They're faster and stronger than girls, but inside they're weak. So, when I look at James, I like him even more. Today? I pulled a small leaf out of his hair. His hair is brown, and wavy. I didn't actually touch him—I did not—only his hair. But it made me feel good and, like, fizzy, and this is an example of why I can't tell Bellamy, who is against boys. Or my sister, who is afraid of everything. So I will tell my secrets only to you, my little CD. My compact diary.

I'm outta here.

Penelope stopped the player with the remote and looked at me. Hair back in a clip, a black tank top and capris, bare feet.

"First of all, Roland," she said. "You can believe what you want about me. But the facts will always be facts and your beliefs don't change them. I'm a fact."

"Thank you."

"You're a hard and immovable man."

"But upgraded from ox."

"That didn't really bother you. Did it?"

"It was funny."

"You win, Roland. I'm done apologizing."

I looked at her with all the impartiality I could muster. I earnestly tried to view her as she was. Only as she was. A subject to be identified. All fact; no fiction. Get to the truth of her.

"Where did you find this CD?" I asked.

"I was going through her room, looking for some clue, *anything* that might lead me to her. I flipped through her music, thought I'd like to hear the Jewel album I gave her. No Jewel in that jewel case, though—just sixty minutes of Daley. I opened every last case and found another disk she'd made. Recent. From last year, when she was thirteen."

"Have you contacted Bellamy?" I asked.

"Yes. She hasn't communicated with Daley since the move. Since just after that recording was made."

"Why did you leave Phoenix?"

"Pastor Atlas had found us again," said Penelope. "He drove past our house. I saw him five times. Once in his bus, the fancy big one. The Silver Eagle. The other times in one of his cars. He loves cars."

I thought again of Penelope's story about Reggie Atlas. Its plausible and implausible horrors. I thought again of the preacher's story about Penelope Rideout. And I recalled the cliché about clashing stories: her version, his version, and the truth.

And of course I thought of Daley's secret sharer, courtesy of Carrie Calhoun and Alanis Tervalua.

A man old enough to be Daley's grandfather, to whom she felt a spiritual connection. Who had told her that they were like ghosts flying through each other.

Whom Daley had known for years, "off and on."

And with whom Daley had started to talk in earnest a few months ago.

I thought of Daley feeling like a puppet in the rain.

And how talking to her secret man was like turning off the rain so she could turn into a woman.

I remembered what Penelope had said about Atlas, her alleged tormentor: "He's more evil than you understand."

"Here she is again," said Penelope. "Age twelve."

She pointed the remote control at the boom box. Stood and began circling her way around the toys and CDs and clutter as Daley's voice took over.

I'm back!

I've got a few minutes before Penny comes home from work. I think it's smart to hide my CD in the Jewel CD case, because that means Pen has to look through every single case if she suspects something. Why should she suspect me of this? Because she suspects me of pretty much everything! But what if she finds the actual Jewel CD between my bed and the springs? She'll go see what's in the Jewel CD case, and I'll be cooked! So I'll just take the Jewel disc to school and throw it away. Tomorrow. Not a problem.

Penny says she got a better job in California. I looked up Oceanside and it looks like a really great place. It's on the water, duh, and it's got a surfing museum, a super-cool library, and it's, like, always in the seventies. Degrees, that is. Pen says her technical editing job there will pay two dollars an hour more than here in Phoenix. And there'll be the beach and good schools.

When I'm doing my homework at the dinner table, Penny pretends she's reading on the couch and she looks out at the street and parking lot every few seconds. This is totally not unusual. This is what she always does, every place we've lived. But we're in a condo complex now, so there's cars coming and going a lot, so Pen looks up from her book all the time. Here I am trying to figure out a math problem or read something but I have to look up at her looking out at the car. I don't know what she's expecting to see. Why look at every passing car? All I know is that she's afraid. And I get afraid, too. And, like, totally distracted. Not that I care about my grades. So I go in my room. But I know she's there, looking out that window.

So it's goodbye to Phoenix and Bellamy. Goodbye to Mrs. Herron, who for a teacher is pretty cool. Goodbye to the Yogurt Yurt and the extra sprinkles.

I saw Pastor Atlas yesterday. He's in Phoenix to preach at a convention. He always lets me know his schedule when he's going to be nearby. He sends a postcard with his picture and the info on it. Drives Penny insane that Reggie always has our address. With her taking away my Facebook, it's harder for him to communicate, so sometimes he just calls. Of course I can't tell Pen, and the pastor and I talk even though I'm like totally banned from talking to him because there's an illness in him, she says, but when I ask her what illness is that—like a heart or gallbladder problem—she just says he has cancer of the soul.

Which is strange because, like, everybody loves Pastor Reggie. And he's got his podcasts and his streaming Four Wheels for Jesus sermons that Penny won't let me watch or listen to. But I do. There are ways. Bellamy loves him. Her mom does, too. And when Pastor Atlas is preaching near home, I always seem to run into him somewhere. Really funny how that happens. Small world! He's usually with his wife and kids. He smiles and stops and we talk. He's always got fans around him, but when he talks to me I can feel all of his attention totally one hundred percent on me. One time when we were alone for a minute at the mall he said that we were like ghosts flying through each other, which I thought was so beautiful. And when he said we could fly together sometime, side by side in Jesus, I said okay, Pastor Reggie, get me a ticket! And he said he had a ticket for me and I just had to pick it up. Whatever he meant by that. He does have a way of making you feel good inside. And that you're close to Jesus.

Gotta go.

"That's how he got to me when I was young," said Penelope, pausing the CD, a faraway look on her face. "Back when I was eleven, he was still coming through Mobile twice a year. He didn't have a church yet. Just his van or motor home. But he always made sure my family was invited to his guest appearances, and his special tent programs. We were a very religious family. Fundamentalists. We went to anything Pastor Atlas did, if it was in driving distance. Reggie paid special attention to my mother and father. But just like with Daley, his private attention was aimed at me. I came to believe that he was truly holy. When he looked at me, he must have seen an adoring little angel. And a willing victim. I had no real idea what he was doing. Neither did my parents."

Penelope still had the remote, worrying it in both hands, the force of her memories showing through. She accidentally hit the play button, flinching when Daley said, "I'm back!" Found the pause, then looked at me.

"But I know exactly what he's doing to Daley," she said. "Reggie Atlas is going to have to go through me first. I taught her from an early age that most men are wicked at best, and some are evil. And I was able to shape that thought into the person of Pastor Reggie Atlas. When she became old enough to understand. To be aware of him. To watch out for him. Should he *approach*. As I knew he would. We moved and moved and moved. My daughter. My sister. My legal charge. The first time I saw him near her was at one of her soccer games. She was nine. I was walking her back to the car after the game, and he was watching us from behind the wheel of a black truck. I acted like I hadn't seen him. Pulled the pepper spray out of my purse, then charged him. He sped out of the lot. His engine had been running, just in case. Cagey Reggie. And guess what I did?"

"You moved again."

"You bet we did. By the time we got to Phoenix I had to admit that Reggie could find us no matter where we went. He was big. He was rich. He had people to keep track of us. We were easy. I was getting very tired. I picked out Oceanside because it sounded so good. *Beside* an *ocean*. And it was close to San Diego and lots of technical writing for me to do. And just after I sign the lease on this place and get Daley enrolled at Monarch, guess what?"

"Reggie Atlas breaks ground on his Cathedral by the Sea," I said. "Pretty much right next door."

A strange expression from Penelope then, hostility, with notes of mayhem. "At which time I decided to stop running. But he began to close his net around her. And I can't control her anymore, and she has no fear of me or anyone. No fear of her teachers or Chancellor Stahl, or her sometimes much-older friends, or of ill-tempered Nick Moreno. No fear of Reggie Atlas, certainly. She told me a couple of weeks ago that she felt like running away with him just to get away from me. He would divorce his wife and she'd marry him and have *hundreds* of his children. Be free of me and my silly rules forever. Get her damned Snapchat and Instagram back."

I watched the anger recede from her face, replaced by a blank long-distance stare at the window and the street. Without breaking that stare, she pointed the remote at the boom box again.

29

////////////////////////////////

DALEY's diary wasn't all about Reggie Atlas. She talked about her "really cool little house in Oceanside," and her new school, and the strict Chancellor Stahl, and two friends she'd already made. And an interesting guy named Nick who drove a van and had a mobile dog-walking business.

I'm back!

So Max is kind of a friend, and this guy Nick and Max's mom picked up Max after school today and Nick smiled at me when he saw me looking at the picture of the dog on his van. And he tells me the dog is called a papillon, which is French for butterfly because of the ears, and I said duh, everybody knows that. And I could see this made Nick feel dumb and a little bit angry, too, and I thought, well, there's your basic boy stuck inside an older man's body. Great face, though, Nick's—alluring eyes and a beautiful smile. Told me Max's mom's car was in the shop so he was helping her out, and did I need a ride home, too? So I said yeah, why not, because Alanis was sick that day and Carrie was going to this club called Alchemy 101 and I just wanted to go home and kick it, maybe play some guitar and have some cookies. And that's what I did.

I'm outta here.

I looked up and caught Penelope studying me. She had known Nick. She understood Daley's proximity to his violent death, how close she had come to brushing up against it. I thought of Nick, too, and the gruesome end that Connor Donald and Eric Glassen had provided him.

Daley wondered how her former BFF Bellamy was doing. Wondered if Alanis and Carrie would turn out to be good friends. Said Nick had given her the ride home and said he could do that the next day, too, because Max's mom's car would be in the body shop the rest of the week.

It struck me that Daley Rideout was talking to herself and her CD recorder because she really had no one else to talk to. In Daley's mind, her "sister" was paranoid and controlling. Bellamy was hundreds of miles away and Daley had had no social media to keep in touch with her best friend. She didn't know Alanis or Carrie well enough to confide in them. Leaving her no one but stern grown-ups and nineteen-year-old Nick Moreno with the beautiful smile and eyes that had alluringly roamed her way.

"A good time for Reggie Atlas to show up in her life again," I said.

"Interesting you would say that."

I'm back!

Been three weeks now and I don't love Monarch, but Nick is turning out to be pretty cool, and Alanis and Carrie really rock and there's this teen club I've heard about that's supposed to have good music. I've been playing a lot. I wrote, like, three songs since we moved to Oceanside! I get true satisfaction from writing songs. I'm hoping Pen gets me the Martin Backpacker I'm totally craving. Only two hundred and twenty-nine bucks. Got a birthday coming up, baby. Funniest thing, I saw Reggie Atlas and two other guys at Monarch today. He gave me a big smile and said he was there to see Chancellor Stahl about a church-sponsored endowment thingy, which I think means money. I said what a small world to see you here, and Reggie said God works in mysterious ways. We all sat for a minute in the quad, had drinks from the cafeteria, then Chancellor Stahl had another meeting and Reggie told his friends let's go see that new athletic field and we followed them over. I know Pen hates him and I don't know why, other than she says he's got cancer of the soul. Must be painful. We fell behind his friends and talked. He said he had been praying for me a lot and still felt like we were ghosts flying through each other and he'd really meant it when he said we could fly together side by side in Jesus. I told him I was still waiting for that ticket and he said can you come to my new church in Encinitas, it's not finished yet, but I'll show it to you and you can see what a beautiful home for Jesus it's going to be. He said he could send a car and driver for me when Penelope wasn't home from work yet. Pen just had to think I was going to go to some usual place for a few hours—like maybe studying at a friend's house, or to the library, or maybe practicing in the music room after school. You're still playing your guitar and writing songs, aren't you? I said yes, and Reggie said, okay, your sister gets home from work tomorrow at five forty-five, so you just be at the corner of Seagaze and Myers at exactly five fifteen. You know where that is, don't you? I said duh, like I haven't lived here for almost a month. Don't you harassinate me, Pastor Atlas! And Reggie smiled down at me and just when I'm getting irate that he's treating me like a child my heart reaches out to him and I say, sure okay, I'll be there, Pastor Reggie.

Later, 'gator.

"He played guitar for me," said Penelope. "He has a beautiful voice. And he gave me the line about ghosts flying through each other, too. I thought it was haunting when I was twelve—these two beautiful wispy spirits moving through each other but not able to stay and unite. I asked Daley if he had ever said that to her. She denied it."

"Did he have other favorites?"

"In Jesus. Everything was in Jesus."

"Something concrete," I said.

"Concrete?"

"I'm fishing here, Penelope. Something physical. Something I can see. That helps me understand what he's doing."

"Well, there was our mansion on the sand. That was physical."

"Tell me about that mansion."

"I don't remember the first time he talked about it. I must have been very young. Eight or nine. I just kind of grew up hearing about it. At first it was a magnificent house he was going to build. On a beach. Maybe in California. Maybe in Mexico. Later, he told me he was going to build a holy mansion on the sand. Over the years, it became a place for him to live in, with all his friends and dogs and cats and whatever other animals he wanted. It would be huge, with a domed roof made of blue lapis, like temples in Jerusalem. White walls, with windows trimmed in shiny red paint. And it would sit on sand the color of gold in the sunlight, next to an ocean that would be always changing, from blue to green to silver to black to blue again. There would be tall palm trees all around. There would be flowers in planters beneath every window. And balconies where he could sit and watch the sun go down. Miles of beach. Whale spouts and seabirds in formation. And horses. Of course he would have pretty horses."

"You were impressed."

"I was *awed*. Over the years, the mansion on the sand became a place for me to live, also. My beautiful home. We would live there, together. A place of peace and beautiful things and love. Love everywhere. In every room. Morning and night and all the hours in between."

A bemused look fell over Penelope's face, then a bitter smile. She shook her head as if to clear a thought she didn't want.

"He said we would come together in Jesus with all of our hearts. As husband and wife. Twelve beautiful children would appear, children in His—Jesus's—image. And our family would become the foundation of the lost tribe of Israel, the true Israel—not the Israel of the Hebrews, who are only half human—but the Israel of Jesus Christ, God's only begotten son."

And so I glimpsed the depth of madness inside Reggie Atlas—if this was all true. Even mostly true. If Penelope was not spinning another convincing, self-justifying fiction.

"What did you make of all that, Penelope?"

She considered, a parade of emotions playing across her face. "I was still young enough to fall for it. He was such an impressive man to a little girl. To a little girl whose parents thought the world of him, who took her to hear him preach every time he was near us. Somehow, Reggie Atlas always found ways for us to be private. Just for a minute or two. In a chapel, while the choir rehearsed. In a church office, with the door open to the hallway. In a Sunday-school classroom, on the break between services. Walking in the woods around the tent. Even with other people around, he created this privacy for two. We talked and prayed. We had special sayings. We had looks and expressions. We never touched. Until. And Reggie would always bring up what was becoming *our* beautiful home. Like a parent telling a child a story. I know now that he was trying to shape my thoughts and dreams. My expectations and limits. He was measuring my portions and tenderizing me. Like a butcher."

In the wake of Penelope's painful memories, the ceiling fan whirred and the boom box sat silent and two boys with surfboards under their arms hustled down the sidewalk outside, voices raised. In that moment, their innocence seemed the most valuable thing on earth. I thought about how the world was made up of things that are here and seen, like the surfers, and also made up of things that are here but not seen, like a man walking in the woods on a warm spring morning with a girl too young to sense his menace, while the congregation gathered in the shade of the tent, awaiting the Word. I felt some of the weight of Penelope Rideout's past bearing down across the years, and her growing torment as she saw it gathering over her daughter. Her sister.

"What did you think when you first saw the Cathedral by the Sea?" I asked.

"Thought it was plug ugly. It's certainly no mansion on the sand. Why?"

"I just had the thought that Reggie built that mansion. Somewhere. I can find it, but it might take time. It would depend how good he is at secrecy. How many layers between his name and the bricks and mortar."

Another long stare from her. "For him and Daley?"

"For himself and his fantasies."

"Why not just rent a damned mansion? See, that's what I do." She gestured to the little beach rental, her hands open.

That was a very practical idea, and I said so.

A blink and a stare from her. The ever-judging, ever-assessing, ever-appraising eyes of Penelope Rideout.

"Let's hear Daley's second CD," she said.

30

////////////////////////////

I'm back!

Turns out Pastor Atlas's Cathedral by the Sea isn't much more than a cut-off hilltop and some cement with those spirally metal rods sticking out. You can see all the way to the ocean, though. It's out between Encinitas and Rancho Santa Fe, I think they call it, lots of twisty roads. Anyway, Pastor Atlas didn't send a car and driver to get me at the corner of Myers and Seagaze at EXACTLY five fifteen. No, he came himself, driving this crazy motor home, all red and silver and shiny. And down the road we went. Just us. I sat up front and it was like being a copilot in a jet. Pastor Reggie started talking about Jesus like he always does, but He's not really my thing, Jesus isn't, though I don't have any problem with Him. That I know of! I tuned Sirius to this oldhead band I totally love, Huey Lewis, rather than the Four Wheels for Jesus channel, which seemed to annoy Pastor Atlas. By the way, I got the Martin Backpacker guitar from Penny for my birthday, EARLY! and I took it with me to see Reggie's church because my story to Pen was I went with Carrie to play guitars in the music room at school with our music teacher at Monarch, Mr. Bob Dillon, that's his real name! And so Carrie's mom would drop me off at home and don't worry. So I had the Backpacker in the motor home and this big window right in front of me and I was playing along with Huey Lewis and the News. Watching the world out the window was more like the world was watching me! I don't really want to be famous, but for a minute it felt great. Everybody looking at me. Reggie trying to tell me how to play the music. Says he's good on guitar, but I've never heard him play a single note.

We walked around the cathedral construction site. I met one of the security guards, Adam, and Reggie said to call Adam if I ever needed anything. Adam would handle it. I thought maybe I could tell Adam that Nick was getting more and more aggro, and maybe he could maybe get Nick to chill. Then I thought, don't be a coward, girl, if Nick is dissing you, then get in his face yourself. Inside, he's a sweet guy, but I frustrate him with the no-sex-until-next-year-when-I'm-fourteen thing. He's all, what about handjobs? But I'm stubborn and have almost no interest in that with him and I don't owe Nick anything. I carry my own weight, except he drives everywhere because I'm too young. Which in the papillon van gets us lots of laughs, but some business, too. Half of what we do I pay for, gas included. If Pen knew how much of my allowance I spend on Nick, she might not be too happy.

Pen made me promise no sex until I'm eighteen, but I renegotiated with myself in case I meet someone better than Nick. Someone who makes me feel more that way. I mean, I do feel that way, and if you judge menstruationally, then I'm all grown up. I mean, someone who makes me really, really feel that way. Like an authentic connection. Physical, yes. But a soul thing, too. Soul mates? I don't know. Out loud it sounds so sappy and dumb.

Inside the construction trailer he showed me the drawings for his new church. We sat on a couch and he spread the plans across our laps. Arms touching. Hmm, I thought. I'd never been that close to him. The architect cost one hundred thousand dollars. It will look

very modern, kind of a mash-up of glass and wood and steel with big
cables connecting things. Reggie said the architecture was supposed
to symbolize the fractionalized world and the cables are Jesus, hold-
ing everything together.

Gotta go now!

Penelope gave me a sickened look.

Daley played some of her songs, accompanying herself on guitar.
Her voice was a soprano, bell-clear, with a girl's sweetness in it. She
didn't hold her notes any longer than necessary, giving the lyrics a
moving simplicity. The songs were grounded in the wonder of physical things: the ocean, which was new to Daley; seagulls contesting
food scraps thrown by a child; the loud power of an Amtrak train
rushing north from San Diego to L.A. Her guitar picking was simple
and timely.

"She has talent," I said.

"She didn't get it from me. Reggie plays beautifully. At least, he
used to. So the talent is more circumstantial evidence that he is Daley's
father. Since my eyewitness accounts are not enough."

"I'll plod into the truth on my own time," I said. "That's just the
way I do things."

She came and sat at the far end of the couch.

"Give me your hand."

With both our arms extended, our hands met, palm to palm, hers
on top.

"I want you to believe me, because what I've told you is true," she
said. "I want you to like me in spite of it."

"I like you very much. You're smart and funny and easy on the
eyes. You brought me some thoughtful gifts that night. And some
home nursing. It all meant something to me, Penelope. Really."

"But you look at me like I'm a pathetic victim," she said. "An over-sexed, low-IQ girl with eyes for a preacher man."

"No."

"Then how, exactly, do you see me? I'll accept nothing but the truth."

She squeezed my hands. Stronger than I'd have thought.

"You know how to put a man on the spot."

"We'll sit here until you answer me."

I imagined different answers, each true and each leading off the same cliff. "A bright young woman with a troubled heart and a tough problem to solve."

"How craftily you avoid my past," she said. "I need you to see it clearly. It's who I am."

"Only partially. Once upon a time. Which marches on."

"Do you believe me or not?"

"I want to believe you."

The hand squeeze again.

"But if you are proven wrong, would you still like me on a go-forward basis?"

"Okay."

Penelope Rideout, peering at me through clouds of doubt. Then a gradual change. Subtle but apparent. A thin ray of sunlight. Another. Willpower? Hope? Acceptance?

"Hmmm. Okay? Okay."

She let go of my hands and aimed the remote.

Daley's voice filled the room again, no songs, but snippets from her days at Monarch, her first time at Alchemy 101, ups and downs with Nick.

Followed by ruminations on *what made Penny so afraid of her own shadow, like every window in every place we ever lived had something bad*

waiting outside it. When I ask her why, she says don't be silly. I think it's
probably something to do with Mom and Dad. Like everything is. When I
look at pictures of them I don't feel very much. I hope that doesn't make me
a sociopath. I remember them only a little, and unclearly. Mom was pretty
and talkative. Dad was quiet. They both seemed huge. There. I just ex-
hausted my memories of them.

Toward the end of the sixty-minute disc, Daley introduced her new song, "Mansion on the Sand." It was brief.

Mansion on the sand
Filled with music and
Waiting for a trusting girl
To lock inside its perfect world
Jesus coming by to chat
Prayers and joy and love you say
All night and all day
Lost together forever bound
In the beauty of God's way
You say it's yours, take it
But why close my eyes to see
The beauty you've made for me?

We sat in a silence longer than the song. The sickened look came back to Penelope's face. She wiped a tear and flicked her hand sharply and the tear shot toward the kitchen.

"Fuck, I'm tired of this," she said. "Can't you just go get her and bring her back? Then Daley and I can turn around and light out for the territory ahead. Move again. And move again and again, a million more times. Move for fucking ever. And you won't have to deal with me and my melodramas, or try to figure out what you think about me. I'll get over you. We'll send Christmas cards. I was happy running away because it was always away from him. Now I've stopped and tried to fight, and I've lost her."

"You don't know that," I said.

"I know SNR Security works for him. I know you're just one man. And you can't go up against them alone again."

"Roger that. Don't lose hope."

31

///////////////////////

THE trail leading to Pastor Reggie Atlas's mansion on the sand wasn't quite as hard to find as I thought it would be.

It took me most of the next day to pick it up through the labyrinthine IvarDuggans.com "Known Associates" and "Doing Business As" listings for Reggie Atlas and his Four Wheels for Jesus Ministry. A Mexican LLC controlled by six known Atlas associates had formed a real estate investment trust and brought shares to market on the U.S. stock exchange.

The trust was called Sand Mansion Investments, and offered shares in properties in Baja California's burgeoning East Cape, just north of La Paz. East Cape was serviced by two good airports, one in San José del Cabo, the other in La Paz.

I knew the area. Once a loose necklace of peaceful villages strung along the Gulf of California, East Cape was rapidly developing into a land of luxury hotels, ecotourism, and tony golf resorts.

I'd even worked a case down there, locating and finally helping a careless gringa get back to the U.S. She had gotten herself into some ugly trouble, an impromptu kidnapping attempt that was both amateurish and potentially lethal. She was very happy to finally board her plane out of La Paz. So was I. As American journalist Ambrose

Bierce had written to a niece more than a century ago, not long before he disappeared in Mexico, "To be a gringo in Mexico—ah, that
is euthanasia." For me, it almost was. For the gringa, too.

Studying the computer monitor in my home office, I saw that
Sand Mansion Investments was a legal shell company comprising
the six known associates of Reggie Atlas, but also of Ronald White,
aka Reggie Atlas, and Mary Lavoy, aka Marie Knippermeir, heir to
the Knippermeir Breakfast Meats fortune and wife of the hatemonger Alfred Battle.

I felt my pulse jump when I saw that one of the Sand Mansion
REIT properties on the Bay of Dreams in Baja California was Casa
de Angeles Caídos. House of Fallen Angels.

I'd fished the Bay of Dreams. A beautiful bay and a rich fishery.
For decades it was known as Bahía Muertos—Bay of Death—because
of the hundreds of head of cattle that had died there in a hurricane.
More recent developers changed the name for obvious reasons, and
the former Bay of Death was one of the most ruggedly beautiful
places I'd ever seen. Like the Middle East, lower Baja California has
an almost otherworldly beauty where the desert meets the sea. The
coast is dotted with mansions, some merely spectacular and others
competitively outdoing their neighbors. Sprawling estates painted in
bright colors, mostly. Extravagant properties.

House of Fallen Angels was a ten-acre, ten-thousand-square-foot
compound overlooking the Bay of Dreams. A main house and two
guest houses, all painted white, with blue domes that appeared—on
the House of Fallen Angel's rental website—to be made of lapis-blue
tiles. The windows were trimmed in red. A wide slope of green
grass. Palms, neatly coiffed. Three crosses towered above it all, high
in a pale blue sky. A helipad, landing strip, two swimming pools. All

offered by the month, domestic and landscape staff included, for fifty thousand USD, serious inquiries only.

So Reggie had gotten his mansion, I thought. Bought it in partnership with a storied white supremacist's breakfast-meat fortune, remodeled it to his own fantasy specs, and offset the costs by renting it to the wealthy when he wasn't using it himself.

Not bad for the rookie Georgia evangelical who'd almost had his career beaten out of him by three black men but was rescued by an angel disguised as an old man, white hair combed back, blue eyes in a haunted face. A pastor who had mixed himself up with an eighth-grade girl who admittedly had a crush on him. And had unleashed his powers of seduction upon her. Although it could very well have been the other way around. Or some of each.

I took the virtual tour of the House of Fallen Angels. Mexican/Spanish/Moorish architecture. Hard to say where one style ended and another began. High windows and sunlight. Heavy wooden furniture. Blue-and-yellow tile mosaics framing the doors. Mahogany window frames. Bold paintings on white walls, elegant ceramics on pedestals, each one singled out by the gallery spotlights. Christs and Madonnas and saints and martyrs of all sizes and postures and materials, from the bloody to the beatific. But mostly angels. Angels everywhere, in paintings and stained glass, as sculpture, as wall sconces and freestanding figures, as candles and dolls, in metals and wood and wax and glass.

Twelve beautiful children would appear . . . and our family would become the foundation of the lost tribe of Israel . . .

And here in the House of Fallen Angels—I had to figure—was where the rest of those beautiful children were to be conceived. According to the gospel of Penelope. Based on sayings attributed to

Reggie Atlas. One down. Eleven to go. And, if they were not to be born of the fallen child-angel Penelope, then why not by her daughter? *His* daughter?

I remembered his words the Sunday morning I'd met him in his office: *The young are our future, Mr. Ford. They will multiply us into heaven.*

From the far side of my spacious oak desk, wasp-cam one from Paradise Date Farm jumped to life on Dale Clevenger's heavy red laptop. I watched Connor Donald striding from the main house toward the large, corrugated metal hangar. Evening by then, the school closed and most of the cars gone. Orange desert light, dust puffing with each fall of his duty boots.

Wasp-cam three picked him up, unlocking the convenience door to the hangar. A moment later the rolling door came up, revealing the dusty ATVs and the shiny John Deeres and the two long work benches behind them. I saw that the hand tools had been moved since I'd first seen them a few days back. The cans of nuts and bolts, too, and the soldering guns. *Elves at work*, I thought, *making presents for Christmas.* Just three months away, and all those millions to provide for.

Connor Donald weaved through the vehicles and past the work benches, then stopped outside the perforated steel security door near the back of the building. He pulled a key ring from his pants pocket, unlocked the door, and pushed it open.

He stepped in and turned on a light and I finally got a look inside. A long stainless-steel table ran almost wall-to-wall in the back, upon which sat a large glove box roughly the size and shape of a coffin. The glove box was clear acrylic or glass, and had two sets of articulating arms on the side facing me. A rolling backless stool for each work station. I could see heavy-looking black hands—somehow both mechanical and human—at rest within the box. There were latches and lock pins at both ends, for loading and unloading from either direction.

Connor Donald walked around the table to the other side and returned with a handheld monitor of some kind, set it on the table near the glove box.

Arranged neatly on the table in front of him, on either side of the long glove box, I saw a flotilla of smaller box-shaped meters with read-out windows—some plugged in to surge protectors and others apparently battery-powered, some with handles and some without; handheld devices the size of large smartphones; handheld devices shaped like a cross between a pistol and a caulking gun; an assortment of what appeared to be tiny loudspeakers in miniature cabinets, no bigger than travel alarm clocks. Plenty of wires, narrow-gauge cable, and the flexible coiled extension cord once found on telephones.

Electrical diagnostic and measuring equipment? Maybe. Hazmat—chemical or biological? Maybe. But what of the pistol–caulking gun contraptions and the small loudspeakers attached to some of the meters? My next thought was radioactive devices. Not voltmeters but radiation dosimeters and radiometers? Not oscilloscopes but radiation detectors?

Burt barreled in, holding up his phone for me to see.

"They're working with radioactive material," he said. "The fume hood."

At Burt's prompt I saw it, suspended from the ceiling over the work table, just visible at the top of Clevenger's laptop screen. For drawing up radioactive particles or gases suspended in the air, invisible, odorless, and potentially lethal. In my attention to Connor Donald, and the puzzling glove box and various gauges and meters, I hadn't registered it.

Wasp-cam one came online, Eric Glassen crossing the dusty farm yard. Camera three picked him up as he entered the hangar and worked his way through the vehicles toward the lab. He moved quickly and lightly, like the athlete he had been in high school. A cornerback, requiring speed, strength, and the ability to hit an opponent—often a very strong running back—at high velocity. With his thick neck and pit-bull ears, Eric was a formidable-looking man. I remembered his brief and disappointing UFC career. And his odd choice of UC Riverside undergraduate degrees in mechanical engineering and history.

Which reminded me of Connor Donald's contradictory curriculum vitae: an athlete-scholar who'd renounced a full football ride to study physics and philosophy at Penn State. Summa cum laude. Followed by his Christian mission in Somalia, where he'd witnessed the slaughter of nine people by Somali rebels. And his subsequent role as a founding member of SNR Security, a company with a proven record of hostility to blacks and Muslims.

So: football; university degrees in physics, mechanical engineering, history, and philosophy; martial arts fighting; and a Christian mission ending in blood, all conspiring to lead these two young men to a secret laboratory outside a small desert town in the Imperial Valley, to work with apparently highly radioactive materials in order to accomplish . . . what? I tried to make some sense of it, find a throughline, discern the narrative through the facts. I tried to put all that into my pipe and smoke it—as Grandpa Dick likes to say. But I couldn't even get it lit.

"What are the pistol-shaped devices?" I asked.

"Dosimeters for measuring penetrating radiation," said Burt. "X-rays, gamma rays, and neutrons. The smaller handheld devices are similar. I don't know why they'd have so many. Triple coverage.

Must be handling some very lively stuff. The larger box-shaped units with the handles are high-end Geiger-Müller detectors."

"How do you know all this?" I asked.

"I took some nuclear remediation training in Olkiluoto, Finland, one summer. All that equipment around the glove box is standard issue in radioactive workplaces."

"Why the loudspeakers?"

"Audio warning," said Burt. "So if your eyes suddenly explode, your skin melts over them, and your brain ruptures, you can still hear the warning. Clever."

"What do you think they're up to?"

Burt smiled, a crooked thing containing something other than amusement. "No good at all, Roland."

Glassen went into the lab, slapped Donald's shoulder, and swept around the big metal table. Donald joined him, and they each pulled on a pair of tight blue lab gloves, then another. Next they shrugged into white lab coats, and each man settled a white hard hat onto his head and swung up the clear protective shield. They came back to the front of the room, talking and smiling.

Then Connor Donald picked his way back through the vehicles, on his way to the roll-up door of the hangar. He touched something on the wall and the corrugated metal curtain closed on the scene within.

Burt and I stared at Clevenger's screen in silence, as if we could will Donald to open the door again so we could watch them work.

Work done in white coats and face shields and two pairs of protective gloves. Using their clear, coffin-shaped glove box with the fume vent sucking up any loose radiation. In their hidden lab on a date farm in an infernal desert at the southern tip of California.

"The wooden crates in the freezers would fit in the glove box," I said.

My phone buzzed and Mike Lark's name waited on the screen.

"What the hell are they doing out there?" he said.

"I was just wondering myself."

"Where exactly is that place?" he asked, his voice fast and sharp.

Burt gave me a doubtful look as I gave Lark precise directions to Paradise Date Farm.

"Have you saved the previous video?" asked Lark.

"All of it."

"Send it over, now. Use my secure line in the field office."

He gave me the number and I got to work on my desktop.

"What in hell are they *doing* out there?" Lark asked again.

"You're the expert, Mike."

"You said something about crates in freezers. Describe them again."

When I was finished, Lark was quiet. I could hear the tapping sound of his fingers on a keyboard. Burt sat on the couch, head down, twiddling his thumbs.

"No labels or serial numbers on the crates?" asked Lark.

"Nothing."

"You said metal bands. Okay—how many per crate, what size and color?"

I described them in detail. *Tap-tap* of Lark's fast fingers on his keyboard. I looked at Clevenger's laptop screen, but the wasp-cams were resting.

"All right," said Lark. "After you told me that SNR did that number on you, I ran the company through our federal interfaces and dug into the structure of the company. You were right—it's privately held. Marie Knippermeir has controlling interest and sixty percent ownership. Alfred Battle's dear, breakfast-meat-wealthy, possibly addled wife. Battle's name appears nowhere in the incorporation. Although his fine humanitarian views on race and brotherhood show through in SNR's behavior."

I pictured Reggie Atlas standing under the grand magnolia tree in front of his Rancho Santa Fe spread, smoking a cigarette while Alfred Battle retrieved the briefcase from the gleaming black Mercedes parked in Reggie's garage. An apparently very valuable briefcase.

"Is SNR profitable?" I asked.

"Very," said Lark. "No debt. They've got eight regional offices and three hundred–plus accounts in fifty states. From plant protection to executive security to mom-and-pop residential patrols. Agriculture to aerospace. School campuses, retail, and churches. Over six hundred employees. SNR invests in and donates heavily to needy Battle-approved organizations."

"Such as Paradise Date Farm."

"There's quite a list," Lark said. "Some of my personal favorites are the Fraternal Order of White Knights, Right Proud, the Christian Century Crusade, and Don't Tread. Most of them are American, but some European groups, too—Lemborg Jugend and C14. It's not illegal."

Legal or not, I wondered at the riches amassed by Reggie Atlas's Four Wheels for Jesus Ministry—cash donations to his church and subscriptions to his podcasts and streaming videos—some of it contributed to SNR, laundered into profit, then sent back out again to Alfred Battle's hate organizations. Wondered that Reggie could afford such largesse to people like Alfred Battle, on top of joining Marie Knippermeir in the purchase of the House of Fallen Angels on the Bay of Dreams on the Baja Riviera. The generosity of the faithful has always impressed me. The rank-and-file believers. The five-or-ten-dollars-on-Sunday-morning people. Sitting in their pews, or in front of their devices, hearing the word, feeling the word, willing to pay for the word.

"Your files on Paradise are coming through," said Lark. "How many SNR soldiers are usually out there?"

"It changes. At least six, the night they jumped me. I've seen as many as eight or ten at a time from the wasp-cams."

"I'm looking at Connor Donald and Eric Glassen right now," said Lark. "The date stamp says four days ago."

"They're the ones who picked up Daley Rideout from school," I said.

"And put a bullet in her boyfriend's head," said Lark.

"If my gut is right, they've got her right now. I don't know where, or even why. But it has to do with Reggie Atlas."

Silence then, as Lark tried to get his head around the hydra: Paradise Date Farm, SNR, Pastor Reggie Atlas, and a missing fourteen-year-old girl.

"How much life do those camera batteries have left?" he asked.

"They're down to half-charge," I said. "Two weeks. Clevenger said the heat will wear them out fast."

"No way to replace them?"

"The Bureau might be able to get inside," I said. "But Paradise has seen enough of me and my people."

"Thanks for this," he said. "If I see what looks like evidence of a federal crime being committed, we're going to be knocking on some doors out there pretty damned fast."

"They won't be happy to see you."

"About as happy as they were in Oregon and Nevada."

"I don't want your job."

"I don't want yours. You're on your own. But it suits you, Roland."

"Thank you for Alfred and Marie," I said. "But Daley Rideout is who I want most, Mike. She's in the hands of bad people. Anything you can find out. Anything."

"I'm sending you a link you'll like," said Lark.

I pocketed my phone and returned Burt's calm gaze.

"Why does the San Onofre nuclear power plant keep coming into my mind?" asked Burt.

"Because it's patrolled by SNR Security," I said. "And because Daley frolicked with her SNR pals on the beach there."

"Why would they take her to that particular beach?" asked Burt.

"Maybe it was a simple diversion to keep her happy and busy and not missing home," I said. "They took her to that particular beach because they know it. Home turf. Remember, that was the day she ran away. She wasn't quite a captive yet. Or didn't know she was."

Burt gave me a doubtful look.

"We need another look at the San Onofre power plant," I said. "Now that we know Paradise Date Farm is bristling with radioisotopes."

"And the same security company is guarding them both," said Burt.

My phone chimed when Mike Lark's texted link came through. I opened it.

WHITE POWER HOUR

Sunday after church

113 Orange Hill, Escondido

Special Guest: Kyle Odysseus

Refreshments and Education

Your Supremacy Is Your Admission

32

////////////////////////////

Late that afternoon, Grandpa Dick made a point of me joining the Irregulars for dinner and a "group discussion," say, around seven o'clock sharp.

"We haven't seen much of you since your last title defense," he said. "We miss you. And Violet spent half the day hand-fashioning raviolis. One of your favorites."

I figured their discussion topic would be Penelope Rideout. She had showed up unannounced at Rancho de los Robles not once but twice, successfully honked her way into the property on the second occasion, invited herself to dinner, dressed my wounds, kissed my split lip, and showered me with gifts. And I had spent a recent night away from home, which my tenants would have duly noted and attributed to Penelope.

The discussion began over shrimp appetizers and Liz's potent martinis.

It was after sunset and a cool breeze came up the San Luis Rey River Valley from Oceanside. Faint smell of ocean, mixed with sage. A half-moon had begun its rise over the hills. I propped my phone against my water glass, to view wasp-cam streams, if any came online.

We sat around the big picnic table, four men, two women, and a pitcher of martinis sunk deep into a bowl of ice. A stray black dog lay at Frank's feet. Somehow the dog had managed to travel the acres of coyote-heavy scrub and chaparral that surround this property. And shown up the previous day, to be swiftly adopted by Frank, who had named him Triunfo, after his home in El Salvador.

"We're concerned for you," said Liz. "We don't unanimously approve of the behavior of your current client. And the bad luck she has brought you."

"We don't unanimously disapprove of her, either," said Dick.

Liz: "Of course not. We're individuals. There are dissenting opinions about her, but the general drift is that you should be careful of deepening your involvement with this woman, beyond the PI-client relationship."

A moment of silence, during which I glanced at my phone and lifted my drink. "To you, my friends," I said. "The Irregulars."

Followed by a careful raising of martini glasses by everyone.

I noted that Violet, usually a temperate drinker, was at least one drink ahead of the rest of us at this early point in the evening. And that she seemed more subdued than usual. Maybe just tired. She had run around the pond for nearly two hours today. I'd seen her from my upstairs office window, while taking brief breaks between my virtual tour of Reggie Atlas's House of Fallen Angels and the wasp-cam action from Paradise Date Farm, and my conversations with Burt and Mike Lark.

"Penelope is an attractive young woman," said Liz. "She's had a hard life. But she's plainly out to claim you. And her aggression reveals neediness."

"Or just knowing what she wants," said Dick. "Liz would be the first to stipulate that she's hard on her own gender."

"Discerning," she answered.

"Well," said Violet, "I mostly agree with Liz about Penelope. She's obviously interested in you. Beyond just hiring you."

Dick: "First of all, women often unionize against other women they don't like. So I think Roland will benefit from a male perspective. I for one think that Penelope is lovely, generous, spirited, and quite a catch for you, Grandson."

Liz: "A *catch?*"

"I'm not hearing wedding bells," said her husband. "Just some loud and low-down rock-and-roll."

"You used that line on me fifty-something years ago."

Dick grinned at her over the top of his martini glass as he took another sip.

"I very respectfully disagree with Liz on one big point, though," said Violet. "I don't blame Penelope for your bad luck. In you getting beat up like that. Luck is an invisible hole into which anyone can fall, and it can be good or bad. You don't make your own luck, and other people don't bring it to you. You fall in."

"*Es verdad,*" said Frank.

Triunfo gazed up at his new master, clubbing his tail against the flagstone. He looked like a Lab cut with a German shepherd, well proportioned and strong. Brown eyes in a black, serious face. Tan brows.

Frank leaned down and petted him, apparently done with his opening statement.

Burt: "We could give Roland enough credit to make up his own mind about her. Last I checked, he was all grown up."

"Of course we will," said Liz. "I just want to be sure that he can see things from a different point of view."

"More talk from the women's Local 666," said Dick. "Really, what don't you like about Penelope besides she's pretty, gets things done, and is half bonkers over my grandson?"

"I know a liar when I hear one," said Liz. "For starters, her husband being a fighter pilot out at Miramar? It didn't ring one bit true, all her *Top Gun* this and Tom Cruise that. Everybody knows the Top Gun school was moved to Florida, anyway. It took Roland a little longer than it took me, but he saw through that one. The night she barged in here, showed us those pictures of her sister? Before Roland and Burt came home? Well, nobody shows a picture of their little sister. They show you a picture of their kids or grandkids. Maybe their dog. It was her own daughter, even just by the looks of her. Roland and I had a talk after his night away from home, and he indicated some doubt as to whether he was searching for a sister or a daughter. Correct, Roland?"

I nodded.

"The girl has run away!" said Dick. "What's it matter if she's Penelope's sister or daughter?"

"What matters are her blithe evasions of truth," said Liz.

Then Frank: "I like Penelope."

"Jeez," said Liz. "Talk about a union."

She quaffed her drink and reached for the pitcher but Frank beat her to it, poured her a fresh martini, and cast her a questioning look.

"She's a lovely person," said Dick.

"She's full of shit," said Grandma. "Don't let her touch you again, Roland."

"*Let* her touch you, Roland. It's time. She's like Justine in some ways."

"She's not fit to lick Justine's parakeet dish," said Liz.

"Justine had a parakeet?"

Liz: "God."

"And what exactly is a parakeet dish?"

Violet lurched up and excused herself to go boil the ravioli. She swayed some on the way to her casita, looking back over her shoulder before going inside. Liz marched off to get the salad. Dick gave me a "What's gotten into them?" shrug and headed to roast the vegetables he invariably burned. Burt and Frank set the table and Triunfo trotted off toward the pond.

I sat and wondered what Penelope Rideout was doing just now. If her ears were on fire. And if so, what she would make of this Judgment of the Irregulars. I thought she'd have some zesty words for them. More darkly, I wondered where Daley was, and who was holding the keys to her cell.

DINNER WAS VERY good. Violet's pasta was stuffed with portobello mushrooms, pork, or duck; Dick's vegetables were just black enough; Liz's salad was her usual bounty, with extra beets because she knows I like them.

The conversation turned lighter when Violet animatedly told about sometimes having the same dreams as her younger sister, on the same night at approximately the same time, which led her to speculate that dreams—like luck—were simply invisible things that you fell into. So why couldn't two people fall into the same dream at the same time, especially if they were sleeping in the same room?

Frank had good news—he'd landed another weekly landscape job in Fallbrook, for a total of three days a week in addition to the three he was working here on Rancho de los Robles. "No more Saturdays I will be sleeping late," he said. He had purchased an "almost new" bicycle to get to work. Bikes are a tough way to get around in these parts. Fallbrook is a sprawling little town, lots of hills to climb and some fast traffic to negotiate.

You could see Frank and his Central American brethren from El Salvador, Guatemala, and Honduras—mornings just before seven and afternoons just after three—pedaling to and from their labors. They were compact men, sometimes just boys, always wearing long pants and work boots—never athletic shoes—and always long-sleeved shirts, absolutely tucked in, their belts wide and their faces dark in the shade of their hats. Frank told us, as he had before, that his wages were for his return to Salvador to avenge the death of his father, and to save his family from the violence of the MS-13 gangsters who terrorized the entire village.

He said all this with a pleasantly matter-of-fact expression. Frank seems to be both guileless and fearless. I wonder what good can come of his small-arms combat training with Burt. I've heard them talking about flights to El Salvador, the physical layout of the village of Puerto el Triunfo—Frank's hometown—and how easy it is to buy quality weapons in El Salvador. Thanks in part to the United States military and CIA involvement there in the 1980s. Thousands of weapons left over from the post-Somoza days, many of which had found their way into the hands of the Mara Salvatrucha—MS-13. It was hard to reconcile Frank's plans for bloody revenge with the bright-eyed innocence of his eighteen-year-old's face. I wish I could tell him that a young refugee from American violence, willing to work six days a week and stay out of trouble, might find his way into a legal stay in this country. But the chances of that are small and, at last check, getting smaller.

"Back to the matter at hand," said Liz. "We're all just hoping you'll look before you leap with this Penelope woman."

"I'd leap," said Dick.

"You dismay me, honey."

"Can I say something?" asked Violet. Which struck me as funny, because Violet was always talking anyway. However, she paused to take another drink from her martini, and Frank couldn't resist.

"Penelope is *muy bonita*," he said with a boyish grin.

Violet: "What I'd like to say is—"

"*Roland still hasn't gotten his heart back from Justine!*" Dick boomed. "And it's time, Roland. More than time. It's *okay*, Grandson. Justine has already forgiven you for moving on. Mark my words."

"How far will you go to miss a point?" Liz said. "Roland can't simply surrender to a low-quality person because she catches his eye! He can't build a future with a manipulating liar. And, *Frank*? You should learn that men are not crows. You can't have every shiny little thing you see."

He smiled uncertainly at her. Triunfo returned from the pond, dripping and pleased.

Violet downed her drink and poured another.

Burt stood. "I want to thank you all for this wonderful evening."

"It was nice, wasn't it?" asked Liz.

"Roland," said Burt, lifting his glass to me, "you'll do the right thing with regard to Ms. Rideout. You always do. Doing the right thing is your gift. And your curse."

"Violet," said Dick, "you're awfully quiet all of a sudden."

Violet sat upright, back straight, hands resting on the table, tears running down her face. Silence. She looked at us in a clockwise rotation, locking eyes with each one of us before moving on. She looked as if she were about to be executed.

"I wanted to say that I have come to love you all very much. You have accepted me, and you have been of good humor with my incessant yapping and nervous tics. Roland, you let me move into casita four without really knowing anything about me.

"Liz plays tennis with me. Frank has shown me some very wonderful Salvadoran recipes. Dick has shown interest in my future. And Burt—in some way I can't quite explain—I know you have my back."

Burt sat. The hush was heavy.

"But I've been dishonest with you," Violet said. "And I want to stop that right now. You all talk about lying, and the truth, and how we go forward. You judge Penelope by what she says about her past. We all judge her by that. It's all the evidence we have to go on."

She wiped her eyes and continued, voice cracking and tears running off her chin. "My name is Melinda Day and I grew up in Santa Barbara. I come from a well-to-do family and I've been advantaged in every material way. I went to Stanford, not Southern Illinois University. I do fly for the airlines, though—that much is true.

"I was all set to be married in June of last year, to my longtime boyfriend, Brandon. But the previous October . . . we went to the concert in Las Vegas. To celebrate . . . And we were there, standing with our arms around each other, I was telling Brandon about this famous writer who lived down the hill from us in Montecito and only wore red athletic shoes everywhere he went, even with a tuxedo . . . and when I stopped talking I heard these pops coming from behind me, from the sky, and I turned and couldn't see anything and people started screaming and running and Brandon slammed into me. All his weight. Pulled me down . . . His shirt was bloody. And some people helped me drag him behind this low wall and I lay down there with him, got all scrunched up close together like we were sleeping, and he said to run. He told me to run. Then he stopped breathing. I did not run. I did not run.

"My heart was pounding and my face was pushed between the back of his neck and the ground and I could smell his blood. It was soaking me. I thought I might be drowning in it.

"Days later, I knew I couldn't be Melinda anymore. It was too ter-rifying. I could no longer . . . inhabit Melinda. So I became Violet. Violet wasn't in Las Vegas that night. She has no Brandon to remem-ber. Melinda Day has not been available for some time now. But she's sorry. She asked me to say she's very sorry for lying to you all."

Burt handed her a napkin, then another. Violet wiped her face. Liz stared at her. Dick folded his hands and looked at the table. Frank crossed himself. Triunfo panted softly.

When she looked at me, I thought I saw a wisp of resolve come to Violet/Melinda's tear-burnt face, but maybe it was only the relief of confession.

"So, about Penelope," she said, "I have two things to say. First, be careful of her, Roland. As a practicing liar I understand her need, though not her reasons. But be careful *with* her, too. She seems both brave and breakable. You can build her up or tear her down. You have more influence on her than you might realize."

A long silence. An owl hooting from across the pond. A strong half-moon dangling light on the water. Justine in a rowboat on that pond, floppy hat, brown arms. What to remember? What to forget?

"Thank you," I said. "Thank you all. I value your advice, whether I take it or not."

"We care," said Liz.

"Hope I didn't overstep," said Dick. "About Justine."

Violet undaintily blew her nose into a napkin, made a fist around it. "I'll now be quiet for as long as I can. I'm trying to teach myself not to talk so much. Obviously."

She smiled as if embarrassed, and sighed. "It's harder than it sounds, because so many things really deserve to be said. Is that just me? Even before that night I was an incessant talker. Melinda Day could carry on without a comma. Brandon was the first guy who actually listened to what she said. She was used to male attention, being reasonably attractive and very much a man fan. But she noted that few men could listen to her closely for more than just part of one date. Let alone a lifetime. Not that I was sizing up every guy as a possible mate, but to be perfectly honest, I was. Rafael came the closest, junior year of high school. What a sweetie. He'd really hang in there. Hour after hour of me. But around eleven, if it was a date night and not a school night, he'd fall asleep wherever we happened to be. Unless he was driving. He had a red Soul—the car. Kept it really shiny. But if he was a passenger in my car, or if we were watching videos at one of our houses, or hanging with friends—there'd go Rafael, nodding off with that little smile on his face. But Brandon? He could listen all night. And not only that, he was a beautiful man. Naturally, I wanted to write our own wedding vows, and he said, *Great, Mel, but they can't be longer than* Infinite Jest. And then when I started actually writing them, you'd never believe it but . . . oh, heck, sorry, sorry, sorry, you guys! I'll stop now. I will stop right now!"

She sighed hugely. "Just one more thing. I totally promise. Please call me Melinda. I have to start somewhere."

She looked back over her shoulder. Everyone else looked there, too.

No bullets. No building and no thirty-second-story window.

Just the man in the moon looking down with that odd half-face of his, like he's eyeing you from around a corner, either groaning or smiling, hard to say.

One by one, the Irregulars and I stood and gathered behind Melinda. She rose and we closed around her. A circle of awkward embraces, a cross between a football huddle and a group hug, Triunfo running around us, hoping to join in.

No words, just this strange new thing between us, silent and strong.

I SAT IN an Adirondack chair down by the shore of the big pond, let the night cool around me. No breeze, the water black with a wobble of silver pointing straight up at the moon. I hadn't expected the Irregulars to lecture me, but it felt good to be cared about. To have things in the open.

Saw my phone come to life, figured something from a wasp-cam, but it was a text.

> Penelope
> (760) 555-5555
> Thanks for being here today
> and listening to Daley. She
> is so sweet and bright and I
> hope that you understand her.
> I've prayed long and hard that
> you can find her very soon. I
> have this black feeling surrounding
> me, and it's getting closer and
> tighter. I feel slightly more
> optimistic when you are around.
>   11:48 PM

I thought about that for a minute or two.

> She is sweet and bright and
> I'm trying my best to locate
> her. Reggie owns a mansion
> in Mexico that sounds much

like the Mansion on the Sand.
I don't think he is in control
of Daley right now. I will
find her and you will get some
peace.
    11:50 PM

Hope you had a good day.
Hope the Irregulars are well.
Hope deferred makes a heart sick,
but a longing fulfilled is a
tree of life. Says that right
in the good old Bible. I feel
better to have stopped running.
Good night, Roland Ford PI,
one of the last good guys.
    11:51 PM

33

////////////////////////

THE next morning, Burt and I sat in a rented white Taurus, parked off Old Highway 101, just outside the north gate of the San Onofre Nuclear Generating Station. A white Taurus is as anonymous as a vehicle can be, and we didn't want to draw so much as a second glance from SNR Security, which knew me as the big guy they'd whaled on outside of Paradise Date Farm, and knew Burt as the little guy who'd showed up a few days later to wash the windows.

I had my phone propped up in the cup holder, waiting for live streams from the wasp-cams. They were quiet. Paradise had been eerily peaceful since Donald and Glassen had donned their radiation suits in order to do who knew what in their hidden lab.

"I didn't know you'd studied in Finland, Burt."

"After Italy and before Japan."

"As a college student?"

"Not exactly," Burt said. "I was in college, but I'd been recruited to do a student-officer program. They didn't call it that."

"CIA?"

"Their Special Activities Division, SAD, sponsored by JSOC. I never knew which acronym was ordering me around. Wonderful years. Young and not a care in the world. I got a college degree out of it. Biology with an emphasis in ornithology. Finland was part of that. Olkiluoto had half of Finland's nuclear power plants and they were trying to figure out where all the radioactive waste would be stored, like we are now. They finally decided on an island."

With these few sentences, Burt Short told me more about his past than he had in the last three years combined.

I lifted my binoculars, balanced my arms on the Taurus's steering wheel, and took a long look at the power plant. It wavered in the late-morning heat, magnified and flattened by the powerful field glasses. The employee parking lot was sparsely occupied. I'd read that there were only a handful of employees here now compared to the days when the plant was producing. And most of those employees were security subcontractors—the friendly professionals at SNR.

They weren't hard to spot. Silver SNR vehicles had the best parking slots, up near the entry/exit hut. Where, I could see, a uniformed armed guard awaited a woman now approaching. Middle-aged, a dark suit, white blouse, and black running shoes. She raised her neck badge to a scanner on a stand, then passed through a tall, steel-ribbed turnstile and entered a concrete hut. Through the open security door, pausing to use the wall-mounted hand geometry reader. She stepped to the guard, who scanned a dosimeter up and down her torso. They talked and nodded and smiled, as if continuing some running gag. A moment later, she stepped through another heavily barred carousel and into the plant.

"More people set off those scanners after getting X-rays from their doctor than from exposure in the plants I worked at," said Burt. "You'd be surprised what they hit you with in a CT scan or dental X-rays."

I watched the woman leave the hut and continue down a wide steep ramp leading to the Security Processing Facility building, a

large structure at the north end of the station. Through the binoculars I scanned the concrete building, with its vehicle barriers set pro-
actively out front, its steel double doors, the delay barriers topped
with gleaming rolls of concertina wire, the anti-grenade-screen windows, and thousands of slender spikes sprouting from almost every
surface of the roof on which a bird could land. In spite of the spikes,
I noted three pigeons crowded into a bare corner of the security
building.

Looming above it was a boxy sniper's nest, perched atop four
steel columns bolted to the concrete beneath. Its retractable stairs
were folded up against the bottom. The nest had firing slots cut into
both sides that I could see from this angle, and pods of floodlights
rising on poles from the flat roof. Another uniformed SNR man,
headset on and an M4 slung over his shoulder, slowly patrolled the
perimeter catwalk, looking down. Gulls circled haphazardly over
him, sharp-winged in the blue.

"Where did you serve, Burt?"

He lowered his binoculars and gave me one of his odd smiles. "Attached but not formal. I was too short, of course."

"That's funny."

"It never hurt my success in business," he said. "My height."

"What business?"

"Various. Commercial fishing back in Alaska, where I was born.
Beef in Kansas City. Later, Wall Street. That's where your rent comes
from each month. I worked for the PGA, too, mostly for the fun of it."

"Law enforcement?"

"God, no."

I didn't want to quash Burt's unusual candor, but I couldn't resist.
"Married, children?"

Burt lifted his field glasses to his eyes. "Roland, I value you. I value your genuine interest in me. What we did that night in the mountains made something rare of us. We have an unusual bond. Over time we might become close in a more conventional way. So I'll tell you just one more thing, to save you time and trouble—though I suspect you've already wasted some time and had some trouble with me. I came to Burt Short late in life. When I rented a home from you. But there is no Burt Short in my past."

Which tracked with all of the IvarDuggans.com, TLO, and Finders hours I'd logged, trying to snatch some truth about my new tenant from the multiverse of data rising daily into the cloud. Plenty of Burt Shorts. But scant information on my Burt Short—a recently issued California driver's license with Apartment 5 at Rancho del los Robles as his home address, and a registration for his Cadillac Eldorado. No prior addresses, no criminal record, no known associates, no Social Security number. The more I looked, the less I found. No hits on their costly facial-recognition program, not even Burt's picture on his CDL.

Until one small piece of luck that seemed warm to the touch: video of a man watching a table-tennis match in Atlanta in 1996. Why was I watching such a thing? Because Burt loved to play table tennis. Like I do. Because he'd once mentioned a restaurant in Atlanta that I'd been to more than once—a modern take on southern barbecue. Because I saw on my screen that the 1996 Atlanta games were listed as one of seven Olympiads since 1988 in which table tennis had been played. Because the Internet to a PI is a porchlight to a moth.

The BBC news clip of the men's championship showed my Burt, ten rows back, in the audience. I plucked a frame of him. His image was out of focus and couldn't be usefully enhanced. But I ran it through the facial-recognition program anyway. No match. Ran it again, same result.

I still think it was Burt. My Burt. The new Burt Short.

"I've known for a while that there's no Burt Short in your past," I said.

"Thank you for telling me now."

"Did you watch the men's final table tennis match in the Atlanta Olympics?" I asked. "About ten rows back?"

He lowered his binoculars again and studied me. "Ninth row. Liu Guoliang over Wang Tao."

Two eventless hours later, a white pickup truck with a shell pulled up to the vehicle sally port. The door decal read:

RaptorLand

Falconry, Breeding & Sales

www.raptorlandisus.com

"This should be fun," Burt said. "In Finland we used *Falco peregrinus*. They're popular for this kind of work."

I looked up at the pale blue sky, misted by the Pacific. Saw gulls again circling lazily.

The guard opened the second sally gate and the truck bumped down the wide concrete road to the security building. RaptorLand Man got out. He was a husky, sun-darkened fellow, wearing cargo shorts, a shirt festooned with pockets, chukka boots with socks almost to his knees, and an Australian safari hat with the starboard flap snapped up.

He went through the first set of delay barriers, spoke into an intercom on a steel stanchion. Both barriers slid open and he walked past them and into the building.

He was out five minutes later, with what looked like a parking pass in one hand. Looked up at the sky while he waited for the barriers to open, then went back to his truck. Set the pass on the driver's-side dash and went around to the back, where he lifted the shell gate and lowered the tailgate to expose the green raptor carrier inside.

RaptorLand Man lifted the carrier by its top handle and set it on the tailgate. He was talking to it. He looked up at the seagulls cruising low over the beach. I could see the raptor's leash extending from a cutout at the bottom of the crate door. The crate was windowless, to keep the bird calm. Even captive-bred falcons retain their wild fears and behaviors. The man pulled a heavy-looking glove onto his left arm. It went almost to his elbow.

He held the leash in his glove, swung the door open with his right hand, and brought the hooded bird into the sunlight. It perched on his upraised forearm, curious but blinded by the hood. I recognized the rusty, black-barred breast and legs of the peregrine, a large falcon but not a large raptor—maybe twenty inches tall. Crow-sized. This was a female, much larger than the male. Its hood was Arab style, red leather with black eye patches. I wondered what her name was.

"*Falco peregrinus anatum*," said Burt. "They're all over the West, from the Rockies to the coast. Some people call them duck hawks, but they're not hawks at all."

I don't know much about falcons, but I do know that the peregrine is the fastest animal on earth. In a hunting stoop they fly more than 200 miles per hour. An alleged record speed of 242 miles per hour was reported by *National Geographic*. They tuck, dive, and club their prey midair with their claws clenched at those speeds, killing it or knocking it out. If the prey is small enough, the peregrine catches it, carries it to earth, and eats it. If it's too large—peregrines kill birds much larger than themselves—they follow it down for dining. I've seen them hunting out on Point Loma; in a stoop, a peregrine looks like a small anvil dropped from above.

Burt and I stood next to the car for a better view. RaptorLand Man snugged a jess around each leg—down by the talons—then removed the leash. With the falcon on his raised arm, he started toward the middle of the plant, where the cooling pools were housed. Gulls circled haphazardly.

Halfway to that building, the man stopped, talked to the falcon for a moment, then unhooded her. She pivoted her head quickly, taking in this sudden new world with her shining black eyes. I wished I had eyes as strong as those. He released the jesses. The bird hunched, turned, and launched with a puff of downy feathers, wings slender and sharp. She flew low over the spent fuel casks until she almost reached the beach, then climbed and shrank into the blue.

If the gulls noticed, they didn't show it. I glassed the pigeons I'd seen earlier, but they were gone. Some of the plant employees had come outside near the switchyard. They stood together, most of them looking up. Behind them loomed the switchyard, the tangled mountain of transformers and coils and relays and the fat black power lines rising over I-5 on their way inland. Three SNR guards watched from outside the cooling pools; four more waited near the sunken casks of fuel rods.

"She's got an audience," said Burt.

Suddenly a small black object dropped into view. It was hard to pick up with the binoculars, but when I locked onto it I saw the tucked falcon bulleting down from the heights. She looked half under control and half out of control, her midair adjustments sudden and tense, like an airplane in a dive too fast to withstand and too steep to pull out of. I thought she might start smoking. The gulls cried and scattered and the falcon angled sharply and a moment later a gull burst into feathers and dropped, pinwheeling through the sky, wings and feet akimbo, the falcon following in relaxed switchbacks, minding her investment on its way to the sand. The three pigeons I'd seen loitering amid the spikes sped over the rooftops like fugitives.

The guards and employees clapped and hooted, some heading back to their tasks, others enjoying a moment in the warm midday sun.

"The seabirds in Finland would stay away for two weeks after a peregrine patrol," said Burt. "I don't know about these Californians. You know how optimistic we can be. But a falcon is cheap security against birds. You get a seagull loose in the electrical or pigeons sneaking inside to nest over the cooling pools, you've got a problem."

I watched RaptorLand Man work his way between the buildings and come to a stop at the security fence. His falcon squatted a few yards away, tearing at the gull.

34

////////////////////////

J UST after three o'clock, a well-worn panel truck pulled up to the
deliveries gate. It was white, with a large cooling unit on top and
a faded Paradise Date Farm graphic on its broadside panel. I noted
the license plate number. An SNR guard with a clipboard stepped to
the driver's side as the window went down. The driver was a young
blond man in a black golf shirt and Ray-Bans who said something to
the guard and smiled. The guard laughed, tapped his sidearm, and
went back into his booth. A moment later the gate rolled open and
the produce truck went in.

"I don't think they're delivering fresh Medjools," said Burt.

"I doubt they're delivering anything," I said.

The produce truck trundled past the security building and down
the road toward the cooling pools, then went out of sight between
the steam-containment domes. Came out farther south and stopped
in front of a small windowless building.

The driver parked, the tall door at the back of the truck rolled
open, and he hopped out. Three SNR guards barged from the squat
building, all wearing heavy gloves with high safety cuffs, bearing a
small but apparently very heavy wooden box.

"Look familiar?" I asked.

"The heaviest thing on earth is the nucleus of a uranium atom," said Burt.

"There are eighteen hundred tons of enriched uranium now in storage right here," I said. "In the form of spent fuel rods. Guarded by SNR."

"Think portability," said Burt. "The rods are titanium and they encase the fuel pellets. Small pellets. Like dog kibble. Break open a titanium rod and you've got death pellets, ready for deployment."

"Think concealability," I said.

"And don't forget pure power," said Burt. "Close exposure to one pellet is enough to kill a man within minutes. I've seen acute radiation syndrome in rats. Brutally thorough and surprisingly fast. Nausea, convulsions, diarrhea, seizures. Hemorrhage of eyes, nose, and ears. Sudden organ shutdown. Like in old science-fiction movies. Over in minutes. "

They hefted the box into the truck, leaning hard to get it in far enough for the door to close. The four men talked for a while, one of the guards gesturing at the sky, one gloved hand the gull and his other hand the falcon, knocking her meal from the sky.

"You think they're selling this stuff?" I asked.

"It's the opposite of valuable," said Burt.

"Except to well-financed players smart enough to work with it."

"SNR wouldn't sell to jihadists," said Burt. "But they might act themselves. So how about a dirty bomb targeting blacks and Muslims, in keeping with Alfred Battle's sociopolitical beliefs? Manufactured in their little lab way out in the desert? Led by SNR's physicists and mechanical engineers."

"For use where?" I asked.

"Again, who do they hate?"

"Blacks. Muslims. Nosey PIs."

"A mosque," said Burt. "A black church. A Black Lives Matter rally. A feast at the end of Ramadan. A nightclub popular with young blacks. A black celebrity. The home of a Muslim family. No end to the possibilities."

The guards and driver touched fists and the driver boarded his truck. The backup warning sounded as he made a three-point turn and headed out the same way he had gone in.

WE GAVE THE lumbering produce truck a comfortable head start down Basilone Road toward the freeway. Stayed far back as it joined the tractor-trailers and the extra-slow drivers all the way down to San Diego and onto Interstate 8 East, bound for the Imperial Valley. Near Buena Vista the truck took the Rattlesnake Road exit, made a left at the stop, then slowly accelerated toward the town and Paradise Date Farm beyond.

I went right on Rattlesnake, swung a bat turn across the median when it looked safe. The Taurus fishtailed severely in the fine white desert sand, and for a moment I thought we'd go under. But the road shoulder rose up to meet us, then asphalt, and I punched the car up Rattlesnake, back to the freeway onramp, and onto the interstate.

"You'd have felt like a real idiot getting stuck back there," said Burt.

"PIs don't get stuck."

I was about to call Mike Lark when Mike Lark called me.

"Ford, the National Center for Missing and Exploited Children just got a tip. A girl matching Daley Rideout's picture and description was seen in the company of three or perhaps four men on the beach in front of Cotton Point Estates in San Clemente five minutes ago. She's even wearing the Beethoven top you said she took with her. San Clemente sheriffs are rolling."

"Here's one for you, Mike."

I told him that the Paradise Date Farm produce truck about to trigger one of the wasp-cams might have just picked up one very heavy wooden crate from the San Onofre Nuclear Generating Station.

"Like the ones in the freezers?" he asked.

"Fresh from the nuclear energy plant."

"Do you know this for a fact?"

"I watched them load it."

"This changes everything," he said. "This is now federal. This is us."

"You're welcome."

"The truck just came on-screen. Tell me what you find at Cotton Point."

Lark rang off and Burt held his phone up for me to see.

I HELD THE Taurus to eighty most of the way to San Clemente, radar detector plugged in and Burt's keen eyes on the lookout.

It's a long haul from deep in the Imperial Valley to south Orange County. Had to gas up in Alpine, wade around a wreck in Del Mar and construction traffic in Oceanside.

I badly needed a posse of deputies in fast radio cars, an aggressive watch captain, and three units on their way, dispatched well ahead of me. And how about a helicopter? All the useful tools I used to have and now do not.

But I did count my blessings. I had me. I had Burt. A six-cylinder Taurus with a radar detector on the dash and a Colt .45 1911 in the console. A concealed-carry permit to make it legal.

I called Lark again, but he hadn't heard anything from the San Clemente sheriffs. Because they'd gotten there too late to intercept

Daley, I thought. Or it was a false tip to begin with. Happens all the time. Sometimes on purpose.

It took a minute to talk my way past the Cyprus Shore guard. I played my ex-Marine card and he accepted it, an ex-jarhead himself.

However, this is a "double-gated community," so that meant I had to get past the stately Cotton Point Estates guard as well. His name plate read Eccles. I produced my CDL and a "Damian Thomas, Locations" business card, which features a logo criminally similar to that of a famous motion-picture studio. Introduced Burt as my assistant. Told Eccles it was a Leo DiCaprio–Jennifer Lawrence picture, Iñárritu to direct, and I had only ten minutes. Smiled and confessed that Orange County wasn't as dull as they said it would be. Eccles seemed to suspect that I was a liar, but the distant scent of Hollywood seduced him.

The beach was sparsely attended for a warm day. It's a public beach but privately accessed. The waves were small and the tide was high, so there were more rocks than sand.

Two uniformed Orange County deputies came down to the beach behind us, a bulky sergeant and a muscular young man with a curt mustache.

When the sergeant asked us for ID, I gave him my PI's license, which brought a long look from him.

"*That* Ford," he said. His nameplate said Ionides. "I thought so."

The younger deputy handed back Burt's driver's license.

"What happened to you?" asked the sergeant.

"I was looking for Daley Rideout and I found six bad guys instead."

"Six. You were lucky."

"I was, but the girl's family is taking this hard," I said. "They're good people. So I'm still here. Did you see her?"

Ionides shook his head.

"Had anyone here on the beach seen her?" I asked. "Besides the tipster? I'd appreciate your help, Sergeant. Daley Rideout is mixed up with some very bad people."

"So I understand."

Ionides had a heavy, unsurprisable face and flat, wet eyes. He sized me up without a blink and handed me back my license. He had what he needed on me. I was the chickenshit cop who betrayed his partner and cost him his career. I was also the stand-up PI who'd helped the FBI save some lives recently, down in San Diego. But it would come down to a fourteen-year-old girl.

"Couple surfers thought they saw her when they were waxing up," he said. "Weren't sure. Mainly focused on the waves. She looked kind of like the picture we showed them. Same top—black, with Beethoven on it. She was with three older guys. She and one of them went swimming, didn't stay out long. When the surfers came back in, they were all gone. Two other witnesses gave us similar statements. All four witnesses said she looked fine to them. Just a girl and a guy who went swimming. One said they looked like brother and sister. Nobody said she looked afraid. We missed her by ten minutes. Ten damned minutes."

I texted my employer and told her there had been a reliable sighting of Daley less than three hours ago on the beach at Cotton Point. She appeared to be at ease and unharmed. She swam in the ocean. I was there right now and Daley was gone again.

Penelope called and I let it go to message.

35

/////////////////////////

BURT and I drove to Cotton Point Estates. Sixteen homes plus Nixon's old Western White House, now owned by a big-pharma go-getter and marked down to $63.5 million. Quite a 'hood. You could see the blue Pacific from almost anywhere, beyond the bright white plaster and stony old-world walls and clay-tile roofs and fountains and cypress and palms and flowers. Beautiful, serene, rigidly coiffed.

There was a private Cotton Point Estates beach path that Daley Rideout might or might not have used to arrive for her swim. The next nearest beach access was more than half a mile away, according to my phone maps. Without using the Cotton Point Estates beach access, Daley and her "friends" would have had to walk more than a mile and a half to and from Cotton Point. A long, rocky walk along a perfectly swimmable beach, just to get here and back. Which suggested to me that she'd come and gone right here where we were parked.

We watched the surfers out on the point. I surfed a lot until I went to war, then not. It was another thing that changed for me in Fallujah. Don't know why. It wasn't as if someone shot me off my surfboard in Iraq. Watching now made me want to do it again.

"She was here just two hours ago," I said. "They escorted her here. They allowed her to come here."

"*They*," said Burt. "Friends or keepers, Roland?"

"Friends the day she left Nick Moreno's condo with them," I said. "She was comfortable with these men. But less than forty-eight hours later, she got cold feet and ran away. Made it as far as the 7-Eleven in San Clemente before they got her back under control."

"*They* being SNR Security."

"Specifically, it's Donald, Glassen, and Revel," I said. "Maybe they're acting on orders. But maybe they've gone rogue."

"On behalf of Pastor Reggie?"

"That's what I thought at first," I said. "We know he contracts SNR to patrol his church. We know he funnels some of his hard-earned fortune to Alfred Battle. We know that's big money, pouring in through the Four Wheels for Jesus Ministry—the cathedral, the streaming sermons, the podcasts. But Reggie tried to hire me to find and deliver Daley to him instead of Penelope."

"Leading you to believe what?"

"That Atlas doesn't know where she is any more than we do."

"Yet SNR Security does," Burt said. "To what end?"

"To shake down Atlas for even more."

Burt went quiet and stared out the window for a long beat. Drummed his thick fingers on the armrest. "But what if trying to hire you was just a way of putting you off his stink and keeping you close? And the SNR gentlemen are in fact already holding Daley for him? And he can get to her whenever he wants? In keeping with Penelope's idea that the man is determined to seduce his own daughter?"

I'd considered that before Reggie Atlas had even left my downtown office. "Then he's more dangerous than I thought."

Burt looked at me, shook his head. "Really? Follow this through,

Roland. If Penelope is correct about what Atlas did to her when she was a girl—and what he will do or has done to Daley—then at some point he'll have to tuck Penelope in, once and for all. He absolutely can't afford not to. And he'll want a dirt nap for you, too—as party to what she knows. So of course he'd ask you to work for him. Keep you handy."

Sitting here in a place approximating paradise, a place of sun and sea and riches, it was important to be reminded that there is a darkness in some men that is unstoppable unto death.

"Thanks for reminding me," I said.

"Of what, Roland?"

"What we're up against."

He grunted.

"My next life I'm going to be a doctor," I said. "Or a farmer. Or maybe I'll learn to dance really well, and teach. Imagine—The Roland Ford Academy of Dance."

"Just be a PI in your next life. Think how good you'll be by then."

We drove past each of the sixteen Cotton Point Estate properties again. The oceanfront lots are big and some of the homes are all but hidden. We drove slowly and loitered when good views of the houses presented themselves.

Spent the next couple of hours parked in different locations. Finally admitted we might be wasting our time.

THAT EVENING IN my upstairs home office I poured a hopeful bourbon. I scoured IvarDuggans.com and my other online data dealers for a Cotton Point Estates property owned by Reggie Atlas and the breakfast-meat maven Marie Knippermeir.

No dice. When I deleted Reggie Atlas and Four Wheels for Jesus

Ministry from the search, I found a brave new world of shell companies with Marie Knippermeir's and Alfred Battle's names behind them. But nothing in Cotton Point. How many more holdings they might have, and what shell companies had been formed to possess them, was anybody's guess. Even the data miners could miss a nugget. I did have an idea who would know, and where I might find her. But getting her to talk to me at all might not be easy.

Nothing under Reggie Atlas as sole proprietor.

I looked out the window, saw Melinda and Liz taking up table tennis positions against Dick and Burt. Could be a good match, with Burt's speed and Dick's defensive consistency against Liz's and Melinda's tennis smarts. Styles make fights.

On my big oak desk, Clevenger's computer slept. It wasn't popping to life as often with the wasp-cam feeds. I worried about the battery life of the cameras, but they still had almost a quarter of their power left. I worried that Donald and Glassen had accomplished something ominous in their large, wicked glove box. But what?

I watched the setting sun pour gold on the pond and called Penelope Rideout.

"Roland, I'm so glad you called!"

Gunfire roared in the background, loud, chaotic, and plenty of it, the reports and echoes thundering through my phone. *"Where are you?"*

"I'm at Iron Sights, practicing up. She's alive. Daley's alive!"

Popopop pop pop popopopop.

Suddenly the gunfire quieted, then stopped.

"Can you hear me? I'm outside now. Man, that derringer kicks like a mule. Goes by the name of Smokey. I was so relieved to get your call today. It was like a window being thrown open in a dark room. Daley is okay and we're going to get her back. I *know* it, I *know* it, I *know* it, Roland."

"Why are you shooting?"

"I practice once a week with the Iron Ladies."

"Practice for what?"

"For all the creeps," she said. "No reason a girl shouldn't have some security. So long as she's safe and sane. Like you know I am!"

"Do you have a concealed-carry permit?"

"As of two weeks ago. Passed the class and got the approval. A hundred and fifty-six dollars and fourteen cents, plus training costs."

I wasn't quite sure what to say. People with guns worry me. Especially ten percent killers.

"Roland, don't worry. I'm not a gun nut. I'm not, like, off my rocker. Did you talk to the people who saw Daley?"

I told her about the call from my contact at the FBI, the anonymous tip to the National Center for Missing and Exploited Children, the sergeant who had interviewed the four witnesses.

"Exactly what did the witnesses say about her?"

I synopsized carefully—the three men in their late twenties or early thirties, Daley's apparent willingness to be there with them, her brief swim. None of the witnesses gave Daley and her companions much thought. One said that Daley and the young man she went into the water with looked like siblings.

"He's brainwashed her," said Penelope. "Stockholm syndrome. Patty Hearst. She's too terrified to resist, so she's psychologically thrown in with him. See?"

"It's possible she's cooperating with her captors. But I don't think Atlas has control of her."

"You're wrong," she said. "Reggie Atlas can convince anybody of anything. *It's what he does.* He convinced you that I tried to seduce him. That he never drugged and raped me. That he didn't father Daley. You *still* don't believe me."

"I'll find Daley and bring her back."

"I wish you trusted me," said Penelope. "I know I've lied. I'm very sorry to have done that."

"Let me do my job."

"A minute ago I put eight nines in the black at fifty feet."

I saw a brief but spectacular trailer of Penelope walking into the Cathedral by the Sea and shooting holes through Reggie Atlas.

"Penelope."

"Yes, Roland?"

"Don't do anything foolish. No matter what you think you know. Let me get Daley back to you. It's what I do."

"Prove it."

I was about to answer when she ended the call.

36

///////////////////////////

THE next morning I decided to have another look at Pastor Reggie Atlas and headed to the Cathedral by the Sea.

Melinda, Frank, and I walked across the parking lot toward the church. We were on the early side because the Four Wheels for Jesus website had warned of an overflow ten a.m. service. Three golf-shirt-and-chino-clad SNR men stood outside the entrance, feet wide, hands folded in front of them, wraparound shades in place even though the morning was cloudy.

Up ahead of us was a young black couple. I saw that they drew the attention of the SNR men, who had three oddly similar expressions on their three oddly similar faces. The couple slowed and the woman whispered something to the man and they stepped away to let us pass. I caught the expression on the woman's face as we went by—uncertainty and resolve. Then brief words rippling among the SNR men, impossible to hear from this distance, but I could sense that the words concerned the couple.

When I turned a moment later, the man and woman were heading back toward their car with some purpose, the man's arm light on the woman's arm, her back straight and her head high.

"I just hate that so much," said Melinda.

A chuckle from the security men as we passed by.

As Reggie Atlas took the stage, a bar of morning sun broke through the coastal clouds and streamed through the cathedral glass. I sensed subterfuge in this but couldn't imagine how Reggie could manipulate sunlight. A countrified rock band played an intro, some good pedal steel guitar. Reggie stopped halfway to the pulpit, raised his arms to the crowd, smiled The Smile. His usual wardrobe: white shirt, open-collared and long-sleeved, pressed jeans, white athletic shoes. His blond mop was purposefully styled.

Melinda—the healing, less garrulous Melinda—sat on one side of me, writing in a small leather-bound notebook that she had begun to carry. She was still running insane distances throughout the hills and valleys beyond my house, but she was looking up and behind her far less than she had before her confession a few evenings earlier. I respected the terror in her soul and the energy with which she tried to fight it. As I respected all the thousands of people caught in the same storm of bullets that night. How were they managing their fear? What about the ones who didn't have Melinda's willpower and gumption?

To my left sat Frank, enjoying his morning off. He had just added a regular Sunday-afternoon account, which meant a six-and-a-half-day workweek. On our drive to the cathedral, he had told Melinda and me that one of his sisters back in El Salvador had told him to watch out for an old friend of his—Angel Batista—who was rumored to be in the San Diego area. Frank explained that Angel was never a friend. He was a scrawny *ratón* who had turned into an MS-13 soldier and went by the nickname El Diabolico. Frank's sisters feared him and his friends, and if Angel was in the San Diego area Frank hoped he wouldn't show up in Fallbrook. *For Angel's sake,* he said. Frank had no fear of him at all that I could see.

Off to one side stood a large screen devoted to Pastor Atlas. He was gigantic but detailed. In spite of this, many of the worshipers around us were tuned in to fourwheelsforjesus.com on their smartphones. I did likewise, watching the live-stream Reggie on the small screen doing everything that the actual Reggie was doing, just in a jerkier, slightly delayed kind of pantomime. I turned the thing off and put it in my pocket.

As before, Atlas welcomed his "family," asked that we all hold the hands of the people next to us and close our eyes for prayer. He praised Jesus our Lord, and gave thanks for the life and love around us. He mentioned several people by name who were in need of special prayers this morning due to illness and accidents.

After Amen, he asked each of us to stand and introduce ourselves to anyone nearby we didn't know. "None of us are strangers," he said. "Remember who the disciples met on the road to Emmaus." I met Dane and Tina, Sophie, Jim and Linda. After we had sat back down, Reggie reported that this past week the Onward Soldiers Fund had donated well over $2,300 to U.S. military deployed worldwide, the most in any week since the Cathedral by the Sea had opened.

Today's sermon was "Jesus Is Action," which Atlas began with a story of a revelation he had at the age of seven. He had been out in his tiny backyard, playing with his puppy, Sparky. Reggie saw that the puppy was happy but only interested in his chew toy. Reggie started wondering what made Christians different from any other religion if all they did was go to church on Sundays, sing some songs and pray some prayers, dropped a few dollars into the offering plate, but never did anything to make the world a better place.

"If all they were interested in were their toys? And I decided as a seven-year-old that being a Christian *is not what you say but what you do*. What. You. *Do*. And what does a seven-year-old Christian with a puppy do? I vowed to find a home for every dog and cat in the Creek Valley Animal Shelter in town!"

Melinda looked at me and smiled, then wrote something in her notebook. Frank sat up straight, hands folded, sleepy-eyed.

So did I. Drifted off a little, as I always do in church. Every once in a while my parents took us kids to a service. Usually Easter Sunday, Christmas Eve, or Memorial Day. A different church each time. Mom was especially suspicious of churches getting their hooks into you, telling you what to believe, with whom you should congregate, and charging you for the advice. Dad always sat with his eyes closed, fragrant with aftershave. A good suit and shoes. I realized I had just shaved for church, too, and put on a suit and shoes I'd had for years but that still looked new.

Reggie humorously recalled taking the dogs from the animal shelter one at a time, walking each on a leash, and pulling a wagon filled with cans of dog food and donated used dog leashes behind him, door-to-door, neighborhood-to-neighborhood, until he talked someone into taking the animal, a few free cans of food, and a complimentary used leash.

As before, Atlas was self-deprecating and self-amused, and it was easy to picture him forty-plus years ago, hustling his shelter rescues door-to-door. I tried my best to reconcile that seven-year-old boy with the staggering evil that Penelope saw in him. It was hard to age the puppy savior into the child rapist he had allegedly become.

It was also hard to believe that sweet, daft, smart, and lovely Penelope Rideout was a chronic liar, or worse.

I let my church-drowsy mind wander from one questionable Penelope Rideout story to the next, like a dinghy drifting from one island to another. From her Navy Top Gun nonhusband to her faked family pictures to her vaguely referenced jobs to her ceaseless moving from one city to the next across the continent to her half a lifetime of telling her own daughter she was her sister.

And I wondered again exactly where her accounts of the pastor's seduction and rape landed on the cold, hard scale of truth.

As I tried to assign answers to these mysteries, Reggie Atlas continued with his theme that Christians don't just talk, they *do*. Jesus in action. Jesus *is* action.

I remembered Penelope's words:

He told me that we would come together in Jesus with all our hearts. As husband and wife. Twelve beautiful children would appear . . . and our family would become the foundation of the lost tribe of Israel . . .

Over the next month, young Reggie had rescued eight of twenty-one dogs, three of nine cats. His takeaway from this was: Plans sometimes don't come all the way true, but don't let perfection become the enemy of action. What if Jesus had cursed the loaves and fishes as not enough, the water into wine as insufficient? I liked that idea. Melinda slashed a big exclamation point on a blank page of her notebook and showed it to me.

We left the cathedral a few minutes later, under a humid blue sky and white thunderheads rising in the south.

37

////////////////////////

A LFRED BATTLE's White Power Hour started approximately two hours after Reggie's sermon ended. I had taken Melinda and Frank home and driven to Escondido. By then, the thunderheads were gray anvils behind Battle's compound; rain was on its way.

White Power Hour. I and my good friend Morbid Curiosity were hoping to see for ourselves what puppy-rescuing Pastor Reggie Atlas—through the generosity of his many followers—was secretly financing for hate engineer Alfred Battle. And maybe even to find some clue to what Marie Knippermeir's SNR Security was doing for the good of mankind out at Paradise Date Farm.

I had guessed my chances of being recognized by the Paradise Farm SNR guards at fifty-fifty. Higher for Burt being spotted as the window washer. So I was alone, with sunglasses and a hat to hide my battle scars, banking that the public setting, the police presence, and the gun at the small of my back would dissuade another attack.

I brought Justine's red Porsche Boxster to a stop at the corner of Holiday Lane and Orange Hill, where the Escondido Police had Orange Hill blocked off with portable bollards. Officers manned a checkpoint, looking through the windows of the incoming vehicles, though it appeared that a roving trio of armed and uniformed

SNR Security men was deciding which cars to let in and which to turn back.

A dozen protesters of various races were corralled behind police sawhorses and yellow crime-scene tape, some of them waving hand-painted signs, while others used their phones to film the cars lined up to enter the rally grounds. Many of them focused on Justine's Boxster as an obvious privilege machine, staring intently through the window at me as they brandished their signs: *#StopHateNow! Nazi-Free Zone, #SanDiego Too Great for Hate!*

When it was my turn to try out for the team, I rolled down the window and said hello to Officer Brantley, while his counterpart on the opposite side of the car leaned down to peer through the lowering window.

"Here for the rally?"

"Yes, Officer."

"Do you have a weapon of any kind on your person or in this car?"

I handed him my driver's license, PI license, and a concealed-carry permit.

He gave me a long stare. "Not the first one of these I've seen today," he said, finally looking at the permit.

He asked where my sidearm was holstered and I told him. As he studied my CDL, I looked over at the three SNR guards who were looking at me. Saw no hint of recognition or anything else on their faces.

The cop handed me back my docs and one of the SNR Security guards waved me through.

The road to Alfred Battle's hilltop compound was narrow, steep, and winding. Through my windshield, the orange grove looked only slightly better than it had the night I'd followed Battle here. Drought-worn trees, not many leaves and not much fruit. I waved to a heavyset older woman in overalls and a wide straw hat, standing amid the trees. She waved back. Work gloves, white and clean. Marie, queen of breakfast meats? I pulled into a bulldozed dirt lot crammed with cars. Followed the hand signals of a blond boy in a bright green vest.

I walked up a dirt path toward the White Power Hour. Smell of kettle corn and barbecued meat. Three open-sided canvas tents staked on a brown lawn. One white, one red, and one blue. Big. People milling around inside. Behind them stood the centerpiece home, a faltering two-story yellow farmhouse half swallowed by ivy.

From a distance I saw Alfred Battle, old, tall, and dapper, standing beside a stage in the white tent. Looked like the same brown suit he'd worn to grab Reggie Atlas's payola. Two men in beige chinos and black golf shirts loitered behind Battle, both with pistols on their hips.

But what mugged my attention was the red, white, and blue banner hanging behind the stage. It was a grand vertical rectangle, long sides down, composed of three red uppercase letters in a heavy contemporary font, outlined in white and set on a blue background:

S

N

R

I thought of the newspaper column by the *Union-Trib* writer who wanted to know what the letters meant, and how the SNR regional office in San Diego wouldn't tell him. I wondered how Alfred Battle had come to name the company his wife had bankrolled.

One of the golf shirts looked across at me. Once again, it irked me that I hadn't seen the faces of my attackers while they were busy beating mine. In a fair world you would at least get to see who's behind the punches. And the kicks and gun butts. Besides being a PI working on a job, I was also a man itching for revenge. I'd seen Connor Donald's snarling-lion tattoo. Maybe that would have to be enough.

Framed by the towering banner behind him, hawk-faced Alfred Battle considered me from a distance.

I drifted into the red tent, joining the audience watching a big-screen TV. Images of Charlottesville raced across it, mobs of haters, mobs of protesters, most of them young, most somewhere between angry and furious. Flying fists, torches, shields. A cheer went up as a white mob and a black mob dashed against each other.

From behind the half-privacy of my sunglasses, I studied the men and women around me. Young and old. Some teens, too, and younger children. All were white and most were everyday-looking people who wouldn't stand out.

But some would. Tattoos were big: Confederate battle flags, iron and Gothic crosses, even a few swastikas mixed in with the bald eagles, American flags, Don't Tread on Me rattlesnakes, and pierced hearts. And plenty of bling: Confederate battle-flag headbands, skull-and-dagger key rings, a young couple wearing matching singlets with images of a screaming Richard Spencer front and back. Trump buttons, Trump trucker and cowboy hats.

A conference table had been set up and furnished with reading material, presided over by a preppie-looking young man, mid-twenties maybe, wearing a dark suit and an open-collared white button-down shirt. Behind him hung a green, black, and white banner, vaguely Nazi in design if not in color, with the letters *KEK* as its focal point.

A poster board stood on the table beside him, and he watched me with a curious, open expression as I took it in. The top of the poster was a meme I recognized, Pepe the Frog, combined with an exaggerated cartoon of Donald Trump. Beneath Pepe/Trump's grinning face was an oversized sheet of paper, yellowed and wrinkled to look like parchment, with what looked like a poem or meditation of some kind, printed in an Egyptian-looking font.

"That's the flag of Kekistan behind me," he said. "And the froggy meme is Kek. Kek is an ancient Egyptian god with the head of a man. And below Kek is our Kekistani prayer."

I read it.

Our Kek, who art in memetics
Hallowed by thy memes
The Trumpdom come
Thy will be done
In real life as it is on/pol/
Give us this day our daily dubs
And forgive those who bait against us
And lead us not into cuckoldry
But deliver us from shills
For thine is the memetic kingdom, and the shitposting,
And the winning, forever and ever
Praise KEK

"We got lots of play in the Charlottesville coverage," he said. "What we're trying to do is have some fun and make a serious point at the same time."

"What serious point?" I asked.

"The United States of America needs chaos and darkness. Tear it all down and build it back again. Honor your ancestors. Don't let our white children go extinct."

"What's the fun part?"

"Don't you think he's hilarious? Pepe the Frog mixed with Trump? There's this whole video where Kek follows Hillary around before the election, then gets inside her and causes her nightmares and convulsions. Remember how old-looking she got toward Election Day? Then falling down, and that whole charade about her being exhausted? No way, citizen—that was Kek, working his magic."

"So it's a put-on to get attention for your cause. Sort of get people laughing?"

"Exactly. I'm not a racist, either. I'm a race realist. To quote my man Michael Enoch, 'Diversity means you're next, white people. Your heads are on the chopping block.'"

He gave me a canny look, trying to see how his story was going over.

"You're a normie and that's cool," he said. "But here's something to think about. Unless we take some dramatic action on all this immigration, our grandchildren will live in a country that hates them. As a result of America's ongoing moronic military intervention around the world, we're digging our children's graves. You have kids?"

I shook my head.

"There's a new website for single whites who happen to like other single whites. Man-woman, no gay crapola, no lesbos. It's all straight white people, ready to breed. We have to replenish, that's a fact. We need men like you. Check it out. I've got a daughter. And I will *not* bring her into a world where it's okay for her to be fucked by darkies who give her drugs, who won't work for a living because of biological limitations, and who'll throw her in the garbage the minute they're tired of her. Would you wish that on your daughter?"

"Well, when you put it that way, I would not."

"Well, then, check out the site. Are you staying to hear Kyle Od-ysseus?"

"Should I?"

"He's the future of this republic. And, hey—if you ever feel down or in need of a pick-me-up or just someone to talk to? Pray to KEK!"

I tipped my hat and moved along, eyeing the hate-lit set out on the table. *The Confessions of Nat Turner, Mein Kampf, The International Jew, Vigilantes of Christendom: The History of the Phineas Priesthood,* and assorted titles by Thomas Dixon, George Lincoln Rockwell, Alfred Rosenberg, Hermann Göring, Ludwig von Mises, H. P. Lovecraft.

On the "What You Should Be Reading" table I noted *Cuckservative: How "Conservatives" Betrayed America; Kill All Normies: Online Culture Wars from 4Chan and Tumblr to Trump and the Alt-Right; Barbarians: How Baby Boomers, Immigration, and Islam Screwed My Generation; Black Lies Matter;* and *¡Adios, America! The Left's Plan to Turn Our Country into a Third-World Hellhole.*

The blue tent was crowded with card tables set up as information centers for various California far-right organizations. I was surprised by how many there were.

"More than any other state," said a young blond woman. She rose from her chair and shook my hand. She wore a sleeveless navy dress and a diamond, ruby, and sapphire bracelet.

"Laurel Davis."

"Blake Hopper, Fallbrook."

"Enjoying the Power Hour?"

"My first time. Lots to see."

"Well," she said, "some of these groups represented here aren't much more than websites. But most of them do meet regularly, have dues and budgets and fund-raisers. Stated objectives and agenda.

We're the Institute for Historical Review of Newport Beach, and we don't deny the Holocaust, but we do question the numbers. Serious historians have been questioning them for decades."

"Do you have a different number?"

"There are several different accounting methods. Just as there are different ways to interpret the same historical events. Our research is continuing, of course, but right now we're at just under eight hundred twenty thousand confirmed Jewish dead."

"Low, isn't it?"

She held my gaze and pursed her lips. She wore diamond, ruby, and sapphire earrings to match the bracelet. She looked like a Fourth of July magazine cover.

"Low?" she asked. "Well, I'll admit that after eighty years of academic, governmental, and Zionist brainwashing aimed at people like you and me, it can be easy to believe so. But if that number offends you . . . like I said, we're finding out new things all the time."

"No offense at all," I said. "I studied some history in college when I wasn't surfing. Only got a BS, but I did learn that the past is constantly being revised. It's human nature. Sometimes they get it right and sometimes they get it wrong."

"That's why we exist," she said with a small smile. "To get it *right*."

"I should have seen that one coming."

"Here's a flyer and a link to us," she said. "We do important work. We are not the Hysterical Review, as lib pundits like to say. We do not hide anything. Not all conservatives are low-IQ knuckle-draggers like some of these people. Come to our site. Listen and learn. We accept Bitcoin donations and good American greenbacks."

"You're persuasive. But save the paper."

She gave me a nod and a look that concluded she couldn't help me, sighed, and put the flyer back on the table.

I continued my blue tent tour: *The Daily Stormer*, the Fraternal Order of Alt-Knights, The Right Stuff, Western Hammerskins, Patriot Front, Soldiers of Odin—LA/Ventura, Crew 38, Alamo Christian Foundation, Conservative's Forum, Jihad Watch of Sherman Oaks, Counter Jihad Coalition of Santa Monica, Traditional Values Coalition of Anaheim, ACT for America, San Diegans for Secure Borders.

Most of the reps were confident and well rehearsed in their pitches and opinions. There were a few knuckle-draggers, as Laurel had pointed out, but most of the White Power Hour presenters were young and well-groomed. They looked like normies themselves until they opened their mouths.

I wandered through a labyrinth of voices:

Martin Lucifer Coon was a fraud and a degenerate . . .

At the core of Jewish Identity is a malevolent supremacy . . . The root of the kike problem is of course sexual inferiority . . .

Stay in your own nations, we don't want you here . . .

Kyle Odysseus says it the best—Islam isn't just a religion, it's an economic, judicial, and military system, too . . .

Whites must be allowed to take their own side in their affairs . . .

Racism has had its day. It's over. The remaining chasms between blacks and whites are natural, biological, and can never be narrowed . . .

38

///////////////////////////

Alfred battle took the stage just before one. The crowd overflowed the shade of the white tent, leaving scores of people standing in the muggy monsoonal heat of the afternoon. I found shade under the less-crowded red tent just as a barrage of heavy raindrops hit the canvas above me and sent a ripple of surprise through the unprotected rally crowd. A moment later it stopped.

Battle stood at the lectern in his heavy brown suit, silver-haired and gaunt. He looked uneasy. Said a few words about the white race ceasing to be the dominant race on earth and likely extinct within a century, perhaps two. This would be a "bleak and self-inflicted catastrophe." And if you didn't believe him, read his book.

Next, he had some advice for his beleaguered race.

"As my writings explain," he said, "our solution is simple in concept, clear in design, and certain to be effective. SNR."

I perked up. At last: the mysterious initials explained.

"Segregate, Nullify, Remove. The inferior. The infidel. The dark and savage, the addicted and addled, the perverted, the weak and the malformed. And so, too, their white enablers, these beautiful children of privilege and Hollywood and Satan. Segregate them. Nullify them. Remove them. Also."

The applause was polite. He shuffled his papers nervously until the applause trailed off.

"But I am an old man," said Battle. "Listen now to tomorrow. God bless you all, and bless this once great nation."

Odysseus looked thirty. Wavy brown hair and a boy's face. Sleek in a trim black suit and a skinny black tie.

"It's difficult to retake and redirect the modern narrative," he said. A clear voice with a measured tone. "But we're going to have to. I'm Kyle Odysseus, a middle-class Orange County, California, boy. My real last name is Smith. But to best redirect one's self, sometimes you need to rename yourself. An ontological fine point, but nonetheless true. We become what we imagine. When I got out of college I traveled the world. I didn't just go to the places people think are pretty or important. I saw it all. I went through thousands of dollars and six pairs of boots. And when I came back I felt like Odysseus returning home from Troy. Kind of tired and pissed off. And like him, when I looked around at my quaint suburban home and tried to recognize the loyal girl who used to be my friend and partner, I was appalled. She had surrendered to sloth and narcissism. I saw the self-absorbed, money-stunned drones who used to be my friends, openly consorting with the black and the brown and the swarthy and the pederasts and the mad. I wanted to slaughter them all. Are you people listening? Do you even fucking hear what I'm saying?"

Whistles and war whoops.

"And slaughter them we must. With their own swords. Let's start with the federal government of the United States of America . . ."

While Kyle Odysseus started in on "our hypocritically egalitarian one-party system," I looked out past the crowd at the old yellow house falling to the ivy and a swimming pool with the patio furniture covered and the big sloping orange grove that continued all the way down the hillside to the road. I saw the cops turning cars away. The protesters were still at it. The old woman with the hat and gloves stooped out of sight for a moment, then rose again amid the scraggly trees, looking up. The rain again thundered into the tent top above me for a few seconds, then again stopped.

I sidled out the back, meandered down to the parking area like a disappointed rallygoer, then cut downslope and into the dripping orange grove. Slipped my sunglasses into my shirt pocket.

Midway to the woman, I took cover under a tree and waited to see if I'd been followed. Raindrops dripped from the trees, silver in the gray day. A distant blaze of lightning far in the south. A grumble of thunder. No one behind me. All fascinated by Kyle Smith, aka Kyle Odysseus, aka a voice for white America. I turned and saw the woman putting something into a white bucket.

I sidestepped down the hill toward her, calling out.

"Marie? Marie Knippermeir?"

She looked at me and set down the bucket. Put her white-gloved hands on her hips as I approached.

"Marie?"

"Yes?"

I took off my hat in a show of manners. "I was hoping I'd find you here. I'm Blake Hopper, with the Family Values Coalition, up in Fallbrook. One of Alfred's groups."

"I love Fallbrook."

"So do I. I like this rain, too."

"Beautiful, isn't it?"

We talked for a few minutes about rain and lack of rain, as Southern Californians often do. I saw that her bucket was about half full of reasonably good-looking oranges. I noted that the ground around us was littered with shriveled, squirrel-chewed fruit, some of it dried black and hard.

"Do you need some help?" I asked. "Looks like lots of fruit to pick."

"I prefer to work alone. Do you enjoy the White Power Hours?"

"This is my first," I said. "We're hoping to get more funding from Alfred, but a lot of hands are out."

"Hate is so expensive," she said. "But worth it to Alfred. He loves his work. He'll die at his desk. Or maybe in a tent. But that's not a cheerful thought."

Under the brim of her big hat, her face was plump and her complexion rosy. Eyes like little blue pools. "What does your group believe in?"

"Exactly that—family values."

"I love family values. Pies and picnics and—when they list the American boys killed in action on PBS? I tear up."

A cheer came from the crowd on top of the hill. As it trailed off, Odysseus's amplified words cut through. Something about "the only meaningful thing Muslims have ever done in America is 9/11!" before the applause flooded over his voice again.

I looked up to see two chinos-and-golf-shirt SNR men staring down at me.

Time to nudge this along. "You like beautiful homes, don't you?" I asked.

"What do you mean?"

"Beautiful properties, like this one. And the House of Fallen Angels in Mexico."

"Why do you ask?"

"We're interested in renting the House of Fallen Angels for a Family Values Coalition retreat," I said. "It has everything we need, except an affordable price. It's one of the things I wanted to talk to Alfred about today."

The two golf-shirted men had become three, still looking my way.

"It's very expensive and far from here," said Marie.

"True, it's a long flight to Cabo. And the Fallbrook FVC isn't exactly drowning in money."

"So much comes down to money with these nervous little haters," said Marie. "Last month at the White Power Hour, our keynote speaker was hawking autographed T-shirts and coffee mugs with his picture on them. Not just a logo. *His face.* But you seem different. Are you?"

I looked up for the men. Still there. "Something closer to Fallbrook would be less expensive, too. For our retreat, I mean."

"When I was young I was idealistic," said Marie. "I married the prettiest, loveliest man. He died of a disease they didn't have a name for yet. He got his own lymphoma named for him and I got a dead husband. Alfred has been miraculous, though. I had no business marrying him at my age, and being crazy. Or so they say. He's much kinder than he looks. Empathetic, too, which is unusual in someone who hates people different than himself. He was raped as a child. He still screams when he dreams. Don't tell him I told."

"Never."

"What was it you were talking about?"

"Renting a beautiful property for a Family Values Coalition retreat," I said. "It's in April of next year. We have a respectable budget, but not a fortune."

The men started down the embankment, heading for the grove, one of them on his phone.

"Come closer," said Marie.

I stopped in front of her. I could hear the distant crunch of the men moving through dead leaves. Marie lifted a white-gloved hand to my face, put her thumb on the hollow of one cheek and stretched her fingers to the other, bridging my mouth with her palm. Her small blue eyes seemed to have iced over. Pupils like pinheads. She turned my face to the left. To the right. Then stared at me straight on.

"What do you want?"

"A good deal on a luxury property. To rent for our retreat."

"I see no hate in you," she said. "But someone has given you a good old-fashioned beating. I'll bet you're plotting something. What? Quickly, Mr. Hooper—what are you plotting!"

"It's Hopper."

"They're coming, Hopper. Answer me!"

"Vengeance."

"Is that a family value?"

"There are some family values in my vengeance, yes."

She let go of my face, stood back, and picked up her bucket. I could hear the men closing in. A burst of rain. I put my hat on. The downpour swiftly turned to a drizzle. I shook the water off my hat, put it back on again.

"Rain in Eden," said Marie.

"Do you have a rental for me or not?"

She looked hurt. "Possibly. I bought another lovely property just recently. It's where a cotton field used to be, up north in San Clemente, I think. I was there for a while. But Alfred brought me back down here last week because he needed it for something."

"I wonder what."

"Alfred doesn't tell me all his business," said Marie. "I'm just his bank. And a good one I am. You two can talk about a fair price. But I am willing to rent our property to your group, Mr. Hopper. I do have some sway here. I like what I see in you. And what I don't."

Through the dripping orange trees the three golf shirts approached, well watered by the last monsoonal dump.

"Marie, is this man bothering you?"

"Not at all. We were just conducting a little business. You look familiar."

"Jason, ma'am. And Bo and Miller."

"Jason and the Argonauts! I remember you."

They were young and fit, and their drenched shirts were tucked in, their half-soaked khakis pressed. I could see on their faces that they were eager to get at me. But no evidence that they knew who I was.

"Mister," said Jason. "Alfred told us to keep the rally crowd in the tent area and off his private property. Last month there was some damage and possibly theft. So, please, let Mrs. Battle pick her oranges. And you come with us now."

I put my hat back on and tipped it to Marie Battle. She smiled and gave me a little wave, brief, half secret.

I started back up the hill, surrounded by Jason and the Argonauts.

"What the fuck are you doing down here?" asked Jason.

"I'm with the Family Values Coalition of Fallbrook," I said. "We're looking for a retreat rental. Something nearby and afforda—"

"Talk to Alfred Battle. He runs the show. Don't pick on Marie. She's got enough problems without shitballs like you trying to pick her pockets. You want something special from Mr. Battle, go to 4chan and get in line with the other phonies. In fact, when we get to the parking lot, you get in your car and get the hell out of here."

"Tell Mr. Battle I enjoyed the rally."

"Beat it, asshole."

39

////////////////////////

G RANDPA DICK's convincing City of San Clemente emblems, attached to both flanks of a rented white Malibu, and a city
Building Services Department business card he'd counterfeited were
enough to get Gerald Mason past the Cyprus Shore security booth.

Dick had worked extra-hard on the vehicle signs, especially on
the city seal. If prosecuted and convicted for this risky trick, he could
draw a hefty judgment for defrauding the public, impersonating a
public official, and copyright infringement, and I could lose my license for five years for conspiracy to defraud.

To up my chances of success with guards who might well have
seen me two days earlier, I'd dyed my dark brown hair. Melinda and
Liz said it now looked like vanilla-caramel-swirl ice cream. I'd added
a realistic costume mustache. And there I was, Gerald Mason: big,
bad, and blond. In chinos, a golf shirt, and a blazer, no less. I could
have applied for work with SNR, helped them segregate, nullify, and
remove those pesky mud people from the rest of us.

At Cotton Point Estates, I had to explain to a tough American
Response guard that a homeowner confined to her house with dis-
abilities had requested city building code requirements and fees and
didn't want her name on the guest list. Worried about the neighbors,

I noted. The guard was a woman. Ruthven. She squinted at me skeptically, the morning sun in her eyes. I lifted my aluminum citation keeper clipboard for her to see—a souvenir from my days in traffic control, many moons ago. The gate rolled open.

Sixteen estates. Sixteen chances to discover if one of them might be Daley Rideout's plush prison. My most recent visits to IvarDuggans, just hours earlier, had once again yielded no clue as to which mansion might belong to Marie Knippermeir, if any actually did at all. I clung to the hope that she had amplified the Cotton Point development to "where a cotton field used to be, up in San Clemente."

If Melinda Day was right, and luck was just an invisible hole into which you might or might not step, then my chances of seeing Daley, or any solid link to Daley, were poor. But if luck is something you make, as I have come to believe, and I could find a way to keep from drawing attention to myself, I might be able to beg, borrow, and steal enough minutes to find her place of luxury internment.

So I hid in plain sight, with the zoom Olympus under my blazer on the passenger seat, just in case. Toured the 'hood, as if looking for an address, working east to west, starting with Via Calandria. My computer search had given me three estates offered for sale that I could likely cross off the list. Price range $5 million to $44 million.

Down to thirteen, just like that.

On Calle Isabella, a dashing redhead in a Porsche convertible swept out of the circular driveway of a Neopolitanesque mansion. Justine had been a dashing redhead once, and had driven a Porsche, too. I pulled over and watched the woman and the car, a painful knot in my throat. Waved politely, as did she. Thought about Justine. Four years and five months. It's harder to picture her now. Not that the images fade, but there are fewer of them to choose from. Some stay.

Some go. They vanish slowly, like snapshots left in the sun. It's how you move forward.

Down to twelve.

From another Calle Isabella home, an older couple walked arm-in-arm under the porte cochere, supporting each other equally toward a black Lincoln Navigator.

Beside a French country extravaganza on Calle Lisa was a blue tennis court surrounded by languorous palms. An instructor fed volleys to a woman at the net. The pro stopped to demonstrate a proper split step, racquet up and out and ready to carve, knees bent. The woman tried, seemed to be getting it.

Ten. Probably.

A young mom ran a stroller down a driveway on Calle Louisa.

Squads of gardeners, rakes raking and blowers blowing. Pool cleaners. A laundry-service van.

On Calle Marlena, two boys flipped a white lacrosse ball back and forth on a big green lawn.

Onward to Calle Ariana, back up to Via Calendria, then onto Calle Isabella again.

By eleven o'clock I had eliminated two more estates, leaving me with six.

I pulled into the shade of a huge coral tree outside one of them, set my lunch bag on the passenger seat, and cracked an energy drink. I set my phone in the cup holder, hoping for wasp-cam action. The less activity we saw at Paradise Date Farm, the more it bothered me.

A text message from Penelope:

Dreamed of you last night. Actually
a rhinoceros in Armani, kind of a

swanky wild-animal thing, but the
rhino was you and we danced and we
were quite good together in spite of
the horn, which at the end of the dance
I swung on like on a jungle gym when I
was a happy girl all those light-years
ago. Don't worry. Freud was right.
Sometimes a rhino horn is just a rhino
horn. Get it? Where is my girl?
Please bring her to me now. Been too
long. I miss her. Make her be here, Roland Ford.

THE SILVER SNR EXPEDITION approached from behind me at 11:48 a.m. I saw it coming in the rearview and faced away as it went by. When it turned onto Calle Marlena I started up my Malibu and slowly followed. Entries and exits are what cook you as a follower. As I eased onto Calle Marlena I saw the SUV pull into the circular drive of a formidable two-story block mansion, headed for the porte cochere. The porte cochere was laced by mandevilla vines, abundant with pink blooms.

I couldn't sit there in the middle of the street, so I crept along, riding the brakes with my clipboard up, looking around as if lost. The Expedition parked. Connor Donald and Eric Glassen headed toward the front porch and an enormous wood-and-iron door. Donald pushed a ringer, and a long moment later Adam Revell pulled open the big door and let his compatriots inside. I caught a glimpse of the foyer, a rustic iron chandelier and a stone wall with sconces leading toward sunlight. Noted the address as I drove by.

I circled back to the shade of the coral tree and finished my lunch.

Stayed as long as I thought I could without drawing unwanted attention from the residents.

Without worrying Ruthven.

Feeling the luck. Whether I'd made it or fallen into it didn't matter. I believed I was onto something good.

Believed for a few more fruitless hours.

BACK THE NEXT morning. The same guards believed the same story but gave me different looks. Ruthven looked ready to challenge me but stood down. I was pressing my luck, but it would have been worse to show up with my third version in five days.

I passed by Marie Knippermeir's stone-block mansion and parked in a shaded parklike border between a Venetian canal house and a Castilian manse. I had a good view of Marie's place, where two SNR vehicles waited under the porte cochere.

Sipped my coffee and kept an eye on the house, and on my phone in the cup holder. Cameras one and two picked up a Paradise Date Farm truck as it lumbered through the barnyard. Then, after the requisite sixty seconds of inactivity, went black. But when nine o'clock rolled around—the time when the SNR "school" was usually busy with students, moms, and dads—there was no streaming video at all. Had the wasp-cams been discovered? Run out of power? Had SNR shut the school down? Why?

Over the next two hours I moved my bogus City of San Clemente vehicle to three different locations, keeping Marie's estate in view and trying not to draw the attention of the locals.

Saw the same landscape workers and pool cleaners I'd seen the day before but working at different properties. The woman hit with her tennis pro. No lacrosse boys on the big green lawn.

At about noon a brightly colored pizza truck brought lunch to an estate just south of Marie's on Calle Marlena. A few minutes later the redhead in her Porsche headed up Via Calandria on her way out of Cotton Point Estates.

It was one o'clock when a shiny black Mercedes AMG sedan swept into Marie's driveway and parked in the shade. Reggie Atlas sprang out and headed for the door. He was dressed in his preaching duds: jeans and white running shoes and a white open-collared shirt. I shot him with the Olympus, shutter sound off. He rang the doorbell and ran a hand through his thatch of heavy blond hair. Waited awhile, checked his watch. Adam Revell finally opened the door and Atlas went inside without conversation. The chandelier and the foyer leading to sunlight flashed briefly, then vanished behind the door of wood and iron.

Alfred Battle arrived less than five minutes later in his Caddy, parked behind the black sedan, and hoisted his tall, thin body from the car with the help of a handle. I took a shot of him as well. He straightened, buttoned his brown suit coat over his shirt and tie. Strode to the door in well-shined wingtips. The door opened and Connor Donald was at his service. I took a shot of him, too.

Two hours went by. I didn't take my eyes off that front door except to check my phone for Paradise activity. Quiet again out there. I wondered what Lark was planning. I knew it would be swift, thorough, and adequately powered—federal-style. I doubted I would be a part of it, though I surely wanted to be. It might be my best chance for a rematch with six men I'd come to despise.

Reggie Atlas came out alone and angry. He slammed the heavy door with both hands and plenty of muscle. I got a couple more good shots. He threw open the door of his Mercedes, stepped inside, and slammed it, too. I watched him head up Calle Marlena toward Avenida de las Palmeras and the exit.

Ten minutes later Battle emerged, unbuttoning his suit coat on the way to his car. He was flanked by Donald and Revell, who held open the door of Battle's CTS. Three more shots with my shutter on silent. When the tall old man had retracted all of himself inside, Revell closed the door and gave a curt salute.

I waited awhile, pondering. Wondering if Daley Rideout really was inside that house. All they had to do was keep her on the grounds, away from phones and computers, and there wasn't much she could do. Keep her from screaming out for help. If she even wanted to leave that badly. But did she? If not quite badly enough, they could always take her down to the beach when she got bored. Out for a good meal now and then. I wondered if they were drugging her. They could have strung her out by now. Locked behind the bars of a narcotic.

And every question led to another: Were Battle and his SNR men keeping her for Reggie? Or *from* him? Had Battle just allowed him a visit? If so, for what purpose?

I knew what Penelope's answer would be. It was a terrible possibility, and I was in no position to refute it. Why would Battle let the preacher do such a thing? Were they charging him for her use?

But Reggie claimed he needed Daley Rideout to prove his innocence. Was that all bluff? What if he'd drugged, raped, and impregnated Penelope Rideout exactly as she'd described? Then threatened violence to keep her silent? In that case, if Battle turned Daley over to Atlas, she would be the living proof of his crimes. And when he was done with Daley, he would have to silence her.

EVENING. TRADESMEN, GARDENERS, and servicepeople leaving in their trucks and vans. Citizens returning in their premium rides. I half expected Ruthven to track me down, driven by boredom and suspicion. Maybe she'd gone home. Or maybe I'm easily forgotten.

Okay. I was hungry. Needed a bourbon.

I had just started up the Malibu when the big wood-and-iron door opened and Connor Donald stepped into the shade of the porte cochere.

Followed by Eric Glassen and Adam Revell, flanking Daley Rideout. She was dressed in shorts and flip-flops and her "I'm not as stupid as I look—Are you?" sweatshirt.

She wore her backpack, carried her little guitar in its gig bag with one hand and pulled a piece of rolling luggage behind her with the other. Her posture was good, her attitude calm.

Where are you going?

I got two shots before the silver SUV swallowed them up and shuddered to life. Traded my camera for my phone and called Sergeant Ionides. Gave him the actors and the make, model, and plates as the Expedition rolled onto Calle Marlena. Told him the three men were likely armed. Ordered my hands *away from the steering wheel* so I wouldn't do something foolish like follow them. I couldn't put Daley Rideout in that kind of danger. At least Ionides could light a fire under Dispatch and they'd get the Orange County sheriffs into action as fast as was departmentally possible.

Departmentally possible.

Which wouldn't be fast enough. The SUV curved out of sight up Marlena. Seconds from now, the SNR men and Daley Rideout would be exiting Cotton Point Estates onto Palmera, just blocks from an interstate highway serving 28.3 million Southern Californians, armies of tourists, and legions of big rigs.

I saw a way to pry Daley away from SNR.

Thought I did.

40

////////////////////////

Hᴵɢʜ on the hill I saw houselights on in Alfred Battle's slouching, ivy-coated home. The winding road through the orange trees was weakly lit. I kept an eye on it for a few minutes while sending three of my Olympus pictures to my phone—one of Battle, one of Reggie, one of Daley and her handlers.

I pressed the intercom and Marie answered.

"Mrs. Battle, this is Blake Hopper, with Fallbrook Family Values Coalition. I talked to you at the Power Hour on Sunday, and you offered to lease me one of your properties for our annual retreat. I was hoping you and Mr. Battle might be willing discuss it."

"You're who?"

I repeated some of my pitch. Heard Battle's stern voice in the background.

"Oh, of course!" said Marie. "Come up, Mr. Hooper."

"Thank you, Marie. It's *Hopper*."

The gate squealed into action and I saw a porch light come on. Followed my headlights up the hill. Parked up near a detached garage in which Battle's stealthy CTS waited in the dark.

Marie welcomed me in. She wore a powder-blue fifties house dress with white buttons and pocket trim, and a new pair of Jack

Purcell sneakers. Hair up, eyes blue and joyful. She led me through a small foyer, then into a faintly lit living room. Mid-century and lots of it—a burnished walnut floor, pale turquoise walls, white acoustic ceiling. Trim chocolate fabric sofas, a glass coffee table, and bulbous avocado-green space-age lamps with abstract atomic-print shades. Bookshelves on three walls, an entertainment center with an enormous TV/stereo cabinet with sliding fabric panels. Marie offered me one end of a long brown sofa, and she took the other.

Alfred, draped in his bespoke brown suit, sat in a low-slung green orange-slice chair, his legs spread wide and his big bony hands on his thighs. The space-age lamplight caught one side of his face and left the other in shadow.

"Ford," he said. "I thought that was you at the Hour."

"You've got good eyes for an old man."

A suggested smile. "All the better to read about you in the papers. Deputy Roland Ford, the indecisive triggerman in the death of Titus Miller. PI Ford, widowed by a whimsical God and a plane accident. Later, the slayer of a celebrity torturer. Most recently, the executioner of two very dangerous terrorists, saving countless innocent lives. Thank you for that, Mr. Ford. They were Muslim scum."

"Glad to be of service," I said.

"This is all very exciting," said Marie.

"What did you think of the White Power Hour, Mr. Ford?"

"I thought it was interesting how the dinosaurs like you led the way for the new generation of haters like Odysseus," I said.

"Spencer and Enoch have learned much from the post–Arab Spring Europeans," said Battle. "We didn't have that same perspective when I was young. We were still looking for the Soviets under every rock. We forgot about the mud people, who the Soviets turned against us so nimbly. We failed to react strongly enough, or there wouldn't be any need for the alt-right today. If we could only have continued the lynchings, expanded them north to include browns and later Muslims, this would be a healthier and more prosperous republic. We softened."

"You didn't get soft, you got whupped," I said. "By people who were better than you."

Battle sighed and adjusted his long frame in the ridiculous-looking orange-slice chair. Smiled bitterly: "Frauds and adulterers. They all claim to have a dream. We don't dream. We have a stated goal. We want to be free in the country that we founded. We want a country in which the white child has opportunity again and is respected as the superior child that he is. If this sounds familiar, it should. It is the foundation of the United States Constitution."

"I thought you were very odd from the beginning, Mr. Hooper," said Marie. "But that's okay. I collected six pounds of oranges that day."

"They're good ones, too, Marie," said Battle. "Now, what can I do for you, Mr. Ford?"

"I want Daley Rideout."

"Then explain who she is, and why you want her, and why I'm in a position to help you."

"Daley is the younger sister and the legal charge of one Penelope Rideout. Daley might be her daughter—maybe—if you're willing to expand your field of interest to your pal Reggie Atlas. Either way, I want to return Daley to Penelope. As you know, your SNR meatballs are holding her."

"Oh?" asked Marie.

"My reaction exactly," said Alfred. He crossed his legs, then interlocked his finger over the top knee.

I showed the three pictures on my phone to Alfred and Marie and sat back down.

Marie frowned at her husband.

"I'm sure you're aware that Daley is all over the Missing and Exploited Children websites," I said.

"But we never appear in the same frame in your pictures," he said. "I had no idea the girl was in my wife's house. Mrs. Battle owns too many homes for me to keep track of."

"You're free to tell that to the fed, state, and local cops," I said. "But these photos are still enough to get you one phone call to a lawyer."

Battle slowly rose, turned his back on me, and walked to a south-facing window.

"If I could deliver the girl to you, you would destroy these photos and say nothing of my company's involvement?"

"The pictures are already in the cloud, Mr. Battle. And my associates know what to do with them."

"Have you been hired by Penelope to find Dolly and bring her back?"

"Good guess. Her name is Daley."

"Pays well, I hope," he said.

"Standard fee."

"May I ask what your rates are?"

"You can ask all you want."

A decisive silence.

"Why does Reggie Atlas want Daley?" I asked. "And why are you allowing him to see her?"

Battle turned, raising a bushy eyebrow, his hawk's face half-illuminated. "If I tell you what I know, will you leave me and Marie and SNR out of your dealings with the police?"

"No," I said. "Although it would dispose me in your favor."

"To what end?"

"Probably none at all. Your ass is cooked, sir."

"When your ass is cooked, make s'mores," said Marie.

Alfred smiled at her, then looked at me. "I love my wife."

"I see why."

"You two," said Marie.

"Ford," said Battle, "exactly what Reggie wants with the girl was never clear to me."

"You should have made it clear," I said. "She's fourteen."

"She plays guitar in her room all day," said Battle. "She hasn't said one meaningful word to me. But, according to Reggie, that girl has been showing up at his church for about a year. Seeking time with him. Making herself . . . available. For what? Reggie fears sexual intent. This behavior is much like her sister, Penelope's, years ago, Reggie says. But Penelope's advances went much further. He rejected her, of course. But shortly thereafter, she suffered a psychotic break with reality—professing that Reggie had seduced and impregnated her. With a baby everybody knew was her own sister. There is some suspicion in Reggie's mind of Penelope's role in the death of her parents, also. There was insurance money at stake. At any rate, Penelope followed Atlas all around the country, wherever his ministry took him, hounding him, demanding money. He has paid her handsomely. Many times. Simple blackmail, effective because of the pastor's public life and extraordinary success. Of course he's offered a final arrangement, and a nondisclosure agreement, but it must include a confidential paternity test, which is exactly what she does not want. End of revenue stream for Penelope. Reggie is very aware that one tweet from her to #MeToo would damage his ministry immeasurably. He's hoping Daley might be able to talk some sense to her sister. And that is what I know about Pastor Atlas's motivations and the girl."

Marie left the room. Alfred watched her go, his face silhouetted in the lamplight.

"Your men took Daley," I said.

Battle looked out a darkened window and said nothing.

"Let me refresh your memory," I said. "SNR Security men took her away from her boyfriend's condo in Encinitas. They executed him in bed. I was the one who found him. Nick Moreno."

"Mud," said the old man. "Consorting with white. Abomination. I know from experience."

Battle gave me a flat stare. I wondered if what Marie had said about a childhood rape was true. Or if she had only been on one of her flights of fancy, making s'mores.

"Here's what I think," I said. "You've known Atlas for years. Like-minded individuals. So you knew his story about crazed Penelope and her sister. Which started ringing false when he took a personal interest in Daley, not the other way around. He offered donations to the White Power Hour if SNR could bring Daley to him. Not a tough assignment, really, for your boys. She even went along for the ride, at first. Literally. A rebellious girl, coming into her own. Eager to get away from her controlling sister. Then your fund-raiser's light went on—why give Reggie what he wants until you've made him pay even more? Keep Daley and raise her price. So Atlas remains *your* revenue stream, but you have to let him see her once in a while. Proof of life. Like today at Cotton Point."

Battle beheld me in the half-light. "We always need funding. And note, the girl has never been in danger. She has always been free to go. My men are upright, moral, and trustworthy."

"Nick Moreno might disagree. And every time Daley slips her leash, your men grab her again."

"They are protecting her from herself."

Marie came back with three glasses of milk on a round tray. Three coasters and three cloth napkins. I set mine on the glass coffee table before me. Alfred sat again, pushed the napkin between his buttoned collar and his wattled neck, then took his glass with an appreciative nod. Marie returned to the far end of the sofa.

"What happened today when Atlas came to Cotton Point?" I asked.

"Happened?"

"As in, what did you do?"

"We socialized as adults. Sat in the living room and talked about current events. Sports, too, of course. Exchanged ideas. One of my SNR employees, Adam, is an excellent cook. Today was broiled ahi, asparagus, and Tater Tots."

"Was Atlas alone with Daley?"

"I don't allow it," said Battle. "I'm not sure I trust him."

"You all talked and had lunch?" I asked.

"And Pastor Atlas led us in prayer. That is the absolute truth."

"How did he behave toward Daley?" I asked.

"He was formal. Per usual. He told her once again that he only needs to satisfy some final obligations, and she'll be free to go with him. They sat well apart from each other. But often, he looked at her with an affection—an adoration, I'd say—that was downright embarrassing to everyone in the room but him. Not the first time."

I weighed what I knew about spirited Daley Rideout against this strange account. "How did she react?"

"She seems both repelled by and drawn to him," said Battle. "A girl, then not a girl. They are very similar, psychologically. Like magnets. With their polarities opposed, they attract. But when aligned, they repel."

"As men and women always do," said Marie. She smiled, drank some milk, dabbed her lips.

This alleged afternoon at Cotton Point was hard for me to

picture. The hatemonger, the preacher, the gunmen, and the girl. A storm of crosscurrents, most of them vile.

"Have you ever talked to Penelope?" I asked.

Battle shook his head, sipped his milk, and waited.

"I have," I said. "Let me give you something to think about. Penelope told me something. It was difficult for her, and I have no good reason to disbelieve her. She's known Reggie Atlas since she was eight. With her family, she attended his services and guest appearances. He was building his congregation. Six years. During which time he developed a faith-based relationship with her mom and dad, and especially with Penelope herself. It included one-on-one conversations, phone calls, emails, and an occasional postcard from Reggie's itinerant preaching. Over the years he convinced her that their relationship was special in the eyes of Jesus. Sacred. She wholeheartedly agreed. When she was fourteen and a virgin, he invited her into his travel bus, where he baptized, seduced, drugged, and raped her. The morning-after pills failed. Daley was born nine months later. Atlas has been keeping track of her and his daughter ever since. Penelope hasn't been shaking him down for money. She's been trying to keep his daughter away from him. Fearing that he will repeat himself with her."

"True monsters always do," said Marie. "I think I read that story in a book once. Some tragic Greek? The Bible, maybe?"

"Interesting," said Battle.

"It's a helluva lot more than just interesting," I said.

Shadow and light on Battle's hate-carved face. Something like pain. "Do you think that's true? Penelope's story?"

"I think it is."

"Oh."

Again, pain on the Old Hawk's face. Penelope's story must have gotten to him. Alfred Battle: moral hater.

Marie collected the glasses and napkins, left the coasters. She winked at me as she made for the kitchen. I heard her set the glasses on the counter.

"Where are they taking Daley?" I asked. "She had her things when they left."

"That brings us to a crossroads, doesn't it?" asked Battle.

"Here's your crossroads, Alfred—I want the girl and you're out of time. Where are they taking her?"

"I own a compound in the desert," said Battle. "As you know, it's difficult to find and has good security. Daley will be safe there."

He squinted at me and smiled fractionally—gauging my fear of returning to Paradise Date Farm. I felt fear, even with Battle as my shield. I also smelled revenge. And, more important, a chance to parse the riddles of the wasp-cams.

"Why not keep her at Cotton Point?" I asked. "Two guard gates. Tough to crack."

"You managed to find her," said Battle. "In truth, I had a premonition that you hadn't gone away. In spite of your down-home welcome at Paradise. Maybe even because of it. Scent of revenge? SNR was proud to have felled a local hero."

"Proud of six on one?"

"I treat them like attack dogs," he said. "Always keep them a little hungry. Psychologically."

"Stand up."

"I'll need to make some calls."

"That's funny. Stand up, old man."

He worked himself up from the chair. Same height as me, gray raptor's eyes boring into mine. I reached inside his suit coat and felt for a gun. Faint smell of milk on his breath. A whiff of the same shave cream Grandpa Dick uses. Dad, too.

The weapon was napping in the small of his back, right side, where I carry mine. I broke it from the holster and held it out and away, taking hold of his necktie while I ran a boot-toe around his ankles for a second gun.

"I haven't been frisked in forty-eight years."

"Miss it?"

"I was contemplating a knee to your face. If you'd knelt down to check my ankles."

"Sorry to have missed that."

I stepped back and looked at the gun, a slim five-shot revolver with an enclosed hammer and a smooth front sight—great for concealment and snag-free on the draw. Old-fashioned and deadly, like its owner. Put it in my jacket pocket.

I heard Marie coming in from the kitchen, new sneakers squeaking, oddly slow in her approach. I turned and she stopped, a nail-studded baseball bat over one shoulder, ready, both hands choked way down on the grip.

"I implore you," she said.

"You disappoint me, Marie."

"I *so* don't mean to."

"Please give me the bat. By the handle. And sit back down where you were."

"Okey-dokey, Mr. Hooper."

I set the hideous club on the coffee table, a wave of adrenaline surging through me. Careful not to scratch the glass.

Took Alfred's phone, turned it off, and slipped it into my pocket.

"If Daley isn't at Paradise like you say, we'll just swing by the sheriff's station in Encinitas," I said. "Where I'll introduce you to Detective Sergeant Darrel Walker. Black dude, good cop. He'd love to see my Cotton Point pictures of you and Daley. He's already got the crime-scene shots of Nick Moreno. He'd enjoy bringing charges against a legendary white-supremacist geezer such as yourself."

"Proving charges could be difficult."

"So could dying in prison."

"Which is why I need assurance that once the girl is in your possession, you will not inform on me to law enforcement. A simple this for that."

"No assurance," I said. "But for tonight I'm your only hope of staying a free man, Alfred. Take me to the girl."

A heavy lift of eyebrow. "Would two hundred thousand dollars buy your silence regarding me and the girl and the boyfriend? Allowing your cop friends to focus on the actual actors—Connor, Adam, and Eric? I have the cash, right here on the property. Or Bitcoin, if you prefer. Almost impossible to trace, as you know."

I was disappointed but not surprised that Battle would so eagerly throw his men under the bus. I had to figure they would throw him under, too.

"You're driving," I said.

Extra sharpness in his eyes as he regarded his wife. "I'll be home shortly, Marie."

"Will you come to me by moonlight, though hell should bar the way?"

Battle looked at me. "That's from her other Alfred. Noyes, the poet. May I say goodbye?"

"Oh, take your time," I said. While Alfred and Marie hugged, I texted Burt and Lark, looking up to the Battles between letters. Alfred kissed her on the cheek. Her chin quivered. She rose and hugged him long and close, plump arms around his thin frame.

"Do nothing foolish, dear," he said. "Do nothing at all."

When he broke away and she looked at me, a tear rolled from her left eye. I looked at the nailed club on the coffee table and I tried to judge her capabilities against her madness. Close call.

"Marie," I said, "would you like to come along?"

"I will not endanger her in any way," said Battle.

"I thought you'd never ask!" said Marie.

I politely searched her for a phone or weapon, found neither. She smelled of lilac.

"That was a little personal," she said, smiling.

Outside, I took the battery out of Battle's phone, then locked them and his revolver in the big tool chest bolted to the bed of my truck.

We got in and closed the doors. Battle in the driver's seat, me on the passenger's side, Marie in back. She had her seat belt fastened first. I set my .45 on my lap and started the engine. Battle glanced at the gun, then adjusted the mirrors slightly. Marie looked through a window and waved goodbye to her house.

"Drive," I said.

We wound down through the orange grove toward Holiday Lane. "I expect some kind of help from you," said Battle. "SNR discovered a runaway girl. They did not abduct her. There was no force involved. No threats or coercion of any kind. They were protecting her from Reggie Atlas."

"Nick Moreno," I said.

"I knew nothing about him. I'd never heard his name until the news."

"Save all that for Darrel Walker."

"I will not be done in by a runaway girl and the timely removal of one muddy sexual predator."

"Don't count on it. What do you think about all this, Marie?" I asked.

"All what?"

41

////////////////////////////

A QUARTER-MOON rose over the In-Ko-Pah Mountains, boulders heaped in the dark. Imperial Valley ahead, heat rising and the brittlebush shivering in the wind. A red Cadillac Eldorado fell in behind me from S-2.

Battle drove the speed limit, eyes on the road and one bony hand relaxed way down at six o'clock on the wheel. He'd been telling me about his boyhood in Houston, his high school days in Yuma, his time in Korea as a rear gunner on a B-29, trying to shoot down MiG-15s the Russians had sold to North Korea. Marie had fallen asleep with her head against the window.

"I had eyes like a falcon back then," he said. "Twenty-ten, and a good sense of leads and trajectories from shooting doves in Arizona. They got me into that Superfortress in a hurry. We shot down two. I got some lead into both of them. Now we got Kias and Hyundais invading us. Should have pounded them to nothing like Japan. We'd have one big clean subservient nation under us. Instead of some nutcase with nukes and a bad haircut."

The heat rose when he hit the valley floor. Flat rows of crops fanning by, the smells of cut alfalfa and onions drawn into the cab by the AC.

Battle gave me a quick hard look, then turned back to the road. "You've got all the fixin's to become a red-blooded American patriot," he said. "A father in the Navy, mother a history teacher and a DAR. You served in Iraq, First Fallujah, if my IvarDuggans search is correct. Law enforcement. Now you're a sneaky PI. Charging money to commit unsavory acts. Deceiving a kindly older woman with a long history of mental illness. What happened to you?"

"I know phony indignation when I see it."

"So it's all okay, what you do?" asked Battle.

"When I can't sleep at night it's not from something I did," I said. "It's always from something I didn't."

"Hmm," he said. "Might your abrupt slide down the moral ladder have been caused by the fact that you should have killed that crazy nigger when you had the chance? Instead of letting your partner do it?"

I'd thought about that over the years, a lot. What I'd done and hadn't done on that cool cloudy day in an alley behind an Imperial Beach strip mall.

"If I could," I said, "I'd not kill him all over again. His name was Titus Miller and he wasn't armed."

"He had a gun in his belongings."

"Some yards away from him, not within his reach. Down in a cart that held all his worldly riches."

"Blah," said Battle. "Coward's talk. Hiding behind the least understood commandment of them all. You want to see true Christianity, get yourself a look at *Judith Beheading Holofernes* by Caravaggio."

"I've seen it. It has what to do with me?"

"It's got everything to do with bringing our race back to its natural leadership of the world," said Battle. "The rest of the world is Holofernes, Mr. Ford. You can see it in his dark, bestial, beheaded face. On some level you understand that. That you are superior. That you are Judith. But you're afraid of it. It offends you because you have been brainwashed into being offended."

I waved him off, indicating boredom. "Hate never changes," I said. "Just the packaging. Hitler. Spencer. Enoch. You. It's the same old whining."

"Hitler?" asked Marie, head bobbing off the window glass.

"How are you back there, hon?"

"Can you turn the AC down a little?"

I reached between the seats to the rear control, turned it down.

Then got another glance at me from the old man, the crags of his face deep in the dashboard glow.

"I need to pee," he said.

"You can pull over. The shoulder looks firm."

"There's a rest stop up ahead," he said.

"No. I don't want you out of my sight."

"He's too old to run," said Marie. "Look at all that dust."

Battle signaled and eased the truck onto the shoulder.

"Make it quick," I said.

"Settle down, now, Roland," said Battle.

We got out and Battle ambled into the desert in his brown suit, the wind whipping his coat. I leaned against the bed with a peripheral view of Marie and watched him. Wingtips raising sand. Read Lark's message: *Paradise search warrant and SWAT in hand.* I saw Battle stop, spread his legs, reach forward with both hands. Old men take a long time to pee. Maybe the wind was a factor. My high school buddy Dirk Ott went fifty-one seconds, no double-clutching, fueled by a twelve-pack. Battle finally turned, zipping up on his way back. The wind gusted and Battle teetered uncertainly.

———

HALF AN HOUR to turnoffs for Coyote Wells, Plaster City, Dixie-land. I felt my nerves rising and the clarity brought by fear. Battle got off on Rattlesnake, went east toward Buena Vista, and turned right onto the familiar dirt road that would take us to Paradise Date Farm.

"Know where you are?" he asked.

"Pretty much."

"I failed world geography," said Marie.

"Scared, Roland?" asked Battle.

"Some," I said.

"How many stitches?"

"A bunch."

"You must want a rematch," said Battle. "Revenge. One of the building blocks of civilization. I wish you were one of us."

"And so do I, Mr. Hooper!"

"You've got enough young men to order around," I said.

"You have a conscience, though."

"Is that good or bad in SNR Security?" I asked.

"It's good, Roland. My people are the deep and strong. The straight and true. Right belief. Right convictions. Right thought."

"There is only one right," said Marie.

"That's the nonsense that trips you people up every time," I said.

"There's the entrance," said Battle. "Oh, *damn*. What is this?"

I looked through the darkness to the faintly lit guard tower and the guardhouse and the twinkling chain-link fence.

Saw the white FBI Suburbans, the black-and-white Imperial County vehicles—six in all—and Mike Lark in a Bureau windbreaker and street clothes, waving us closer. In the side mirror, Burt's red Eldorado swept in from the darkness behind.

"You've betrayed me," said Battle.

"I told you I couldn't help you."

"For a fourteen-year-old runaway?" said Battle.

"And the crates you've been smuggling in from San Onofre."

"I have no idea what you're talking about."

"Let's go see about that, Alfred."

I pointed to the gate. He pulled behind Lark's Suburban, handed me the key fob, and shook his head. Lark started toward Alfred's side of the truck.

"This has federal overreach written all over it," said Battle.

"You're about to meet FBI Special Agent Mike Lark."

"Him? He looks like he's still in high school."

We climbed out of the truck and into the gusting wind. The Paradise Date Farm sign shuddered in place on the gate, and the desert dust swirled in the cones of the floodlights.

Introductions made and search warrant served, Battle agreed to lead us onto his property. He entered the code and the tall steel-pole gate opened on squeaky wheels. When he turned to face the rest of us, a dozen headlights blanched his face.

Marie was boarded into the back of an armored sheriff's Bearcat, accepting a hand up from a hefty black deputy. No sooner had Lark ushered Battle into his Suburban than Burt slipped into my truck, a red PGA windbreaker twice his size billowing around him.

"This is going to be a good one," he said. "It's got some O.K. Corral going for it."

"What I want," I said, "is Daley Rideout in one piece."

42

///////////////////////////

The road to Paradise was dirt washboard that kept our speeds down and a steady blizzard of dust blown by the vehicles ahead. I wore shooting glasses against the wind and sand, yellow lenses for low light. We were fourth back, behind the Bureau Suburbans, and ahead of the sheriff. I guessed ten FBI agents, including their SWAT, and ten deputies.

No surveillance drones in the sky that I could see. The gusting wind would keep them down, ditto law enforcement helicopters, in case Lark and the sheriffs had any airborne ideas.

The old boxing scar on my forehead burned, and the swirling black night seemed to sneer at my hopes. I wondered if Battle had fooled me. If his bargaining over Daley was cover for luring me away from her. And into an SNR ambush. Burt had sensed it, thus his Tombstone remark. And why not a trap? Battle had known full well that I'd deliver him to the police. His $200,000 hush money having failed, maybe an ambush was his only option. Send me to the sandman. Literally. Plenty of places out in this desert where the pesky PI would never be found. Ashes to ashes and sand to sand. *Not too deep, boys. Let the sun and the critters do their work.*

I had assumed that my multiagency backup would surprise him. Feds, no less. But maybe SNR had standing plans for such a raid.

We pulled into the floodlit center of the compound, the buildings forming a loose circle around us. Lark dropped to the ground, then Battle, who buttoned his coat in his oddly formal way and stood facing the farmhouse. The rest of us scrambled from our vehicles as a unit, everyone but Marie.

The farmhouse door swung open and out marched Connor Donald, followed by Eric Glassen and Adam Revell. Each wore chinos and black golf shirts and yellow shooting glasses, and each carried an M4 machine gun on a sling over his shoulder.

The shuffle of guns, safeties, and slides. My hand back and ready. Burt with his feet spread, the windbreaker rippling.

The three SNR men stopped ten feet short of their boss.

"Bring out the girl," he said.

"Yes, sir," said Donald, raising an open hand into the air.

Daley stepped onto the front porch between Flat-Top Woman and Tattooed Forearms, guns on their hips as before.

She wore the same shorts, flip-flops, and comedy hoodie. Same backpack. She pulled her rolling carry-on behind her and carried her backpacker guitar in its gig bag.

My heart sank.

She was ready for me.

They were ready for me.

Battle had ordered them to have her ready to go. How and when?

And what else had he ordered?

A rifle shot cracked from the darkness behind us and a sheriff's deputy pitched forward. I hit the dirt as Daley broke away into the darkness and Flat-Top Woman and Tattooed Forearms drew their guns and were cut down by agents and deputies not thirty feet away. The Bearcat tore back toward the gate.

Then a barrage of fire from the main house, and more from the barn and the metal hangar and the row of bunkhouses behind us. Slugs clanged into the FBI Suburban and the sheriff's vehicles, sparks flying and windows collapsing in the twang of ricochets. Battle strode toward the hangar as if invincible, Connor Donald and Adam Revell backpedaling beside him, M4s rattling rounds back at us.

Burt and I crawled under my truck and out the other side, jumped to our feet and zigzagged after Daley.

I made the darkness and saw her running through the swirling desert sand, not fifty yards away. From behind me came a fusillade of law enforcement return fire, and, looking over my shoulder, I saw their tracer rounds punching through the home and the metal hangar and the barn and bunkhouses. Teargas rockets arched and plummeted. Lark bellowed orders and men screamed in agony.

"Daley! Stop! I'm here to help you."

In the sand-blasted dark I saw her stop and turn, then take off again toward the exit road.

We caught her halfway there and I took hold of both her shoulders to brake her, then pushed her to the ground as lightly as I could.

She rolled onto her back breathing hard, eyes wide and glittering behind her windblown hair, drawing one leg back to kick if we got too close.

Behind us the battle popped and sputtered on, but from the slowed rate of fire I knew that lives were being taken. The rhythm of First Fallujah, the tempo of death.

"I work for your sister. She hired me to bring you home. I'm Roland and this is Burt."

"I don't trust you."

"That's too damned bad," I said. "There are men back there getting shot because of you."

She scrambled upright and ran off again, but we caught her quickly, circled, and herded her to stop.

Burt cuffed her with a plastic tie, hands behind her. Tripped her backward with an outstretched boot and guided her rump-first onto the sand. Then stepped away.

"Take her to your car," I said. "I'll bring the truck if I can get it started."

"Roland, the three of us can make the Eldo in twenty minutes," Burt said.

I saw that the barn and the farmhouse had caught fire, the wind drawing the flames from the windows and whipping them back and forth like rags. I heard the slowing gunfire and the moaning of wounded men. I thought of Lark and Marie.

"I need to go help."

"You've done your work. Not worth it, Champ."

While the gunshots popped and the flames swept high above the floodlights and the smell of teargas wafted over us, I considered the fourteen-year-old girl handcuffed in the desert.

She considered me. I saw Penelope's face. Penelope's anger and suspicion. Was I looking at Penelope's sister, or her daughter? Her sister, or living proof of the rape of a girl and the child she bore from it? Then where was Reggie Atlas? In that swirl of light brown hair? The firm jawline, maybe, or the expressive mouth?

"Burt, if I'm not there in thirty minutes, you and Daley hit the road. Don't let her out of your sight. I'm ready for this to be over."

"I won't run away again," she said.

"No," said Burt. "You won't."

Building by building, wall by wall, I worked my way back into the battleground. Sporadic shooting to my left and right, someone wailing from inside the flame-clenched main house. I fell in with Lark and four of his SWAT men behind an armored Suburban as they waited for Battle and his lieutenants to come out of the big hangar.

The SWAT leader was calling to them through a powerful megaphone when the hangar door rolled up and two ATVs came howling into the barnyard. Battle drove one of them, with Eric Glassen on the passenger seat behind him, his M4 hacking away at us, rounds bouncing off the bulletproofed Suburban as the ATV skidded off into the darkness through tattoos of gunfire. Connor Donald followed, steering the other ATV with one hand and firing at us behind him like a cowboy as his mount bucked and bounced across the rough desert floor. The six of us piled into the armored SUV, Lark at the wheel. The back end slid hard and the tires threw up a rooster tail of dirt as I slammed the rear door shut.

We came up hard on Battle as Glassen tried to reload the M4, the Suburban's powerful searchlights illuminating the scene like a stage. Battle tried a hard right turn, but Glassen's weight sunk the back tires and the ATV rolled across the desert floor like some huge mechanical tumbleweed, the men flying off and the tires spinning fast as it turned over and over again, finally crashing to a stop against a hillock of rippled white sand. We slid to a stop. Glassen rose from the chaos, drawing his sidearm, when two of the SWAT men riddled him with bullets so powerful they kicked up dirt behind him before he even had time to fall. Alfred lay on his stomach, arms outstretched, as Lark and two of his men approached. The old man rolled over and groaned and tried to struggle up. A cell phone slipped from a suit coat pocket in a cascade of white sand, and I understood why it had taken the old man so long pee, and why SNR had been ready to greet me. Marie's phone, passed in their long, tearful embrace? It had to be. My pat-down had been a good one.

I watched Connor Donald vanish into the night, headed for Rattlesnake Road.

By the time we loaded Glassen and Battle into the Suburban, picked up the road, and stormed our way to the Paradise Date Farm guard gate, the Lion of the Lord was gone. Not even a cloud of dust to point his direction on the asphalt. And no red Eldorado.

Lark threw the big armored Suburban into a U-turn, gunned it onto the road and back toward the burning compound.

THE HOUSE AND barn burned without a fight, flames billowing through the windows, their frames and interiors dried to kindling by decades of Imperial Valley sun.

A young SNR man sprawled faceup on the front porch of the house.

Tattooed Forearms and Flat-Top Woman dead in the floodlit dirt.

Another body lying near the small house where SNR had stored the mystery crates imported from the San Onofre Nuclear Generating Station.

Two burnt, bullet-shredded corpses were heaped directly under the shattered windows of the barn loft where they had fallen. I wondered how many more were inside.

In a remote patch of the barnyard, under heavy guard, sat the captured ambushers, tied at their wrists and ankles, propped up in a line with their backs against the bunkhouse—Adam Revell and eight men I recognized from the wasp-cams but didn't know by name. They looked like POWs, defeated and hostile, smeared with dirt and blood, their eyes flickering orange.

Lark and a SWAT sniper escorted Battle from the Suburban, cuffed him, and propped him up next to his SNR followers. Two of the SWATs dragged blood-dripping Glassen out of the vehicle and into the barnyard dirt.

Lark had a brief confidential word with one of his agents, who nodded toward two tarp-covered bodies that lay in the middle of the loosely circled law enforcement vehicles.

A rear door of the Bearcat swung open and Marie got out and clambered toward her husband in her blue dress and new Jack Purcell sneaks. Two sheriff's deputies caught her and pulled her back.

Then sirens in the wind, sounding far away. Flashing lights coming our way on a distant road.

My bullet-holed truck started right up and Lark let me go.

43

///////////////////////////

I PICKED UP Daley in El Centro. Steered west through the black night, eyes fixed on the yellow dividing lines. We climbed the boulder-piled mountains, my thoughts crowded with death and destruction, my mood calm and bad. Burt behind us in the Eldo.

Daley dozed beside me after talking briefly but emotionally with Penelope. Burt scanned the road behind and ahead of us while trading messages with Penelope: Daley's frame of mind and physical condition, our own conditions, our estimated time of arrival in Oceanside, would we have to stop for gas or food?

The road signs accelerated into my high beams. A small owl lifted off from the road shoulder.

Burt on the phone. "What was the body count back there, Roland?"

"At least six SNR guards, one FBI agent, and a sheriff's deputy are dead. Battle rolled an ATV, but it looks like he'll make it. Marie's fine. Connor Donald is in the wind, waving a machine gun."

I needed some hard intel. "Daley, did you leave Nick's place with Connor and Eric willingly?"

"I knew them. I called them to come get me. I felt safe at first."

"Did they force you to stay with them after that?"

"Yes."

"Did Reggie Atlas sexually assault you?"

"He did not. He often looks at me very strangely."

"Do you have any idea how much torment you've put your sister through?"

"She lives in fear," said Dailey. "Because of me. As she constantly reminds me."

"She'll be glad to have you back."

OCEANSIDE WAS MISTY and cool, a world away from Imperial Valley. I could see Daley registering the city, her neighborhood, her street. She looked exhausted and unhappy, and I had the thought that I didn't want to be Penelope Rideout tonight. We passed the sprawling Oceanside Transit Center, lit but quiet at this late hour. "You turn at Myers," said Daley. "I take it you've been here before."

I nodded.

"Did you go in my room?"

I nodded again.

"How's my Gibson?"

"Looking good," I said. "Penelope has really missed you. I hope you can find some kind words for her."

"I lost my Martin, half my clothes, and my backpack full of CDs," she said dreamily. "Back in all that gunfire. That was really scary."

"Did you hear me about the kind words?" I asked.

"I can find some good words," said Daley. "Sisters always fight. I'm happy to be home again. I think, maybe, I'm about to be really happy."

When we pulled into the little driveway, Penelope burst through the front door, charged across the porch and down the drive toward us.

Daley met her halfway and they collided in a hug that sent them spinning like dancers. Both of them yelping and crying at once, hands on each other's faces, words rushing over words.

"No Toto," said Burt at my window. "But you did well, Roland. You've earned some overtime pay and a good long vacation."

For a moment I watched them through the windshield, then checked the rearview and stepped from the truck. Penelope came over and threw herself into my arms and locked on like a constrictor. Over her shoulder I saw Daley coming toward us with an amused smile.

INSIDE, I SET the window blinds for a good view and the four of us crowded around the dinette. Burt and I sat facing the small living room and the front door. Penelope thanked God for the food and for Daley's return. Then served hot rolls and butter and a stew she'd made.

Daley shoveled down her dinner, then brought her Gibson into the living room and started playing. She stopped and looked at us once, briefly, then dropped her attention to the guitar again, devoted to her instrument, as musicians always are.

"You shouldn't be here tonight," I told Penelope. "Too much mayhem in the air."

She eyed me. "I feel it."

"You two can come home with us. I've got a casita free. Or the Hyatt Grand downtown has good security. We can drive or follow you there. Talk to Daley if you'd like."

"We'll go with you," Penelope said. "I want us all to be close."

Burt smiled, staring through the living room window, then broke open another roll.

EARLY-MORNING DARKNESS STILL over Rancho de los Robles, the stars fading, coyotes yipping not far away.

Francisco stood in the porchlight of his casita, strapping a cooler of food and water to his bike rack for the very long workday ahead. He had groomed and dressed as would any Central American beginning his workday in Fallbrook: showered and cleanly shaven, hair recently cut, long-sleeved shirt tucked in and buttoned up, long pants, wide belt, and boots. Triunfo watched us, tail wagging. They came down and Frank greeted Penelope with a charged smile. She introduced him to her sister.

"You are the girl is loved," he said.

"Sounds like a song," said Daley.

Penelope and Daley got casita three, two small bedrooms with a shared bath, a sufficient kitchen, and a cedar-walled living room with a fireplace and a view of the pond and the sunsets.

An hour later we were all sitting side by side along the western edge of the big patio, facing the pond and the rolling acres and the hills.

An odd eight-pack: Burt and me, Penelope and Daley, Dick and Liz, Frank and Melinda. Coffee and English muffins. Small talk with big pauses. A softly murmured account from Melinda, of a pleasant dream from which she'd just awakened, about riding a horse facing backward and guiding it by the tail. From behind us the rising sun touched its light to the hills, and the sky above them went from black to gray.

Francisco excused himself, got on his bike, and rode down the driveway toward the gate.

I got two hours of sleep, snores thundering from my bedroom, I am told.

I LEFT BURT in charge, and three hours later met Mike Lark at the entrance of Paradise Date Farm.

I looked out at the legions of disgruntled reporters and their vehicles, all having baked in the sun for hours by then, with more hours to come if the reporters wanted the story. I saw Howard Wilkin, my friend at the *San Diego Union-Tribune*, and he saw me, not necessarily a good thing for a PI with privacy for himself and his clients in mind.

Lark picked me up in one of the armored Suburbans, the thick plexiglass windshield chipped and cloudy with dust, its flanks well dented by recent bullets.

"You wouldn't believe what these people were going to do," he said.

"I thought dirty bomb," I said.

"Worse. How's the girl?"

"I think everything's all right. I think."

He glanced at me, then gunned his shot-up Suburban toward the compound. Even from a distance I could see that the barnyard was crammed with vehicles that weren't there just a few hours ago. I saw new people, too—futuristic clomping men and women in white hazmat suits, helmets, masks, and breathing gear. Geiger-Müller counters, dosimeters, particle detectors, radiation meters, from wands to wheeled. A team of two push-pulled an explosives containment vessel toward the wide-open metal hangar.

Lark reintroduced me to FBI's Western Region director, Frank

Salvano, whom I'd worked with under comparably violent circumstances less than a year ago. Older, gaunt, with short silver hair and round wire-rimmed glasses.

"Not you again," he said, with a wrinkle of a smile.

"In fact."

Followed by a moment of silence for the agents he had lost in those dark and terrifying days we had spent together. A shadow drifted across Lark's good young face, Joan Taucher reaching out from whatever lockdown he'd assigned her to. I know the tricks that memory plays. How it can surprise you.

"Don't touch anything," said Salvano.

"I won't even breathe."

"We need to suit up," Lark said. "We're still not sure what we're up against."

After being scanned by an Agent Fromm—who noted our preexposure levels in her notebook—Lark and I encased ourselves in antiexplosion and antiradiation bulk, tightened the boots, pulled on heavy breathing helmets, and checked our oxygen flows and communications. Last up, gloves.

Lark led me into the hangar, past the clutter of ATVs and tool-strewn work benches I'd seen on the wasp-cam video, all the way to the back of the big building, where the security doors stood closed. An explosion-and-radiation-proofed agent let us in.

"This is the heart of it," Lark said. His voice came through the tiny speaker in the helmet, clear and bright. "You remember the big glove box. We speculated that those coffin-shaped crates would fit perfectly into this baby. Look."

Through the curved, clear window I could see one of the wooden crates from the San Onofre power plant lying open in the glove box. The wooden lid lay beside it, with loosened steel bands encircling it like ribs. In the middle of the glove box was a long, shiny steel tube with three black, metallic-looking pellets that had either spilled from the tube or been shaken loose from it. Fuel pellets, I was all but certain. Also, a battery-operated Sawzall with what looked like a diamond blade. Two locking wrenches.

"Here's what Washington has kicked loose so far," said Lark. "Seven years ago, Marie Knippermeir's American Agriculture Enterprises bought Paradise Date Farm from Imperial Farm and Mine. Cheap—two million six, plus the debt. Paradise was still productive but running in the red. Poor management. Their main account was Eid-al-Mawlid Co., specializing in Muslim events and holidays—birthdays, weddings, the breaking of the fast of Ramadan. A thriving company. They need plenty of dates, a centuries-old Middle Eastern staple. Fresh, frozen, dried, preserved—packaged in mail-order gift baskets for Muslims all across the United States. Eid-al-Mawlid is kind of like Harry and David, but they specifically market to Muslims."

In the dimmer caves of my imagination I saw the truth beginning to take on its terrible form. I studied the strange tableau inside the curving clear dome of the glove box: the clumsy hands suspended on their robotic sleeves, awaiting their next deployment, diamond-bladed saw, a small electric grinder like a jeweler might use, the wooden crate with its sprung lid, the shining zirconium tube, and the three black uranium pellets either spilled or shaken loose so they could be . . .

Behind his mask, Lark's face was impossible to read; his voice was dry but urgent. "Fast-forward to 2016. SNR gets the San Onofre contract to guard the plant during the actual physical decommissioning. Decommissioning will take a decade. First, they have to cool the *spent* fuel rods in wet storage for five years before they can even weld them into steel-and-concrete casks. That's how hot they are, both thermally and radioactively. Battle offered San Diego Gas and Electric a sweet deal for SNR. He had good men—most with military or law enforcement experience. At a good price, too, because Battle and SNR weren't guarding the spent rods at San Onofre just to make money."

"They wanted the pellets."

"And they've got four freezers of them out there in that storage building. Each freezer holds one crate. The crates are fitted with concrete molds that surround one fuel rod, which contains fifty-six pellets. The concrete keeps the radiation shielded, and the freezers keep the pellets cool enough to be worked on in the glove box. Specifically, to be ground. Note the diamond saw for getting through the concrete and titanium, and the jewelers' grinder, and the locking wrenches to hold the pellets to the wheel. The end product is ground fuel pellets the consistency of beach sand. They've got this whole process on video in the farmhouse library. And more. Adam Revell got talkative when I told him a conspiracy to kill people with radiation could get him a death penalty."

"Radioactive dust," I said. "To be sprinkled on the dates before they ship to Eid-al-Mawlid, which will wrap the fruit up real pretty and ship the baskets out to their Muslim customers."

A moment of silence as I considered the consequences of such a thing. I could hear Lark's breathing through my speaker.

"Thousands of innocent people," said Lark. "Women and children. Anyone who ingests the smallest amount, touches it, breathes it. The Eid-al-Mawlid employees would be the first to report symptoms. A matter of days, depending on dose equivalent and Gray levels. Then, acute radiation syndrome—blistering skin, convulsions, vomiting, diarrhea, bleeding from the eyes, nose, and ears. Death within two days to two weeks. Agony itself. It would have taken days for us to even figure out what was happening. This is one of the most depraved and disgusting things I've ever seen attempted. The bosses are still arguing whether or not to even acknowledge it publicly."

It took a long moment for that depravity and disgust to really settle in.

"In Arabic, the words *Eid-al-Mawlid* mean 'birth of the prophet,'" said Lark. "It's one of Islam's holiest days and biggest celebrations. This year it's November ninth. The big Paradise shipments were set to commence two weeks from now—in time to be made into gift baskets for the Sunni Mawlid on November ninth. We beat SNR to the punch, Roland. Barely. Thanks to you and Daley Rideout and those wasp-cams."

My moment of glory came and went and I enjoyed it briefly, but all the way to my bones.

44

///////////////////////////

For the rest of that day and the next, I accompanied Penelope and Daley on their several missions. Penelope wanted me on the clock for my time, which was fine with me. She wondered out loud how long she could afford my services before she went broke. I noted that Daley seemed exasperated at times like that, as if Penelope were *her* little sister.

I enjoyed their company, especially when they seemed to forget that I was there. I listened to them as you might to a pleasant mountain stream or the sound of waves. I was pleased to know I could stand between them and most wickedness that might come. In spite of being pounded senseless by six men, I felt needed and capable. Stitches out, hitting the bags again. I thought of Connor toting his machine gun and Reggie Atlas his lust.

I took them to their family doctor so Daley could be examined. Everything was fine. Then to a conference with Chancellor Stahl and attorneys for the Monarch Academy, followed by visits to Alanis Tervalua and Carrie Calhoun, and a sad few minutes with the parents of Nick Moreno.

I also escorted them to and from interviews with Darrel Walker, Mike Lark and his roomful of FBI agents, and the Center for Missing and Exploited Children. I sat in if welcome, waited in lobbies and hallways when not.

Nearly everyone who talked to Daley treated her with warmth and mild awe at what she'd been through—though her story of running away was vague and incomplete. *Mostly just hanging out with friends and playing my guitar, stuff like that* . . . Only Lark and Walker knew enough to depose specific truths from her, much of which would become a part of the kidnapping, murder, and conspiracy to commit terror charges being readied against Alfred and Marie Battle, and several of their SNR employees.

An alert KPBS reporter noted that Daley Rideout had been suddenly dropped from the missing-children websites and wanted to know why. Penelope handed off her phone to me, hissing, *"Her story is not to be told!"* I wasn't sure if that was meant for the reporter or for me, or maybe even for Daley, who was riding in the back seat of a rental car at that time. I told the reporter that Daley was now home in good health but didn't want to be interviewed. The connection was bad and the reporter was insistent but I prevailed, having identified myself only as a family friend.

Fortunately, at about the time I was finishing up with KPBS, the Associated Press—after hundreds of social media accounts, rumors, speculations, and images of distant buildings burning in the night—broke the story of the bloody raid on Paradise Date Farm. Some harrowing photos. It was everywhere, leaving a runaway fourteen-year-old girl lost among the "two law enforcement officers and six homegrown extremists killed in a gunfight in a hidden Imperial County compound."

Which was how I learned that Lark and his DOJ bosses had decided to let the homegrown terror plot out of the bag. And realized that many of the roughly 3.45 million Muslims living in the United States would dream that night—and many nights after—of lethal radioactive gift baskets arriving in their homes in celebration of the prophet's birthday.

The cops and the FBI may have prevailed at Paradise by body count.

And yet, in its way, hate had won.

AFTER DINNER THAT night we all sat under the palapa and streamed the San Diego news on Dick's laptop.

Near the end of the hour, which the station likes to conclude with a brief, uplifting story, the anchor noted that a missing Carlsbad Monarch Academy student had been found unharmed and was returned home following a tip that came in to the Center for Missing and Exploited Children. The fourteen-year-old had been gone for nearly two weeks.

"Nice to have a story with a happy ending," she noted. "We don't release the names of minors in cases such as this, but the student's guardian told us earlier today that the missing girl's story is about to be told. We look forward to that. That's San Diego tonight and I'm Monet Reese."

"I said her story *is not to be told*," said Penelope.

"*Not* sounds like *about*," said Dick. "She misheard you."

"And I said it to Roland, not that reporter. Now look what she made me do." She wiped a piece of strawberry that had somehow landed on her periwinkle dress, the same one she'd worn to shower me with gifts and nurse my wounds. "Can I get a retraction?" she asked.

"Nobody consulted me about my story being told or not," said Daley.

"Oh, let it go," said Dick. "They can't change it now. It's no big thing."

A look from Burt.

No big thing unless you were Alfred and Marie Battle, Connor Donald, or Reggie Atlas, I thought. Then it might be a pretty damned big thing after all.

WITH DESSERT I drank coffee and mostly listened to the conversation at the table. After all the drama—the bloody shoot-out at Paradise, and the evil plans of SNR, and Daley's dramatic reappearance—the talk was sparse and polite. A poet once remarked that after great emotion, a sense of formality sets in. Another noted that sooner or later everyone must get stoned. Which is true, but I was sick of being hit by them.

I helped myself to brownies that Liz and Melinda had teamed up on.

Daley played guitar, her voice beautiful.

Frank provided erratic accompaniment on Dick's old guitar, sometimes finding notes to go along with Daley's melodies, sometimes not. He told us that his father had bought him a two-dollar guitar when he was ten.

Burt offered to stay with them while I drove Penelope to Oceanside to get some things they needed. Dick said he'd be here, too. For Irregulars, they're exceptionally reliable.

SHE SAT WITH the white purse on her lap, hands folded over it, hair up on one side and held with a comb. She took a tissue from the bag and fussed with the strawberry stain on her dress again, then dabbed it with finality and put the tissue back.

"It's really nice to be alone with you for a few minutes," she said.

"Daley and I will check into the Hyatt tomorrow, as you recommended. We don't mean to wear out our welcome."

"You can have the casita a few more days if you'd like."

"No. I feel complete again. Daley is better. I'll be able to sleep at night. My soul won't feel eaten alive. Thank you for finding her." She cleared her throat. "Thank you."

I nodded.

"You certainly earned your pay."

"Thanks for being generous."

"You should be the most expensive PI in the world. In my opinion."

I steered my rental truck down Highway 76, west toward Oceanside. Managed to hit all the red lights. Didn't mind.

"Sorry I came on so emotional and ditzy and full of evasions," she said. "I was totally freaked by Daley running away from me. And I liked you as soon as we met there in your office. I didn't know how to behave. I don't know the first thing about men. Got off to kind of a bumpy start with you guys, as you may or may not know."

"I know."

"I hope you do," she said. "Because you're the only one I've ever told. But drop it. I am what I am, no matter what you choose to believe. Well, damn, another red light. Guess we'll have to sit here and talk about the next thing. What do you think of those Padres?"

"Have you given any thought to outing Atlas?" I asked. "Talk to Daley, get a lawyer? Call that reporter who asked about Daley? Get it all out there once and for all?"

She glanced at me, then looked straight ahead for a long while. "Someday. Roland, that's pretty much all I've thought about for fourteen years. That, and how to stay away from him. As I explained to you, I don't want Daley to grow up knowing that her father's a monster and her mother's a victim. She believes her father and mother were kind and loving parents. There's a hole in her, but that merciful illusion helps to fill it. Each year the hole becomes smaller. I want to wait until she's ready. And you know Reggie said he'd kill me if I speak out. On four separate occasions he promised to. I know him well enough to believe him."

"That's part of the story you need to tell," I said.

"Not until Daley is ready."

"And you."

"Yes. And me."

"Times are better, Penelope. If you act now, you can take him down before he can hurt you. You can blow him out of the water with one tweet. You could do it in less than the time it takes us to get to Oceanside. You two can stay with me while the cops investigate and the courts order a paternity test. Then it's all she wrote for Pastor Reggie Atlas. SNR is broken and Battle will die in prison."

She gave me a long, frank gaze. I returned it in parts, trying to read her expression in the colored glow of the traffic lights. I wondered again if the paternity test was stopping her. If she knew it would reveal the innocence of Reggie Atlas.

I couldn't read her face or her mind. My heart believed Penelope because it wanted to. My reason doubted her because it had to.

I parked in her driveway, behind the cheerful yellow Beetle. A motion light came on. The night was damp again and the streetlamps glowed through feints of fog.

Her eyes were gray and cool in the dashboard light. "Come on in, Roland. This won't take long."

She unlocked the front door and we went inside. A lamp was already on, weakly illuminating the little living room and its plaid couch and director's chairs, the upturned orange crate/CD stand, the small collection of photos on the wicker stand, the TV.

"Getcha a drink if you'd like," she said. "I'll be back."

She walked into the hallway and a light came on. I heard her footsteps on the old wooden floor, the creak of boards, a closet rolling open.

I poured a conservative drink, added an ice cube. Sat in the living room, where I could keep an eye on the yard and the street. Sipped the good, smooth bourbon. Heard the Amtrak Surfliner groaning into the Transit Center just a few blocks away. Then Penelope, coming back up into the living room, clothes on hangers dangling from each hand. She laid them over one of the director's chairs, balancing the load so as not to tip it over. Gave me a matter-of-fact nod.

"One more load," she said. "Daley's."

I sat in the still, small room and listened to her bumping away in Daley's room. Her sister's room. Her daughter's room. I told myself it really didn't matter, but of course it did. One was ordinary human grace, the other a rape of it. I wondered if there was a deeper wisdom in Penelope's refusal to tell her daughter this alleged and awful truth. If I was failing to see the bigger picture. I tried to think what it might be. But I was a childless widower with a history of willing violence and an incomplete understanding of this world.

Penelope brought out another handful of clothes on hangers, Daley's—lots of black and pink—and a paper shopping bag of toiletries.

"Almost," she said. "And how's that drink?"

I made her one and away she went.

I heard her shower go on. A few minutes later she came padding down the hallway, feet bare, by the sound of them, and stood at the threshold of the living room. She was wearing a brief pink robe with white daisies and a price tag dangling from one sleeve. Matching slippers. A black camisole. The empty highball glass in hand.

"I'm not sure what to do next," she said. "Will you take over?"

"You left the price tag on the robe," I said.

"Maybe in case I have to do that."

"Don't do that."

SEX CAN BE tender, passionate, urgent, formal, animal, awkward, sudden, kind, brief, long, sad, alien, familiar, punitive, unselfish, inspiring, competitive, exhausting, heart-pounding, electric, empowering, embarrassing, ornate, dreamy, martial, surprising, disappointing, rambunctious, lonely, purposeful, greedy, funny, furtive, loud, languorous, acrobatic, ambitious, required, frequent, rare, once.

Or many combinations thereof. Dealer's choice.

If I had to describe those hours with Penelope Rideout, I would start with wonderful.

45

///////////////////////////

WE dressed, Penelope remarking that consensual, un-drugged sex wasn't all it was cracked up to be. I thought she was being funny, then wasn't sure. In the living room Penelope got her house key out, then shouldered her purse. I took all four hanger loads in one hand—feeling like a strong and capable man after all that loving—and picked up the toiletries bag. Managed to turn the knob and elbow open the door.

Atlas put the gun to my forehead, walked me back, and slammed the door with his foot. His eyes were wrong and he smelled bad.

"If you go for your gun I'll blow your brains out," he said. "Don't move. Don't let go of that stuff. Penelope, you drop the keys or I'll shoot you, too."

I measured my chances. If I tried to draw, Atlas would have drilled out my life before the hangers hit the floor. Penelope next. The desperate energy on Pastor Reggie Atlas's face made these things appear certain. His gun looked to be a semiauto .40-caliber with a short barrel.

"Nice to see you, Pastor Atlas," I said.

"Don't start in on me," he said.

He considered Penelope briefly and I saw an expression on his face that I couldn't fathom.

I heard Penelope's keys hit the floor behind me. I dropped the clothes and the bag of toiletries well away from my feet.

Atlas lowered his aim to my chest. The gun was shaking. "I didn't tell you to do that," he said.

"Reggie," said Penelope. "You stop this right now."

"Leave your hands up and out like that," he said to me. "And remember how far away from your gun they are. Remember that."

In the academy, they teach you to keep them talking.

"Been waiting long?" I asked.

"Cruising, mostly," he said. "I had this vision you two would be together here tonight. I'm still capable of visions."

"You must have seen PBS, too," I said.

"Yes." He sneered at Penelope. "You, so eager to tell Daley's story."

"Atlas," I said. "What you want is to not spend the rest of your life in prison for murder."

"And how do I go about that, considering I'm going to kill you both?"

His gun barrel was now moving in a small slow circle, my chest the bull's-eye. Sweat filled the lines of his face and he wiped his brow with his free hand. His wad of fine blond hair was soaked at the temples and the stink of fear came off him.

"Haven't you already destroyed enough for one lifetime?" asked Penelope. "Go. Go away, Reggie Atlas."

"I gave you everything you love," he said. "I gave you the true path and a child."

"It astonishes me every day that she could have come from you," said Penelope.

A minor smile on Atlas's face, then, filled with what looked like genuine pride.

"I could have enjoyed that astonishment with you, and with Daley," he said. "The thousand times I asked. I was prepared to leave my life. And create a new one around you."

"What about the times you threatened to kill me?" said Penelope.

"You brought this on yourself, Penelope! By trying to hide my daughter in the bulrushes of my own cathedral. Here on the edge of the ocean, where you stopped running. And tried to tempt me with her just as you tempted *me*."

Atlas pointed the gun at Penelope. I heard the catch of her breath. Then the shaking front sight found my chest again.

"Then you hired this idiot, a man who suffers for money and sees no difference between the sacred and profane? With you two gone, there's nobody to even suspect me. Nobody to keep me from bringing my daughter into the fold. As I did you. And I will not lose her."

"I'll take her and run a thousand miles away," said Penelope. "You go back to your family. And our secrets can stay right where they are."

"Oh, no, no, *no*, Pen. It's way too late now."

A chill down my scalp as I wondered what condition Reggie's wife and children were in.

I lowered my arms by half. The circling of Atlas's gun barrel had widened. He wiped his brow again, snapping the sweat to the floor.

"Don't doubt that I will kill you," said Atlas.

"I believe you will," said Penelope.

"I don't," I said.

Which brought Reggie Atlas's best smile to his face, his preacher's, actor's, can't-resist-me grin. I'd never seen such derangement on a face, and I had seen a lot.

"Why wouldn't I?"

"You're too smart," I said.

"You flatter me to control me."

"No flattery, Reggie," I said. "You're the most repulsive human I've ever met. You really did it, didn't you? You raped a girl of fourteen in a bus. Four Wheels for Jesus. Threatened her and your own daughter for years after. I think you should put that gun to your head and prove how sorry you are, once and for all. End your life with a shred of dignity instead of this groveling. Jesus would agree."

"Roland, he'll—" said Penelope.

Reggie gave me a concerned, cagey look. "Do you really think Jesus would agree?"

"I know he would," I said. "And on a practical level, if you use that gun to do the right thing, you won't spend a day in prison. You won't have to face the world as a child rapist and a fake holy man and a murderer. You'll be remembered as Pastor Reggie Atlas, a brave but troubled man who did what he had to."

"Roland—"

"You know, you're right," said Atlas. "I can do what you suggest. It would address those issues head-on. But it wouldn't be fair."

"Give me one reason why it wouldn't," I said.

Atlas held the gun with both hands, but now the orbit of the barrel had lost its shape. The mad ellipsoids terrified me.

"Well, for one thing, I was innocent once," he said. His voice wavered and desperation widened his pupils.

"Yeah? Explain that."

"Did you tell him how you singled me out, Penelope? How you came to me for private moments of talk and fellowship? How your hands trembled in mine when we prayed? Did you tell him about the looks and the smiles you gave me, and the poems you wrote and the clothing you wore for me—the black sweater and the little pink skirt? The lotions and perfumes that smelled like coconut, because you knew how much I liked it? Because it smelled like the mansion on the sand, where you agreed we were going to live and produce holy children. You haven't said anything about that? How you tempted and seduced me. *Systematically?* How you enjoyed what we finally did together? I know you did. You were eager. You were *wet!*"

I heard movement behind me, then Penelope stepped into my peripheral view. Reggie swung the pistol at her, then back to me, the breath in his nostrils short and fast.

"You know I was too drugged to fight," she said, her voice seething with contempt. "I've told you and you've heard, Reggie. I was dizzy and afraid and trapped. I told you to stop. I hit you and nothing happened. Wet? That was my body's defense against you! Autonomic, like throwing up a poison. It took me years of shame before I understood that. I wanted to be *baptized*. I wanted to be *accepted* and *loved*. I didn't want to be touched like that, Reggie. It was the only thing I *didn't* want you to do! You knew it, too. You one hundred percent *knew*."

Again Atlas looked to her, then back to me, but this time left the weapon pointed at my heart.

"I loved you more than I'd ever loved any earthly person or thing," he said. "And you loved me that much, too. I knew you wanted me and it was time. Our time. I never meant to harm you. In the big picture, I have not harmed you in any way."

Penelope took a deep breath and let it out slowly. Her voice hitched into a sob and she continued. "You tricked me and raped me . . . You threatened me if I told. You tracked my daughter. No more, Reggie. Enough."

"You seduced a humble man of God."

"You used God's name to fuck a girl."

"I have suffered, too," said the pastor.

"Tissue," she whispered. Swung the white purse around and took out the strawberry-stained wad and pressed it to one eye, then the other.

"You used me," said Reggie.

"I adored you," said Penelope.

"You stole my soul and corrupted my flesh," said Reggie, pointing the gun at Penelope again, the barrel wild. "I want them back."

"Me, too," said Penelope, stuffing the tissue into her bag and pulling out a plump pink derringer.

I saw his flinch and launched into Reggie with all the speed I had. Grabbed his gun in both my hands and forced it up and away so Reggie blasted the ceiling instead of Penelope. Her handcannon quaked the room, then boomed again as Reggie crashed back into the wall, his gun clattering to the floor. Eyes wide in the gunsmoke and breathing hard, blood blossoming through his clean white shirt, Reggie gazed down at himself with what looked like disbelief. Then collapsed, the wall behind him pocked by two closely spaced holes.

"Smokey only takes two rounds," she said. "I'll reload."

"Not necessary," I said.

I took her gun and ushered her into the kitchen, helping her into a chair at the small table. Her face white as snow and her body shaking badly. Over the half-wall I could see Reggie trembling on the living room floor.

"Now what?" she asked.

"Get ready to answer a lot of questions."

"I'll tell them the whole truth."

"That's all you need to do, Penelope."

"The whole damned miserable truth."

Back in the living room I knelt beside Atlas. Watched his breathing stop. Saw his eyes surrender their terror and then their light.

Through the blinds, I saw lights coming on in the houses across the street.

Stood and found my phone.

46

///////////////////////////

I N spite of our accepted beliefs and earnest hopes, things really don't happen for a reason.

There is no master plan, only private notions—both yours and others'—some of which work out well, while others explode like pipe bombs.

Everything else is out of your control.

So you wipe your eyes, chart your beliefs, and fly again accordingly.

I flew *Hall Pass 2* up to the Bishop Airport, rented a Jeep in town, picked up some camping and fishing gear I needed. Turned off my phone and listened to the news station fading into static as I climbed into the Sierra Nevada mountains.

Fished alone, as I prefer, really nailed the browns on the East Walker, let the fish go free, ate canned food, and drank good bourbon. On the San Joaquin, I crawled out of my tent at sunrise just as a black bear swatted my coffeemaker off the fire-pit grill and into the trees, then lumbered away.

In Reno I took second place in the amateur all-ages category at the Reno Ballroom DanceDown, teaming up with a woman I found in the hotel bar whose regular partner had sprained an ankle just that morning. I'd been hoping for luck like that. Lenore was a delight to dance with, much better than me and utterly regardless about winning trophies, which, as a youngish male, I covet beyond reason. The trophy was a dandy. Our barely rehearsed country-swing dance to "The Last Worthless Evening" was good enough. Justine cut in for a few steps. Said she was proud of me for how I was treating Penelope and Daley. Sticking up for them. Giving them a second chance. Wished she could have a second chance, too.

Lenore, her partner Wayne, and I drank late on victory night, until Wayne, limping badly, took me aside and threatened to kick my ass all the way back to San Diego if Lenore looked at me like that again. I told him not to bother, I was headed home early the next day anyway.

As I DROVE from Reno back down to Bishop Airport through the fragrant sage and the spotty cell signals, Burt and Penelope brought me up to speed.

Federal prosecutors were readying charges against Alfred Battle and several of his SNR henchmen/-women for kidnapping, conspiracy to commit murder, conspiracy to use weapons of mass destruction. And more. Lark had declared the indictment would be "aggressive and comprehensive," and there would likely be some very long federal prison sentences handed down. Lark told Burt off the record that Adam Revell was singing like a parakeet.

Penelope told me that Daley had been so shocked by her true bio/history that she had spent four days rocketing between belief, denial, and outrage. Threw a lot of things. The emerging mother and daughter had spent hours hiking the rolling hills of Rancho de los Robles, and hours in casita three cooking meals, listening to music, talking, arguing, crying, and remembering.

"My blood ran cold when she told me she'd sometimes wished that Reggie Atlas was her father," Penelope said. "That he reminded her of someone wise and kind and probably a lot like the father she never knew."

I'd wondered along those same lines: Might an unknowing daughter feel an instinctual recognition of her father? A blood instinct? Even dimly? And, believing that her father was another, what name would the daughter give that curious, strong, instinctual pull? Might she name it affection? Curiosity? Attraction, even? Might she pursue it? Was Reggie Atlas counting on blood instinct? Had he been using it against her?

"And, of course," said Penelope through the static following me down Highway 395, "I have to forgive myself for taking a man's life. Self-defense, yes. But still a man. A man whom I as a child once adored. Father of my daughter. A husband and father of his own children. My soul feels stained, Roland. I hope it fades some. The stain. I hope Daley can truly forgive me for what I did."

"He came there to kill us both."

"I know. But what I did changes everything about me. I think you know what I mean."

Penelope went on to tell me she'd read to her daughter from some very long journals she had kept. She told me she'd waited a lifetime to do this. She told me that when the "waves of truth" had finally broken on Daley enough times, Daley surrendered her doubt and began to accept who she was and where she'd come from and the idea that, in some ways, she would be starting her life over again as a different person. With a different history and family. With a reviled father and a world eager to invade her past and exploit her privacy. Was there an upside? Penelope said the last few days had been better. And that Melinda and Daley had become close quickly,

Melinda's violent loss helping Daley handle her own wrenching changes.

Speaking for herself, Penelope said she was "elated and exhausted." She and Daley would be returning home to Oceanside soon. Between Penelope and me there was much to be said, but little of it could be done by phone. She asked how the fishing was. Then ventured that she was glad her "second virginity" had ended with me.

Burt told me Connor Donald had been killed in a shoot-out with police outside the Newport Beach offices of Historical Review. On the link he sent me, Historical Review spokesperson Laurel Davis— the cool, bejeweled beauty who had harangued me at Alfred Battle's White Power Hour—said that Donald was a security guard who occasionally worked for the Historical Review, and said the Review had no reason to believe he was involved in the Paradise Farm terror plot.

I came home a few days later to bad news: Frank, walking his bike up a narrow, tree-lined road in Fallbrook at the end of his workday yesterday, had been stopped by three MS-13 gangsters. He knew one of them from Puerto El Triunfo—El Diabolico, the kid he'd gone to school with who had connections to the people who had killed Frank's father. The El Triunfo boys brought greetings from Frank's two sisters in Salvador. They'd shown Frank machetes and a gun and asked him for eighty dollars to protect the girls. Gabriella was eight and Filomena eleven. Eighty dollars was exactly what he'd made that day, plus a sandwich, an apple, and a bottle of water for lunch. He'd told them he'd pay only this one time. *Solo una vez.* They had laughed and told him they'd see him here next week, and his old El Triunfo friend had given him back one of the twenties. He'd told Frank that he might want to change his mind about the one-time-only payment, then they had scurried off to their aging black Nissan.

"Thus, Frank has a meeting with them next Friday," said Burt as we walked down to the patio that evening. "I've got some ideas how we should handle that, and Frank agrees."

He gave me a mischievous but sincere welcome-home smile, leading the way to the palapa on short bowed legs.

The rest of the Irregulars greeted me with a smartphone concerto of the first verse of "Money for Nothing." This, a common attack on my slowness to make improvements while still collecting the rent on time. There's some small truth in it. So I stood there and took my medicine while four phones tinnily chimed the song so out of sync I could hardly tell what it was.

"Thank you," I said. "Thank you very much."

After the Irregulars had drifted off to their casitas, Penelope and I walked the pond in the minor moonlight. The October nights had lost their heat and the damp cool of fall hung around us.

"I'm taking Daley to New York tomorrow, early," she said. "We have a nonstop out of San Diego."

"I'll take you, if you'd like."

"I'd like. I hope I'm doing the right thing, Roland."

"My offer stands," I said. "You both can stay here. Dodge everybody, hang low for a few weeks, then get on with your lives."

"They want me to do a silhouette interview on *60 Minutes*, so nobody can recognize my face. I need to do this one thing, Roland. I need other people to know they don't have to get raped and hide it forever. No matter how rich and famous and holy the rapers are. Just this one statement, then back to Daley and we'll figure out our lives."

"Tell your story, Penelope. Daley will be fine here for a few days."

"She wanted us to do this thing together," said Penelope. "I wouldn't let her."

"Good call," I said. "She needs to be a girl again. Not a cause."

I thought of Jake, the young surfer at Old Man's, who had looked through all of Daley's inner turmoil and seen simply a cute girl he'd like to hang out with. I thought: *She wouldn't mind being that girl. Not at all.*

"Are they going to turn me into a freak show?"

"Well, a show, anyway," I said. "Just remember it's your story. You tell it. Don't let them put words in your mouth."

"I've got plenty of my own words. "

"You're going to be a busy woman for a while."

"Yeah, a busy little me."

I took her hand and rounded the water. Ahead of us, frogs plopped and barn owls screeched on the hunt. A light fog had rolled in, a bit of chill in it.

"You know the best part?" she asked. "I finally get to be a mom to my daughter. We're going to get to know each other for the first time, as such. Under the banner of truth. I'm going to be a mom, Roland!"

"You'll be outstanding," I said.

"Roland? I do have one regret. You only got the stripped-down version of me. You got the base model. I want you to experience the limited edition. The best Penelope Rideout you can stand. Get it?"

"I think I can handle that," I said.

I like her, too, said Justine.

"I'll see you early, then," said Penelope. "Tonight I need to spend some time with Daley."

Under the palapa we held each other for a silent while, then she set off for casita three. She was wearing the same black sweater as she had the night she'd searched downtown San Clemente so thoroughly—door-to-door—looking for some sign of her daughter. Tonight she had her arms around herself like she had then. Against the chill. Against the world.

Halfway there, she stopped and turned and gave me her hard blue stare. And that awkward wave of hers, part "Hi" and part "See you later."

Then continued to the casita, worked the door lock in the halo of the porch light, and went inside.